37½ Cents.

THE HEIR OF WAST-WAYLAND.

A Tale.

BY MARY HOWITT.

NEW YORK:
HARPER & BROTHERS, PUBLISHERS,
82 CLIFF STREET.
1851.

DEO REIPUBLICÆ ET AMICIS
George Duffield A.M.
In tali nunquam lassat venatio sylva.
A.D.1884.

THE

HEIR OF WAST-WAYLAND.

A Tale.

BY MARY HOWITT.

NEW YORK:
HARPER & BROTHERS, PUBLISHERS,
82 CLIFF STREET.
1851.

THE HEIR OF WAST-WAYLAND.

CHAPTER I.

As travelers from distant points, unconscious of each other's existence, set forth in the morning with one common object in view—the reaching a certain hostel at night, or the visiting some spot of interest, so occurs it daily in the great journey of life. At one and the same moment various individuals, as yet unknown to each other, are drawn together by circumstance, or destiny, toward one common meeting point.

These meeting points are curious: we advance toward them as if with our eyes shut; we seldom know when they will occur, and still less how much they may involve. From them arise the most momentous incidents of our lives; often sad enough, often strange enough; often completely altering the after course of our existence, and exercising an influence which extends beyond time—into eternity.

I am about to make you *clairvoyant* with regard to three such unconscious groups of pilgrims on the every-day journey of life. You shall see them all in their various places of abode, on one particular evening in April, and you will then perceive how they are all advancing unconsciously toward each other, and toward one object, literally and metaphorically, toward a certain landed estate, called Wast-Wayland in the North of England. Here, having once arrived, like the travelers at the hostel, they shall remain together for a period, and then, as by an irresistible fate, be again separated, as if to the four winds of heaven; for there are separations which divide more completely than half the globe—while the influences which brought them thither shall remain in their effects forever.

Our first little group consists of but two women, Mrs. Mildmay, and her daughter Honour. They are sitting in a small but neat room looking upon the sea at Hastings; the tide is out, the slant rays of the setting sun light up the beach, and the sea, and the low gray rocks which rise above the level of the low-water sands, with a golden radiance. It is a lovely evening, warm and balmy as June, and many people are out picking up shells and pebbles, and enjoying the finest sunset of what has hitherto been a late and ungenial season. Even the poor invalid, with his close wrappings and his anxious attendants, had ventured forth, either to pace slowly, or to be drawn in his wheeled chair along the sun-illumined esplanade. The two ladies, however, of whom I have spoken, both of whose countenances wore the quiet and subdued expression of sickness and sorrow, seemed indisposed to leave their little room this evening, fine though it was. The mother sat on the sofa at her needlework; the daughter in her little bow window apparently gazing on the lovely sunset and the groups of people on the beach below.

The feelings of both mother and daughter were much alike at this moment; each had a communication to make, and each felt reluctant to make it; we fear so much to distress those we love, we avoid touching upon painful subjects even when the poignancy of the pain is past; so sacred to the affectionate heart are the feelings of the beloved.

The daughter's eyes were fixed on the objects without, but her thoughts were not employed by them. The mother glanced up from her work from time to time, with that sick, sinking sensation which every anxious spirit knows so well. A writing-desk stood open on the table before her, and she thought painfully of certain papers within it, the contents of which must be communicated; and now the time was come when that communication could be no longer delayed. She had so often put off this painful duty, she must put it off no longer. She thought over the weary words she would use; how she would try to soften that which was hard, how she would endeavor to cast a cheerful coloring over what she too well knew was dark and dispiriting; and above all, how she would never reveal to what an extent she herself had suffered.

She made two or three attempts to speak, but her tongue or her heart failed her, and perhaps she might have deferred her communication till the morrow—till the morning, that her daughter might at least have one more quiet night's rest, as she had so often done before, had not Honour herself risen from her seat, and placing herself by her mother's side, said in a low, but firm tone of voice :

"I have long wished to have some talk with you about many things, dearest mother. I wish you really to understand and to believe that there is no longer any need for anxiety on my account. I have been now for some time quite reconciled to things as they are. I acknowledge that it requires a great effort, perhaps also a great amount of suffering, before we can submit to adverse circumstances, but the effort is not beyond our strength ; and then, when once we are submissive, there comes great peace of mind, and new paths are opened to us, and new sources of pleasure which fully compensates for what we have lost. When once, dearest mother, we attain to this state of submission and faith, we are not only contented, but we see that every thing is ordained for the best, and that if we had the ordering of our own destiny we should make blundering work of it, and have but little cause to rejoice, after all. I have come to see this, dear mother, very clearly, and now I beseech of you to have confidence in me. Do not wear that sad, anxious look which is not natural to your countenance, and which distresses me much more than any of those old troubles which at one time so completely occupied me, and worse than that, made me apparently forget you. Pardon me, dear mother, for all this ! The worst of such trials as mine, is, that they are so self-absorbing. And now I want really to convince you that I see all these things very differently to what I did. I am no longer unhappy. I shall no longer be selfish."

"My dear child," said her mother, interrupting her, "do not be so unjust to yourself. You have not been selfish ; you have behaved heroically. You have had a great trial to bear, and thank God ! he has enabled you to bear it."

"Yes, indeed he has," continued Honour, who was anxious to resume the conversation which it had required a great effort to commence, "and your goodness also, and your patience with me, have done much—have many a time strengthened me when otherwise I must have sunk. And there is no one in this world so true and kind as yourself, and so worthy of my living for. I see this, I know this now ; and now I feel it as my greatest blessing and privilege to be a life-long companion to you, to be able to devote myself entirely to you, and to my duties as a daughter—to making you happy : and I know, dearest mother, that in so doing I shall be happier than I ever have been, or ever should have been.

Happy in another way—in a way that God has appointed for me, and not myself; and that is much better, for God is wiser—oh, so very much wiser than we! Will it not be so, dear mother; shall we not be very happy together?"

Honour paused and gazed into her mother's face with her large, beautiful eyes full of emotion, though not of tears. Tears, however, were in the mother's eyes as she lifted the trembling hand which she pressed to her lips, and Honour continued:

"But, mother dear, you must promise me one or two things: firstly, you must cease to be anxious about me, for indeed, as I told you before, there is no cause for anxiety on my account. It is only while the mind is wavering and tossed about that we are unhappy; only while a single regret remains, a single longing after that which God has forbidden to us, are we unhappy; but when the mind is calm, is submissive, when we can conscientiously say, 'I have given up all; thy will and not mine be done,' then that which was dark becomes light, the difficult becomes easy, and the uncertain assured; then there is nothing left but to advance straight forward in peace, and even perhaps in great joy. This is what I feel at present, and you, dearest mother, must feel it with me, and you must still strengthen me as you have hitherto done; and more than this, you must cease to be anxious for me, for that you are so I can see plainly enough. Yes, dear mother, you press my hand; you confess it; you have not faith in me; you have seen so much weakness in me that you can not believe in my strength. Ah! what can I do to prove to you that I am contented, that I am happy! Believe this, my mother. There is, therefore, no need for anxiety; nothing but happiness lies before us—happiness in our united affection, in our friendship, in our love for each other, for there is nothing in this world to compare with the affectionate, confiding intercourse of mother and daughter; there is no friendship, no love like it. Yes, of this I feel sure: a new life lies before us, a better life than the old one, because it will be so much truer; and if I can only see you looking as carefree as you used to do, then, indeed, I shall be happy; very, very happy!

"But then, dear mother," continued she, in a tone of less exultation, "I have to ask from you a sacrifice; perhaps it is selfish, but I hope not—I think not. Do not let us return to Northbridge. There is something very painful to me in the thought of returning thither. There we should again fall into the old routine; and seeing the same people, and living among the same old scenes, would recall daily and hourly old associations to keep alive old habits; habits of mind, trains of thought I mean, from which I must dissever myself if I would live up to the new and better knowledge which I have acquired. The trials which God ordains for us we must bear, be they ever so painful, but those of which I speak are not his trials; we *may* put them from us; it is a duty which we owe to ourselves."

"I do not wish," continued she, after a pause, "to meet Frederick's—Mr. Horrock's friends," said she, correcting herself, and with a peculiar tone of voice, which her mother well understood; "it would be very painful and unpleasant. Therefore I have thought if you would consent, and if it were not asking too great a sacrifice, that we would not return to Northbridge at all. Let us go abroad for the summer; let us quite change the scene, and you will see how I shall rise above that which has made me so unhappy: and what a beautiful new life will begin for us both. I mean from this time to put myself, as it were, to school again: in fact we are scholars all our life long; but I mean literally what I say. I shall study hard; I shall read none but solid, improving works, so that I may strengthen my mind, so that the heart may not run riot in very idleness, as women's foolish hearts too often do. 'Love in idleness' has a deeper meaning than people think, therefore I will not be idle. I will work hard, and give a purpose to my life, and in this way I shall be very happy. I feel something of this happiness already; and this I believe seriously, that there is nothing better for us than to have to overcome some enemy—some weakness or besetting sin; for if we seek in sincerity to overcome, strength is given to us, and one victory over ourselves insures us many others. In this way there is no fear of sliding backward, because at every step forward additional strength is given for the next. Is it not so, beloved mother?"

"Bless you, my child!" said the mother in reply, "bless you for these words, for this assurance of strength; but have you ever thought that God in his wisdom may see meet to try you still further, to lay yet other burdens upon you—upon us both?"

"What does this mean?" exclaimed Honour, with a flushing cheek; "what new trial is there? for such your words imply. Tell me all. Let me know the worst. It can not be so very severe since you are spared to me."

Honour looked into her mother's face, and it seemed to her as if that beloved countenance had at once become twenty years older;

every line seemed furrowed; a deep pallor overspread it, and the lips quivered.

"O, gracious Father in Heaven!" exclaimed Honour, "be merciful to us! Tell me, my mother, are you ill, or what fearful calamity is impending. But fear not for me. I am stronger than you think. I will, with God's aid, help you to bear it, be it what it may."

"God will strengthen you to bear this, as he has strengthened you to bear other sorrows," said the mother, speaking slowly from her unwillingness to reveal tidings for which she knew her daughter to be wholly unprepared; "but I feared to tell you, because I would not willingly have added one feather's weight to your troubles. But I keep you in suspense. Yes, my child, you have yet other troubles to bear. Nerve yourself and be strong. We have lost, my darling, our comfortable little income; the firm of Harriman and Payne has become bankrupt; and thus, not only is my annuity gone, but your two thousand pounds. My child, how can you bear this? Oh! it is more on your account than my own that I am distressed!"

Honour made no reply: this intelligence was to her like a thunderclap. For the moment she felt stunned, and all the gloomy weight of poverty seemed crushing her brain. Sterner causes than the indulgence of her own wishes would now compel them to give up their former pleasant and comfortable home, which but a moment before her own inclinations had advocated. How different was the aspect which every thing now seemed to wear! There was no romance in poverty; she understood too well the realities of life for any such delusion; and though she appeared outwardly calm, her mother's tidings had fallen on her spirit with a crushing weight.

Her mother, however, who had expected a more visible effect from her communication, seeing her thus apparently self-possessed, continued in a calmer tone herself:

"Yes, it is a very dreadful thing for us who have now no other dependence than your poor godmother's legacy, forty pounds a year. Most unfortunate was it that your poor, dear father, left his money in this old house of business, instead of investing it where it would have been safe; but, then, he had such confidence in them; and I should as soon have expected the Bank of England to fail as their firm. You know it was only two or three years ago that Mr. Payne had thirty thousand pounds from his wife's uncle, all which, it was said, was to go into the business;

but, instead of that, it now turns out that this money is settled upon her and the children, so that, though a bankrupt, he leaves the business, still a wealthy man; and they are all gone into South Wales, where she has an estate. I do not know if one can altogether blame Mrs. Payne, as many people do, for not giving all up to the creditors; for there are six children, and, as Mr. Bellairs says, by this money she may enable her husband again to enter trade and make a good fortune; and even, perhaps, if he is so disposed, to pay something handsome to his creditors; whereas, if she gave up every penny, and reduced them all to beggary, it would be no great matter among the claimants, for the house has failed to the amount of two hundred thousand pounds. It has been a dreadful thing, dear Honour, and has caused the ruin of many, many families. I could not tell you at the time, dearest, for it was just after we came here, and when you were so ill. Mrs. Woodley wrote and told me that there were some suspicions of the house; that was the first intimation I had; and then in January, when the payment was not made as usual, I wrote to Mr. Harriman begging him to remit me the money here, but of course not hinting of what I had heard. He sent me the money immediately, and wrote saying, that, owing to great failures abroad, they would be compelled to stop payment, but that, considering the hardness of my case, they at once made this remittance to me. The next week their bankruptcy was gazetted. Of course, every body at Northbridge knew our altered circumstances, but I took care that no hint of it reached you, for I thought that at that time it would have been the death of you."

Honour pressed her mother's hand, but spoke not, and her mother continued:

"I am convinced that some knowledge of this must have reached Frederick Horrocks, and that this is the true explanation of his conduct. And, darling, as I am now speaking of him, I may as well tell you that he has left Northbridge, and is now settled somewhere in Warwickshire; they say he has entered into partnership with a solicitor there. And if I am right, dear Honour, in my belief as to his mercenary views, it is a blessing that you were not united to him before this loss of property occurred, or yours might have been a miserable life; he had no generous, noble affection for you, and such a union could not have been happy. Ah, you are weeping, darling! Well, I do not object to tears; they will relieve you; only lay your dear head on my shoulder, and let me support you, and I will go on; for I have had a deal to do, as you may imagine; and now that the ice is once broken, as I may say, and you know the worst, it will be a great relief to me to unburden my heart to you."

"Ah! I ought to have borne all this heavy burden with you, my mother!" said Honour, sorrowfully.

"All in good time, my dear child," returned her mother, speaking more cheerfully. "But you must not be cast down, for a new path of life seems opening to us; but I will tell you of that presently; there are other things which I must speak of first. When I saw that my annuity was gone, that we had lost those means which enabled us to live so handsomely and so independently, and with them all prospect of any after provision for you, and that, literally, we had nothing left but your poor godmother's money, I determined to give up our house at Northbridge, to which place, for many other reasons, as you say, it was undesirable for us to return. Mr. Boydell Grainger took our house at once off my hands —you know he always admired it so much; every thing was sold by auction, and sold much better than I expected. Mr. Boydell Grainger bought many things which suited the house, and Mr. Woodley very kindly took the business management of every thing on himself. Every body was kind; the Bellairs, the Walpoles, and the Woodleys wrote very kind letters to me. I shall show them all to you some day. I hardly knew that we had so many friends. Several of our poor neighbors bought little articles at the sale, because they said that they would have something which had belonged to the Mildmays. Poor Sally Randal has the cat, and old Mrs. Miggs bought Dickey; she paid fifteen shillings for him and the cage; I could not have believed that she had so much money to spend; but Mrs. Woodley says that the old lady is delighted with her purchase, and that Dickey hangs in her little parlor window between her red curtains, and looks quite smart; but what affected me most of all was, that poor old Job Wood wrote to me here to say that if five-and-twenty pounds which he had saved would be of any service to us, we should have it, and he would never trouble us about it while he lived; for he said, poor man, that nothing was too much which he could do for us; and every body was so anxious about you, darling; and even the school-children, Mrs. Trimmins said, spoke of you continually, and many of them cried when they heard that you were not coming back and would never teach them again."

A sentiment of tender yet pleasing regret passed through the heart of Honour. "Poor, dear children!" she said, in a low voice, and her mother continued:

"Yes, dear, people were very kind; and it was in the midst of all that trouble, some little consolation to see that there were kind and genuine hearts in the world; nevertheless it was altogether a sad, anxious time, as you may believe, for me, and you so ill."

"But I am now well," interrupted Honour, raising her head from her mother's bosom, "and had I only known all this before I should have roused myself. I only needed the motive. We women so often only need the motive to rouse ourselves, when without it we droop in sentimental sorrow, and are a burden to ourselves and others. You will see now, dearest mother, that I am strong—now, with God's help, it is my turn to care for you—to work for you."

"Yes," continued her mother, without replying to her daughter's words, "it was an anxious time, but I put my trust in God, and He, my darling, is ever a faithful friend; He, I believe, will never forsake us. But I must now proceed with what I have further to communicate. One evening, when I was very much out of spirits, and all the more so because I was forced to keep every thing to myself, I wrote to Mr. Wilbraham, and told him exactly how our affairs stood, and asked his advice. I do not know exactly why I wrote to him, unless it was that your father had so high an opinion of him, and he knew our circumstances so well, and as it has turned out, I think I was right in so doing. He was then on the northern circuit, and my letter was sent after him, and lay somewhere for some little time before it reached him, so that I did not get his answer till about a fortnight ago. But even in this very delay there seems to me a providence, as I will tell you. It appears that after he left York, professional business took him to the residence of a friend of his, a Mr. Elworthy, of Wast Hall; somewhere on the borders of Westmoreland. Now, as I said before, my letter reached him there, and as he and this Mr. Elworthy seem to be old and confidential friends, as well as for other reasons, which I will tell you presently, its contents were fully discussed between them. Mr. Wilbraham represented this Mr. Elworthy to be a man of high character and great wealth, although of singularly secluded habits. He lives very quietly on his estate, and has devoted himself for many years, indeed since the death of his wife, to the improvement of his tenants and the poor people about him. He has very liberal and enlightened views on education, and having successfully established a boy's school some years since on his estate, is about to establish one for girls also. He has built a school-house, to which is attached a cottage for the mistress: he will pay a hundred a year, besides which there will be the house rent-free, with a garden, and a little croft for the keep of a cow."

Honour sighed, and her mother remarking it, observed, "You think, my beloved, that this is very humble. It is so, no doubt, but for my part I have looked at it so long that I am accustomed to it; nay, can even see something attractive in it. Mr. Wilbraham writes me that the cottage is extremely pretty; the country round beautiful, and the people among whom we should live, simple and kind in their manners. There have been, of course, many applicants for the situation; not a clergyman or dissenting minister for many miles round but has some candidate to recommend; none however have come up to all his requirings; for, as I told you before, he has very exalted notions of what a teacher ought to be—even a teacher for the poor."

Again Honour sighed; and Mrs. Mildmay, without appearing to notice it, continued:

"Mr. Wilbraham laid my letter before him, warmly recommending you, dear Honour, and myself, and that so successfully that Mr. Elworthy himself inclosed a letter in one from Mr. Wilbraham, offering us the situation if we chose to accept it. Mr. Wilbraham, who writes in the kindest manner, and who I believe to be sincerely our friend, most strongly advises it;" and here Mrs. Mildmay opened her desk, and taking out the two letters, put them in her daughter's hand.

"Read them," said she, "and you shall decide. I have done nothing definite, for I wrote to both gentlemen, saying that it must rest with you entirely, and that as soon as you were sufficiently recovered, I would lay the proposal before you. Therefore, read them, my love, and I think you will agree with me that we ought to accept the offer; for then, at all events, we shall have a little independence, although we may have to work for it, and that among strangers."

Honour read the letters, and decided as her mother had already done.

It was astonishing how little the loss of income seemed to affect the mind of the younger woman. The motive for exertion, as she herself had foretold, raised her above her former enfeebling sorrows. No well-constituted mind can prostrate itself long before one idea;

it may be bowed to the dust for a time, but a reaction will take place, and it then raises itself with more than its ordinary force, as if to compensate itself for its late abasement. Honour's soul seemed now to breathe a purer and a more bracing atmosphere, and her whole being was as if renovated.

It was soon settled that they should immediately remove to the north, and enter upon their new duties. There was, therefore, no time to sit with folded hands and drooping head, pondering upon the painful past; both mother and daughter, in the midst of occupations, looked, as it were, only upward and onward, and cheerfulness and hope, which had been strangers to them for many months, now again found entrance into their hearts, and began to beam upon their countenances. Mind and body were alike regaining health.

At this wholesome point we must leave them for the present, and return to that same April evening when we saw them first.

CHAPTER II.

While Mrs. Mildmay and her daughter were, on that same April evening, arranging their plans and discussing their future prospects, which were as new to Honour as they were unexpected by her; and while much thought was expended on the letter which was that same evening written to Mr. Elworthy, accepting the situation of village school-mistress in Wayland-dale, another family circle was gathered round their fireside tea-table, busy also with their future life, prospects, and plans, all tending toward this same Mr. Elworthy—toward this same Wayland-dale.

This latter family party, which is met at Woodbury, a small country town in Warwickshire, has a very bright external aspect. It consists of Mrs. Dutton, a handsome, middle-aged, and most respectable widow lady, and her four daughters. Of these four daughters, all handsome women, the two oldest are already married.

Mrs. Dutton is a managing woman with a small income. Her husband held a government situation, which was obtained through the influence of a remote aristocratic cousin, among the collateral branches of whose family the name of Francis Dutton may be found in the peerage. After the death of her husband, Mrs. Dutton removed to Woodbury, his native place, and on his claims to rank, took a high position among the gentry of the neighborhood. She visited a great deal; her inclinations led her to this, as well as what she considered her duty toward her slenderly-portioned daughters. She dressed well, which she held also to be her duty to them, and in reward for her many maternal virtues, was marrying off her daughters as much to her own satisfaction as to the envy of her acquaintance.

The business of Mrs. Dutton's life was, and had been for some years, the marrying these daughters. She had the natural solicitude of a mother on this subject, besides which, she entered into all the joys, fears, excitements, and final triumphs of her daughters' courtships with the deepest interest, living over in them her own youthful days. The history of each daughter's heart was to her like a new novel, in which the reader is willing to be plunged into the deepest seas of uncertainty and bewilderment, so that the heroine is but rewarded at last by marrying the richest of all her suitors.

Of the marriages of the elder daughters a word must be said. Mr. Beauchamp, the husband of the eldest, although merely a surgeon, had an extensive country practice, and made a large income, and it was through him that Mr. Cartwright, the husband of the second daughter, had been introduced to the family. Mr. Cartwright was only one remove from a baronetcy, and though he was—even Mrs. Dutton was obliged secretly to confess it—a coarse-minded man, and though his wife was not happy, yet these were only flaws in the matrimonial prize, which, as she averred, never was perfect, never came up altogether a prize. So she talked proudly of her "daughter Cartwright's carriage," and of "her son-in law, Mr. Cartwright, the nephew of Sir Peter," and looked forward to the time when her other daughters, Natalie and Ellinor—"the pretty Ellinor Dutton," as she was called, might furnish her with other means of self-exaltation.

And now the pretty Ellinor was sought in marriage. Alas! poor Mrs. Dutton! she was considerably disappointed on this occasion. Ellinor, who was so pretty, was wooed and willing to be won by no person of more elevated rank or station than the new young partner in the old law firm of Cheatham and Bragg, solicitors of Woodbury. Mrs. Dutton made resistance for some time, but Mr. Cartwright overruled her objections; he decidedly favored the match; and the pretty Ellinor was invited to spend a week at Fircoates, the residence of the Cartwrights, where Mr. Frederick Horrocks, the young lawyer, came to dine very frequently. When Ellinor, therefore, returned home, it was soon understood that Mrs. Dutton must give her consent; and accordingly the family party of which I spoke was assembled this same bright April evening to meet the gentleman for the first time as Ellinor's accepted lover.

I have spoken of Mrs. Dutton's daughters as being slenderly portioned: that is true; and yet, had this lady had twenty daughters instead of four, she would soon have married them all, and married them well, according to the world's opinion. The reason of this was that the whole world believed, on her confident assurance, that they would inherit the large property of their Uncle Elworthy, in the North of England. The good people of Woodbury, therefore, always spoke of Mrs. Dutton's daughters as heiresses, and as such the attentions and the kindnesses which they received from every body were untold; they had presents without end; they were invited to every party and pic-nic which took place throughout the year; they were courted, admired, and flattered; in short, they were the most popular young ladies in Woodbury.

So confident was the public opinion with regard to the golden prospects of the Duttons, that even tradespeople, who would not have trusted a poor, honest man's daughter to the amount of twenty shillings, vied with each other as to who should have the largest amount in his books against them. And although the bills for Mrs. Cartwright's wedding-clothes were not yet paid, yet it would be very edifying to see how assiduously every body would press wedding purchases upon Mrs. Dutton, as soon as it was generally known that the pretty Ellinor was to be married to Mr. Horrocks, the new partner in the old firm of Cheatham and Bragg—Mr. Bragg having retired with a hundred thousand pounds, as it was said.

The advent of Mr. Frederick Horrocks, with his handsome person and popular manners, as one who was henceforth to divide profits with old Cheatham, caused, some six months before, a vast excitement in Woodbury, especially among the mothers and daughters there. It might indeed be said, in scarcely a metaphorical sense, that he was received by the ladies with open arms. He was immediately as popular as the Duttons themselves. Mr. Cheatham gave dinners to introduce him to the gentlemen of the neighborhood, and these dinners, of course, led to a great deal of visiting and gayety, in which, as a natural consequence, the Duttons, the Beauchamps, and the Cartwrights were included.

Mr. Cartwright, whose property had been, one way and another, in the hands of Messrs. Cheatham and Bragg, for many a long year, showed very early a decided intention of favoring the young solicitor, and, as I have said, a prodigious intimacy grew up between them, under the fostering care of which Ellinor's love affair prospered immensely.

But before the little world of Woodbury began even to gossip about the pretty Ellinor Dutton and Mr. Frederick Horrocks, that young man, who was greatly elated by his new prospects, was for a time considerably perplexed by an old love-engagement into which he now persuaded himself he had entered very unadvisedly True, Miss Mildmay loved him—at one time he believed that he loved her.

"What fools young men are!" exclaimed he to himself, when he now recalled his passionate vows and protestations, and bethought himself of all the ardent letters he had written. He thought, too, heartless young man though he was, how good, and sweet, and lovely was Honour, and how little she deserved such treatment, how little she expected it. For the moment he was almost staggered. Then, on the other hand, the gayeties of Woodbury, the golden prospects of the Duttons, the fascinations of the pretty Ellinor, the unmistakable purport of Mr. Cartwright's friendship, operated like magic upon him, loosening, as it were, every old bond—and he resolved to be free. And though he should be a villain, and though he should break the heart of Honour Mildmay, and though it was a case for a duel or for an action for breach of promise of marriage, yet many a man was a villain, and Honour had neither father nor brother to call him out; nor were she and her mother the people to make the affair public in a court of law. No! on all those points he was safe. The question lay between himself and his conscience; it hung, as it were, in a balance. Miss Mildmay had property, but she was no heiress; she was quite as lovely as Ellinor Dutton, but then she was no heiress; the question hung, as I said, in a balance. At length it became suddenly decided. The dubious state of Messrs. Harriman and Payne's affairs was one of those professional secrets which was confided to Mr. Frederick Horrocks soon after he became associated in this law-firm. With the ruin of Harriman and Payne, which the lawyers considered to be inevitable, Honour Mildmay and her mother would become penniless.

Therefore, before this great commercial bankruptcy was dreamed of by the public, the true woman's heart of poor Honour Mildmay received a deep wound. Her lover, without assigning any reason, excepting a parade of his own unworthiness, of which he professed himself to have been long aware, begged to restore to her the faith she had plighted to him. The blow was like that of a thunderbolt. Pride and wounded affection, nevertheless, sustained her for the moment. The plighted troth, so unworthily bestowed, was retaken with apparent equanimity, but then she sank prostrate, and to her agonized and outraged feelings, death alone seemed her refuge.

If the Bellairs, and the Walpoles, and the Woodleys—friends of the Mildmays at Northbridge—were full of indignation at the false-heartedness of Frederick Horrocks, who, like Honour, was a native of their town, though he had of late years lived in London, still his uncle, who had brought him up, was a man of considerable consequence in the place, and as he did not seriously resent his nephew's breach of faith, neither did they quarrel with him on that account. The Bellairs, the Walpoles, and the Woodleys, visited with the Horrocks as usual, satisfying themselves by showing an increase of personal kindness to Mrs. Mildmay and her daughter, during the short time they remained there, and by remarking whenever the subject was mentioned among themselves, "Poor Honour Mildmay! she was shamefully used by Frederick Horrocks; and if she had had a brother he would not have dared to have done so. But, however, he was not worthy of her, and that is one consolation."

It is always easy for mere lookers-on to console themselves for other people's troubles, even those of their best friends. Still Mrs. Mildmay and her daughter saw nothing but kindness on their countenances and in the behavior of those who surrounded them, and leaving Northbridge as they did soon after, in consequence of Honour's illness, they took with them no sentiment but that of the earnest sympathy of their friends; and the letters which Mrs. Mildmay afterward received from them, on the loss of her property, only tended to strengthen this belief.

These circumstances occurring however at least a hundred and fifty miles from Woodbury were wholly unknown to the good people there. Frederick Horrocks came among them from London as a young bachelor with a heart at his own disposal. He said that he was free; Mr. Cartwright began to manœuvre, the little town began to talk, and in an astonishingly short time the pretty Ellinor and all her family were impatient for the proposal. As a matter of course, it came.

It had been made in form to the mother this morning—it was a mere form, for they all understood one another; and now, on this particular evening, Mr. Frederick Horrocks drinks tea with the Dutton family for the first time, as the openly accepted lover of the pretty Ellinor. The married daughters were there. The two husbands were to come later in the evening, although it was possible that they might not come at all, for Mr. Beauchamp was very little at home, and Mr. Cartwright seldom went where his wife was, least of all to her mother's, to whom he had very early ceased to show any regard, the cause of which coolness will be mentioned afterward; nevertheless, Mrs. Dutton continued to behave to him as the most amiable of mothers-in-law, speaking of him invariably as her "son-in-law Mr. Cartwright," and magnifying his prospective advantages from his uncle Sir Peter, and most religiously shutting her eyes against all his defects. He would not, indeed, have been at all expected to-night excepting on account of Frederick Horrocks' visit; Mrs. Cartwright spoke, therefore, confidently of her husband's coming, and Mrs. Dutton had lobster salad for supper, which was a favorite dish with that gentleman.

The tea was now ready; the water bubbling in the handsome urn, and the silver tea service on the best tray, while the table was covered with cakes and muffins, and marmalade, and the most delicate bread and butter; for though it was but a family party, yet the occasion was rather ceremonial.

Mrs. Dutton wore one of the best of her many best silk gowns, and had a profusion of white French satin ribbon on her cap. She looked really handsome as she sat, tall and gracious, in her large crimson chair, with her feet on a footstool, watching her yet unmatrimonially-engaged daughter Natalie, preparing tea.

At that moment the door opened, and Ellinor, with her long, dark ringlets drooping to her bosom, entered the room leaning on her lover's arm. The two young people had been walking together in the garden, for the evening at Woodbury had been as warm and splendid as at Hastings, and they seemed now to bring into the room with them a feeling of fresh air.

"Well, my love," said Mrs. Dutton to Ellinor, when they were all seated at the table, "have you told Mr. Horrocks about your uncle Elworthy?"

"Not one syllable," said Ellinor, laughing.

"Naughty girl!" replied her mother.

"I thought we could do it so much better all together," said Ellinor. "Caroline can tell about her visit, which was so comical; and you mamma, must tell Frederick about that horrid Mr. Richard Elworthy. I never can bear his name! All I shall tell is, that our revered uncle Elworthy is an eccentric old man, as cross as possible; that he has a great rambling estate consisting of peat-bog and stony sheep-walks in Wayland-dale; that the climate there is so bad that, when I was there last, it rained for a whole three weeks without ceasing; that there are horrid caves and 'pots,' as they are called, in the neighborhood of Wast-Wayland, which is where he lives, and that he makes every body go and see them, as if they were the most beautiful things in creation; that the people there are as rude as savages, and do nothing but knit, both men and women, and that our excellent uncle has schools where he tries to civilize them, and where he takes you every other day; and that I never was so tired in all my life as when I was there last; and mamma was obliged to set off and come away before her visit was ended, lest, as she said, I should affront him, but in reality because she was as tired as I was."

"Nonsense!" said Mrs. Dutton, laughing. "You must not believe a word she says, Mr. Horrocks. My brother Elworthy is a fine original character, and the most benevolent man living; not one of your alms-giving philanthropists, but one who has the real well-being of the poor about him at heart, and who spends a deal of money to promote it; though I must confess that many of his schemes are chimerical, as is so often the case with your poetical-minded reformers, and Mr. Elworthy is one of these."

"Only think!" exclaimed Ellinor, interrupting her mother, "of his benevolence toward his savages being so great as to make him try to persuade mamma, after Emma's marriage, to take Natalie and me to manage his girls' school for him! I never heard of such a thing! And if it had not been our uncle Elworthy's scheme, how affronted we should all have been!"

"You silly child!" returned her mother, "when I get you all off my hands, I'll go and manage his schools for him. There is nothing that I should like better than to be settled down for the remainder of my life in that beautiful place. It is really a noble estate, Mr. Horrocks!" said she, "and such shooting! With my brother-in-law's management, he must have at least seven or eight thousand a year, and the old tenants live on at mere nominal rents. However, he does not spend much, so that what is lost on the one hand is saved on the other, and it will be all the better for my girls one of these days. It is a beautiful place, Mr. Horrocks, quite a little territory, for nearly the whole of Wayland-dale belongs to him. The upper part of this dale is called Wast-Wayland; and there, on elevated ground, stands the house, Wast Hall. It would be a very fine place if it were kept up, but he only occupies a part of it; the principal rooms have been shut ever since his wife's death—in fact, have never been finished. The situation of the Hall is very striking, as I said. Behind it, and screening it from the north, lies a high hill called Hibblethwaite Fell, on the foot, as it were, of which stands Wast Hall. This Hibblethwaite Fell may be considered less as the termination of the hills which inclose the valley, than as the majestic commencement of a wild district which runs northward from this point, consisting of savage glens and black rocky moorland, in the depths of which lie caves, and that wild Druidical scenery of which Mr. Elworthy is so fond, and to which, as Ellinor says, he drags all his visitors, poor man, without any mercy. But as to Wayland-dale itself, if you know any thing of the Yorkshire dales in general, you will know what it is, only that Wayland is perhaps the most secluded, as it is certainly the loveliest of them all. I am somewhat of an enthusiast," said Mrs. Dutton, apologetically; "if I was an artist, I should certainly be a landscape painter, and Wayland-dale would furnish beautiful subjects for my pencil. There is the beck, as they call it, that is the rocky stream winding along the bottom, with its lesser tributaries collected from the peaty morasses on the fell-heads, as they are called, and which run gurgling down the broken stony sides of the hills, bordered with alders and ash trees, and which, as in most of these dales, form the boundary lines of proprietorship, each farm being inclosed between gill and gill—for these little streams, in the dialect of that country, are called gills; but as Mr. Elworthy owns the greater part of the Dale, this division has reference only to the tenants. I know all the people in the Dale, for I made a point of becoming in some measure personally acquainted with them; but I can not say that I like them much. Their manners are simple and very old-fashioned. I should think the most primitive in the kingdom, and their dialect something like the Lowland Scotch. Mr. Elworthy calls the dialect pure English, and has I believed studied it very much—he has a great turn that way. But the people, with all their simplicity, have a vast amount of cunning in them, and have found out the way of imposing dreadfully on poor Mr. Elworthy."

Mr. Frederick Horrocks, who was really interested in hearing of one, from whom he hoped to derive a great advantage at some future time, requested Mrs. Dutton to give him the history of this their excellent relative.

Mrs. Dutton had pleasure in gratifying him, for there was nothing which she liked better than speaking of Mr. Elworthy and the Wast-Wayland property.

"The grandfather of the present Mr. Elworthy," said she, beginning in true historic style, "had two sons, William and Richard. William, the eldest, the father of our Mr. Elworthy, inherited the Wayland-dale property, where he continued to reside till his death; Richard, the second son, like the prodigal of the gospel, took the portion which fell to his share and went to London. He was a born spendthrift; married, somewhat late in life, a woman without property; died and left a son, his only child, penniless. In the mean time, his brother William was left a widower also, with an only son, our Mr. Elworthy, who came early into the possession of his property. As I have said, he was a man of a most noble and generous heart, and very impulsive by nature; therefore, no sooner was he master of his own large property than he sent to London for his penniless cousin, who, his mother being also dead, was friendless as well as poor, and adopted him almost as a son, or as a younger brother. It was very noble of him; but, as it turned out, the most unfortunate thing he could have done. He was bred to the law, and is, I am told, a very clever lawyer, but worthless and unprincipled; one of those men who, with considerable talent, yet turn it to no good account. Oh! he is a very bad man; you will have much to hear about him, I fear."

"Richard Elworthy?" inquired Frederick, interrupting her; "is he called Elworthy Elworthy?"

"The very same!" said Mrs. Dutton. "Only think of the arrogance, the foolish assumption of his being called Richard Elworthy Elworthy! It provokes me!" said she.

"I know something of him," said Frederick Horrocks; "he is of the Middle Temple; every body knows him; a black-haired man, with very white teeth, who has the most astonishing amount of antiquarian knowledge—nay, indeed, has knowledge of every kind; is member of I don't know how many learned societies, and is always going to dine with some lord or other, and asks you to lend him half-a-crown for cab fare, as he has forgotten his purse. I have seen him. He is a clever fellow, but a worthless scoundrel. I know that he has great expectations from somebody. So *he* then is the famous heir-at-law of which Mr. Cheatham has spoken?" said Frederick Horrocks, as if thinking to himself.

"But Mr. Cheatham does not believe that there is any chance of his having the property?" remarked Mrs. Dutton, with undisguised impatience.

"No, certainly not!" returned Horrocks; "but I can not help being so astonished. I have heard this Richard Elworthy himself speak of it; every body who has been with him for only half an hour has heard the same. Would you believe it? he carries a pocket map of the property about with him, and has contrived to gull Jews and money-lenders out of their gold by his pretended claims of heirship; I know not how many *post-obits* he has not abroad.

But, my dear lady," said he, addressing Mrs. Dutton in a very business-like tone, and with the intention of persuading every one of his entire disinterestedness, "this man *is*, unquestionably, the heir-at-law, is he not? Would he not take every farthing, if Mr. Elworthy died without will, or if the property descends alone to heirs male?"

"That it does not!" said Mrs. Dutton, eagerly; "my husband saw the title-deeds before his sister's marriage, at the time her settlement was made; and, besides, I have heard Mr. Elworthy say so himself, times without end; and I have heard him say, quite as often, that Richard Elworthy shall never possess one farthing of his property; and he has good reasons for this. I know very well how his property is to be disposed of; I therefore make myself as easy as if we had, or as if my daughters had, possession already. Mr. Elworthy is a most conscientious man, with a great deal of that feudal feeling toward his tenants and dependents which made the old baron a father and friend, rather than lord and master, to his inferiors. Oh! he is a very unusual character, Mr. Horrocks, and one which you will know how to appreciate: a very superior character is he! who could not leave his old, respectable tenantry in the hands, and to the mercy of an unprincipled wretch like his cousin Richard, to whom, independently of other causes of dissatisfaction, he always attributed the death of his wife!"

"You amaze me?" said Frederick Horrocks; "pray, proceed; how could her death be attributable to this man?"

"Oh! it is a long history," said Mrs. Dutton, "and quite a tragedy, I assure you; and so dotingly fond of her as as he was! But I don't feel equal to telling it to-night; you shall hear it on some other occasion. But it was a terrible thing! You know she was my husband's sister, and he, too, was greatly attached to her, for she was a beautiful woman—Ellinor is reckoned to be very like her. Poor Mr. Elworthy's mind was so much affected by her loss that he shut himself up for a long time, and would see nobody but the nurse and the baby that she left. It was the general opinion that my husband must give up his appointment—we were living in London then—and remove to Wayland-dale to take charge of the property for him. It was what we were quite willing to do, for we would have made any sacrifice to have served him. However, he preferred keeping the management in his own hands, and it was better that he did so, for the exertion that was requisite, both of mind and body, was good for him. But, between you and me, he never has thoroughly recovered the full tone of his mind since, and hence, like the Catholic with his penance, he is, and has been for years, striving to put away the memory of this woe, and to atone for faultiness in his own character at the time, by establishing schools and doing so very much for the people about him. Beautiful traits these are of character, I grant you, and in poor, dear Mr. Elworthy's case they are particularly so, because by nature he was proud, somewhat imperious, and extremely hasty in temper. However, as I was saying, he preferred managing his property, although he felt my husband's offer most gratefully, and he told him, some years afterward, that he had made his will, leaving the whole of his property to himself and his children, whom he looked upon as his own blood relations. They were, in fact, the nearest relations of his wife, and he knew, he said, that this disposition of the property would be in accordance with her wishes. His health was greatly shattered by her death, and he became subject to that terrible heart-complaint which will one day remove him. This circumstance rendered it additionally incumbent on him to prevent, by will, his property descending to Richard Elworthy; my husband was, therefore, requested by the physician to inform Mr. Elworthy of the fatal nature of his complaint. It was a painful duty, but he did it. Mr. Elworthy, however, was aware of his own danger; he told my husband, with the utmost calmness, that he was so, that death had no terrors for him, that he should henceforth live as if in his daily presence, and with regard to the future disposition of his property gave him solemnly to understand what I have told you.

"It is my firm conviction," continued Mrs. Dutton, after a considerable pause, and now speaking the long-cherished wishes of her heart, "that he will not be a long-lived man. He has hardly attained middle-life, it is true, but then he is extremely imprudent. He is an ardent sportsman, and walks immense distances in his shooting excursions, which is the worst thing for him. But he is, poor man, very obstinate on the subject of his health, which is not unusual in such cases."

"Henry left him a prescription when we were there last," said Mrs. Beauchamp, "and laid down a system for him as regarded regimen and exercise, but he was so dreadfully angry about it, that I begged him to leave him to himself."

"Do tell Frederick about your wedding visit, Caroline," said Ellinor, "and of all the sins that you and Henry committed."

"Nonsense, child! how can you be so foolish," interposed Mrs.

Dutton who disliked the idea of representing Mr. Elworthy as capable of being offended by her daughters; "you, all of you, owe love and obedience to your uncle; he stands in the place of a second father to you; I always regard him as such, and consult him on every important affair. There is the letter, Mr. Horrocks," said she, pointing to a sealed letter on the chimney-piece, "which I have written to inform him of your proposals for Ellinor, and I repeat to you now, what I said before, that if he knows of any valid objection to this connection, it must be given up, for I will never give my consent if Mr. Elworthy withholds his."

"Oh mamma, how can he?" exclaimed Ellinor, gazing with beaming eyes on her lover.

The lover made no reply; he was questioning with himself whether this Mr. Elworthy could possibly know any thing of his broken faith to Honour Mildmay; it was an unpleasant cogitation, but he said, in a manner which appeared perfectly natural, "I have heard that he is a man of a wayward and arbitrary temper. I shall therefore be cruelly anxious till his reply arrives."

"You need not fear him in this case," said Mrs. Cartwright, whose domestic unhappiness made her temper unamiable. "He will neither give his consent nor withhold it; he will just do as he did when mamma wrote to him about Caroline's marriage and mine; he will say that, as he had no part in bringing us up he can have none in giving us away. I believe he has a stereotyped blank which he fills up on these occasions; he will conclude by offering his good wishes, and sending a couple of hundred pounds for wedding-finery. That's what he'll do, and mamma expects nothing more formidable."

"A capital uncle! a very good uncle, on my faith!" said Frederick Horrocks, laughing; "such a letter as that will quite satisfy us, will it not, Ellinor?"

Mrs. Dutton, who saw that, from some cause or other, her daughter Cartwright was out of humor, and who feared that she might, as she did sometimes, say something which was undesirable to be heard, resolved to take possession of the subject herself, and therefore, again addressing Frederick Horrocks, she began:

"You spoke just now of our relative being a man of wayward and arbitrary temper; probably Mr. Cheatham may have spoken of him as such. Naturally he was so, as I told you; naturally he was a man of the most violent and uncontrollable temper. Poor man! this was the cause of great suffering and sorrow to him. And as we are on the subject, and as neither Mr. Cartwright nor Mr. Beauchamp make their appearance, we will have the tea-things removed, draw round the fire, and I will tell you about it, as shortly as I can, and by the time I have done, the gentlemen will no doubt be here for supper."

When the little family group were seated in great comfort on the sofa, and on low easy chairs, round the fire—Mrs. Dutton continued :

"I said that Mr. Elworthy was naturally of a violent temper; he *was* so, but is very different now. He is now an amiable recluse—a recluse by the force of circumstances, rather than by any natural aversion to society. But I must give you a little idea of some passages in his life.

"The Dutton family, that is to say, my late husband's family, old Mr. and Mrs. Dutton and their daughter, then about twenty, were in Paris when Mr. Elworthy first made their acquaintance. The daughter was very handsome, was considered, indeed, the handsomest English girl in Paris; and as her father was known to be a wealthy man, she had, of course, a great many suitors. Among the rest were Mr. Elworthy and a Mr. Chinnery, a young lawyer, who was most desperately in love with her, and who was favored by her father; she, however, preferred Mr. Elworthy, and, of course, it was soon settled that they were to be married.

"The Duttons were exceedingly gay people, and their life in Paris was as delightful as it was possible to be. It was fixed that they were to remain in Paris through the winter, to be married in the spring, and then return to England. It was rather singular, perhaps, but Mr. Chinnery, though a discarded lover, still continued his intimacy with the family; and when, from some cause or other which I do not remember, but which is altogether unimportant, they removed to Cassel he followed them there.

"It is probable that Mr. Elworthy, who was a man of quick resentment and hasty temper, grew jealous of Chinnery's familiar intercourse with his bride, but to that I can not speak certainly; this, however, is certain, a quarrel ensued between them, a duel was fought in which Chinnery was wounded, and Elworthy was obliged to fly, because the German police were at that time very severe against any breach of the peace, especially by foreigners. Ellinor Dutton, who had a great deal of spirit as well as beauty, resented the part which Elworthy had taken: the marriage for the time was broken off, and shortly after she and her family returned to England.

"However, I suppose," continued Mrs. Dutton, smiling on her

auditors, and more particularly on her daughter and her lover; "that true lovers can never be parted, they *must* come together in the end. You know that all good love stories end in marriage, and this case was no exception to the rule. They were true lovers, sure enough, and Mr. Elworthy, though he did fight a duel, and though he, perhaps, was jealous of his unhappy rival, was a man full of the most generous sentiments, and, therefore, some six or eight months afterward they were married, and the love-romance of their life came to an end.

"Mr. Elworthy was passionately attached to his wife. Indeed I never knew a married couple so entirely happy—so entirely devoted to each other. She was very fond also of her brother, my late husband, and I have got a packet of her letters which I found tied up and labeled, for he was a most methodical man, among poor, dear Mr. Dutton's papers. I had read them, of course, when they were received, but after their deaths—for, poor thing, she died before him—I went through them all again, and I never read any thing more affecting. She had the gift of writing beautiful letters even on the most trifling subjects, and these are full of little, simple, touching incidents of their daily life; they describe her home and the people she lived among; she would give a grace and an interest to every thing; she was, in short, a creature full of genius. In these letters she speaks also of my children, and calls them her darlings, for she had been married three or four years before she had any prospect of becoming a mother. In one of them she says how much she wished to have one of my children to bring up as her own. My Ellinor, who was born soon after this marriage, was baptized Maria, but, to please her she was christened, when three years old, Ellinor, by which name she was ever after called.

"My brother Elworthy has seen all these letters; for I was sure he would like to know what were *her* feelings toward those young people who will become his heirs; not that he needs any thing to prompt or strengthen his affections for them, but because it could not fail of gratifying him to see her sentiments so fully and beautifully expressed.

"At the time of their marriage, and indeed until the very year of her death, they lived at an old rambling place, like an old manor house, half-way down a valley, standing in a recess of the hills among old sycamore and fir-trees; you never saw such a romantic spot. It is still standing, and let now as a farm-house. This was the old family residence of the Elworthys, from the time of one of the Edwards or Henrys—I don't know which. Soon after his marriage he pulled down an old house on the Wast-Wayland estate, which was a purchase in his father's time, and as I told you, at the foot of Hibblethwaite, looking over a lovely little lake, called Wastwater, stands the new house, Wast Hall, which he built for himself, and to which they removed the very year of his wife's death, and indeed before it was completed.

"Happy, however, as was Mrs. Elworthy in her married life, there was yet a little drawback, and this was no other than that very Richard Elworthy Elworthy, of whom we have been speaking. Even after his cousin's marriage, in the absence of children, he regarded himself as the heir of the property; his home still continued to be with them whenever he was away from London, and some way or other he contrived to do a deal of mischief. I can not tell how it was; I never knew, nor wish to know; only this is certain; he was treated with just severity, I doubt not, by Mr. Elworthy, who had early learned the baseness of his nature, and that it was a serpent whom he had fostered in his bosom; but she, poor thing, with the kindest heart alive, and knowing, as she did, how violent was the temper of her husband when excited, became an intercessor for him, concealed his faults, perhaps, or perhaps never believed in them, for she was the soul of purity herself.

"A nature like that of Richard Elworthy's would only abuse connivance or indulgence. One day a dreadful quarrel occurred between Mr. Elworthy and Richard. Poor Mrs. Elworthy, who was near her confinement—the confinement of her first child—endeavored as she always did, to be a peace-maker between them."

At this moment an interruption occurred in Mrs. Dutton's narrative: a loud knock at the door, a bustle in the hall, and Mr. Cartwright and Mr. Beauchamp were come. They came together—Mr. Cartwright in wonderfully good humor, which produced an instantaneous effect on his wife. Supper was ordered in; the lobster-salad was pronounced excellent, and Mrs. Dutton was in her glory.

The ladies told the gentlemen that they had been talking all the evening of poor, dear Mr. Elworthy; they feared Frederick Horrocks must be tired of the subject.

"I had just got to that dreadful quarrel," said Mrs. Dutton, "between him and Richard Elworthy."

"There have been so many dreadful quarrels," said Mr. Beauchamp, laughing.

"But I mean that fatal one," returned she.

"Ah, poor man!" said Mr. Beauchamp again, "if he had not learned to curb that extreme excitability of temper, he would have been dead long ago. Nevertheless," added he, with the grave authority of a medical man, "that disease of the heart will kill him. He will be found dead in his chair, or his bed, one of these days."

Mr. Cartwright then related how he had walked him twenty miles across the moors without pausing, one hot day in September, but that at last he had turned restive, and would stop for the night at a farm-house, where there was nothing to be had but milk and oat-cake.

"You might have been the death of him!" said Mr. Beauchamp, who was really a good-hearted man. "I would not have done as much on any account. If you'll only wait patiently, he will die one of these days."

"Pray do not talk so, my dear Mr. Beauchamp," said Mrs. Dutton; "I can not bear to hear it!"

Excellent Mrs. Dutton! Yet she had herself often built beautiful castles in the air, based on this same disease of the heart, which was to leave her worthy relative dead in his bed or chair one of these days. Every body knew that she did so, although she outwardly expressed many a hope that his sad complaint would spare him many a long year to the full enjoyment of his beautiful property. She often said that there was nothing in this world that she should like better than to end her own days in Wayland-dale; she said that the air there agreed so wonderfully well with her, and that when all her daughters were married, she should want exactly that amount of occupation which a country life would afford her. It was remarkable also, that she never seemed to think of any of her children enjoying this charming country life with her. No, she always said, Henry would not give up his practice; Mr. Cartwright—nobody called him James—could not be expected to leave his own beautiful property, and of course, it would be much more to Frederick Horrocks' interest to stick to his profession: when Natalie married it would be the same with her husband, no doubt; so of course, all the actual enjoyment of the Wayland-dale property was to be Mrs. Dutton's, and nobody else's.

Poor lady! if such were her intentions, she reckoned without her hosts. The Wayland-dale property would have been an apple of discord, if it had fallen among these expectant heirs.

Mrs. Dutton's communications to her intended son-in-law were very satisfactory. It must not, however, be supposed that they were at all new to him—the main fact, the confidently-expected heirship of the Miss Duttons to their uncle's fine property—was well known to him; the minor detail was of very secondary importance. One idea, however, had suggested itself to him, as it had done to other people—namely, suppose, after all, that Mr. Elworthy should marry again? It was not impossible; he had hardly attained middle age, although it was a notable fact that the Duttons always spoke of him as an "old gentleman," or as their "dear old uncle." They wished to persuade themselves that he was old. He was also apparently hale, and strong, and active, and likely enough for life, spite of that affection of the heart, the danger of which they would so willingly have magnified, at all events in imagination. Now, this being the real state of the case, where was the Duttons' chance any more than the chance of Richard Elworthy Elworthy, provided he married again and had direct heirs? Frederick Horrocks did not put this important question to Mrs. Dutton herself, but he put it before he made his proposals for her daughter, not only to the wise old lawyer Cheatham, but to other parties equally disinterested, some of whom knew Mr. Elworthy personally, and all agreed that he would not marry; that he was not at all a marrying man; and that if Mrs. Dutton would only have gone with her daughters and looked after his schools, and could have been contented with the simple, secluded life that he led, they might have had a home in Wayland-dale, at Wast Hall itself, and literally have come into possession of the place during his life. That, at least, was what people said.

But good Mrs. Dutton, she had walked according to her own wisdom, which was, to get her daughters well married. It was very natural; nobody could blame her; certainly not Mr. Elworthy. But as to *his* marrying, people were quite sure that he was the last man in the world to marry again, and quite sure that the Miss Duttons would be his heirs.

Very satisfactory was this universal opinion. Mr. Frederick Horrocks, therefore, proposed for the pretty Ellinor Dutton, her uncle's favorite, it was said; the one who bore the name of his beloved wife; and, as we know, he was accepted.

CHAPTER III.

We must now glance into a melancholy room in Clement's Inn, on a dreary morning in January. The room was ill-furnished and dirty, and its present occupant, Richard Elworthy Elworthy, who writes himself barrister-at-law, has just finished his noon-day toilet. The earlier hours of the morning, which he spent in bed, were occupied by a female who calls herself his wife, in various preparations for this toilet. She was a thin, haggard, and anxious-looking woman, whose countenance bore traces of former beauty, and still retained that clear, blooming complexion which belongs to a wholesome country life, and which will often remain, amid want and squalor, as the early-taught prayer of childhood clings to the memory when the crimes of life seem to have blotted out even the very consciousness of God.

Richard Elworthy's toilet was now complete. He was appareled in his best attire, although the boots which he wore, as well as sundry of his other garments, had been mended with black thread that very morning. His waistcoat was double-breasted, and buttoned to the very chin, where it met a large black silk neckerchief, thus rendering all appearance of white linen most conveniently unnecessary. Spite of the literally threadbare condition of his habiliments, his black whiskers and hair were perfumed and glossy; his teeth were splendidly preserved, for he prided himself on his teeth, as well as on his white, well-made hands.

At this point of his toilet the door of the room opened, and the woman entered in a shabby, wadded silk cloak, a straw bonnet, and green vail.

"Have you brought them?" asked he, impatiently.

She replied in the affirmative, shaking out, at the same moment, a gentleman's blue cloth cloak, which she had carried as a bundle under her arm. This she hung on a couple of chairs before the fire, as she said, to air and freshen; and then, taking a pill-box from her pocket, opened it, and gave him a handsome seal ring, engraved with crest and initials.

"The time was up," said she, speaking with a slight provincial tone; "I've had fifty-seven shillings and sixpence to give; there's only half-a-crown out of the three sovereigns, and that you'll want, I reckon."

Richard said that she might keep it; and, putting on his ring, and taking another look at himself in the glass—in fact, to observe the effect produced by this ring—he threw his cloak over his shoulders, and went out. He had an important appointment, and was now on his way to keep it.

At three o'clock that same afternoon, he was driving in a cab with a certain unworldly, unsuspicious man, named Thomas Young, from the county of Devon, a poor, independent minister, as simple as a child, whose life had been spent in preaching the Gospel of God's love to the poor, and in the profoundest scientific studies. This good man was now, for the first time in his life, in London, whither he had come for the purpose of obtaining a patent for a great practical discovery which he had made in science, and over which he had spent many years and much money—*much*, at least, for one so poor as himself. He knew, personally, not a single soul in London, although the great scientific minds of the age were as familiar to him as his own thoughts, and he had been for some years in communication with several of them; but he was timid and diffident, and was unwilling to trouble any man. I said that he knew not a single person in the great human wilderness of London; I ought to have excepted a cousin, a baker, named Smallcake, who lived in Bishopsgate-street: a shrewd, money-making man, who kindly promised him the loan of five hundred pounds to work his patent with, as soon as he could meet with a responsible man to give good security for the money. Mr. Young's invention, or rather discovery, was of that general application which, when once known, would be used in a thousand different ways, all equally important; so that the profit to be obtained from it would be immense, could the discovery be only kept secret until it was placed in its perfected state before the public. Much money and much skillful management was requisite for this purpose, and poor Thomas Young, a very child in worldly wisdom, was the last person to manage this successfully. He had brought up with him all the money he could raise, somewhat above two hundred pounds, which would be immediately wanted for the obtaining of the requisite patent.

It was very unfortunate for this simple-hearted man, that his cousin was not only so completely occupied by his business, as to be unable to act as his guardian amid the snares of London, but also, that from his education and pursuits, he was quite incapable of understanding the importance and originality of his discovery. He was thus left to take his chance, and chance led him, on an evil day, to make the acquaintance of Richard Elworthy Elworthy in a coffee-house. Richard Elworthy was the most plausible of men; his general knowledge was immense; to the metaphysician he was deep read in the study of mind, to the antiquarian in antiquities, to the man of science his scientific knowledge appeared wonderful. True, it may be thought that, spite of all this mental wealth, a man whose exterior bore traces of that shifty poverty which is so suspicious, could not impose on any one very seriously, inasmuch as the very appearance of his neediness would put all on their guard. Let it, however, be borne in mind, that poor Thomas Young was blind, as it were, to outward things, and very unsuspecting of evil; besides which, Richard Elworthy possessed an extraordinary knack of diverting people's attention from his clothes to his face. His conversation riveted their minds, and they forgot that the speaker was shabby. This was especially the case with Thomas Young; and Richard Elworthy, who soon saw the nature of the man he was about to make his victim, declined for the present any introduction to the London baker.

To prove the effect which Richard Elworthy had produced on his mind, we will see a portion of a letter which he wrote to his sickly wife and daughter.

"I could believe, my beloved," wrote he, "that your prayers on my account have been answered. By the merest accident—the upsetting of a cab—which occasioned me to go into a coffee-house hard by, I became acquainted with one of the best-informed men I ever met with, and one as well qualified, as any in London, to aid me in the present state of affairs." And then the simple-minded man went on to describe Richard Elworthy as he believed him to be; a man of education; a good lawyer, understanding perfectly all the business of obtaining the patent, which, to poor Mr. Young, had appeared perplexing and senseless; a man of great scientific knowledge, who at a glance could comprehend the great importance of the discovery, and above all, a man of probity and of property, the heir to a large estate in the north of England, from the present possessor of which he had undertaken to obtain the necessary guarantee, so that his cousin Smallcake would forthwith advance the money. He wrote this letter, he said, hurriedly, for that every moment he was expecting his new friend, by whom he was to be introduced to some of the first scientific men in London; indeed they were going that very afternoon to meet one of these gentlemen in Westminster.

Thus wrote the good man to his wife and daughter, and the letter made them very happy.

"God never forsakes those who trust in him!" said the pious women: and they went to rest that night with songs of rejoicing in their hearts, and rose the next morning betimes, that they might communicate the good tidings to their friends and neighbors.

Richard Elworthy, wrapped in his cloak, and with his handsome ring on his finger, drove in a cab to Thomas Young's lodgings and thence to Westminster, on their visit to that first-rate scientific man of whom the letter had spoken. Nothing could surpass Richard Elworthy's agreeable attentions by the way. Every object, every spot of note or interest, as they passed along, was pointed out, and commented upon in his best manner. Mr. Young was very grateful; he promised his friend the half of one of the twelve shares into which it was proposed to divide the property of the patent, and this was no trifling gift. Richard Elworthy told of the handsome office that should be opened at the West End, and of the honor as well as the profits which would accrue to all parties concerned, and to the fortunate patentee especially

In the midst of such interesting conversation Richard Elworthy interrupted himself, for they were just passing one of the best eating-houses in London.

"By-the-by," said he, as if the idea had just struck him, "let us stop here, for I have not dined!"

"Bless me!" said the other, "I dined four hours ago. Yet stop, by all means, and I will have a cup of tea."

Richard ordered the best of dinners, to which he drank a pint of port, while Mr. Young sat by and modestly took his tea; but when the question of payment came, an astounding discovery was made. Elworthy had forgotten his purse! How could he have done such a thing! "It was of no consequence," said good Mr. Young; he would settle for the dinner. It so happened, however, that the dinner, which was rather costly, exceeded the change which Mr. Young had in his purse; he therefore took a five-pound note from his pocket-book, which he handed to the waiter. He naturally looked for the change; but Richard Elworthy, having glanced at the time-piece on the chimney-piece, and discovered, as he said, that they should be after their time, and perhaps miss seeing their scientific friend, put the whole change into his own pocket, and hurried Mr. Young into the cab. The good man sat and thought for a few minutes what he ought to do in this case; of course the money was his, but then his excellent friend, Mr. Richard Elworthy, had, in a fit of abstraction, put it into his own pocket; many clever men were liable to these fits of abstraction or absence of mind. It was an unpleasant circumstance, reasoned Mr. Young with himself, but he must let it pass; he believed that he owed much more than five pounds to his friend for the service he was about to render him.

Mr. Richard Elworthy feared they might be too late for their scientific friend in Westminster, but there was no fear of it; he would have waited several hours for them.

A few weeks went on, and Richard Elworthy's plans somewhat changed their character. It had been his first intention, merely to obtain, under the pretext of expediting the business of the patent, the whole, or the greater part of that small amount which Mr. Young had brought up with him. A portion of this had already been so obtained; chambers in Lincoln's Inn were taken, where, as Mr. Elworthy said, the business of the patent should be temporarily transacted, and as Mr. Young placed implicit confidence in him, he neither wondered that a man of so much intelligence and influence, had both time and thought to devote to a stranger; nor yet did he notice the great change which had taken place in his outward appearance, by the handsome suit of good broadcloth in which he now presented himself. No, none of these circumstances awoke any suspicion in his honest heart, and if the money seemed to vanish fast, he believed it to be in the legitimate business of the patent, which once obtained, and his discovery brought into operation, would make a thousandfold return.

Peculation, on a comparatively small scale, had been Richard Elworthy's first intention, but when he gained a sufficient knowledge of the discovery to see the immense advantage to be obtained through it, he determined, if possible, to become an actual participator in the larger and more honorable profits. Many, however, had been the phases of his villainy before he arrived at this point. At one time he thought of ousting the original discoverer altogether, but that was not easy. Mr. Young, though simple as a child regarding money, was yet tenacious of his secret; nor was it of any use to depreciate the value of the discovery, nor to pretend, as he had done for some time, that the scientific friend in

Westminster was about to make the same discovery public by patent. Mr. Young disproved this at once, for no such specification was on record, and for the credit of his useful scientific friend, Richard Elworthy was obliged to confess his error. Thus far, with regard to his discovery itself, Thomas Young was secure.

Richard Elworthy, therefore, under these circumstances, remembered the old adage, that honesty was the best policy, and zealously set himself about to obtain the patent, the management of which he determined to keep very much under his own control, so that the profits should come into his hands. Accordingly, now in his excellent suit of clothes, on which there was no sign of suspicious poverty, he had frequent interviews with Mr. Smallcake, the baker, in Bishopsgate-street, and contrived also to impress him with the idea of his being a very clever man of business. The baker's five hundred pounds was now greatly wanted; but, spite of his favorable opinion of Richard Elworthy's business talent, the wary baker refused to make the advance on other than landed security. For obvious reasons, Richard Elworthy was jealous of any other parties being brought into the concern. He offered himself, therefore, as guarantee on the strength of his heirship to the Wast-Wayland property. Mr. Smallcake professed his willingness to advance the money, provided it should be satisfactorily proved to his lawyer that his reversionary claim to this property was valid, and the old gentleman, the present possessor, really was in the precarious state of health which was represented. All this was good; but Richard Elworthy declined to meet Mr. Smallcake's lawyer. He had, he said, a friend whom he believed would advance the money at once, and that was no other than his cousin, the present possessor of this large property.

It was a bold and desperate thought; but, at all events, had this advantage, that it was the lesser of two evils.

He wrote accordingly, in the month of April, to William Elworthy, upon that very evening when Honour Mildmay and her mother, and Mrs. Dutton and her family, were so much occupied by thoughts of the same gentleman—he had not now written to his relative for several years—stating to him, in the most business-like manner, in the manner most likely to have an effect upon him, that an opportunity was now offered to him of making an independence, of becoming an honest and a creditable man. He gave him the names of the parties, described the greatness of the discovery, and ended by requesting that his cousin would generously forget the past, and so far befriend him as to advance him a thousand pounds, for which he offered him a share in the patent; or at all events, if he objected to advance the money, to become his guarantee to Mr. Smallcake for half that sum.

This letter, and this application, were too much like many similar ones in former years, not to be received with the utmost suspicion by Mr. Elworthy. It is the misfortune of the unprincipled man whose tricks have been detected, not to be believed honest even if he really is so. Richard Elworthy's intention at this moment was to behave uprightly as regarded the patent, although the patentee himself might derive but a very subordinate advantage; his cousin, however, gave him credit for nothing but deception. He disbelieved every word that was written, and refused to advance a shilling, excepting on better authority than Richard Elworthy's.

Mr. Smallcake, from having been very lukewarm, all at once became enthusiastic on behalf of the patent. This alarmed Richard; and then came his cousin's letter. He read it with the deepest vexation, yet he was not surprised, for he knew only too well what grave reasons there were that he should not be trusted.

"Have you got your answer from the north, yet?" asked Mr. Smallcake, a few mornings afterward. Richard Elworthy's reply was in the affirmative; and forthwith he produced a letter purporting to be from his cousin, which assured him in the kindest manner of his readiness to become guarantee for the required five hundred pounds. All parties were immediately in high good humor. Mr. Smallcake's lawyer said that nothing further was needed, and the five hundred pounds were immediately deposited in the bank of Messrs. Smith, Payne, and Smith, in the name of Thomas Young, and for the business of his patent: Richard Elworthy being introduced by him there as his agent, fully empowered to draw out the money.

The offices were now immediately taken in the most appropriate part of the city, and the whole thing begun to be carried on with spirit. Richard Elworthy was at the head of the management; every body trusted in him, and he promised every body that within twelve months they should find themselves possessed of an El Dorado.

Mr. Young returned into Devonshire on account of his wife's illness, Mr. Smallcake went on merrily with his baking, and Richard Elworthy, in a very short time, drew out from the bank the sum of five hundred and thirty-five pounds, the whole amount of money deposited in the name of Thomas Young, and the very day the last money was drawn out he left London, leaving behind him an amount of debt on the concern which was incredible.

Where he was gone, and why he was gone, no one could tell. It was supposed for some time that he was away on the business of the patent, for Mr. Smallcake was as reluctant as poor Thomas Young to believe that they had fallen into the hands of a sharper.

CHAPTER IV.

IT was the beginning of June when Honour Mildmay and her mother having, as it were, wound up their accounts, in the great debtor and creditor ledger of life, struck a balance, and found in their favor, spite of many losses, sundry not unimportant items, such as recruited health, renewed hope, trust in heaven, and increased affection for each other.

This was, to continue the metaphor, the little capital on which they were about to commence life. The godmother's small legacy and the hundred a year, with house rent-free, and croft and garden in Wayland-dale, being also set down at their full value, which was by no means small to those who otherwise were without a home.

At this beginning of June I hardly recognize our friends as we saw them in April, so greatly are they improved in appearance. The daughter has begun to live again in the strength of clear-sighted duty; the mother has thrown off a burden of unparticipated anxiety which had bowed her like the weight of age. It is ever a glorious sight to see the human being rising above the cares and troubles of earth which God never intended should utterly crush and confound his immortal creatures. He has given them wings, as it were, to lift them upward, even in this world, if they will but use them. Honour and her mother raised themselves on these spirit-wings, and their oppressed hearts expanded in the purer atmosphere of love and faith.

Henceforth they advanced forward by a new, though a humbler path, mostly amid sunshine and flowers.

They had received from their unknown patron directions as to their journey, together with funds sufficient for that purpose. It was a long and tedious journey, for it was before the times of universal railways, and would occupy two days and a night. They came to London from Hastings, and taking the night coach to Kendal, arrived there in the afternoon of the following day. Thence they proceeded by post-chaise.

The letter which contained these traveling directions was one of great kindness, and gave an agreeable idea of the writer. None but a generous-hearted, thoughtful man, could have taken into consideration, as he had done, every circumstance, however small, which could contribute to their comfort. He evidently did not regard them as poor dependents who were to scramble, as best they could, through the wearinesses of a hard life, but as friends who were to aid him in accomplishing a scheme of happiness for himself and others. He seemed to feel himself as the obliged party; he was grateful to them, and, in this spirit, joyfully met them with benefits.

The tone of this letter not only removed much anxiety from their minds, but filled them with a joyful anticipation for the future. The journey seemed one of pleasure; the season was beautiful, the very youth of summer, and their spirits rose with the necessity for exertion. They had no sorrowful leave-takings to undergo. They had already, before the full amount of their trials were known, parted from their old acquaintances and friends at Northbridge; there were, therefore, now no condolences to dishearten them, and no pity to wound; their few tried and valued friends wrote to them, but their letters were only those of encouragement and congratulation. They were about to leave the old and the painful behind them, and to begin a new and a cheerful life. They were placed in those circumstances which the way-worn and sorrowing pilgrim of life often wishes for in vain.—"Oh!" sighs he hopelessly, "could I but begin my life anew, with all the benefit of my past experience, how differently, how much more wisely would I act! How much sorrow and repentance would I spare myself!"

They were, indeed, beginning life anew; they had been rooted up from the old place where the storm had scathed them, and they were about to be planted afresh, where the fulfillment of duty, rather than the smile of fortune, should make their happiness and insure their reward.

They reached Sedburgh, and here commenced the last stage of their journey.

It was a lovely evening; the song of the thrushes in the leafy tree-tops sounded into the very streets, where healthy children, with their ruddy complexions, and clear, ringing voices, were at play. The landlady at the little inn expected them: she came out to meet them, smiling and courtesying; the chaise, she said, would be ready immediately to convey them forward, and refreshments awaited them in the best parlor; for Mr. Elworthy himself had been there only a few days before, and had ordered every thing.

And then the good woman began to talk as though she never would cease. She was herself a dales-woman, she said, and her father had been tenant to "the Ha' folk," and so was her brother-in-law at that time. He was Christie o'Lily-garth, a right good man, and much esteemed by the maister, and he had a fine family of his own, whom he had brought up at Lily-garth, and that was where the maister had been brought up himself. The ladies did not know the dale-country? Oh, but it was a fine country, and there was not a bettei homestead than Lily-garth in all the seven Yorkshire dales, and Christie's lasses were bonny as all Yorkshire lasses were. Mrs. Thwaite, the good, communicative landlady, who thus talked, had evidently herself, been one of these bonny Yorkshire lasses in her youth.

The ladies were well pleased to have these anticipatory glimpses of their future neighborhood; they smiled, and she went on.

And they did not know Mr. Elworthy? Had not seen him in London even, where he was gone some three or four days before? Well, they would know him in time; but this she could tell them beforehand, that it would be a hard matter to find his equal—say nothing of his superior. And she, Mrs. Thwaite, had seen the new school-house, and she knew the cottage where the ladies were to live; it was the one in which the curate used to live formerly, but of late years it had been uninhabited, or nearly so, and Mr. Elworthy had bought it, with some other property at Dale-town, and done it up, and built the school-house just by, only not on the premises; and it was a mighty pretty place, with a flower-garden and a nice little parlor, with mahogany furniture and a looking-glass over the mantle-piece; and one of the tidiest lasses in the Dale was to be servant there; and old Mrs. Hawes from the Hall had been down there putting all to rights, and airing the rooms, though it was summer, for the squire says to her, says he, 'you must let them find things somewhat as they've been used to, for it is so pleasant to feel home-like in a strange place.'

The chaise was getting ready, but still Mrs. Thwaite talked.—The new school-house was prettier than that which was built in the mistress's time for the boys. The school-master lived under the same roof with the school; but it was a nice place for all that. The school-master had been there a matter of a dozen years, he was a poor scholar from Oxford, a friend of the maister's; and what a school he had! and what scholars he turned out! He taught them not only to read and write, but a power of things beside. Had not the ladies heard of Dr. Benson, who got such honors at Cambridge, and was professor of some kind? No! Well he was a great man, though, and he had been one of Mr. Walker's Dale-town scholars. And how he taught them to sing! Why, people came for miles and miles to hear the choir at Dale-town church! They were called Mr. Walker's singing-boys; the landlady's own son was now one of them. And so well as all the boys turned out! the very parents themselves were ashamed of being rude and wicked before their children, for he taught good manners as well as book-learning; that was what Mr. Elworthy insisted on; for "good manners," said he, "were as much a part of religion, as the fruit was of the tree."

The chaise at length could be detained no longer. With many smiles and courtesies, Mrs. Thwaite saw her guests depart in the direction of that wilder district, which commences a few miles out of Sedburgh.

After crossing a region of stony moorlands, the travelers entered amid the soft gloom and stillness of approaching night, that wild, and almost savage district, where, amid broken rocks of a stern Druidical character, and in the deep shadow of sycamore trees, lay at various distances, those caves of which Ellinor Dutton had spoken, and from the wooded heights above which rushed down the tumultuous waters of the Wast, which thence flowed onward, accumulating as they flowed through the various windings of Wayland-dale.

The rushing sound of the water, as it fell from ledge to ledge, resounded through the deep solitude of the scene, and the perfume of innumerable flowers and flowering trees filled the air. While our travelers were remarking upon the impressive character of this scene, a wood-lark suddenly poured forth its gushing flood of melody, to which an echo, like another bird, replied. It seemed like a song of welcome, and while yet listening to its strain, they wound round the huge base of Hibblethwaite Fell, still keeping on the level ground, and in less than a quarter of an hour were in Wayland-dale.

At the commencement of the Dale, and beneath the huge back of Hibblethwaite, they seemed to drive for some time through a wood of sycamores and birches, and then emerged into the open moonlight on the banks of a little silvan lake, on which the moon was reflected as if in a mirror. It was like a bit of fairy-land.—Honour suddenly bade the driver stop, and asked the name of this little lake.

"It is Wast-water," said he; "the beck flows out of it. We

passed the Hall gates about five minutes since, among the sycamore-trees; you'll see the Hall a little further on."

He again drove on, and then stopped: the Hall was now in sight on the other side of the little lake.

"Yon's the Hall," said the driver. "Squire Elworthy's. It's a fine place, is Wast Hall. The dale-head is called Wast-Wayland; that's Squire Elworthy's property. He has some, to be sure, lower down, but this, all compact together, is Wast-Wayland."

Again they drove forward; now among shadowy sycamores and birches, now into long intervals of moonlight, down the valley toward the new school-house, a distance of about three miles. With wondering and admiring eyes they looked around them. The road kept the level of the valley, through which the little river, or beck, as it was called, ran with devious course, sometimes in company with the road, at others, taking, as it were, a playful sweep, or concealing itself among the masses of trees. It was sufficiently light for them to distinguish the neat white homesteads scattered on the hill-sides, and also that, midway in the valley among shrouding trees, stood an old water-mill with its picturesque buildings, and large, slumbering water-wheel. Peasant people were occasionally met or passed on the road, to all of whom the chaise and its occupants seemed objects of interest. The smell of burning peat here and there, filled the air, giving that pleasant sense of mountain homes which is so attractive to a poetical fancy.

"I shall love this place. I feel that I shall," said Honour, with a spontaneous emotion of delight.

At that moment, as if in response to her words, the chimes of the village church which they were just passing began to play. It was nine o'clock. The tune was one of holy rejoicing, and the hearts of the two strangers ascended on the wings of its soft and heavenly melody toward God.

They were at the door of their new home. A tall, kindly-countenanced, and middle-aged woman stood there to receive them.

"It is Mrs. Peggy, from the Hall;" said the driver, as he opened the chaise-door.

Mrs. Peggy, or Mrs. Hawes, as she was indiscriminately called, wore a dark cotton gown, a fine white linen apron and cap, a plaited frill round her neck, and a buff muslin handkerchief, with a reddish border, pinned over her shoulders. I describe her dress thus particularly, once for all, for she never varied. She was a dales-woman, with just enough of dialect in her speech to give it raciness.

Mr. Elworthy, she told them, was now from home, and she did not justly know when he would return; but she knew his mind about the ladies, and all that he wished to have done. That she was there, by his orders, to receive them, and she hoped they would find all things comfortable.

Any one must have been harder to please than our friends really were if they had not found much to admire in this new home. It was too late to take any thing like a general survey that night; they retired, therefore, early to rest. Honour, however, spite of the fatigue of her long journey, slept but little, and in the early morning arose and dressed herself, in order to look round by daylight.

She then found that their little demesne occupied a pleasant knoll which lay in a cove of the hills, and which was scattered over, as if by the hand of a skillful planter, with the most beautiful groups of sycamores and birches, the native growth of the Dale, with here and there a splendid oak, now in the rich amber of its early leafage. The road from the adjacent village of Dale-town, which led up the western side of the valley, immediately passed their house, but being only little frequented left it still in a pleasant solitude. The new school-house, partially concealed by trees, stood below the garden, by which it was approached from the cottage. About the cottage itself there was an air of elegance and simplicity which made its appearance very pleasing, although in extent it hardly exceeded that of many a well-to-do dale peasant's dwelling. Honour stood on the door-step and looked around her. The soft white mist which, a quarter of an hour before, had hidden the level of the valley as with a vail, now ascended in the beams of the morning sun, which had already risen above the hills, and the lower portion of the valley, with the old gray water-mill and the village of Dale-town, with its blue wreaths of curly ascending smoke, and its low-towered massive little church, lay before her. It was a scene of the loveliest rural seclusion and peace. Here and there glimpses of the little winding river shone out in the sun; the thick-leaved masses of trees cast deep shadows, and the meadows which bordered the stream were either knee-deep in grass, which was ready for the scythe, or golden with flowers, and furnished abundant pasturage for the milch-cows of the dale farmer. On the hill-sides were planted white homesteads, with their cultivated fields about them, while the whole upper region of the Fell was an extensive sheep-walk, uninclosed, and common to all, and affording pasturage also to herds of wild mountain ponies, which might be seen even now in the sunny distance dotting the soft green of the hills, as well as later in the year to immense flocks of geese, which constituted a source of wealth to the dale farmer's wife, as the sheep and the ponies did to her husband.

After surveying this scene for some time with sensations of exquisite pleasure, Honour walked round the house and seated herself upon a rustic bench which she found in an elevated part of the garden, beneath a large birch tree, and which commanded in still broader amplitude the scene I have attempted to describe. Skylarks were singing in the clear sunny air above her ; the dew still lay glittering on leaf and flower, and peeping through the leafy branches of trees, she saw the little gable of their new home, with the white-curtained casement-window of the little chamber where her mother still slept.

The deep, consoling consciousness of a loving and guiding Providence, which had brought them hither, where the hands of friendly strangers had provided for them not only comforts but indulgences, filled her heart with an inexpressible joy and gratitude. She felt no regrets for the past; she had gone as through the darkness and uncertainty of night, and she stood now in the light and security of morning, and, like the lark on the hill-tops, she poured forth her soul in thanksgiving.

"Oh ! my God, I bless thee !" said her silent aspiration. "I bless thee for the evil as well as for the good ! Thy hand it is which has led me hither, and from this hour I will dedicate myself to thy service ! I bless thee for the beautiful scenes in which thou hast placed me. I bless thee that at this beautiful season I am come hither ; that I am come when thy sunshine casts a glory over all things, and when the lark carols to thee his morning song. For all this I bless thee ! and if one as poor as myself may promote thy good work on earth, let me, amid this simple people, find an abiding home, and here become thy servant, thy humble minister of joy and blessing !"

Again the chimes of the little church filled the air with their harmonious voices. It was six o'clock.

Honour returned to the cottage, but not to her bed. Their little maid-servant was now up, and singing in a low voice at her work ; the parlor casement was open, and, early as it was, the breakfast table spread.

"I did not know at what hour you ladies would like breakfast," said the girl; "even gentlefolks are often early in these parts. The maister is up at six at the Hall, though he does not breakfast till eight, and as I heard you a-stirring, miss, I thought, ma'ppen, you breakfasted betimes." Honour said she had not slept well; besides she was fond of the early morning.

"Oh, it's the heart of the day is the early morning!" replied the girl with animation; "then the air is so fresh, and the birds sing, and all is so young-like! I'm an early riser myself, for there's plenty to be done even in a small family. I've the cow to milk now; and have you seen her, miss?" asked she; "she's a prime cow; not one of your great milkers, though, for the maister said you would not want so much milk, only it must be of the best. She's one of Christie o' Lily-garth's breed, the maister will have no other sort at the Hall. You'd ma'ppen like to see her?"

Honour said she should. She followed the girl with her milking pail to the little adjoining croft, at the gate of which stood a small, beautiful black cow, with a ruddy tinge on her ears and about her muzzle, waiting to be milked, with so amiable an expression of countenance, that Honour was at once inclined to believe far more than the girl had said in her praise. She stroked and caressed her, called her fond names, and fed her with fresh grass which she gathered while she was milked. She then took a draught of warm delicious milk from a china basin which the girl brought her, and certainly never before had enjoyed any beverage so much. A feeling of almost child-like joy filled her soul, and prophesied to her of a beautiful, simple life, of which this was the fresh unsophisticated morning.

"And you have not seen the little poultry-yard, miss, have you?" asked the girl, who seemed greatly prepossessed in her young mistress's favor, by the genuine pleasure she appeared to take in the cow.

Honour had not; she did not, indeed, know that there was a poultry-yard.

"Oh! dear, yes, miss," said she, "and poultry too; three hens and a cock; one hen sitting on twelve eggs, and the others are prime layers. Mrs. Hawes," continued she—"that's Mrs. Peggy that was here last night—she has the best poultry in all the Dale; and she brought down these herself in the market-cart when she came down with the feather beds."

If Honour had been conveyed at once into Arcadia it would not have seemed more delicious to her than did now this little rural home with its rural wealth. She stood watching the two hens and the handsome cock picking up their morning meal, which she herself had given them, when she was joined by her mother, who being also early awoke by the universal joyous clamor of singing birds in the trees around her window, had risen and looked abroad with feelings somewhat akin to her daughter, and on finding that she was up and dressed, had followed her example, though it was long before her usual hour for rising. Honour saluted her with a beaming countenance, and took her the round of the little homestead, not omitting to walk down to the school-house, which, however, from its being locked, they were unable to enter, and then returned to the cottage to breakfast, which the maid had by this time fully set out, with all the usual country dainties of new-laid eggs, fresh butter, delicious cream, to say nothing of sweet home-made bread, and various kinds of dale cakes—a breakfast fit for a prince in that very Arcadia of which this seemed a type.

The school was not to be commenced until Mr. Elworthy's return. He had written to them from London to this purpose; the business, he said, which had taken him there, would in all probability delay him longer than he at first expected. It would be a fortnight, at least, before he could be back, but in the mean time, he begged his unknown friends to make themselves at home; and if the cottage was not entirely to their minds, to avail themselves of the Hall during his absence.

But their new home was entirely to their mind, and their first employment, after arranging their small possessions, was to make themselves better acquainted with the valley than their moonlight drive along it enabled them to be. Let us accompany them to the Hall. They had already had a glimpse of it in passing, and knew its situation. Advancing now toward it, on a splendid summer afternoon, they found it to be a handsome, somewhat irregular mansion, built of the stone of the district, standing beautifully on a wooded upland, behind which rose, as it appeared, to an amazing height, the stern, stony back of Hibblethwaite. This hill, though pastured to its very top, was so brown with patches of peat, so rugged with gray craggy masses, and so torn into deep, black gulleys, by the wild impetuous torrents that in the winter season poured down it, that its character was rather that of savage grandeur than of pastoral fell and moorland which belonged to either side of the valley. It stood like a huge giant at the entrance of the Dale, and at many points of the road seemed entirely to close all exit. The road, however, having crossed the river, which might be called the playful daughter of the hill, by an old and picturesque stone bridge, insinuated itself along the thick wood which clothed the giant's foot, and stole quietly, as it were, through a narrow pass out of the valley.

Approaching the Hall by this beautiful road, Honour and her mother soon stood upon the banks of Wast-water and contemplated the scene. The grounds of the Hall sloped down to the other side of the lake, and all around it lay verdant pasture fields, and meadows in which the hay-making had already commenced. A boat-house, and a small green boat that was moored within it, testified to the proprietor taking at times his pleasure upon this beautiful little lake, and the occasional glimpse of a summer-house, or rustic shed, on the hilly grounds near the Hall, or more distantly in the woods, proved that he had more than an angler's delight in the rural seclusions of which he was master.

In this higher part of the valley, or Wast-Wayland, as it was called, the views were by no means extensive, for though the hills on either side were not lofty, their bases locked, as it were, into each other, and while they somewhat contracted the Dale, caused it perpetually to wind, and thus to present rather an infinite variety of exquisite bits of rural scenery, than views of any great range.

Honour and her mother reached the house; the large handsome windows of its principal front, looking toward Wast-water, opened upon a grassy terrace which led by a broad flight of steps into an exquisite flower-garden below. The whole of this front was in the most excellent preservation and order, which caused an extension of the house, forming, in fact, a second and still handsomer front, to strike the beholder very singularly and almost painfully, from its somewhat neglected and wholly uninhabited appearance. The lower windows were altogether closed by outside Venetian shutters, which had evidently been for many years unopened, while the upper ones as evidently belonged to rooms which were either unfinished or wholly unused and neglected. There was something singular, something unpleasing, in this close approximation of order and neglect; it was a discord where all otherwise would have been in harmony.

Mrs. Hawes was soon aware of their arrival, and received them with much cordiality, with which, however, a certain degree of ceremonious respect was mingled. The truth was, that she found them to be of a class so much higher than she expected, that she could only behave to them as to her master's equals. On the evening of their arrival, when she was down at the cottage to receive them, she became instantly aware of the circumstance. Mr. Elworthy, it is true, had told her that the strangers were gentlewomen, and must be received and treated as such; still they were merely the new schoolmistress and her mother, and Mrs. Hawes thought of them as persons whom she might patronize and be kind to in a somewhat condescending way, and receive to a pleasant cup of tea in her parlor at the Hall, during Mr. Elworthy's absence. But the first sight of them dispelled this agreeable idea.

"Very nice ladies they are," said she to Mrs. Fothergill, of Lily-garth, having called there on her way back in the market-cart, for she very naturally wished to tell the good people there what the new-comers, in whom the Dale had so great an interest, were like, and more especially as they were so different to what she herself expected; "very nice ladies they are, I can tell you, but they are *real gentlefolk;* for one can tell in a minute what people are, and what they have been bred to. They were never born nor bred to keep school among poor folks, and I wonder whether th' maister knows it. He said, says he, 'Mrs. Peggy, you must make these ladies very comfortable, and let them feel at home among us'—you know that's just like him—'and you must do all you can for them while I am away.' Those were his last words before he set out, so I did the best that lay in my power; and very nice I thought I had got every thing, and they seemed so pleased and satisfied, and said all was right, and were much obliged by all I had done; but then, when I saw them, and *felt* how they must have been used to something so different, it seemed to me as if nothing had been got ready as it ought to have been, and I wished they had come to the Hall instead. But th' maister will be back soon, and then he'll put every thing right in a minute!"

The report which Mrs. Hawes had left of the strangers at Lily-garth soon spread through the Dale. The utmost curiosity was excited and the utmost interest also, which was only the more increased by the appearance of the ladies themselves. The sturdy, and somewhat rude peasant farmer, as he met them on their first walk up the Dale, uncovered his head, and passed them with a greeting which was meant to express at once his good-will and his respect; the women courtesied, looked long after them, and then ran to the nearest neighbor to communicate the agreeable impression they had made, while such of the children as were not too bashful offered them flowers.

They were now at the Hall; and Mrs. Hawes, who had given up the thought of the pleasant tea-drinking in her own parlor, led them at once to Mr. Elworthy's favorite room, where, no doubt, he himself would have received them. This was a large, lofty, and handsome apartment, to which a very cheerful character was given, from its windows facing the south, and opening directly upon the smooth, grassy terrace and the beautiful flower-garden. Large well-filled bookcases lined the walls, leaving, at regular intervals, spaces for casts of the finest antique sculpture raised on pedestals; the upper portion of the walls was covered by portraits the size of life, many of them by excellent artists. It was a room which suggested agreeably of its possessor; fine taste and solid judgment seemed combined with domestic comfort. The hearth was particularly cheerful and inviting; sofas and easy chairs stood about, as if offering every incitement for fire-side enjoyment. A writing table, on which stood a large closed writing desk and materials for writing, with a quantity of newspapers and books, stood midway between the fire-place and a remarkably pleasant window, and a large chair covered with green leather, drawn near to it, pointed it out at once as the familiar seat of Mr. Elworthy.

The strangers naturally felt a strong interest in all they saw, and they looked around for such small characteristics of domestic and every-day life and habits, as might, in some measure, make them acquainted with the tastes and pursuits of the man himself.

It was afternoon, and though good Mrs. Hawes had quite abandoned the idea of inviting them to tea in her parlor, she yet so cordially pressed them to take that meal, in the name of her master, that the ladies consented. The good woman was again in a perplexity. She was not accustomed to sit in Mr. Elworthy's presence, neither did it seem right to her to sit in theirs; but they insisted upon it, and even said that she must take tea with them. To sit and take tea in Mr. Elworthy's room, seemed an unheard-of liberty; fortunately Honour unconsciously obviated all difficulty.

"Let us take tea in this beautiful garden, just within shade of this arbor-vitæ, and within sight of Wast-water—it is so very lovely!" said she, stepping from one of the windows which opened upon the smooth, warm turf, in which flower beds, like brilliant gems, were set.

Mrs. Hawes felt relieved from her dilemma. She followed Honour to the green terrace, saying,

"Maister likes his tea also i' th' garden, but he mostly takes it under th' cedar tree, round th' corner; he reckons th' view much better there."

The tea was set out in Mr. Elworthy's favorite spot, and Mrs. Hawes felt quite at her ease, more especially as the ladies seemed much interested in all she told them of the Dale, and the life of the people there, as well as about Mr. Elworthy himself.

Mrs. Mildmay inquired, if there was in the house a portrait of this gentleman, and from this simple question Mrs. Hawes ramified into a good deal of family history.

"Th' maister's pictur," said she, in her Dale dialect, which I will not too literally follow, "hangs in what we call the little green room up-stairs; that was th' mistress's dressing-room, but th' maister has th' key with him. The mistress's portrait hangs there too; th' room opens out of his chamber, and he mostly keeps it locked. Her wardrobe's in that room, and there her jewels are, and her desk with all her papers, just as she left them. He was very fond of her, the maister was, and she was deserving of his love."

Mrs. Mildmay and her daughter were wholly strangers to the details of Mr. Elworthy's private life, and they listened with great interest, and without any sense of impropriety, to all that this faithful old servant was willing to communicate.

"You see, ladies," said she, "I lived in the family in old Mr. Elworthy's time, afore this Hall was built, when they lived at Lily-garth, which is the old family house, where th' Elworthys lived time out of mind, and where th' maister wer' born. I knew him as a young man afore he wer' wed; and I thought when he brought th' mistress home, that I had never clapped my eyes on a prettier woman. She wer' a Miss Dutton, from London, but no fortune; but that mattered nothing to th' maister, for it's worth, not money that he looks at. Well, as I said, a prettier woman never came into th' Dale."

"What kind of beauty was she?" asked Honour.

"Why, miss, if you'll excuse my speaking of you in your presence," said Mrs. Hawes, "she wer' not unlike you. There's a something about you that reminded me of th' mistress th' first minute I saw you. You've her black hair, and th' same expression of eye, though hers wer' brown and yours are dark gray, and she stood about your height. Th' maister, ma'ppen, may not see th' likeness, though I do, and though I reckon there are others i' th' Dale that will, for th' mistress has never been forgotten among us. Dale folks don't soon forget their friends."

Mrs. Hawes having once begun to talk, did not cease until Honour and her mother were in possession of all she deemed it right to tell. I question, however, whether the whole particulars I am about to relate were told by her. For the sake of succinctness, however, I will put her various communications into a compact form, adding thereto what is requisite to make the family-story complete; and this may be done in my character of novelist, for the novelist is a diviner, who knows not only what is privately said and done, but who can trace the springs of action, and who knows what is secretly felt and suffered.

Mrs. Hawes told all that Mrs. Dutton told to Frederick Horrocks, of the father and uncle of the present Mr. Elworthy, and of the son which the spendthrift uncle had left. She told how this man, although he had run through his share of the paternal property, and spite of a great burden of debt and sorrow which he laid upon the family, still made large demands, and had given to his son the baptismal name of Richard Elworthy, thus making the name twofold in his case. She told that after his father's death he was adopted by his cousin, and brought hither to be educated as an acknowledged member of the family.

"He was a tall-grown, handsome lad," said Mrs. Hawes, "when th' master brought him from London down to Lily-garth; but there wer' something hard, and proud, and selfish about him even then. Th' master, who wished to do by him as if he had been his own brother, sent him to a good school that was kept by a clergyman i' Kendal. There he was a matter of three years, and all his holidays he spent at Lily-garth, and had good clothes and pocket-money, and a horse to ride when he was here, and fishing and shooting, and just what he liked. At seventeen he wer' a manly chap, and looked like to twenty. Th' master wer' fond of him, and very indulgent, and yet he wer' a hot-tempered man, th' master wer'; that was just his one failing; he had not patience, like; but then Richard wer' given to wild ways, and if any thing was said, he wer' insolent, and had always such a deal to say for himself; besides which, he wer' extravagant, and spent a power of money. All this drove th' master a'most mad with him. 'He'll be his father over again!' he would say; 'and what satisfaction can I have for all my trouble?' And yet he went on behaving to him like a good parent. If he had only been worthy of it! At last, young as he was, he got into debt, and then many things came out that nobody had dreamed of: among the rest he had forged the master's name, and got money in that way from th' bank. He had done enough to transport him, and many peo- think, even now, that will be his end; but he was young, you see, and, mad as the master wer' against him, it wer' hushed up: nobody was defrauded of money but him. So Richard was sent out of these parts, and for three or four years nothing was heard of him."

His good cousin, however, had not deserted him, even then.—Once more he gave him a trial, the condition of forgiveness being his future industry and good conduct. He was penitent apparently, and made abundant promises. His talents were unquestionably great; he was entered a student of law of the Middle Temple, his cousin furnishing not only the money requisite for his studies, but for his maintenance during them, and so creditably did he pass through this time of probation, that once more the doors of Lily-garth were opened to him with affectionate cordiality.

Peace was now confirmed in Europe, and William Elworthy, like the rest of the world, went abroad. Before long the agreeable news reached Wayland-dale, that he had met with a lady in Paris whom he was about to bring home as his wife, and great was the satisfaction which this news caused. Richard, at first, disbelieved it; at length the tidings were communicated to him by a letter from Elworthy himself; and at the same time he was informed henceforth Lily-garth could not be his home, although he would be welcome there as an occasional visiter. Richard, who was indolent and luxurious, received this intimation with great dissatisfaction. There was an end now of his prospective heirship; he must battle his way through life by the means of his own industry and professional talents.

Without replying to his cousin, he immediately left Lily-garth, hastened to London, and thence to Paris, where he presented himself, and with the utmost apparent frankness and good-will offered his warmest congratulations. Elworthy, at that time, in the very heyday of his propitions love-suit, and in good humor with all the world, received his unexpected relative with great kindness, and introduced him to the family of his betrothed, by whom he was likewise cordially welcomed.

Of the Dutton family, at this time in Paris, a word must be said in addition to what has already been related by Mrs. Dutton of Woodbury. Mr. Dutton was a gentleman in trade, who was supposed to have made much money. He had brought his wife and daughter with him to that gay capital, which had been for so many years closed to the English, not so much for their amusement as for his own convenience. His wife took care of him; she had been severely drilled into a knowledge of his will and requirements through a hard apprenticeship of five-and-twenty years; it was long now since any idea of rebellion had crossed her thoughts. She was well-dressed, because she was the wife of Mr. Dutton, and it would not have been creditable for her to be otherwise; she dined at a good table every day, because her husband dined at home. Poor soul! she was very meek; a crust of bread and a draught of water would have satisfied her, could she but have had peace therewith; but she was doomed to have the stalled ox and the strife also, although she herself was full of meekness and submission.

Mrs. Dutton's would have been the desolate, weary, joyless life of a slave, had it not been for her daughter, who, gifted with her own affectionate and amiable disposition, possessed, nevertheless, sufficient of her father's dominant will to insure a degree of freedom of action for herself, in which she not unfrequently included her mother, such as that mother would never have dared to assert for herself.

Ellinor's beauty, and the reputed wealth of her father, brought her, as Mrs. Dutton of Woodbury had said, many suitors, among whom was the young Englishman, Chinnery, whose gay, social qualities made him a welcome guest to every member of the family. To Mr. Dutton, because he made himself useful in a thousand ways, and was a very entertaining companion; to the mother and daughter, for the same reason—he had the power of keeping the fire-side despot in good humor. Before long, however, it was evident that other motives brought him daily to the house than the mere pleasure of amusing the father: he loved the daughter.

A terrible anxiety filled the heart of Ellinor. To refuse him would, she believed, call forth the whole force of her father's despotic will against her. Fortunately, however, it was his ambition that she should marry a man of landed property, which Chinnery was not. He did not conceal his intentions on this head; and Chinnery, knowing his own disqualifications, and unable to remove himself from the idol of his heart, redoubled his efforts as a good after-dinner companion, and spent the half of every day in transacting trifling business for her father, not doubting but that, sooner or later, success would crown his wishes.

In the midst of these hopes and calculations, a formidable rival appeared in the person of William Elworthy. He was then about five-and-twenty, remarkably prepossessing in person, frank and generous of disposition, with the simple, unpretending manners of the well-bred independent gentleman, rather than the man of fashion. He was the very opposite of Chinnery.

Elworthy, like many another who entered that little charmed circle, loved the fair goddess of it at first sight. But, although early comprehending the painful circumstances of the family relations, he did not, like Chinnery, seek the daughter by homage to the father; he devoted himself to the meek and suffering mother, by whose side stood the affectionate daughter, and was soon rewarded by the unqualified gift of that daughter's entire affection.

There was a something in the grave, earnest, yet frank demeanor of Mr. Elworthy which at first favorably impressed even old Mr. Dutton. He listened to his proposals with patience; and when he learned the extent of his landed property, the amount of his income, and what settlement he proposed to make on his daughter, his consent was immediately given. The lovers were made happy.

An hour afterward Chinnery came in with his arm full of newspapers and books which, with great labor, he had been hunting out at various libraries for the old gentleman: he was unusually gay.

"You must dine with us to-day," said Mr. Dutton; "I have just given my consent to Ellinor's new lover, Elworthy; you've seen him; he will dine here too."

All Chinnery's mirth was gone; he sank down in a chair, and laid his forehead in his hand.

"Come, now, don't be a fool!" said old Dutton. "I dare say you have a fancy for her also; it's perfectly astonishing what offers that girl's had! I wish upon, my soul, I do! that I had another daughter for your sake. But you'll come and dine here; Elworthy will be so taken up with the women that I shall have no one to amuse me. I can't do without you! And as to Ellinor, why, my good fellow, you should have spoken; and besides, 'there's many a slip between the cup and the lip,'" said he; holding out, as it were, this faint hope, with the apparently kind, but yet selfish wish, of raising his spirits.

But it was no easy thing to raise his spirits; he had lost the very inspiration of his mirth and wit; and before long, Mr. Dutton, who had also lost his amusing companion and useful servant, and who found that he had greatly the worst of it in this new bargain, was out of humor too, and more than commonly irascible and tyrannical. Elworthy, who was often an unwilling witness of these painful scenes, sympathized naturally too much with the weak to please the strong. There was no chance whatever of his taking Mr. Chinnery's place with the old gentleman; in fact, the more probable chance was that the two would come to an irreparable quarrel, for Elworthy as the reader has heard, was by no means a man of phlegmatic temperament.

"God help us!" said poor Mrs. Dutton, one day, in her weak and somewhat querulous voice, to her daughter, after some violent outbreak of temper on the part of her husband, in which he had spoken of Ellinor's lover with very little patience—"I don't know what is to become of us if your father and Elworthy quarrel!"

"They will not quarrel!" said Ellinor, in that firm, cheerful voice, which always operated like a healing influence on the wounded and sensitively-suffering heart of the mother—"Elworthy will never quarrel with my father. Quick tempered, he may be, but for our sakes he will allay the storm rather than excite it. Have, therefore, dearest mother, no fear, as I have none!"

Mrs. Dutton tried to cast out fear and anxiety, but she was so timid and nervous, and stood in such awe of her husband, that if any one entered into the merest argument with him, she trembled as if she stood on the brink of a gulf, and it seemed impossible to her but that Mr. Elworthy's quick, resolute, uncompromising manner, must excite him sooner or later. She knew her husband better than Elworthy did, and therefore she lived in constant apprehension.

It was about this time when Richard Elworthy, having received from his cousin the intelligence of his intended marriage, made his appearance in Paris; and from that time, strange to say, things began to mend. Ostensibly Richard's object in leaving England was to congratulate his cousin on his approaching happiness, and to enjoy a little of the gay Paris life before settling down to hard work in London.

Elworthy was too happy himself not to make the young man heartily welcome; he liberally supplied him with money, and introduced him to old Mr. Dutton as a merry companion, in the place of his late favorite. Richard's powers were somewhat similar to Chinnery's; he drank freely without becoming intoxicated; sang merry songs, told witty stories, and satirized every body, not omitting his cousin, greatly to the old gentleman's amusement. He was in Paris for a deep and secret purpose: for no other than, if possible, to prevent the marriage taking place. He came without the slightest knowledge of the family with which his cousin was about to unite himself. He now keenly studied every character. He appeared frank, and all trusted him. He heard much of Chinnery, and in him he saw the tool of his purpose; but he was now supposed to be absent from Paris. Richard was bent on finding him and gaining his confidence. The opportunity at length occurred.

One day the Duttons made a party to Versailles, and there met Chinnery alone, and looking very melancholy. Old Dutton, who was leaning on Richard Elworthy's arm, saw him first, and delighted to find his young entertaining companion once more, most kindly accosted him, and introduced him to Richard Elworthy, laying an injunction on the two young men that they should become not only well-acquainted with each other, but dine with him on the morrow.

Chinnery, spite of his melancholy, was by no means disinclined for a renewal of intimacy with the gay and social old gentleman, which would also bring him again into the society of his daughter, for whom he still entertained the most violent passion. Richard Elworthy believed that he had now the game in his own hand; but he kept his designs entirely within his own breast, while he manœuvred with the most masterly skill. He by no means concealed his close connection with the hated rival of his new friend, on the contrary he spoke of William Elworthy in the most natural and unreserved manner. He spoke freely of his many virtues, and equally freely of his failings, always dwelling forcibly on his quick and choleric temperament, of which he furnished many highly colored details, carefully studying, nevertheless, to give a comic turn to all, so that his descriptions might appear amusing rather than serious, and thus wholly without sinister intention. He would then, as if to prove to his listener how truthful a limner he was, dash off, as a companion-piece, the tyrannical and testy-tempered Mr. Dutton, the fidelity of which Chinnery could immediately recognize.

"Good heavens!" exclaimed Richard, one day, after having entertained his friend as above, "to think of these two powder magazines standing side by side without blowing one another up. Some little explosions there have been, I understand; but there will be a terrific scene one of these days, if some good-natured soul, or even chance, perhaps, should drop a spark between them. Think only of Mr. Dutton, the worst-tempered man in the world, vowing that his daughter shall never marry any but a good-tempered man, and she, with more reason, vowing that she never will either; and yet the father has given his consent to, and she is ready to marry William Elworthy, a man whose temper is as ungovernable as a wild horse. Elworthy is my relative, and I am under some obligations to him, yet nevertheless, I should like to see an explosion. There could be no harm in it beyond the bluster, for Elworthy loves that pretty daughter of his too well, not to take care both of himself and her, and old Dutton is too well pleased at the prospect of his daughter marrying a good English estate, to break the connection, spite of all his threats."

Richard laughed, and so did his companion.

"I tell you what though," continued Richard, as if growing confidential, "if it was not for those English acres, old Dutton would rather his daughter married you. He likes you while he is afraid of Elworthy. There is something dignified and reserved about Elworthy; he doesn't laugh at the old gentleman's jokes as he should do; nor sit over his wine with him; they are the very antipodes of each other, and yet are alike excitable in temper."

No more was said; it was merely seed dropped by Richard, as if by chance, but it fell, as he hoped, into fruitful ground.

From this day Chinnery's spirits returned; he and Richard Elworthy were frequently together, and again he was a frequent guest at the Dutton's; again he told his witty stories, and used every effort to ingratiate himself with the old gentleman. Richard now withdrew, as if into the back-ground, leaving ample space for Chinnery's operations, and satisfied himself by merely standing by and watching the game. No one suspected him. He was in favor with all: he seemed to have restored good-humor and the former calm state of things. Chinnery was obliged to him for giving, inadvertently, as he believed, a clew to his rival's character, by means of which he might be inveigled to his ruin; Elworthy was obliged to him, because in restoring Mr. Dutton to a better state of temper he had added essentially to the happiness of Ellinor and her anxious mother, and for the same reason *they* were obliged to him, and expressed their gratitude in words of genuine emotion.

A short time of general happiness and equanimity intervened, during which Mr. Elworthy, who was impatient for his marriage, pressed for its consummation. This pause, however, was only the lull before the storm, the time necessary for the germination of those seeds of discord which the enemy had dropped in, like the tares of evil, while the unsuspecting husbandman slept.

Not a hint of Richard's was lost on Chinnery. Spite of Elworthy's sincere wish to avoid dissension it appeared next to impossible;

he and old Mr. Dutton seemed opposed on all subjects, politics, religion, or the merest event of the day. When they met it seemed as if the devil of discord were between them, and contention was inevitable. Mr. Dutton evidently disliked him, and sought occasion of quarrel, and at length it came. A dispute originating about the root of a Greek verb, between Chinnery and Elworthy, was taken up by the old gentleman, and called forth such an excess of temper, that Elworthy, anxious to close it, rose, and was about to leave the house, when Mr. Dutton, transported beyond himself, ordered him never to enter it again.

Richard had now his wish gratified. The two powder-mills had exploded and blown each other up.

He looked very grave the next evening as he remarked this to Chinnery, adding, "But it is really more serious than might have been expected. Miss Dutton, of course, is very unhappy. But what a hot-headed man is Mr. Elworthy! Who would have thought him fool enough to contend with Mr. Dutton, and yet I must confess, in his defense, that you have had a hand in it all. I have looked on, and seen how artfully you have fomented discord."

Chinnery did not laugh outwardly, but he was well pleased with what had happened, and when within a few days, at old Mr. Dutton's peremptory commands, the family left Paris and removed to Cassel, he almost immediately followed them.

On the night of the unhappy quarrel with her father, Ellinor had a long, and as it turned out, unhappy interview with her lover. Their tempers were both excited, and, in a moment of irritation, she said that she held it to be her duty to take back the faith that she had plighted. She had mistaken his character: he was overbearing and unreasonable, and she had unhappily seen too much domestic misery from these causes to risk her own happiness when her judgment warned her. What was the suffering of separation now, in comparison with a life-long warfare and misery?

Astonishment, pride, and indignation, aroused the whole force of his vehement spirit. He gave her back her faith as a thing of little value, and they parted, as it seemed, for an eternal separation—only, however, to feel the next moment, when recall appeared impossible, that each had been too precipitate, and that the affection of two kindred hearts could not be crushed even by offense and wrong. The spirit of concession and forgiveness awoke in each, like an avenging angel, and drew their souls nearer, in fact, than they had ever been before, only they knew it not.

When the family had been but a few days in Cassel, Ellinor surprised Mr. Chinnery by requesting half-an-hour's conversation with him in the public gardens. It was a splendid summer evening, and the gardens were crowded with pleasure-seeking people, walking, talking, and drinking coffee. Chinnery, astonished and delighted—for he too was about to request the same favor—joined her in one of the most retired walks.

He offered her his arm, which she declined, and then, in a cold and somewhat haughty manner, she addressed him:

"I can not allow you for one moment, to mistake my motive. You know the unhappy state of my affairs with William Elworthy."

He bowed.

"William Elworthy," continued she "has been forbidden our house by my father; and more than that," added she, with a perceptible tremor of voice, which by no means escaped Chinnery's notice—"I have, perhaps, voluntarily seen him for the last time. Under these circumstances, I understand from my father that you have his permission to solicit my hand. My amazement and indignation at this announcement were beyond words! Can my father believe it possible for me hastily and arbitrarily to transfer my affections, or that you could consider them worthy of acceptance if they were thus transferable? You could not; no man could! There must be no misunderstanding among us on this, to me at least, so grave a subject. I have told my father, within the last hour, and thereby I have excited his stern displeasure, that I am in no condition to accept a new lover. I have told him, as I now tell you, that William Elworthy is the only man I have ever loved; I love him still; it is possible I may love him to my death. He has many noble and beautiful qualities! God forgive me if I have done wrong!" said she, her voice sinking almost to a whisper, and then clasping her hands together, as if to keep down some struggling emotion, she stood, as pale as marble, before him.

Chinnery was not an ungenerous man; he loved her ardently, he was now deeply touched by her emotion, and he spoke sincerely, as far as himself at least was concerned, when he replied:

"If Elworthy had truly, nobly loved you—loved you in the spirit of self-abnegation he would not have angered your father;

for your sake he would not! What have I not done for the sake of peace ?—concealed my true sentiments, coincided with what I did not believe, acted a lie to my very soul—"

"Mr. Elworthy was too noble to be a hypocrite, was too genuine, too upright to act a lie!" returned Ellinor interrupting him.

"Let me be properly understood ; do not let my words be taken as an offense," said he, warmly. "You know not how I have loved you ! I have seen that your life was embittered by domestic tyranny. I would have made you so happy ! I had vowed with myself to God to compensate for the sufferings of your youth, by the love which I would have lavished on you, by the indulgence which should have left no wish ungratified. I bore and forbore with your father. Elworthy could not do as much ; he could not, even for your sake ! I know him, Miss Dutton, better than you do : let there be no offense in my words when I ask you, can a wife be happy with a tyrant-tempered husband ? She can not, you know she can not ! Elworthy is a tyrant in temper, a capricious despot—"

"Villain ! traducer !" exclaimed Elworthy himself, who having been led by a singular chance to that very spot, heard the last energetic words of his rival, and now confronted him. "Lying scoundrel !" cried he, and at the same moment struck him with his riding-whip.

Ellinor, pale as death, sunk on a seat motionless. The two men, now fierce enemies, rushed to her, each attempting to thrust the other aside. But Ellinor had not fainted, though a sickness of horror, as it were, passed over her soul.

"Madman ! infatuated madman !" exclaimed she, in a low but firm voice, rising at the same time and addressing Elworthy. "Ah, what have you done ! God in heaven sustain me ! Elworthy, you have parted us forever !" and with these words she again sank on the seat and burst into a flood of tears.

The rumor of an encounter between two jealous English rivals spread through the gardens, and people came thronging toward the spot. In the mean time, Ellinor, who saw instantly the dangerous position of her lovers, as regarded each other, made a violent effort to master her feelings, and in some measure to justify each to the other. But it was no easy matter ; the words which Elworthy had heard justified, in his then excited state of mind, the violence of his conduct, while the very violence of his conduct seemed, on the other hand, to justify the words themselves.

Sick at heart, and overwhelmed with yet more terrible apprehensions, Ellinor reached home. Both her parents were absent, and throwing herself on her bed, she endeavored to compose her mind, and come to a clear judgment as to what was right for her to do.

It was late before her parents returned, and then letters from England, which awaited her father, awoke new anxieties.—Something of fatal presage in the state of his affairs summoned him home; he was thrown into a state of strange depression of mind, which greatly increased his natural irritability. Her mother was overwhelmed with nervous fear: something dreadful was about to happen. Ellinor roused herself to sustain her mother, and for that night, at least, not a word was said of her own terrible anxiety. The next morning Mr. Dutton gave orders for their immediate return to England, and instant preparations for their departure began. A note was brought to Ellinor. It was from Elworthy: a duel had been fought between himself and Chinnery. Chinnery was slightly wounded, and he was about to leave Cassel—to leave Germany, and he now bade her farewell. He deplored any sorrow or annoyance which he might have caused her; thanked her for the glimpses of brief happiness which he had enjoyed with her; begged her forgiveness, her prayers, and, if possible, her remembrance, with forbearance, if not with love. "Ellinor," said the letter, in conclusion, "your image will never leave my heart. I have loved you with an imperishable love; yet you are free. I only am bound—bound by my love and by the tears which I have seen you shed; surely, I did not misunderstand them!—they have been my consolation. God, at some future time, will perhaps make me more worthy of them."

Thus he wrote, yet he asked no interview, and was gone.

The disturbance of Mr. Dutton's mind was extreme. He was not in the habit of being confidential, as regarded his business affairs, with his wife and daughter; it was sufficient for them to know that his son, still in England, but no way connected with him in business, urged his immediate return. Ellinor had enough to do to sustain her anxious and alarmed mother without asking for sympathy in her own troubles. The duel between the two rivals apparently excited more interest among the good idle gossips, English and German, of Cassel, than it did in the Dutton family. Two days after it occurred they were on their way to England, in consequence of it, as it was generally believed, and even as was believed by Chinnery himself. Elworthy knew not of their departure, for he too had left Cassel, and was traveling post to Italy.

Four months after this he learned in Rome, from an English newspaper, of the bankruptcy of Mr. Dutton, and leaving Italy with the same rapidity that he had entered it, he returned to England. No sooner in London than he sought out the brother of Ellinor—the husband of our Mrs. Dutton of Woodbury—who, holding a government appointment, resided in London, and to whom Ellinor was much attached. A frankness of manner in the junior Mr. Dutton instantly prepossessed Elworthy in his favor, while he, on his part, was well-disposed toward Elworthy, spite of the unfortunate termination of his acquaintance with his sister, from what she herself had communicated.

Elworthy's intentions were of the most noble and generous character. He came as a friend of the family, the first moment any knowledge of their misfortunes had reached him; and a warm heart and a liberal hand were now at their service. He came, indeed, at a critical moment. The affairs of Mr. Dutton were extremely embarrassed, and the expensive manner in which he had lived abroad, at a time when any prudent, or even honest man, would have diminished every unnecessary outlay, had irritated his creditors extremely. He was well aware of the desperate state of his circumstances even while abroad, and this circumstance, while it excused and explained to his wife and daughter that unhappy state of temper which had caused such an increase of domestic misery, only tended to exasperate his creditors. Ruin and disgrace stared the unfortunate family in the face.

It will readily be believed that Elworthy stood among all parties as an angel from heaven. The amount of Mr. Dutton's liabilities was too great for him to take upon himself, but it was easy to arrange with creditors who had hitherto expected nothing; all were satisfied, even the most irritated among them. The real amount of sacrifice which Mr. Elworthy made was, however, never known; it was, indeed, so far beyond his expectations that he never spoke of it.

There was no formal renewal of courtship between him and Ellinor; they met as though they had not parted in grief and anger. He laid his peace-offering on the altar of affection, and it was sufficient for him that it was accepted; he himself was too grateful to receive their thanks.

In the midst of the deepest humiliation of the Dutton family, Mrs. Dutton's health gave way; her nervous system, too long excited could not sustain this last blow, and she sank under it, nor was the unexpected deliverance able again to raise her. She had become feeble as a child both in mind and body, and the physician said that she could not last long. Elworthy was like a dutiful son to her already, and as such she loved him.

One night, taking his hand and that of her daughter, she said that she only wished to see them united; that she prayed God she might live so long.

Those feeble words were all-sufficient. Without any ceremony, or marriage preparation, they were united. This event gave her great pleasure. She now said almost incessantly that God was very good to her; that she was surrounded by blessings; that she was ready now whenever she was summoned.

The summons came as gently as the falling of the dew, and she passed away, holding to the last the hands of those beloved ones. After her death, William Elworthy and his bride removed into Wayland-dale, which Ellinor as yet had never seen. Old Mr. Dutton, who, spite of the unexampled nobility and generosity of his son-in-law's conduct, never really liked him, and to whom the obligation seemed rather as a burden, removed after his wife's death to London, that he might be near his son, whose wife, he said, he liked. He lived in lodgings the remainder of his days, on an annuity paid to him by Mr. Elworthy, though he never chose to acknowledge it.

The reader is now in possession of such portion of the family history as was not related by Mrs. Dutton of Woodbury, or which was beyond the knowledge of good Mrs. Hawes, to whom we now return.

"A very pretty woman was Mrs. Elworthy," said Mrs. Hawes; "and every body in the Dale took to her, for she had no pride, and she had as great a liking for the Dale's people as if she had been born among them. She fell into all their ways, and learned to knit and spin, and a beautiful spinner and knitter she was; and she had such pretty ways of doing every thing! It was quite a picture to see her sit at her wheel, and then the thread that she spun was finer than any body else's. The master was very proud of her spinning. I remember one day, when lots of fine London folks came, the master goes up to her wheel and draws out the fine silken thread, which he holds between him and the light, 'and doesn't my wife spin beautifully?' he says. 'Oh! she's a beautiful spinner!' They all looked so surprised; and when she came down they expected to see her, I reckon, in linsey-woolsey, because she spun; but she came down in silks like the first lady of them all, only more beautiful, and as blooming as a rose. She loved the Dale's folk, as I said, and came to their sheep-shearings and weddings, and kept up all th' old customs at Lily-garth, as if she—the greatest lady in a' th' Dale—had been only a farmer's wife. How fond every body was of her, and th' master more than all! One great trouble, however, there was, and every body felt it, and that was, that she wer' not likely to be a mother. *Every body,* I said, wer' troubled at it, but I should have said every body but one, and that wer' Mr. Richard, the master's cousin, who wer' looked upon as his heir, if he had no children.

"Richard by this time seemed to have sown his wild oats; he lived mostly in London, but now and then came down to Lily-garth for shooting and pastime, and the mistress wer' very fond of him; she'd known him abroad, and had taken a great liking to him. It wer' very strange, but after his marriage the master seemed to take a great dislike to Richard; he had less patience with him than ever. No doubt he had his reasons, but th' mistress wouldn't believe any harm of Richard, and he always wer' mighty agreeable with her, which wer' displeasing to th' master. Ay, it's a sorrowful thing to think of, 'at that fellow had even then power to make an unhappy minute between these two, but he had; and many an hour and many a day too!

"Th' master, you see, was hasty, and that always troubled her; she tried to keep peace, and to set Richard in a good light, and he was as artful as deceit could make him. He was as smooth to her as oil; she could not think ill of him. 'You're too hasty, William,' she used to say, in her sweet, but positive way; 'you know you are; I shall take Richard's part, for I know he's right!' Oh! it made th' master very angry to hear her talk so; but he could not turn her; she wer', poor thing! as hasty and as determined in some things as he wer'.

"Well, they'd been married a matter of four or five years," continued Mrs. Hawes, "when there was great joy in th' whole Dale, for she wer' expecting to be a mother. In th' summer of that year, they had gone from old Lily-garth to th' Hall, which had been building two years or more, and to buy chimney-pieces and furniture, for which th' master and she had been up to London, for he would have every thing done to her liking, and she wer' very fond of th' new Hall; she had laid th' fundation stone of it herself; nay I'm not sure but it wer' built to please her altogether; for Lily-garth, you see, was an old-fashioned house, wi' low rooms, and this wer' made large and lightsome. So though the Hall was not finished they moved into it; 'for,' says she, 'our first child shall be born in this new house: it will bring a blessing to it!' So she said many a time. Oh! what joy she had in the prospect of being a mother, and how glad was every body i' th' Dale! For, spite of her partiality to Richard, none of them liked the thoughts of his being one day th' master's successor. They said, no! we shall have now one of his own flesh and blood, born and bred among us, and one of ourselves, as it were. And there wer' not one of the tenants that did not get something ready for th' mistress or th' baby that wer' coming; one made a pillow for the cradle, another a fine pair o' blankets, another a quilt; there wer' not a mother among them 'at did not feel as if she wer' working for her first-born.

"When th' master and mistress moved to th' Hall, Christie Fothergill went to Lily-garth; he wer' eldest son of old Peter Fothergill of Birks-mill down i' th' Dale: Peter wer' a Quaker, and had two sons, Christie and Caleb; Christie married Margaret Gilson o' Dent-town; she wer' not a Quaker, but a notable, pretty lass wi' money; her father wer' a shopkeeper. Old Peter Fothergill wer' angry wi' Christie for marrying out of his society, 'a woman o' th' world,' as he called her; so Christie left th' mill, though he wer' to have had it, and as he wer' always a favorite o' the master's, and had now money to stock a good farm, the master says, says he, 'Christie shall have Lily-garth; and it's amazing how that pacified old Peter; he said no more against his son's marriage, not a word! So Christie had Lily-garth, and Caleb turned miller; he married a Quaker. She wer' a widow named Broadbent, out of Lancashire, and had two lads of her own Thomas and Samuel; they are young men grown now—very steady—and as Caleb Fothergill had no children of his own, he wer' a right good father to them. One o' them, Samuel, is a tanner i' Lancaster, and the other attends to th' mill with his step-father; and well-doing folks they are i' th' Dale, and much respected by the master. But, however, all this is neither here nor there to what I was saying, only Christie went to Lily-garth, when the master and mistress moved to the Hall. Christie wer' then hardly twelve-month wed, and his young wife, like th' mistress, wer' expecting her baby late i' th' autumn, so there wer' a great rejoicing in th' two houses, and Christie said 'at he would give his mistress twenty pounds for her own self and th' baby, if hers war' a lad bairn and born afore the squire's.

"Th' young mistress war' never so happy in all her days afore, and what does she do but writes a letter to Richard and tells him her joy, and bids him come down fra London that autumn, and see them in their new house. Th' master wer' ill pleased at this, but he let her have her own way in most things; and then she says, in her positive way, 'I can't think what makes you take agen Richard so; but he *shall* come to see me in our new house that I take such a pleasure in; of that I am determined.' So th' master said no more, only one could see 'at he wer' ill-pleased. Poor thing! she *did* take a pleasure in the new house! She went from room to room, looking out first at one window and then at another. She wer' very fond o' me," said Mrs. Hawes, with a deep sigh, "and as she wer' not over strong, she leaned on my arm many a time, as she walked up and down, 'and ah, Peggy,' says she, 'I hope it is not a sin to be as happy as I am!'"

"Wae's to me!" continued the good housekeeper. "Richard came down that autumn, as she had asked him, and to my thinking, it wer' like Satan entering into the Garden of Eden. He came down for th' long vacation, as they call it, and th' mistress 'at thought he would rejoice in her happiness, little knew how mad he wer' that there were likely to be a bairn.

"And now I must tell you that there were i' th' Dale a farmer—a man with money, that had lived on an old leasehold farm—one Dannel Garr, o' Tod's-gill. He wer' a hard, money-getting man, who was always in a quarrel wi' somebody; and if there wer' a man in the Dale that th' squire could not abide, it wer' Dannel o' Tod's-gill. He had a son that wer' a butcher as well as a farmer; a hardened, godless fellow, just the moral of 's father, and one daughter, a handsome lass, that could ride over the Fells on an unbroken filly. She had plenty o' lovers, for her father wer' rich, and bragged that he would give his old night-cap full of ginneas with her if she wed to his liking. Richard knew well enough that th' master could not abide Dannel o' Tod's-gill; you may think, then, how mad it made him when he heard, afore Richard had been many weeks at th' Hall, that he wer' a-courting old Dannel's daughter, and that i' th' spring, when he wer' down last, he had' been with her i' Swale-dale where th' Garrs came from, and where they had lots of relations—the rudest people in all these parts. Richard stoutly denied it; he said that she wer' a pretty lass, and that he had only had a bit of talk with her, one day, on the Fell-head among the sheep.

"'There's no such great sin in that,' said he, and appealed to the mistress. She said, 'no, for sure not;' but she hoped he would mind what he wer' about, for that she wer' a wild lass, and might bring him into trouble, and that the Garrs wer' rude, desperate folks, who would not take an affront and say nothing.

"Th' master, however, believed not a word that Richard said; but without saying any thing to him, he set about to find out the truth, and by little and little, a long history of villainy came to light. Richard had kept company with her ever since spring, and they had been together into Swale-dale, among the old Garrs. Old Dannel, the father, knew it, and the son knew it, and both had been willing enough at the time, believing that Richard meant honestly by her, and that he would one day be th' master of Wast-Wayland, and thus Isabel Garr be made a lady of. But Richard had no honest intentions toward th' poor lass, and now a day of reckoning wer' at hand. As soon as th' master began to make inquiries, old Dannel found all out, and now he swore 'at Richard should marry his daughter, or the Lord above knows what vengeance he would have!

"Both Richard and th' master were great sportsmen, and were often out on the moors for days and days, with their dogs and guns, although they never went together. Well, Richard set off one morning, and said he should not be back for three days, and th' master went out also. He took his gun with him, and his favorite dog, and made th' mistress believe that he wer' off shooting; because of the delicate state she wer' then in, and not far from her time, he did not wish her to know what he had heard about Richard's villainy to old Dannel's daughter. So, instead of going to th' moors, spite of all his mislikings of th' Garrs, he went right up to Tod's-gill; and afore he got there he heard th' old sinner a-cursing and swearing enough to carry th' house end off. His daughter was gone, nobody could tell where, and his rage was out of all bounds. She wer' off, he said, with Richard, and he now had not words bad enough for him; and, strange to say, no sooner did he see the master, whom he hated, enter his house, than in the blindness and stupidity of his passion he taunts him with the very fact which otherwise he would so carefully have kept from his knowledge. He calls Richard not only a villain to his daughter, but a thief and a swindler, and says that he has drawn money out o' th' bank i' th' master's name, and has given checks that other folks have got money by, and that he'll get hanged one of these days ; and then, altogether forgetting himself, and to prove his words true, he tore open his old greasy leathern pocket-book, and thrust before the confounded eye of Mr. Elworthy a page on which was written sums of money, which the wicked old man had made Richard enter in his own hand.

"Dannel had known well enough all along, that Richard had come by this money unjustly ; and what sort of money-dealings there had been between them, God knows ! but he were an old scoundrel, wer' Dannel ; and his son, the butcher, had got into trouble, and so Richard had helped him, that they might wink at his acquaintance with Isabel ; at least, so it seemed, and yet, now when it came out that Isabel ought to have been his wedded wife, and was not, he wer' so enraged that he wer' ready to murder her, and even betrayed himself in taking vengeance, as he thought, on Richard. Folks are such short-sighted fools when they are in a passion !

"How th' master, with his hasty temper, wer' able to keep his hands off the old villain, is more than I can say. Most likely he felt so hurt and confounded at finding that Richard was still following his old, wicked, youthful practices, and that he wer' so completely in old Dannel's power, that this overmastered his own passion. However this is certain, without even telling th' old villain what a trap he had laid for himself, he turns round as quiet as a lamb, as if he had not a word to say for himself, and sets off to Kendal that very day to find out th' truth at th' Bank. He did not say a word to th' mistress ; he wer' very still-like when he came home ; looked pale and vexed, ordered his horse, and set off to Kendal. There he found it, sure enough, as old Dannel had said. Richard had been drawing money all that year in his cousin's name ; he knew 'at his cousin had always a balance at the bank, for Mr. Elworthy always lived under his income, and so it never wer' suspected. Th' bank people brought out all th' checks, and th' hand-writing were so cleverly managed, that it wer' hard for th' master to say which wer' his signature, and which wer' not. By this you may know what a dangerous man wer' Richard.

"It wer' late when Mr. Elworthy came back, and th' mistress, who had not been quite well that day, and wer' gone to bed, as wer' quite natural, the master determined to tell her nothing, for as she had a liking for Richard, and thought well of him, this would be too great a shock for her at that time. But he could not hide the trouble that wer' in his face, though he tried to laugh it off as if there were nothing. However, as they sat at breakfast, who should walk in but Richard himself! He had come back quite unexpectedly late last night, without the least notion of what had happened, and he now came in in his gay, careless manner, and drawing a chair, sat down laughing and joking. It wer' more than th' master could bear. All at once he forgot himself; he wer' in a fearful passion, pushed his own chair from the table, started up, called Richard a villain, and went out of the room. Mrs. Elworthy, poor soul! thought for sure he wer' gone mad; she wer' terrified out of her wits; but Richard, though he must have known in his own mind, that the truth had come out, kept as cool as possible, and pretended to be hurt by th' master's anger.

"As to th' mistress, she wer' hurt no trifle. She herself had a deal of spirit, and she thought it wer' unkind of him to alarm and distress her just then in that way, and that made her take part wi' Richard. 'And what is this all about?' says she to him, 'what have you done to make my husband so angry?' Richard, who had no notion that th' master knew aught worse than his connection with Isabel Garr, confessed at once what it wer'; but,' says he, in his smooth, plausible way, 'it's nothing but a flirtation. Bless me! did Mr. Elworthy himself never take a fancy to a pretty girl? 'But,' says th' mistress, 'tell me honestly, Richard, have you made no promises to this girl, that may bring either her or you into trouble? The Garrs are terrible people; they'll be murdering you if you have deceived Isabel! As to Mr. Elworthy, you know he is hot-tempered; you must excuse him; if you are innocent it will all be right.'

'Richard swore to her he wer' innocent, and then got angry himself about th' master's temper, and said he would not bear it, and that he wer' a tyrant and had always been so, all which made the mistress very unhappy, and which in her state, wer' a dreadful thing. However, she tried to pacify Richard, saying she would not hear any thing against th' master, and 'at he wer' good and noble, and always meant well, though he wer' hot-tempered, which she did not deny, and 'at she would talk with him, and try to set all right between them. And so they sat ever so long together over th' breakfast things.

"Th' master, in th' mean time, who had only left th 'breakfast table, because he could not bear to sit there with Richard, and yet would not out with what he knew before th' mistress, stopped till he thought she wer' gone to her room, and then went back, looking, as you may imagine, as angry as could be, and meaning, no doubt, to order Richard into th' library, which wer' his own room, that he might then make a clean breast to him. But, you may think what were his feelings when, on opening th' room door, there sat Richard close by the mistress, and holding her hand, and looking into her face, as if he wer' on the best terms i' th' world with her.

"I wonder he did not strike him dead upo' th' spot, and I fancy he looked ready to do it, for up rose th' mistress in a minute, and going toward him, she said, in her positive way, 'You shall not be angry with him, William! I shall stand between you and him!'"

"'Go to your own room!' says he to her, in a voice as angry as that in which he had spoken to Richard; 'no one shall interfere between me and this man!'

"I myself was at th' door at the very moment. I never heard any thing so fearful as was his voice. A crimson flush overspread her face for a moment, and then she turned pale as death; but she didn't drop, she looked very resolute, and taking my arm, she said, as if nothing were amiss, I'll go to my own room, Peggy.'

"What passed between th' master and Richard I know not; this only I know, that an hour afterward, Richard went out of th' house as cool as could be, with his gun over his arm and with a couple of dogs at his heels. Th' mistress was leaning on my arm, and walking up and down the long gallery; she had been doing so for the last hour, but she did not speak a word all th' time, and seemed to be thinking to herself and listening to every sound i' th' house; and if a door opened and shut she seemed considering about it, and when Richard went out she watched him from th' window go right up th' shrubbery to a bridle-road that led out upo' th' Fells. As soon as he wer' gone out o' sight, 'Peggy,' says she, 'I think it will do me good to walk out this fine morning; I feel poorly, and the air does me good.' So I fetched her bonnet and shawl, and a book, as she told me, and we went out. It's a mighty pretty walk up th' shrubbery the way Richard took, and she said she'd go up there and sit i' the moss-house, which was a very favorite spot of hers, and where she and th' master had sat together hours and hours. So there we went, and hardly had she seated herself, and said she would sit and read there for an hour, and 'at I must go and fetch my sewing and come back directly—for she did not like to be left alone—when up came th' master by the same path, with his gun in his hand, and his old favorite setter, Bess, at his heels. There wer' something very terrible in his look; he wer' pale, and his whole face seemed a deal older, with a dark expression in it. He did not seem to see us, but as if he had some dreadful purpose in view, he walked right past th' little path 'at led to th' moss-house, and up th' wood toward th' gate that led to th' bridle-road; th' very way Richard had gone. Th' mistress, when she saw this, and 'at he wer' not coming to her, sprang forward as light as if she had no burden to carry, and 'William,' says she, again speaking in her positive way, 'you shall not follow him now! You *shall not*,' and she took hold of his arm, 'you'll lay up bitter repentance for your after-life if you do! You are unjust to him! You are more to blame than he is; and even were it not so, remember, William, that we must forgive if we would be forgiven!'

"Ah! I shall never forget them words as long as I live!" said Mrs. Hawes, "nor will th' master either!

"He made her no answer, not a word. Lord above! 'at any one should let passion so far carry them away. But he wer' very angry; he snatched his arm from her; he seemed almost to thrust her from him, and went onward faster and more determined than ever.

"He wer' only going out for a day's shooting on th' hills, and did not know 'at Richard had gone that way before him; but she, poor soul, in her then weak state, seeing them both going out with their guns, and how angry her husband wer', and knowing too, how passionate he wer', terrified herself with the fear that something dreadful wer' about to happen.

"She sunk down upo' th' seat i' th' moss-house, as if there were no strength left in her, and cried bitterly. She wer' not a woman that cried; I never saw her shed a tear afore, and that troubled me all the more. I knew not what to do.

"'Peggy,' says she, after a while, and when she was calm again, 'I feel very poorly; I must go back again to th' house,' so I helped her down, and she went into her own room, and lay upo' th' sofa. About two hours afterward, she rings her bell, and 'Peggy,' says she to me, looking very pale, but still speaking in her clear, resolute way, 'you must send one of th' men to th' Fell-head to look for th' master, and another to Sedbur' for th' doctor, for I feel very badly.

"All th' house wer' up, for there wer' not one who would not have laid down his life for her. Th' doctor fra' Sedbur' wer' soon i' th' house, and two or three men wer' out upo' th' Fell-head in all directions looking for the master; but he wer' nowhere to be found. He had not stopped for shooting, but had walked on to a farm of his, some miles beyond Garsta', and that wer' a long way.

"All that day she wer' very bad. It wer' a month afore her time. Th' nurse, who wer' a very clever woman, and who by good luck wer' at home, wer' fetched frae Dale-town; it wer' then evening and the baby were born. She had a very bad time, and she got worse and worse. She kept asking for th' master. 'For God's sake let him be fetched!' said the doctor, 'for it agitates her so, and I can not answer for the consequences. And then he sent off post for a physician fra' Kendal, and by that it wer' plain to see 'at he were no little frightened himself. All th' Dale wer' up; there were such running and riding about into th' neighboring dales and every where, but nobody went th' right road.

"In th' evening the physician came, and me and th' doctor never left her; th' doctor said 'at she wer' getting worse every quarter of an hour, and 'at we *must* fetch th' minister. By that time she wer' past asking any questions; she lay as if she wer' dead, as white as marble, and the two doctors sat together by her bed, feeling her pulse every now and then, and whispering to each other.

"Although every body wer' in such a state of mind, yet we determined to break it gently to th' master when he did come; so th' doctor said 'at he would go down to see him first. But, however, it wer' not so to be. It wer' late at night when th' master wer' met by somebody coming homeward, just at the foot of Hibblethwaite, and they out at once and tells him that th' mistress wer' just dead. He wer' a strong, stately man, wer' Mr. Elworthy, five feet ten at least, and very strong knit, and though he often showed anger afore folk, never liked to show any other kind of feeling, for he wer' very proud; but when he heard this, a child might have knocked him down. It wer' a bright moonlight night, and his face wer' as pale as death; he couldn't stand, and somebody who were just then coming by, held him. Th' next moment he wer' off, and into th' house, and those who saw his face that night will never forget it to the latest day of their lives.

"Wae's to me!" sighed Mrs. Hawes, "what a dreadful time it wer'! I wonder I've th' heart to tell it! It's not often I do, but I'm in th' story now, and I'll e'en finish it, though it's like tearing open old wounds."

There was a pause of some minutes; both Honour and her mother were deeply affected and interested. Mrs. Hawes saw it, and continued:

"When he came to her bedside it seemed as if his very presence recalled her from death. 'Ellinor, my Ellinor!' cried he, in a low voice, as if his heart wer' broken, and bending over the bed. She opened her eyes and fixed them on him with such a look! and then a smile, like a faint beam of sunshine, came to her white lips. They could see how pleased she wer' 'at he wer' safe and wer' back again with her, and 'at she felt nothing but love for him, but she never spoke nor moved. Th' feeble light in her eyes seemed to fade away, and th' finger of death parted th' smile from her lips. She wer' dead!

"He threw himself on his knees beside the bed; he kissed her, he spoke to her in the most loving tones, but words never passed her lips; she never more opened her eyes; th' beautiful loving spirit wer' gone; nothing but th' dead body remained!

"What a change had a few hours made!

"For four days and nights he never left the room where she lay, nor appeared to sleep through all that time. He took no notice whatever of th' child. He was heard by th' household pacing up and down by th' hour together, and at times outbreaks of agony too wer' heard. Oh, it is a frightful thing to see a strong man shaken by agony! But his grief wer' almost too much for him. As to Richard, he wer' still angry with him, but it wer' in a different way. I reckon 'at, sinner though he knew him to be, he wer' willing to leave his punishment to others. 'God, himself,' said he, 'has punished me, for I too have been a sinner!' Nobody, however, saw him during that time of agony, but th' minister, and he only twice, and that wer' what he said to him. 'Let me be,' says he to th' good man, 'I am in no fit state to be comforted. God has seen meet to punish me when I was about to punish another. I must be able to submit myself to his judgment afore I can receive consolation.'

"That was th' way he talked to th' minister, and then he went back again into th' dead chamber, and th' minister, who wer' a good man, urged him no further, although he remained in th' house th' whole time, for he said, 'if he need me I will be at hand; in the mean time I can pray for him.'

"The brother of th' deceased lady, a Mr. Dutton, of London,

followed by some other kinsmen, came hither as soon as th' news of her death reached him. He wer' a very good sort of gentleman, very fond of his sister, and her sudden death wer' a great grief to him; but Mr. Elworthy would only see him for a short time, and th' others not at all. He sent his compliments to them, and said he was not equal to it then. So they took upon themselves all the necessary arrangements for th' funeral, which was a great relief to him, no doubt, for he seemed to have no thought whatever about it.

"When th' day fixed for th' funeral came, it wer, feared 'at violence might be necessary to part him from the body. But they did not know Mr. Elworthy. I said all along how it would be, for I could feel in myself how he would act. But they were astonished. Th' night before, Mr. Dutton informed him that the funeral was fixed for the next day. He made no reply: but th' next morning he went to his own room, rung for hot water, shaved and dressed without any help from his man, and putting on th' deep mourning 'at had been prepared for him, and which wer' laid ready, walked, just before th' appointed hour, into th' room where th' funeral company wer' assembled, about to depart with the dead. He spoke to no one, but shook hands with them all. And oh! how he was changed in those few days! He looked, at th' least, twenty years older; there wer' deep lines as if they had been scored into his thin, haggard face—and he wer' a very handsome man; his very hair looked thin, and had begun to turn gray; it has just the same touch of gray in it to this day; you'll see it, ladies," said Mrs. Hawes, "and then you'll remember that until this dreadful time, there wer' not a white hair in it.

"Th' next day he said to th' servants, 'it's my wish 'at th' window-shuts of all th' unfinished rooms should be left closed.' He paid off the work-people as had been employed there, and in watching whom she had found so much amusement. I reckon he couldn't bear to see them about. So th' work wer' stopped, and all that beautiful part of th' house has never been finished to this day, and th' trees have been let to grow up thick on that side, and shut up th' view, which is very beautiful, and of which she wer' very fond. Th' rooms themselves are full of beautiful things, many of them unpacked, which she and th' master had bought up i' London that very summer. You shall go into th' rooms some o' these days, ladies, and you'll see beautiful furnitur' and carpets and hangings, all of her own choosing, which cost a power of money.

"When he'd given these orders about th' window-shuts," continued she, "he went up to th' room where th' baby were, and took it fra' th' nurse: he had never had it in his own arms till then, and he sends her out of th' room, and tells her not to come till he rings for her. I reckon he did not like to show his feeling afore her. Th' baby wer' just gone to sleep, and it wer' nigh upon two hours afore he rings for her again, and from that time, as long as th' baby lived, he seemed to have no thought but about it. It wer' a lad-bairn, a weakly child, but very like th' mother.

"But, however, afore I go on wi' th' poor baby, I must tell you about Richard. When he left th' house that dreadful morning, it's my opinion, knowing what he did, 'at he didn't mean to come back again in a hurry. However, let that be as it might, no sooner wer' he on th' moor at th' back o' Hibblethwaite, than who should he see but old Dannel Garr, knitting his stocking upo' th' Fell, looking after's big flock o' geese. Desperate angry wer' old Dannel—calls him all the names he could set his tongue to, and tells him he'll live to see him hanged, even though he himself should get hanged too, because he had made a fool of Isabel.

"Well, that frightens Richard even more, I'll be bound to say, than what Mr. Elworthy had threatened him with that morning; because, no doubt, he knew 'at th' master wouldn't disgrace his own blood-relation, but there wer' no knowing what old Dannel Garr might do when he wer' once enraged. Isabel Garr wer' gone, that was certain—no doubt it wer' all an understood thing—and it wer' long afore Richard wer' again seen in these parts.

"When, or how soon, the news of th' mistress's death reached him, I know not. I reckon, th' master buried all thoughts of vengeance against him in th' grave with his dead wife, for nothing of that ever was spoken of; and yet, it wer' well known 'at Richard had drawn out money in th' master's name, and 'at young Dannel Garr and received a pretty penny, for all he made such a piece o' work about his sister.

"Th' news of th' mistress's death filled the Dale with sorrow; it wer' as if death had come to every body's fire-side; and th' next Sunday, when th' minister preached her funeral sermon, the whole church was in mourning.

"There wer' a deal for folks to talk about, just then; the mistress wer' dead; Richard wer' gone off with Isabel o' Tod's-gill, and old Dannel, what with rage at his daughter, and fear of what the master might do at them, because of the money his son had had from Richard, had taken to his bed, and lay there cursing and swearing, and afraid of dying and leaving his money, and having to give an account afore God of how he had got it. Oh! that wer' a fearful deathbed! Th' old man wer' a fortnight in dying; and they took him off his bed, and laid him upon a mattress and blankets on the parlor floor, for they thought there must be pigeon's feathers in th' bed, and 'at that was the reason why the breath couldn't leave the body.

"All these things together took such hold on Nelly o' Lily-garth, Christie Fothergill's young wife, 'at she got her bed some weeks afore her time, and so there wer' a baby also at Lily-garth. But, waes to me! Nelly got no twenty pounds from her husband, for the baby, though it wer' a lad-bairn, died, and then Nelly—ay, she wer' a good creature and so wer' Christie! forgetting all her own sorrow, wer' wrapped up in blankets, and laid on her bed in a cart, and came up to th' Hall to nurse the poor motherless baby here.

"Th' squire's nature seemed to be quite changed: he 'at had been like a masterful lion afore, wer' now as gentle as a lamb. I've often heard tell of these sudden changes; some folk's hair will turn white in a night's time, other folks will lose their speech and be dumb, all which is natural like. But other more wonderful changes there are, which are the work of God's grace, for if He sends sore trials He sends likewise blessings and mercies. And to my thinking, it must be no common blessing, when a fiery, masterful spirit, which has been tempested like troubled waters, finds itself calm and still, as was the sea when Christ stayed its raging with a word; ay, that was a great mercy and a miracle! And mercies and miracles are not so uncommon in our days as we think, only we don't open our eyes to see them!

"Well, as I said, the master wer' now gentle as a lamb. I shall never forget his look when he saw Nelly o' Lily-garth take his poor, motherless baby in her arms and lay it to her breast. Nelly, poor woman! wer' crying herself; she wer' thinking, no doubt, of her own baby 'at she might have been nursing; he wer' thinking of the mother of his own bairn, and there wer' not a feature in his face 'at wer' not full of agony. He struck his forehead with his hand and dropped into a chair, and then, leaning his head on a table, cried like a woman. It wer' th' only time 'at I ever saw him shed a tear, but those tears took a strong hold on me. I vowed 'at I would be his servant to my dying day, and so, by God's mercy, I trust I shall!"

Mrs. Hawes here made a long pause, she was overcome by her

emotion, and then wiping her eyes, carried away the tea-things which had been standing before them all this time; came back with a more cheerful countenance, and then resumed.

"The best room in th' house wer' given up to Nelly for her and th' child, and nothing wer' too good for her. Christie wer' permitted to come just as he liked; and this I must say, 'at it wer' a great giving up, and he a young man as had been wed hardly twelve months, and very fond of his wife—but Christie and Nelly, and all th' rest of th' Dale, would have thought nothing too much 'at they could do for th' master. Th' child might have gone to Nelly at Lily-garth, but when somebody talked of her going back and taking it with her, 'Nay,' says she, 'it would be like a second death in th' house, to take away th' baby; it's th' only comfort that is now left for th' master!' And it would have been cruel to have done so. He would sit with it sleeping on his knees for hours, and never take his eyes off it. It wer' as she said, th' only comfort 'at wer' left for him in this world.

"I have said 'at th' master wer' changed. It wer' not such a change as often comes from lowness of spirits, or from the body being weakened with sickness, 'at lasts only for a time. No, the change in him wer' as earnest and lasting as his affliction had been great and uncommon. He wer' a good man; and you see he took it all as from the hand of God, and the blessing of God wer' on him, even in that great sorrow. From that time, he wer' full of pity, and gentleness, and forgiveness of wrong; he wer' still the strong, resolute man, but a new nature wer' added to his: kindness as of a woman. It seemed to me something quite unusual; as though the tender, loving spirit of his wife had united itself to him—as if now, more than ever, they were one.

"And now, and for many a long year past, if any body throughout the whole country has any trouble or affliction, they come to th' master; and if there's any quarrel, it's he 'at must set it to rights. He has established schools, and savings' clubs, and he has lending-libraries in ever so many places, so 'at folks 'at love reading can have good, entertaining books at their own houses, and it's wonderful what good he has done in this way! In short he is the best landlord, the kindest master, and the surest friend in all these parts.

"But to go back to th' baby," said she. "It wer' but a weakly thing to begin with, but so good and quiet; it never cried, nor seemed to ail any thing, but just faded and faded away, till when spring came it wer' no more than a pale shadow.

"Th' master had made up his mind to part with it long afore it wer' taken, and th' last day 'at it lived he had it for hours in his arms, wrapped in a shawl, and walked with it up and down in th' warm sunshine, and when it died, it wer' lying on his knees. The death of this poor bairn made no great difference in him. It wer' not sudden; it came so gradually 'at he had time to prepare for it; and when it wer' dead and buried—buried in th' grave with its poor mother, he wer' more calm, and almost cheerful, and set about doing all th' good he could; and if there wer' one thing 'at th' mistress had liked more than another, that he did. She had began a lad's school in Dale-town: she wer' very fond of schools, and there wer' none here when she came, and all th' lads had to go over into Dent-dale, to Dent-town, to school, and that wer' a long way, even in summer. She laid down th' whole plan of th' new school, and a mighty good school it is! Th' master did not care much about it in her lifetime, only he gave her leave to do what she liked about it, and paid for building the school, and th' house for th' master to live in; but when she wer' gone he endowed it with a good bit of money, and bought land thereabout, and took great interest in it, and sent for a college friend of his, one Mr. Walker, and put him in, and soon there were more scholars than they had room for; and all th' gentlefolks, and folks from a distance, now come to see it, for it is very much talked of, and has been the means of other such schools being set on foot in other such out-o'-the-way places. It was in this way that th' master honored the mistress's memory. I reckon he thought it would be pleasing to her if she knew it, and I doubt not but it would.

"But I must not forget to tell you about old Dannel o' Tod's-gill. He lay dying, as I told you, for a fortnight, and the minister came and prayed with him for hours, but th' old sinner had such a knack of cursing and swearing, that th' minister many a time wer' stopped in his prayers, and could not go on, it wer' so shocking to hear him. You remember, ladies, 'at I said th' master could not abide old Dannel, and he'd never been but that once under his roof, but what does he do now, when he heard what trouble they were in? Why-a, he goes up to Tod's-gill again, all in his deep mourning; and they were so astonished to see him, for there wer' a great crowd in th' house, not only of th' neighbors, but some of th' Garrs wer' there, come all the way out of Swaledale—horse-dealers, and butchers, and such like—and old Thomas Garr, Dannel's cousin, wer' there, th' greatest miser in all these parts, and such of 'em as didn't know th' master took him for a minister, 'and ay,' said they, 'we're glad your reverence is come, for you'll ma'ppen set him at liberty.'

"'I'm no minister,' says the master, 'but I wish to see your unhappy friend. I can may-be, with God's help, be of some use to him.'

"So they led him into th' parlor where old Dannel wer' lying upon th' boards, and all th' bed-clothes in rucks and heaps about him; he tossed so, and wer' so uneasy. A whole lot of folks followed him in, and stood in a crowd round th' door-way, for them 'at knowed it wer' th' master wer' curious to see what would happen. Th' master didn't notice them a bit, but kneels down upon th' bare boards and takes the old sinner's hand—a big, bony hand it wer' at best, but now it wer' lean and cold as a skeleton's. Th' master took it in his, and, 'Dannel,' says he, 'if it will be any comfort to you at this last moment, I am come to tell you 'at I forgive you all 'at I have against you; and for your daughter's sake, who has had a great wrong done to her by my relative, I will forgive him also, and endeavor, as far as lies in my power, 'at he shall do right by her.' Dannel turned his head round and stared at th' master. His wer' always a hard face, but it wer' now harder than ever, and he said in a hollow voice, speaking thick at th' same time, 'I's niver forgive her! divvent ask me! I niver will—niver, niver!' and then he tried to curse, but his tongue seemed stiff, and th' words wouldn't come out.

"'Dannel! my poor unhappy friend!' says th' master, taking hold on his hand again, and laying th' bed-clothes smooth over him, 'hearken to my words. God has laid great sorrow of late upon me, and I now speak to you from experience; pray to God to forgive you—the forgiveness of God is better than money, better than houses or land, Dannel—pray to God, it is never too late, and pray that he may enable you to forgive others.'

"'I's niver forgive *her;* niver, niver!' cried he, and again some dreadful curse stopped his utterance.

"Young Dannel had got th' father to make his will in this illness, and he had left Isabel only a shilling; and th' old man wanted to have put in a curse also, but that the lawyer wouldn't do; he said he wouldn't write it in, for it wer' more than he dare; and when th' master heard this from some of th' women-folk 'at were there, he tried to get th' old man, then and there, to alter 's will. But it wer' no use; he wer' too far gone and too hardened to be turned, and if th' master spoke about her it only set him on trying to curse. So he bade him good-by, commended him to God's mercy, I doubt not, in his own mind, and came away.

"And God, of his great mercy, did not forget even him; for one of th' women 'at sat up with him that night after th' master had been, heard him trying to say th' Lord's Prayer; he couldn't bring it out himself, so she said it out loud to him, speaking very slow, and while she wer' saying it, he died.

"That wer' th' end of old Dannel. Young Dannel had now got all th' property, and a pretty little spot is Tod's-gill, and a power o' money beside; for th' old sinner had, unbeknown to any body, money lying out at interest i' th' bank, and on mortgage up and down, and all came to Dannel. Isabel had not a penny. She wer' off with Richard Elworthy.

"Scarcely had th' old man been two months in 's grave, when Dannel brought home a wife. She wer' his cousin, Jane Garr, and th' very night 'at she came home, when they wer' all merry, a great company of them, lads and lasses, and many of the Garrs, as usual, sitting supping their parridge and eating currant bread, there comes a loud thump at th' door, as made 'em jump up. Th' women were frightened out o' their senses; 'it 's old Dannel,' they said, 'he's come again!'—and there was such screeching and fainting as nothing wer' like it. Some of th' men-folk went out, but there wer' nobody there 'at they could see; they looked all about, wi' candles and lanterns, for there wer' no moon—and then, at last, somebody stumbles over a big basket, 'at stood upon a flower-bed just under the kitchen window. They opened the basket, it wer' a big butter basket wi' two lids, and what should they find in it but a lad-bairn, not a month old, wrapped in a new fleece! At first there wer' a deal o' laughing about th' bairn 'at were come so soon to th' new-married couple; but it wer' no joke neither, to have a bairn brought in that fashion. Dannel Garr wer' as mad as could be, and said 'at it wer' Isabel's, as mayhap it were; for I ought to have told you afore, 'at Isabel had gone to th' old aunt in Swale-dale, and there had got a lad-bairn, and that th' old woman—she wer' a desperate old woman; as strong as a man, and looked very like one too—she sent for Richard and made him promise in black and white to marry her, which he did, and then she promised to leave them all her money when she wer' dead. All this Dannel knew, so his first thought naturally wer', that this wer' Isabel's bairn, though how she came to do such a fearful unnatural act is more than I can tell. However, th' bairn stopped at Tod's-gill that night—there were plenty o' women folk there as could take charge on it—and th' next morning, Dannel Garr took a horse and th' basket, and rode over to Swale-dale to th' old woman, where he expected to find Isabel; but she wer' not there. Th' old woman said 'at she wer' gone with her bairn and her husband, Richard Elworthy, to London, above a week afore; and then she fell to calling Dannel all the names she could lay her tongue to, because he had got all th' money, and she said 'at Isabel would be a lady for all that, for 'at th' Wast-Wayland property would come to Richard. Dannel stopped not to hear her out, but set th' basket upon th' house floor, mounted his horse, and rode home again. Whether th' old woman knew any thing about the bairn I know not, but scarcely had Dannel reached home and wer' fallen asleep by th' fire when th' basket and th' bairn were at the door again. Th' old aunt had sent it back again, with a message that a'most blew th' house-roof off. 'It wer' none of Isabel's bairn,' she said, 'but some poor lass's bairn, and that Dannel wer' its father, and it wer' but come to its own home, and more shame to him!'

"Th' woman 'at Dannel had married wer' well-natured enough though she wer' a Garr, but this message of th' old aunt's put her into a great rage, for Dannel wer' well known to have been wildish afore he wer' wed; so she would not have the bairn in th' house. Th' man wer' gone as had brought it, so Dannel, to make short work of it, sets off with it to th' poorhouse at Sedbur', where they wer' forced to take it in. Poor bairn! what with riding from one place to another, what with cold and neglect, it did not live long to trouble any body. Th' overseers of th' poor made inquiries every where, but nothing could be made out; th' old aunt swore 'at Isabel had taken her bairn with her to London, but whether they sought it out in London or not, I can't say; London's a big place, and ma'ppen Richard and Isabel wer' not so easy to light on. However, the bairn died, and no more wer' said about it, though some believe to this day 'at it wer' Isabel's, others 'at it were Dannel's; and Dannel's wife throws it at him to this day, as I've heard.

"Th' old aunt in Swale-dale wer' as good as her word; she never turned her back on Isabel, who she always said wer' married to Richard, though nobody but she believed it. It wer' said that, like old Dannel, she had money in th' bank, and up and down in the country, at interest; but when she died, about ten years afterward, there wer' not as much as wer' expected, and there wer' a mortgage upon th' land to another of th' Garrs; however, what she left went to Isabel. Dannel o' Tod's-gill, threatened hard to dispute th' will, because, he said, that Isabel wer' not married, and that th' law would therefore give every penny to him as heir-at-law. Ma'ppen it might have done so if he'd tried it, but he never did, and it went to Richard Elworthy, as Isabel's husband; and he, ma'ppen, because he was afraid of what Dannel might do, made it over to Thomas Garr, him that had the mortgage on it. He wer' cousin to old Dannel; and there he lives now, for he moved there as soon as he got possession, because he could let his own place for more money, and we've heared 'at Isabel has been there within these three years, and 'at she and Richard, and old Thomas, and all th' Garrs in Swale-dale, make a boast that, some day, Richard will come in for all this beautiful Wast-Wayland property, which is th' master's. But that," said Mrs. Hawes, lifting her hands and eyes, "may heaven forbid! It had fifty times better go to th' Duttons and Cartwrights than to a villain like Richard Elworthy!

"However," added she, after a pause, "it is something about this Richard which has now taken th' master to London. I know 'at he had a letter from Richard, for he said so, and I put th' answer to it into th' post-bag myself the very day after; then there came other letters which seemed to trouble th' master. I can always tell when he is troubled; and I know it must be about Richard; it could be nothing else, unless it were about some of th' Duttons—ma'ppen about that Squire Cartwright. Well, I know not! and ma'ppen, it's no business of mine—nor is it! only it always hurts me to see th' master in trouble."

CHAPTER V.

Mrs. Mildmay and her daughter could not but feel great interest in all they heard respecting the life and character of their unknown friend.

One day they inquired from Mrs. Hawes to whom it was probable that the Wast-Wayland property, which appeared to be very considerable, would go in case of Mr. Elworthy's death; as fortunately it appeared not to be entailed, and therefore need not, of necessity, descend to his cousin Richard Elworthy, in case its present excellent possessor died without children.

"There are plenty that are looking after it," replied Mrs. Hawes, "plenty besides Richard Elworthy, to whom, however, it would go by law if th' master died without a will; plenty, I promise you, keeping a sharp look-out after it, and yet there is not one of them that is fit to lift up his shoes, much more stand in them!

"No, not one of them!" repeated Mrs. Hawes, with a peculiar expression of countenance, which was intended to imply a great deal; her auditors did not, however, solicit information; and therefore, after a pause, she continued, unasked:

"They are no favorites of mine, these Duttons, nor do I think 'at th' master is over fond of them: not that he ever said so, for he is as kind and generous to them as if he loved them ever so; but they are not of his sort; and yet our poor mistress! she were own sister to Mr. Dutton. He's dead now, and this his widow with four daughters, all very handsome ladies, and Mrs. Dutton herself as handsome as any of them; but, somehow, I never think that they'll get th' property. Sometimes I think 'at th' master will, ma'ppen, leave it to schools and charities; sometimes I think one thing, sometimes another; but one thing is sure, th' squire is a sharp-sighted, clear-headed man, for all he is so good and gentle; and though nobody can put him in a passion, and though Mrs. Dutton does not give him credit for half th' 'cuteness that he has, and never thinks 'at he can see through her. But he does, though! But th' Miss Duttons, you see—there are four of them—were th' nieces of his wife, th' children of her only brother, and she wer' very fond of him; and there's a natural leaning toward them in Mr. Elworthy's heart, and he is, and always has been, ready to do all for them that he could. It runs in my mind that he allows them something handsome to live on, but, of course, I can't say for sure. This, however, I *do* know, that, if they had chosen, they might all have been living here now. For you see, after Mr. Dutton's death—it's about ten years ago now—when she wer' left a widow with these four daughters, and but little for them, I take it, he offers for her to come here to overlook all his schools, only he did not want her to teach, and I reckon he would have built her a nice house at Dale-town, and he would have been like a father to her children. But she would not listen to it, unless she might have come and lived at th' Hall, and been at th' head of every thing. That, however, was not what he wanted; he had got over the freshness of his grief, and he wanted, I reckon, cheerful people near him—not always at hand, as one may say, but to see when he liked—to fill up just as much of th' void in his heart as he wanted filled; people 'at he might love and make happy, and yet be in some sort independent of. But Mrs. Dutton, as I've heared, wer' offended at his wishing her to attend to his schools; she liked better to be left at her liberty, to go about from one watering-place to another with her gay daughters; so she had her way, and lives down at a place called Woodbury, in Warwickshire, and comes up here now then with her daughters.

"Mrs. Dutton is a lady who knows as well as any body on which side her bread is buttered, so, though she wer' not willing to give up her own pleasure for th' sake of th' master and his schools, she never lets him lose sight for long of either her or her daughters. For one while she took to coming here twice a year as a regular thing, and besides this, when the children wer' young, she wer' always writing to say 'at one of 'em had th' measles, or th' hooping-cough, and wanted change of air, or they were come from school and wanted relaxation, and so they must come to their 'dear, kind uncle's.'

"Th' master soon got tired of that, for at that rate they would have been here the whole year round; and that was what she wanted, but at that time he could not bear it; the mistress hadn't been long dead, and they moithered him out of his life.

"After a while th' eldest wer' married; they went to Scotland for their wedding-trip, and came here on their way back, to spend the last two weeks of their honey-moon. She had married a

Mr. Beauchamp; a fine young man, a doctor; but they had no more manners than a couple of school-children, and rampaged about the house, and put every thing at sixes and sevens. There wasn't, perhaps, any great harm in them, but they put th' master sadly out of th' way. She'd very high spirits, and acted more from want of thought than any bad intention, but it was all the same. To give an instance now: she begged all kind of things from him—first this and then that; things that had been th' mistress's, and that he set store by. And one day, when th' master wer' out, what must they do but open all th' window-shuts, and look at th' things which had come from London afore the mistress died, which were all of her choosing, and which he wer' so tender of, that he could not bear to look at them himself. Th' master, as I have said, never goes into passions now, but when he came in, all unexpectedly, and saw what they had been after, and found her, as hot as fire, unrolling a handsome piece of carpeting, and when she runs up to him, and begins coaxing and flattering him, and begging him to give her that beautiful carpet for her new drawing-room at Woodbury, it wer' enough to make a saint swear. It wer' more than he had patience for; so, without saying a word, what does he do, but turn her out of th' room, and shutting the door behind her, locks himself in, fastens th' window-shuts, and goes to 's own room, and did not see her again all day.

"They were soon tired of th' place after that, and set off to th' Lakes, but not before he had given her a handsome sum of money to buy a new carpet with for her new drawing-room, as Mrs. Dutton herself told me. Next year th' second daughter wer' married, her name wer' Emma, but her husband called her Nelly, which was meant to please th' master, for so he used to call his wife, whose name was Ellinor; and there was no end of Nelly-ing and Nelly-ing all day long. I wonder they wern't ashamed of it, and I always thought it hurt th' master rather than pleased him. Well, she'd married a gentleman a good many years older than herself, but of a good family, they said, with a title in it; his name wer' Cartwright. I couldn't bear him from the time I set my eyes on him; that wild, young doctor wer' worth a score of him. He wer' a bad man, and I've heard 'at he does not use her well. They, however, did not behave amiss here; but in th' autumn—that wer' in th' spring—he sent down to say that he should like to come here shooting; and, as he did not wish to give trouble at th' Hall, he had written for lodgings at Lily-garth. Th' master had no objection, and to Lily-garth he came. Now, Christie and Nelly had a fine family, as fine as any in these parts—two of them are lasses; the eldest, Agnes, the handsomest lass in the Dale, and the apple of her father's eye. Would ye believe now, that it wer' for this lass 'at that villain had come, and he only married in the spring? The lass herself, for she had th' spirit of a lion in her, ups and tells her father at once, and Christie wer' fit to shoot him. Th' master, from that day, forbade him to set foot in th' Dale as long as he lived. But not a word of it was said to Mrs. Dutton, or to Mrs. Cartwright, for so th' master wish'd: he wer' so sorry for th' young wife.

"Two or three weeks since, th' master says to me, 'Peggy,' says he, 'we shall be having another wedding-party up here afore long, for Mrs. Dutton writes me that her youngest daughter is engaged to be married.' This youngest daughter is th' handsomest of all Mrs. Dutton's lasses; she wer' born two or three years afore the mistress's death, and she wer' christened Ellinor after her. Th' master wer' very fond of her as a child, and she wer' a nice sprightly little thing; but, to my thinking, she's grown rather out of favor. Th' last time she wer' here, it's about twelve months ago, she and Natalie, th' other sister, wer' here together with Mrs. Dutton, and she would have no nay but her uncle must take her every where. They set their minds on going to Kendal race-ball, so he gave them all handsome new dresses, and took them and Mrs. Dutton, and very beautiful they looked. They thought it very dull here, so he took them all to Harrowgate, and brought them back again, and they pic-nic'd in th' wood, and rowed upon th' water, and did all they could to divert themselves; and, lastly, he took them to the musical festival at York, and there he parted with them. He never spares expense to make their visits pleasant, but Mrs. Dutton told me that they thought it very dull, so she wer' forced to take them away, to keep them in good-humor.

"When they are all married, th' old lady, I take it, will be for coming here altogether; and yet, if I am not mistaken, she loves gayety as well as th' poor lasses, though she lays it all on their backs. I think she means to come, because she talked so much of 'th' beauties of nature,' and 'th' sweet peace of th' country,' and how, as she grew older, she longed more and more for retirement, and that she wished, of all things, to end her days in th' country. Then she wer' forever at me about th' master, and wer' he not solitary, and wer' not he very poorly and suffering; and didn't I feel afraid that he might suddenly die of that heart-complaint, and that her son-in-law, Beauchamp, who was a very clever medical man, though he was young, thought that Mr. Elworthy ought to have somebody with him—some friend that could look after him.

"All this she said to me, and no doubt said th' same to th' master himself, only not, perhaps, as plainly spoken out. Then she was always pumping me about th' will; and didn't I know how he had left his property; of course he had a will; when was it made, and who was present at the making? And if I didn't know how the property was left, she did; Mr. Elworthy was very partial to his nieces, and, of course, he never would think of marrying again! She does not like me, and yet she is mighty civil to me always, for she thinks 'at I know more about th' master's affairs—that is, about his will—than I choose to say; but bless you, I know no more than the babe unborn! Mr. Elworthy is not one who talks with such as me about his affairs; I know nothing, only I feel sure that Richard Elworthy will be kept out of th' property. Th' master is too good ever to put his poor tenants into his hands; as to the rest, I know nothing, only it seems to me natural that he should be sorry that his fine property should go into no better hands than those of the Duttons, who, to say the best of them, are not fit to carry his shoes after him; and that makes me think sometimes that he'll ma'ppen leave th' bulk of it to schools and charities. Sometimes I wish—and so does Christie o' Lily-garth, and many another beside—that he had married again, and had a family of his own, so that some one who understood his plans, and would have felt it a sacred duty to fulfill his wishes, might have come after him, and not some mere hungry money-hunter. But his fondness for his first wife, and the circumstances of her death, left him, I reckon, no heart for marrying again for many a long year; and so time went on, and now he's getting upon fifty, and men are hard to please then. So I've given up all thoughts of his ever marrying now; besides, I should like to know where is the woman that would be worthy of him, for he's one in ten thousand!"

CHAPTER VI.

One day, soon after these long communications had been made, Mrs. Hawes walked with Honour and her mother through the Dale. They wished to see the various places of interest connected with her narrative.

The road down the valley ran to the left of the little river, which was crossed at either end by a bridge. The one near the Hall had been built by Mr. Elworthy himself, that at the Dale foot was the old village bridge, and at this point the road branched off, leading, on the one hand, into the more open and level country, on the other, over what were called the Lower Fells, into Ellerdale, one of the largest and finest valleys of the district.

Besides these two bridges, the river, for the convenience of the inhabitants, was crossed here and there in the summer season by stepping-stones, which the naturally rocky bed of the stream seemed to have provided for the purpose. One of these rustic crossings was just opposite to Tod's-gill, where, in fact, the most picturesque scenery of the valley lay.

Tod's-gill, in modern English, the Fox's-glen, took its name from the wild ravine which formed its southern boundary, as Hiblethwaite was its boundary to the north, so that it lay in the immediate neighborhood of the Hall. It was, in truth, a portion of the Wast-Wayland property, although it had long been in possession of the Garrs, having been taken on a lease of three lives from the present Mr. Elworthy's grandfather, so that, he being the last life, it would at his death revert again to the general Elworthy estates. A wild and tumultuous little brook, which was never dry in the dryest of summers, came sliding and leaping down the Tod's-gill among huge masses of rock and through tangles of wild roses and brambles, and then, as it approached the bottom, bounded forward like a frolicsome child toward its mother, through a wild copse of birch and alder trees, and flung itself into the arms of the beck. Below this juncture of the lesser and larger stream, the beck, as if taking a character from its tributary, became much more picturesque, and was marked at every step by ever-varying features. Here it was churned up into fury by tumbling over huge piles of rock, which it had worn into fantastic shapes, and among which, even in the bed of the stream, grew trees of large size, which cast deep shadows over pools of great depth, which lay sleeping in sullen blackness, and to which more than one tragical story was attached.

This wild and romantic scenery was, however, confined to the upper and middle portions of the valley. About half a mile, lower down, it again became less striking: soft, green meadows bordered the beck, and the rocky bed of the water was not more abrupt and rugged than to furnish here and there those convenient stepping-stones of which I have spoken. Immediately at the commencement of this tamer scenery, stood the picturesque old valley-mill, which presented an object of rural as well as rustic beauty. It was built of gray stone, and looked as old as the valley itself, while its shrouding birch-trees, which gave it the name of Birks-mill, had especially at this season a look as of perpetual youth.

On the other side of the valley, and somewhat lower down than Tod's-gill, lay the old house of Lily-garth. Unlike all the other habitations in the Dale, excepting the mill itself, Lily-garth stood low, and on the level of the valley, and between the outstretching feet of two hills, so that it was completely unseen from a distance, nay, in fact, it was unseen until you were immediately upon it, when it burst upon you, surrounded with its old wood, among which were several foreign trees, as the Spanish chestnut and the plane-tree, and backed by the soft green of the ascending fell. This, as has been said, was the old house of the Elworthys. It was somewhat small as the residence of a large landed proprietor, but it must be borne in mind, that at the time of its first possessor, the Elworthy property was scarcely one-third of what it was at present, and their thrifty and more simple style of life, made it an ample, if not a luxurious abode. Small as it might be, as the residence of the present Mr. Elworthy, it was large as a farm-house, to which purpose it was now applied. It was a picturesque old place; the stone of which it was built, was dark with age, and weather-stained, and spotted all over with various colored lichens, which gave to it a rich and mellow tint. Its windows were small, with heavy stone mullions and window-heads; there was a large, projecting porch of heavy stone-work, with little glazed windows on either side, and to which an easy flight of stone steps, with low balustraded walls, ascended; the chimneys were tall and massive, built of dark red brick, with a considerable elaboration of masonry.

which gave a more important and substantial character to the whole place than it otherwise would have had. It was, in fact, a respectable, picturesque old country house, that bore evidence of substantial proprietorship at some former time. On two sides of of it lay what had formerly been a pleasure-garden, inclosed by a low stone parapeted wall, but which was now appropriated to other purposes. It was a grassy croft where, however, ornamental shrubs and trees, and upspringing flowers, which neglect could not destroy, testified of olden times. Here calves now took their first lessons in grazing, and motherless lambs were turned out in the spring; and here also the farmer's wife hung her linen to dry, In the direct front of the house, however, that portion of the old garden was kept up with considerable care; in one corner was a large yew arbor, with seats within, where the farmer on Sunday afternoons in summer, smoked his pipe and drank his glass with a friend; it was clipped carefully once a year, as was the thick, broad, foot-high box-edgings of the flower-borders, which same flower-borders, at the time Honour Mildmay and her mother first entered the garden, were very gay with gilly-flowers, tulips, large blue irises, peonies, and such like brilliant children of summer.

As there was much more room in this old house than the family of Christie Fothergill required, some of the better rooms were mostly occupied, during the summer and autumn seasons, by strangers, often from a distance, who were attracted hither by the quietness of the country or by the great rural beauty of this neighborhood. Sometimes artists from London came here, who transferred many of these lovely scenes to their canvas; now and then a country-loving poet, who was so fortunate as to have money enough in his pocket for such an indulgence, would come hither, and very frequently sportsmen. Hence it was that the libertine Mr. Cartwright had found easy entrance to Lily-garth, when he came, like a spirit of evil, to destroy.

Honour Mildmay was soon at home in the Dale. She and her mother made early acquaintance with the class to which their labors were to be devoted. Every body was greatly taken with them; for although, like Mrs. Hawes, they immediately perceived that they belonged to a rank in life greatly superior to their own, their mild and conciliating manners won their confidence and their respect. They soon ceased to feel either fear or constraint before them, and in every case no other impression was left than admiration, and pity that ladies, so noble and good, and with "the manners of real gentle-folk," should be brought down to teaching a country school of poor children; for whatever may be the vices of the lower class, there is, in the hearts of all of them, excepting the very degraded, a generous pity toward those who, from a higher station, have fallen into their own grade of suffering and hardship.

"You must be good bairns," said many a poor mother to her little daughters, somewhat later as to time, when speaking to them of the new school just about to be commenced, "and learn your best, and always be pretty behaved, for Miss Mildmay is a real gentlewoman, and knows what good manners are."

Mrs. Hawes was right also in another respect, for Christie o' Lily-garth, the good people at Birk's-mill, and some other of the dale's-people also, fancied that they saw a resemblance between Honour Midmay and the still lamented lady of the Hall, "the mistress," as they called her, and it was astonishing not only what favor this gave her in their eyes, but what a warm, familiar place in their hearts also.

"I am sure that we shall be happy here! I feel that here our lives will be good and useful, and therefore that we must be happy!" said Honour, repeating almost the very words she had used the very first night that she drove into the Dale. "I never felt before as I do now," said she, "it seems as if I were now come home; as if, someway, I had never been home before. This is real happiness, is it not, dearest mother? and it will not vanish from before us; it will not deceive nor disappoint us, because it is founded on duty!"

There was no resident clergyman in Wayland-dale, nor even a curate, as there used to be. The little church of Dale-town was merely a chapel of ease to the larger church of Ellerdale, and service here was performed only once in the day, alternately morning and afternoon. Mr. Langshaw, the present incumbent, who held two livings, one still more distant than Wayland-dale, lived at an excellent rectory-house in Ellerdale, and had, therefore, quite enough for himself and his curate to attend to, without devoting much time individually to his parishioners, especially his more distant ones. Besides this, though a really good man, he was very shy, and therefore not socially inclined, and the distance which he had to come for the performance of his duties left him no more time than he had inclination for intercourse with his people. He was married, but his wife unfortunately was an invalid, who had been confined some years to her room, and who consequently never left home.

Mr. Langshaw made a hurried call on his new parishioners, whom he soon perceived in church, after the first Sunday's service, invited them to his rectory, and lamented that his wife was unable to call on them ; but his gloves were on again for departure the moment he had said thus much, and that was all they saw of him. The next Sunday, Mr. Derwent, the young curate, performed afternoon service, and he seemed as hurried as his employer, for the moment it was over he mounted a rather lean horse, which stood ready for his use at the church-yard gate, and rode away.

Excepting Mr. Walker, the master of the boys' school, therefore, for the present, the Mildmays had no acquaintance but the simple peasant-people, the good farmer's family of Lily-garth, and the honest Quakers of Birks-mill ; but it was all sufficient for the time, and besides there was a novelty in it, and a wholesome simplicity which had no inconsiderable charm.

They drank tea one afternoon with Caleb and Elizabeth Fothergill in the neat drab-curtained mill-parlor, and had much talk about the customs and occupations of the dales-people. They had arrived just before the commencement of the hay-harvest. In these dales, however, it was an occasion of no great festivity; hay here was of less consequence than in most other parts of the country, for the land being mostly open-fell, which was appropriated to the wild ponies and the vast flocks of sheep, the wealth of the farmer consisted almost solely of these, and the small portion of meadow-land in the valley was not more than sufficed for the cattle which each family needed for their own use, or if so, young stock were reared and sold off. Around each homestead, which in every case, excepting Lily-garth and Birks-mill, stood at some distance up the fell, lay land which had long been brought into cultivation, and here corn and potatoes were grown for family use, and not unfrequently flax and hemp, which were dressed at home, and then spun by the winter's fire. Higher up still lay here and there a piece of land, called an "intake," inclosed from the brown moorland or green and stony fell-side, by a rude stone fence, the work of some industrious cultivator or daring encroacher, who had possessed himself of it in defiance of the common claim to the pasturage of the fells. As the top of the hill was approached, the land became in many parts spongy with bog; here were the "peat-pots," as they were called, which, like the fell-side, were common to all. Here, during the summer, as suited his convenience, the farmer cut his peats and reared then to dry, or, as the dales-people termed it, "*footed them*," or he purchased them from a poorer man than himself, who gained his living, in part, by this employment. Such being the nature of the dale farmer's and peasant's life, it will be seen that the hay-harvest could be but of secondary importance. Very different was it with the sheep-washings and sheep-shearings, as the greater part of the farmer's wealth consisted in his flocks; these, therefore, became rural festivals from one end of the Dale to the other. On these occasions there was not only community of mirth, but community of labor also, for the flocks were so large that the farmer was obliged to call in the aid of his friends and neighbors, he himself being ready to return the obligation in kind, perhaps the very next day. The men labored thus all day, in large social companies, in the sheep-washing pools of the beck, or upon the hill-side, being provided during their work with plenty of good cheer, and in the evening all assembled at the farm-house to which the flock belonged, to close the day with a bountiful supper and a merry dance, one or two itinerant fidlers always finding their way into the Dale at this season.

The two ladies had unfortunately arrived just too late to witness these pastoral occupations and merry-makings; but they heard a great deal about them, for to people whose lives were so uneventful as these dale peasants and farmers usually were, sheep-washings and sheep-shearings, and their attendant festivities, furnished abundant material for gossip. They were told of some rural love affairs which dated their commencement from these occasions; among these, that Thomas Broadbent, the young Quaker miller, had declared his love to the pretty Agnes o' Lily-garth, when they two sat so demurely in the parlor at Lily-garth, while the rest were all dancing in the big kitchen; every body supposing that they had merely withdrawn from the gay scene because the young man, being a Quaker, did not dance. The Mildmays, however, did not hear this at Birks-mill, but elsewhere, and people now wondered what the Quaker mother and the step-father would say, seeing that Agnes—though otherwise so unexceptionable—was not "of the society." They heard, also, that Mr. Elworthy was always invited to the great merry-makings, at which he was also occasionally present, but that he never staid long, as his coming among them was rather to show his good-will to them all, than for any pleasure he himself would be expected to derive.

One afternoon, when the hay-harvest was in progress, Honour and her mother were invited to drink tea at Lily-garth, and in order to make it less ceremonious to Mrs. Fothergill, who was not yet quite at her ease with the ladies, Mrs. Mildmay encouraged her to invite, also, Mrs. Peggy from the Hall. This was done, and the tea-drinking was anticipated with pleasure by all parties; but it must not remain untold what kettle-cakes and other good things were made for the occasion. They were invited for half-past four o'clock, and were received by Mrs. Fothergill and the pretty, blushing Agnes, all in their "Sunday-best;" Mrs. Fothergill having a constrained, subdued, Sunday feeling about her, which did not leave her at her ease until Mrs. Hawes making her appearance banished all ceremony and formality.

Mrs. Hawes came brim-full of news. She brought word that the master would be back from London either that day or the next, and that she had been busy all morning getting things ready for him. She brought other news, which seemed still more interesting to the Lily-garth people. She said that she had just reached the stepping-stones below Tod's-gill, when she saw a tall woman advancing up the road toward her. As soon as the woman saw her, she turned abruptly into the field which lay between the road and the beck, getting over a stone fence to do so. This circumstance, which showed a knowledge of the locality, taken in connection with her dress, which was not of dale fashion, attracted at once Mrs. Hawes's attention. Evidently she was no stranger to the place, yet she wished to avoid meeting any one.

"Who can it be?" related Mrs. Hawes of her own cogitations, looking after the green parasol, handsome scarlet shawl, and black silk gown, which moved rapidly forward through the uncut grass, in the direction of the alder copse by the water-side, through which, though very indirectly, she might reach the stepping-stones. "It must be Isabel Garr!" replied she to herself; "nobody but Isabel has such a gait; and yet I have not seen her for these many long years. Yes, it must be Isabel, the poor sinner, all bedizened as she is; and she's going to Tod's-gill! There's something in the wind! I know it was business connected with that wicked Richard Elworthy that took the master to London."

Christie and his son came in from the hay-field to tea; they were told the news of the apparition in the red shawl and black silk gown; they had seen nothing of her, but then the meadow in which they had been working did not lie by the road-side. Every one agreed in the opinion that it was Isabel Garr, and no other subject was talked of during tea.

When tea was over, Honour was to take her first lesson in

knitting, because as a teacher of dale children she insisted upon it that she ought to understand practically this universal employment of the dales. She could knit, it is true, as many a pretty, elaborate piece of knitting in their cottage at Dale-town could testify, but she could not knit in the authentic dale fashion; she could not jerk her needles and give to her body a quick see-sawing motion, as if keeping time to the operation, as the dales-folk did; and this peculiar, and somewhat ludicrous mode of knitting, she declared she would learn, as she meant to become a perfect dales-woman.

The two girls went into the large porch, where there were seats, that they might be free from interruption; and while Agnes was wavering about, and making her needles fly with the rapidity of her fingers, Honour was somewhat slowly and awkward imitating her novel movements. All was mechanical to the dale-maiden; she looked about her, and sang in a sweet, monotonous voice, one of the old, foolish knitting-songs of the district:

"My dog's gone a-barking,
Hunting up the sheep on the fell-side.
One, two, three,"

When, suddenly interrupting herself, she started up and exclaimed—

"Mother! yon's Mr. Elworthy! Th' squire's coming, mother!"

In a few moments Mr. Elworthy opened the garden-gate, walked up the gravel path, and stood on the steps of the porch.

"Miss Mildmay," said he, bowing to her, and then offering his hand, for he at once surmised that it could be no other than Honour. She blushed as she gave her hand, she knew not why, unless it was because having heard so much of him, she felt now almost ashamed of knowing so intimately, as it were, one who was an entire personal stranger to her. The next moment a mingled feeling of pleasure and anxiety passed, as quick as lightning, through her heart, but pleasure predominated.

At Mr. Elworthy's approach, good Mrs. Hawes rose and left the parlor where she had been sitting. He entered the room, and introduced himself to Mrs. Mildmay; the little tea-drinking party was dispersed. Mrs. Fothergill, said that both the parlor and house-place were dark, because they were so shaded by trees and lay from the west; she therefore told Christie to carry a table out into the cheerful and roomy porch. The move was a good one. Mrs. Mildmay and Mr. Elworthy were soon seated at it, and deeply engaged in conversation. Nelly and her daughters busied themselves in preparing in the kitchen, where Mrs. Hawes bore them company, all kinds of simple yet delicious eatables, which were destined very soon to be on the table, although a most bountiful tea was but just over. Christie and his boys were again in the field.

Honour, laying her knitting on her knee, rested her cheek on her hand, and listened to the conversation of her mother and their new friend, without feeling as if she herself could say one word. Every now and then Mr. Elworthy glanced at her; he was scrutinizing her, and the scrutiny must have produced pleasure, for his countenance beamed with kindness and satisfaction.

She had known no one as yet who bore any resemblance to him. He looked fully fifty, but his person was commanding, and his features handsome. There were deep lines on his countenance which indicated the sufferings he had passed through, but over all, like the rugged and furrowed earth which is covered with flowers, there was the expression of a calm happiness, which had its origin rather in a deep sentiment of the soul than in any casual incident of the moment. It was the light of a pure, noble, and chastened spirit radiating from within, and which no soul capable of a kindred feeling could see without feeling its attraction.

Their conversation was only on subjects connected with the school and its business. It was now to commence, immediately, and Honour again felt that a large reward would compensate her humble labors.

CHAPTER VII.

It *was* Isabel Garr who crossed the little meadow on her way to the Tod's-gill stepping-stones, and Mrs. Hawes was right also in believing that it was her wish to avoid recognition which sent her thus indirectly toward them. Her eyes at the time were red with weeping; for it was twenty years since the poor prodigal had left her native valley, and the sight of its familiar scenes wholly subdued her. She had suffered much in that long interval; suffered in a hundred ways. Worthless, fallen creature, though the world might reckon her, she was not without her redeeming qualities: very few are. Spite of many hardships and cruel wrongs, she had remained faithful to the man whom she had loved in her thoughtless youth, and for whom she had been guilty of more than one crime. He was a far greater sinner than she was; he had cast her off in his prosperity, and returned to her in his sickness and want; and she had nursed him, worked for him, clothed him and comforted him, only to be again deserted as soon as the smile of fortune again beamed on him. With all her weaknesses and all her sins, Isabel might have been saved—might have been raised like another Magdalene, had there been a Saviour at hand—but there was none; therefore she still lived on, sinful and suffering. But God, who permits such things, measures all with a higher, purer judgment than that of man who does them.

Of the smaller sums of money which Richard Elworthy became possessed of from the funds of poor Thomas Young, and with which he replenished his own wardrobe, a certain portion came also into the hands of Isabel, who bought herself new and gay apparel in which she might appear in the Parks like a lady —like Richard Elworthy's wife, as she called herself. How Richard came by the money she knew not—she never inquired, and such matters he did not communicate to her.

Richard's purse for some time was well filled; at length it was necessary for him to fly. He left her, as he said, on important business, and the next post brought her from him a bank bill for twenty pounds, contained in a letter bidding her farewell forever.

He was about, he said, to sail for America, and he recommended her to return to her relatives in the north, as henceforth she would receive no further support from him.

She had been deserted before. She cried passionately, as she always did in her sorrow, and hoped and believed that, when the tide of his good luck had ebbed, and he was stranded on the bleak shores of misfortune, he would come back to her once more.

In the mean time, while her spirits were very low, and some money yet remained in her purse, an indescribable longing came over her to return to her native dales and to live once more—or, as she said, to die, for she persuaded herself that her days were numbered—among the scenes and the simple people with whom her youth had been spent, and which remained to her imagination like the garden of Eden peopled by angels.

Isabel, did not, in the first place, go to Tod's-gill; there had been no intercourse between herself and her brother since her old aunt's death, when Dannel had threatened to dispute the little inheritance with her. She went to Swale-dale, to the house which had been left to her by her aunt, and where lived Thomas Garr, or "Cousin Thomas," as he was called. Their last intercourse with Cousin Thomas had not been of the most friendly kind, for he had refused to lend Richard Elworthy money; and, at the time, Isabel had vowed never to exchange another word with him. Some years, however, had passed since then; and now, once more, was she presenting herself, not as a suppliant, but in her good London clothes, and with a plausible story on her tongue.

Whatever might be her own secret fears with regard to Richard Elworthy, she never expressed them to any living soul: while she would have shared her last crust with him, she believed herself very jealous of his honor. She told Cousin Thomas, therefore, that one of Richard's noble friends had given him a government appointment, which had obliged him to go abroad, where he would remain for some time. That he had left her plenty of money, and would send her more, but that during his absence she had come into the north to see her relations, and especially Cousin Thomas, for whom she had a warm affection. "Although hard words had passed between them," she said, "she hoped that he would let by-gones be by-gones, and let her sleep in the little chamber in the roof, which he did not use, where she had slept when the old woman was alive; and that she would keep house for him, and try to make him comfortable till Richard came back."

Cousin Thomas was unmarried, and the miserly spirit of the old aunt and of many another Garr, had descended upon him. He was growing now into a proverb: "as close fisted as Thomas Garr," or as "miserable as Thomas Garr, who hoards up his nail-parings," were the every-day expressions which showed the estimation in which he was held.

At the door of this hard old man Isabel presented herself, looking in his eyes, like a very fine lady. It was mid-day when she came, and he was sitting in the sunshine on a stone bench outside his house, in a cotton night-cap, and with large steel-rimmed spectacles on, knitting a gray worsted stocking. Though he owned a considerable quantity of land, he was not a farmer; he let every inch for which he could get rent; he bought the small quantity of milk that he needed for himself, because that was cheaper than keeping a cow. He had neither horse nor pig, nothing alive about the house but a pale gray cat, which either provided wholly for herself, or lived on very short commons, for Cousin Thomas never fed her; a flock of sheep he kept, however, but they grazed on the Fellhead, and were kept because he had common right there, which if he had not thus used he would have had no advantage from.

Cousin Thomas could not be said to make Isabel welcome; he grumbled out, however, a sort of permission for her to "stay a bit." She accordingly settled herself down, taking possession of the little chamber in the roof, though it was half full of fleeces, and not being very particular, made herself tolerably comfortable, if she could only manage not to wear out her welcome. For this purpose, she immediately set about to make herself useful, kept the house-place clean swept, the fire a-light, and began in various ways to endeavor to make the old man more comfortable.

She kept herself as busy as she could; but there was very little to work with in the miser's house. Nevertheless, she wound his yarn, mended his two or three old shirts, washed his linen, brought an old rickety wheel out of a quantity of lumber, paid a shilling for mending it, and began to spin wool. She had forgotten none of her skill as a dales-woman, and any one but Cousin Thomas would have seen all this active assiduity with satisfaction; but he did not. For some time, however, he said nothing, and Isabel, who was haunted by many sad and dark thoughts, busied herself more and more that they might be expelled by occupation.

One day an unappeasable longing came over her soul to see Tod's-gill once more; she had been thinking of the green hilly crofts at its back, of the wild glen down which leapt the sparkling waters; of the beck below, and its gray stepping-stones; but most of those dark still pools, overshadowed with trees, where more than one miserable human being had found oblivion for their earthly sorrows.

"I wish I had drowned myself like poor Bessy Blane, twenty years ago, in yon water!" sighed Isabel, and at once she determined to see the place, and Tod's-gill, and her own folk.

"I think I shall set off," said she to Cousin Thomas, next morning, "to see them at Tod's-gill; ma'ppen Dannel will be friends with me now!"

"Ay," replied the old man, ungraciously, for he was angry from two causes; firstly, because the free use of things in his house had vexed him; and secondly, because she spoke of going to Tod's-gill. "Ay, thou's better go to Tod's-gill, and mac it up wi' Dannel: thou's mair claim upo' him than me! Dannel ma'ppen like tha Lunnon ways! Why-a m' fire's nivir been out sin' thou's been here! Thou's burnt mair peats in a week than I burn in a month; and thou's ta hands nivir out o' th' wash-tub, which is a waste o' soap! and thou must ha' th' old wheel mended, tho' it cost a shilling! and thou's used up a' my yarn! There's no keeping tha in things! Thou'rt wasteful and extravagant! Be off wi' tha, and welcome! Dannel's a weel-doing man, I reckon, and he can afford to keep tha, and thou'll ma'ppen mac thyself useful in's family!"

And without hearing a word in reply, he rose up hastily, thrust on his old hat, took up his knitting, and putting on his big spectacles, began to knit vehemently as he crossed the door-sill, and so walked up the fell to look after his sheep and his peats, which he had cut some days before, and left to dry on the ground.

Isabel was by no means displeased with all this; she received it rather as a sort of rude welcome to return; so raking out the fire completely, and leaving the old man's bed not only made but neatly turned down, she dressed herself in her best, and putting the house door-key under a big stone by the horse block, the usual place for depositing it, she set off with a yearning, anxious heart, toward her native valley. Without taking the round-about high road, she crossed the hills by tracks well known to her, and early in the afternoon, sat down on the Fell-head beyond Lily-garth, and saw Tod's-gill, with its green homestead fields; its wild uplands and picturesque woody glen on the opposite hill-side. At the sight of its beloved, familiar features, the past stood livingly before her, and the memory of her father's cruelty and her brother's injustice, awoke a passion of anger in her soul that at once overpowered all the misery which uncertainty, anxiety, and remorse had awakened. She felt no fatigue, no self-reproach; nothing but anger, which, for the time, gave her strength both of mind and body. She walked on rapidly down the Fell-side, taking a considerable circuit to avoid Lily-garth, and then came upon the high road of the valley. Here a violent re-action of feeling took place; she became depressed and timid; she feared lest she should be recognized; she said to herself that she was an outcast and a stranger; that she was like Cain with a brand on his forehead, and she wished that she were dead! The valley road appeared deserted, it was afternoon and the people at work in their fields; there was no danger of her being met. She sat down in the angle of a gate-way that led to a field of uncut grass, with her back to the road, and wept, after which she rose up and walked onward, and then it was that she saw a woman advancing toward her. She did not know who it was, but she avoided her, and taking her way through the uncut meadow, she hastened to the well-remembered alder copse, while Mrs. Hawes stood by the stone wall and looked after her.

Isabel crossed the beck by the stepping-stones, and then, not having courage to go directly to the house, she walked up the Wast-Wayland side of Tod's-gill, which, as she well knew, could be crossed higher up, and though this led her considerably too high on the Fell, that was of little consequence, as it gave her time, and would enable her to approach the house at the back, which she greatly preferred.

She was, as Mrs. Hawes described her that same afternoon at Lily-garth, somewhat gayly attired; at least her straw bonnet, green parasol, and scarlet shawl, would look gay to the old-fashioned dales-people. Very gay and very attractive, indeed, did they appear in the eyes of Betty, one of Dannel Garr's poor, simple daughters, one of the "daft lasses o' Tod's-gill," as they were called. Betty was "tenting" two calves as they grazed on the grassy border of a little corn-field which bordered the gill, and when all at once she beheld, through the thick-leaved trees and bushes that filled the wild hollow of the glen, what appeared to her a splendid apparition moving on the other side, she uttered a short, quick exclamation of idiotic wonder, she forgot the calves, which immediately turned into the green corn, while she hurried on with her quick jerking pace and dangling hands, to keep so novel an object in sight. Isabel was immediately aware of her, stopped, and calling to her across the glen, bade her go back to the calves, which were "trampling the green corn;" but though, as seemed quite natural to her in these familiar scenes, she addressed her in the broadest dale dialect, the poor, simple creature was only the more startled, and at once set off at her quickest speed, carrying home the strange news, that there was "some girt lady fra' Lunnon, peering for bird's nests, among th' bushes!"

"Fool!" said the mother angrily, "it's nobody but one of th' new ladies fra' th' school; they've naught to do but peer after bird's nests! Go back to th' calves, or they'll get into th' corn and burst themselves."

Poor Betty moved off, as if to return to the calves, but not having quite wit enough to know what was the actual danger of leaving them to help themselves, she only slunk round the corner of the wash-house, and leaning on the pig-sty wall, looked up the Fell in the direction of the gill, on the opposite side of which she still hoped to see the beautiful red shawl and green parasol. Isabel had heard in Swale-dale of Dannel's two daft lasses, and had said it was a judgment on him for his injustice to her. Now, however, when she saw the poor girl, who, though foolish, had a clear, healthy complexion, and not unpleasing face, a sentiment hitherto unacknowledged in her breast as regarded her brother's children, warmed her heart toward this one, though so poorly gifted by nature. She saw her as a creature kindred to herself; her heart yearned toward her, she felt that she could not only love her, but forgive her father for her sake. There was a great void in poor Isabel's heart which she would have given worlds to fill with one young life; she would have given worlds also to have stifled the voice of unappeasable remorse within her soul, but she could not; the voice cried aloud within her, and seemed to impel her onward. She crossed the little glen, and was soon seen walking down the Fell toward the homestead. At the first glimpse of her, poor Betty rushed in, regardless of her mother's displeasure, shouting that "the girt lady was a coming down to th' house."

Dannel and his eldest son were at Sedburgh market, but the wife and the rest of the children rushed to the back door to see the wonderful sight. She neared the house without being recognized, and then, as bashful country people do, Mrs. Garr and her children hurried into the house, shutting the door after them, to await there the stranger's approach.

Isabel walked in without ceremony, and without speaking

stood within the doorway of the kitchen. Mrs. Garr eyed her sternly; she had heard of her being at Cousin Thomas's in Swale-dale.

"What it's thou, is it? thou bedizzened street-walker!" exclaimed she, in a cold contemptuous voice; "and what may hae brought thee to Tod's-gill, prithee? We've enough of beggars and baggages without thee; so thou'd better hae waited to hae been sent for!"

With these words she turned herself round, and busied herself with her housework, leaving the children, both the wise and the foolish, staring at Isabel with open mouths.

As yet Isabel had not spoken; she came into the house with more affection in her heart toward her relations than she had felt for years; the kindly impulse was now checked, and for a moment she stood mute with passion.

Dannel entered by the front door; he was just come back from market. At the sound of his steps his wife addressed him from an inner room, whither he had gone to fetch oatmeal for the afternoon's porridge,

"Here's my lady come fra Swale-dale. I reckon 'at Cousin Thomas is tired of her; but I've told her we'll hae no such baggages under our roof. Let her go back to Lunnon—to Richard Elworthy; he took her and he may keep her!"

The wife was the ruling power at Tod's-gill, and this was said that her husband at once might know what reception it was her pleasure that he should give to his sister.

Nobody asked Isabel to sit; she still stood in the door-way between the back kitchen and the house-place, and Dannel said to her, without a smile or the slightest cordiality of voice,

"We heared 'at thou wert i' Swale-dale wi' Cousin Thomas; he's a weel-doing man, wi' neither wife nor bairns; he's made thee welcome no doubt."

Though neither the countenance nor the voice expressed kindness, there was nothing repulsive in the words themselves. Isabel therefore, went forward a few paces, and seated herself on the old, wooden-backed, well-remembered settle. Dannel sat opposite to her in the very chair which had been her father's; it seemed not to have been moved an inch, and as he sat there he bore a strong resemblance to his father, as Isabel remembered him when Dannel and she were both children.

People of her class are not sentimental, but their feelings are strong; she instantly felt angry that every thing which had been her father's, even to his old oaken chair, was gone to Dannel, but she checked the expression of her feelings and replied to his words.

Cousin Thomas, she said, had made her kindly welcome; that she might stay with him, no doubt, as long as she liked, but that she wanted to see them at the old place; she was very fond of the old place; that she did not want to trouble them or any body for any thing, for that she had plenty of her own, and a spirit above being beholden to any one; and that perhaps they had not heard of the great appointment which Mr. Richard Elworthy had abroad; that he had plenty of money now, and so had she!

"I's glad to hear it," said Dannel coldly, and then called to his wife, who still remained busied in the parlor, and asked whether his porridge was ready.

Isabel started up. "I see that ye are none of you glad to see me!" said she, with angry emotion; "but, Dannel, I am your own flesh and blood, and you've had all the property; not a stick, nor a stone, nor a single penny ever came to me!"

"Th' old man made his own will," replied Dannel. "It wer' no fault o' mine 'at he left thee nothing! Prythee, don't come here to be digging th' dead out o' their graves; let 'em lie still! let 'em lie still!" repeated he with some anger. "Th' old man made his own will, I tell thee, and thou'd ha' had thy share if thou'd ha' deserved it! So, prythee, be off, and don't be stirring among th' old mud, or thou'll ma'ppen get more than thou likes!"

Isabel fixed her large fierce eyes upon him, and yet said with apparent coolness, "Ay, thou hast got every penny, Dannel, but God has cursed it to thee: look at your daft bairns—"

At these words Dannel started up, and the wife rushed from the parlor, and the two silenced her by their loud recrimination. They dragged from the miserable past all the sin that it contained, whether the accusations were just or not, as regarded her—the "lad-bairn" that she had deserted, the wicked life that she had led in London with a man that was not her husband, and lastly, Dannel upbraided her with having come with a lie in her mouth about Richard Elworthy and his grand appointment. Was not he just come from Sedburgh market, where it was the talk of every body that he was off for forgery on his cousin, the squire, at Wast-Wayland, who was up in London about it? No, no! Isabel must not come with her lies to them; for Dannel had seen that very morning, a man out of Ellerdale, whose cousin was a trader between the Isle of Man and Whitehaven, and he had seen

Richard Elworthy at Douglas, where he was well-known to be among a set of gambling blacklegs! And as to Cousin Thomas, said the wife, they knew, and every body knew, that he wanted to be rid of her; no doubt he had turned her out of the house, and so she was come to them, but they wanted her not! She might go to her grand Richard Elworthy; she had better do so, for that London, or even the Isle of Man, was a fitter place for a painted Jezebel like her than either Tod's-gill or Cousin Thomas's! Dannel talked and the wife talked, upbraiding her and taunting her, and finally accusing her of coming among them like a painted peacock or a player-woman.

Isabel swore in passion that she was neither a painted peacock nor yet a player-woman, but the wife of Richard Elworthy; that it was a lie both about his forgery and his being in the Isle of Man; but that, as sure as she stood there a living woman, the day would come when Dannel and the rest of them would go down on their knees to him, and be ready to kiss his feet, for all they begrudged her the shelter of their roof or a morsel of bread now. He would have all the Wast-Wayland property one of these days, and then she would take care that they were turned out of Tod's-gill, stock and stone, although the old man had left it to Dannel, and cut her off without a penny! Yes, the time of her revenge would come, and she prayed to God that it might come quickly.

"Begone!" shouted Dannel, who, with somewhat of the coward's feeling, dreaded the threat, though he did not believe that Richard Elworthy would inherit the property—"begone with thee!"

Isabel slowly crossed the threshold. The brother banged the door behind her and even bolted it, while the children, who had stood by, gaping with wonder, crowded to the window to look after the painted peacock or player-woman whom they had mistaken for a "fine lady fra' Lunnon."

The return of Isabel Garr, or Mrs. Richard Elworthy, as she called herself, occasioned no inconsiderable excitement in her native valley. Every body wished they had seen her; some few of them had had "a glint of her green parasol," or of her red shawl, and they made the most of it.

The Tod's-gill people, however, said very little about it; they appeared to disbelieve the rumor that was getting afloat, that Richard Elworthy had committed forgery to a great amount on his cousin, and had been seen in the Isle of Man, whither he had fled. They were very silent and discreet, and no one knew at that time what was the reception they had given her, How or where Isabel passed the night I know not, certainly not in Dale-town, nor at any of the homesteads of the valley. Somewhat more than a week afterward she once more made her appearance at Cousin Thomas's, foot sore and weary, and with so haggard and dejected a look, as moved even that hard old man to something like pity and a welcome.

Perhaps, indeed, during her absence he had found himself less comfortable, and was therefore not displeased to see her return ; be that as it may, he thus accosted her—

" What ! thou'rt back again, art ta, like th' bad penny ! No-body'll have tha' ! Well, sit tha' down and get a bit and a sup ; I reckon tha' knows where to find 'em. Ay, ay, wench ! I thought thou'd soon be back again ; there's no getting shut of th' bad penny !"

With this welcome she was satisfied. For the present Cousin Thomas's was her home, and here we must leave her.

CHAPTER VIII.

The new girls'-school was commenced at Dale-town. Mr. Elworthy went down very frequently to watch its progress; he went in the afternoon mostly, generally walking, and not unfrequently he staid to tea with Honour and her mother.

He soon found in these two women the companionship for which he had so long sighed, and which he had wished to find in his sister-in-law and her daughters, but in vain. He took the utmost interest in this little household. They were new to a purely country life, and their enjoyment of it was intense; the milking of the cow, the feeding of the poultry, the gathering of fresh vegetables and flowers, had all a novelty which gave them a double charm.

Very cool, and pleasant, and inviting, at the close of a hot summer's day, seemed that little sitting-room, with its simple decorations of a few choice, well-bound books, which Honour and her mother had brought with them, and flowers out of their own garden, or wild-flowers which Honour had gathered, or which some flower-loving little scholar, whose heart was anxious to please, had brought to her. Yes, it seemed to him an attractive little room, with its walls of soft green, and its pure white muslin curtains; and when he saw the little tea-table set out, and Mrs. Mildmay seated at it, waiting for her daughter, to whom this was the pleasantest meal in the day, because her day's work was then done, he seldom could resist the temptation of entering and joining them.

On such occasions the conversation was rarely about the school, but on general topics, on which he found them well-informed. There was a freshness and originality of character, combined with life-experience and sound judgment, both in mother and daughter, which made them most agreeable companions. Nor was their knowledge of books inconsiderable; they were not only well-read in the best literature of their own country, but in that of France and Germany, which Honour read in their original languages. She was also a proficient in music, and sung and played with great taste. Mr. Elworthy heard her first at the Hall, when, at his request, she sang a few songs which he pointed out to her as favorites with himself. She knew not, at that time, the charm which those particular songs had for him: they were such as his beloved wife had sung to him in long past years. He had never heard them from that time to the present, for though his nieces sang, and sang well too, he had not asked the favor from them, and as it was believed by Mrs. Dutton and her daughters that he could not bear to hear his favorite songs, they purposely avoided them.

Why he, at this early period of their acquaintance, thus associated Honour with the memory of his wife, was not perhaps very clear to himself; perhaps, almost unconsciously, he perceived an affinity between the two, and thus tenderly associated them in his mind. One day he told Honour how precious the memory of these particular songs was to him, and from that time she secretly practiced them that she might be more perfect in them.

It was not long before they had a small, beautifully-toned piano in their little parlor; it was a present to them from Mr. Elworthy. He said that it would be a recreation to Honour, and that as he wished the poor children to learn singing, it might be useful to them also. From this time Honour had a little singing-class at home; and that and every thing else connected with the school went on admirably. It was astonishing what interest Mr. Elworthy took in this singing-class; he was often present when it met, and mostly remained through the evening at the cottage, that he might have the pleasure of hearing a song from Honour.

Nor was Honour apparently the sole attraction. Mrs. Mildmay and he became sincere friends; he opened his heart to her on many subjects; she was at once like a beloved sister, and it seemed wonderful to him how he could have lived so long without her society. He was thankful to heaven that these two excellent women, who were daily becoming more valuable, had at length found their way to him: their very nearness to him made his life brighter and better. At times a strange and melancholy feeling crossed his mind; the fear that they might leave him, and thus he would be thrown back again upon the old solitude—that solitude which had been so joyless to him, and which now seemed insupportable in recollection.

The success of the school was equal to Mr. Elworthy's hopes. Christie o' Lily-garth declared that "the lile lasses would grow into angels in time, if they went on improving as they had done in so few months." The poor parents were delighted, and there was nothing that they were not ready to do for the ladies of the school. One would send a present of fruit, another of flowers, a third of new-laid eggs, or a piece of honey-comb; one good wife began to knit for them, and another to spin. It seemed as if they had awakened a spirit of generous and grateful sympathy in every heart. Wherever Mr. Elworthy went among his tenants he heard nothing but praise of the ladies, and gratitude to him for having brought them there to do them and their children so much good. They praised them for being thorough gentlewomen, and yet without pride. They said among themselves that they were not like Mrs. Dutton, who, though she meant well, was always domineering and fault-finding, which nobody liked. No, they were as friendly and pleasant in their manners as the late Mrs. Elworthy herself, or as Lady Lonsdale, who had visited her, and had gone with her to their houses to see the sick, and had even danced at a sheep-shearing supper at Lily-garth, where the family lived then.

One day, when Mr. Elworthy came to the school, he told Mrs. Mildmay that his sister-in-law, Mrs. Dutton, was coming to the Hall on a visit to him. He had expected, he said, two of his nieces with her, but they had joined a party of their friends to Switzerland that summer, and would still remain some weeks at Paris; their mother, however, he said, very kindly preferred his society to the gayeties of Paris, and would stay with him till their return. He hoped, he said, that Mrs. Mildmay would find an agreeable acquaintance in his visitor; and then, after giving a slight and, upon the whole, favorable sketch, of the lady's character, he ended by saying that, though a worldly woman, she had many good qualities, had been a most devoted mother, and was the widow of an excellent man, to whom he had been greatly attached. She was, in short, what was called a clever, managing woman, and it would be extremely agreeable to him if Mrs. Mildmay would show her some little attention.

Mrs. Mildmay and Honour, therefore, walked up to the Hall as soon as they heard of Mrs. Dutton's arrival. Mrs. Mildmay was not strong, and a walk of three miles and back was fatiguing to her; nevertheless, she wished to show every respect to their kind friend's relative, and more especially to prove her readiness to oblige him on this first occasion of his asking a favor from her.

Mrs. Dutton had already heard of the new school, and of the ladies who managed it, but, as yet, she took little interest in it. These "schools on an improved principle," were, she said, one of good Mr. Elworthy's crotchets, and these ladies, of whom he spoke so highly, were only somewhat better than the ordinary class of village school-mistresses; good women they were, no doubt, but not people to go into raptures about. She should see them herself before long, and form her own judgment, and she should hear what Mr. Langshaw, the vicar, said about them, for she would rather go by his judgment than dear Mr. Elworthy's.

When, however, she saw Mrs. Mildmay and her daughter enter the drawing-room at the Hall, a few days after her arrival, her first impression was, that they were ladies of rank out of the neighborhood, who were come to pay their respects to her. She received them very graciously. The next moment she was undeceived; they were but the poor schoolmistress of Dale-town and her mother, and a revulsion of feeling took place. Still it was impossible to treat them with rudeness, and for Mr. Elworthy's sake her manners remained gracious, although a little condescending and patronizing. She professed great interest in the school, and promised in a few days to drive over and see how they were going on. It was a difficult, an almost impossible thing, for Mrs. Dutton to place the young schoolmistress and her mother on a scale of equality with herself; yet she knew not how to treat them as inferiors; it was a relief, therefore, a sort of medium step, to take an interest in their occupation, for in this way she at once became a superior. She said, in her most conciliating manner, that she might probably be able to suggest something in the management of the school, for that she had always taken great interest in the Church Sunday-school at Woodbury; that her eldest daughter, Mrs. Beauchamp, had been one of its best teachers before she was married, and that she herself, and her married daughters, all subscribed to the national-school of the place, and that, at her suggestion, many improvements had been introduced. She then very obligingly propounded some of her views regarding the instruction of the lower classes, and dropping her voice almost to a whisper, as if she were confiding to them a great secret, she said, that her views and dear Mr. Elworthy's, though he was one of the most excellent men that ever lived, were somewhat different; he often took poetical views of things, which was owing to his living so much out of society, and believing that every body was as good as himself. She was sure that Mrs. Mildmay and her daughter must have become already aware of his peculiar, and somewhat exalted opinions of the lower classes; but, however, she doubted not but that they, who had lived in the world, and knew what human nature was, and what the established common-sense opinions of society required, would be able to produce practical and useful results even from a very Utopian system. "However," added she, laughing, "I must come and look after you, and give you the benefit of my experience, and I have not a doubt but we shall get on excellently together."

"She is a worldly woman, indeed, and a cold-hearted one, into the bargain," said Honour to her mother, as they returned home. That was their first impression; they endeavored, nevertheless, to find good points in her; they said that she was Mr. Elworthy's relative, whom he wished them to like, she must, therefore, be estimable. They regretted that their first impression was unfavorable, and resolved, if possible, to improve it by future knowledge.

Mrs. Dutton made the freest use of her brother's carriage when ever she was at Wast-Wayland; in a day or two, therefore, she drove down to the school. She was very gracious and agreeable in her manners; admired the cottage and its garden, suggesting, nevertheless, various alterations; told various anecdotes of one or two curates who had formerly lived there, and inquired significantly whether Mr. Langshaw's present curate, who was, she heard, an excellent young man, was not an occasional visitor at the cottage. With the school she was apparently delighted, although here, again, she proposed various alterations as to the general system.

For some time, hardly a day passed without her visiting the school; she took it in her way as she drove to or returned from Mr. Langshaw's of Ellerdale, where she frequently went to visit his invalid wife; or she merely drove to the school-house, the carriage waiting for her while she paid her visit of inspection, and then taking her back to dinner. In a while, she began to assume an authority which was both painful and unpleasant to Honour. She heard the children read herself; examined them herself, especially in the Bible and Catechism, and even began to punish them; set them tasks, and came the following day to ascertain how they were learned.

There never had been so much punishment required, nor so many tears shed, in the school before. Honour was often almost in despair. She was ready to ask, like the irritated children themselves, "when will that horrid lady go?" But she went not.

What added still more to the unpleasantness of this time was, that Mr. Elworthy now very rarely made his appearance. Mrs. Dutton, to hear her talk, appeared to be as much taken with the young schoolmistress and her mother, as her brother-in-law had ever been. She told him she was delighted with the choice he had made; that she thought them very estimable women. She said that she herself was fond of teaching, or rather superintending instruction, for which she considered herself admirably qualified, and that she could spend half her time at the school. He must permit her, therefore, to come frequently; for that her little suggestions, she found, were very useful, and that, when Ellinor was married, next spring she and Natalie would come, if he would invite them, for a long visit; she would not object to spending the whole of next summer here, and regularly devoting herself to the school; Natalie could go down every other day, and she herself once a week or even more frequently, and by that time, she did not doubt, but that the school would be quite a model school, and might be made an object of attraction even to the goverment Board of Education, which she understood was about to be formed.

Mr. Elworthy smiled, and said that her ambition for his school went even beyond his own, but that he had no doubt that she and Miss Mildmay would make something out of it between them.

Mrs. Dutton let slip no opportunity in which she could praise Honour and her mother. She said that she found them sensible, clever, well-educated women, a little above their station, perhaps, but still unassuming and conscientious.

Mr. Elworthy quite agreed with her; on another subject, however, he was not acquiescent, but he said not a word. Mrs. Dutton asked him if he did not think Honour exactly suited for a clergyman's wife. Mr. Langshaw, she said, seemed to think most highly of her, but it was not, of course, of him that she was thinking, although she did not think poor Mrs. Langshaw was very long for this life. It was Mr. Derwent, the curate, that she had in her mind, and she was sure that Mr. Derwent was in love with Honour; he could not help looking at her even during his sermon, and she had found him twice at the school catechising the children; and only the last evening he was playing on his flute in the garden as she drove back from Ellerdale, and no doubt he would stay to tea with them. And, of course, it would be a very good match for her, for Mr. Derwent had expectations of a comfortable living, which was in the gift of his uncle, after the death of the present incumbent, who was an old man. Did not Mr. Elworthy think she would make a good clergyman's wife?

"No doubt but she would," replied he, somewhat curtly.

And had not Mr. Elworthy remarked Mr. Derwent's attentions to her? Had not he seen him walk home with her and her mother after service only the last Sunday? No? Well, perhaps there was no wonder in it; gentlemen were not always thinking of love and love-making as women were, and as to herself, she had had only too much experience in such things with her four daughters. She assured Mr. Elworthy, with a merry laugh, that she was quite an oracle in the affairs of the heart, and had never once been wrong, and by this same oracular skill she could assure him that Mr. Derwent was in love with Honour Mildmay.

"Indeed," replied Mr. Elworthy, with but little expression of interest in his voice; "and does she entertain any preference for him?"

"Of that I can not speak as certainly," said she, "not having seen them together; but she would be a fool if she did not. He is an excellent young man, very good-looking and agreeable, with good expectations. Of course, she will be only too glad to have him."

Mrs. Dutton thus oracularly delivered her opinion, and her brother-in-law pondered on her words.

It was now the middle of October, during a remarkably fine and prolonged autumn, and Mrs. Dutton, as usual, took her daily drive. One splendid afternoon she passed the little school-house, where Honour was busy with her scholars. Mrs. Mildmay sat at the parlor window at her sewing, with somewhat of the look of an invalid. A drive would do her good, thought Mrs. Dutton kindly, to herself, and instantly ordered the carriage to stop. Her manners were so sympathizing, and her words so friendly, that Mrs. Mildmay did not hesitate for a moment. A drive would certainly do her good; she had so frequently wished to see something of this beautiful country beyond the limits of the Dale, that she would most gladly avail herself of her friend's invitation, and perhaps she might thus be able to make a call on Mrs. Langshaw, to whom she wished to pay this compliment.

Honour nodded gayly from the window of the school-house, as the carriage returned past it with her mother and Mrs. Dutton; they were now taking the road out of the Dale, over the Lower Fell, in the direction of that beautiful Ellerdale, of which so much had been said, but which was to them as yet an undiscovered land.

Mrs. Dutton was extremely kind and affable, and was delighted to make a call at the Rectory, and inquire after the invalid, Mrs. Langshaw. "And suppose," added she, significantly, "we bring back Mr. Derwent; he has always some sick person or other to visit in Wayland-dale; he is an excellent young man, and takes great interest in the school." Mrs. Mildmay, who was very unsuspicious, admitted most cordially, that Mr. Derwent was an admirable young man, and possessed of great musical talent, of which he occasionally gave them the benefit; indeed, that they found him a very agreeable neighbor.

The call was made at the Rectory. Poor Mrs. Langshaw was visited in her bedroom, and the young curate made very happy by a seat in the carriage; it happening rather singularly, he said, that he was just about to set out for Dale-town, where he had a sick family to visit, and where he was intending also to carry some books to Miss Mildmay, for which she had expressed a wish. The evening was beautifully warm and bright, and the drive greatly enjoyed by every one. As they approached Wayland-dale on their return, Mrs. Mildmay invited Mrs. Dutton and the curate to take tea at the cottage, where they would find Honour awaiting them. Every body kept early hours in the Dale—even Mrs. Dutton conformed to these simple habits; therefore, as no dinner interfered with the invitation, it was cheerfully accepted, and the carriage drove to the cottage-gate, where all alighted.

Mrs. Dutton was very gay in spirits; the curate gave Mrs. Mildmay his arm at her bidding, and the three advanced up the steep garden path to the house. It was getting dusk, but the evening was so warm that the parlor window was open, and Honour's clear, delicious voice was heard singing the German words of Beethoven's "Adelaide."

The little party outside advanced in silence, listening with delight to the rich exquisite voice which warbled forth one of the most beautiful songs that ever was composed, as if her whole soul spoke in every tone.

"What a lovely thing that is!" said Mrs. Dutton, softly; "poor Mrs. Elworthy used to sing it; but she must not let *him* hear it; he can not bear to hear any of her songs sung, not even by my girls. I must warn her of this."

The singing ceased as soon as their steps were heard on the gravel-walk, and the next moment Honour was at the door to receive them. Mrs. Mildmay said that she had brought company to tea; Honour was delighted, and ushered them into the little parlor where the tea-table stood ready. Mrs. Dutton was full of her warning about the song, which she was impatient to give, but on entering the room, what was her surprise and chagrin to behold Mr. Elworthy himself, who, with a countenance of unusual animation received them all gayly, and declared it made him happy to be thus unexpectedly one in so pleasant a party!

Candles were lighted, and all looked happy, excepting poor Mrs. Dutton, over whom had fallen a sudden cloud. Honour Mildmay had been singing one of those very songs to Mr. Elworthy, which she knew were sanctified to him by a sainted memory, and which neither he nor herself had allowed even her own daughters to sing in his presence. What was the meaning of it? Was Honour Mildmay alone privileged to enter, as it were, the very recesses of his soul by the witchery of an exquisite voice? Ah! it was a dangerous thing, and must be prevented. But, perhaps, after all, it was a mere accident, and she knew not what she was about; she must be warned, however, and prevented from doing mischief, and in the mean time here was Mr. Derwent, that excellent young man, ready to fall in love with her; he must be encouraged, and her heart must be interested in him. There was a great deal for Mrs. Dutton to do, and she now thought it fortunate that her daughters' stay in Paris was yet delayed a few weeks, for in the present state of affairs she could not leave Wayland-dale.

Her inclination to remain to tea suddenly left her, and in the hope of taking Mr. Elworthy back, she spoke of it getting late, and of the trouble there would be in the carriage returning for them; but every one conspired against her. Honour said she must stay and hear Mr. Derwent's flute by moonlight; and that they had just churned, that they had baked that very afternoon, and had some of Mrs. Hawes's excellent marmalade for tea; and, besides, Mr. Elworthy had already promised. He told her he had come down on purpose to take tea with them, and he must not go back, for it was now so long since he had drunk tea with them. Mrs. Mildmay joined her entreaties: she was sure, she said, that Mrs. Dutton must want some refreshment, for that their beautiful drive had given her, herself, quite an appetite. Mr. Elworthy settled all in a summary manner. He said it was impossible now for Mrs. Dutton to do other than stay, because he had already sent the carriage back, with orders for it to return for them at nine o'clock.

She submitted with a somewhat perplexed and unsatisfied feeling, and all drew round the tea-table. Mr. Elworthy was unusually cheerful, so were Honour and her mother. Mrs. Mildmay had much to tell of her drive. The country, she said, looked now so beautiful in its autumn dress. They had driven all the way down Ellerdale, and seen the great waterfall, before they called at the Rectory; and what a beautiful place the Rectory was! looking now quite splendid, with its masses of dark green ivy and rich scarlet Virginian creeper, which, when lit up, as they saw it, by the golden setting sun, had a most extraordinary effect. As to the views from some of the heights, before they descended into Ellerdale, she knew not how to describe them, with all the rich coloring of the autumnal woods, for the woods in Ellerdale were really remarkable. She hoped that Honour might see them before the leaves had fallen. There were bits, she said, which reminded her of certain pictures of Turner's, which they had seen at a friend's house near London, and which she recalled to her daughter's mind. She said that perhaps some half holiday soon, Mrs. Dutton would have the goodness to take Honour the same drive.

Mr. Elworthy said that Mrs. Mildmay was right with regard to the fine woods and scenery of Ellerdale, as seen from what are called the Lower Fells, and which was not by any means a long walk from Dale-town, not certainly above three miles; that Miss Mildmay might walk as far, and he should himself be very happy to attend her; or, on second thoughts, added he, I had better drive you all there myself; there's a little estate in the Dale which I have some thoughts of purchasing; we will all go together some afternoon next week; Wednesday or Saturday it must be, on account of the school."

Mrs. and Miss Mildmay were delighted, Mrs. Dutton remarked that it must indeed, be considered as a great honor, for she never knew her brother-in-law make such an offer before, not even when her daughters were there. No, he returned, with entire sincerity, it was not often that he did so; he very seldom used a carriage himself, as he preferred riding, but this was merely the exception to the rule.

Mr. Derwent and Mr. Elworthy now began to lay out a route for this memorable drive which was to take place on the following Wednesday afternoon, Mr. Derwent being invited to make one of the party. They were to set out at three o'clock from Mrs. Mildmay's; to cross the Lower Fells, where, at the old guide-post, they were to be joined by Mr. Derwent. They were to drive along the moor-head by the waters of Swaithe, and if the road was passable for a carriage, which Mr. Derwent undertook to ascertain, they were to come up the Combeback, which was a remarkably wild, picturesque hill which lay at the further end of Ellerdale, and in that manner enter the valley, which would be unquestionably the finest route. By the time they reached this point it would doubtless be five o'clock. Mr. Derwent therefore begged that the party would honor him by taking tea at his cottage; he would order all to be in readiness, so that no time should be lost; the horses would be tired and require rest after the long pull up the Combeback, and it would make him unspeakably happy to have such guests; besides, from his parlor window the sunset was seen to advantage through the opening of two hills, just catching on the northern rim of Lenn's-water, and lighting up the great woods of Eddiscombe, which were the very woods of which Mrs. Mildmay had spoken; and, nothing could be better than this arrangement, for, while the ladies were resting, he would walk over with Mr. Elworthy to Oakenshaw, which was the little estate he wanted to look at, and which was only a short half mile's distance.

Mr. Elworthy thought the arrangement good; but he demurred as to stopping for tea any where. "It would make them too late," he said; "they should have it quite dusk before they drove back, and he wanted Miss Mildmay to see the situation of Oakenshaw; he had always thought it the most picturesque place in the whole country; he should like her to see it when the sunset lit up the windows of that old house, as he had often seen it himself; and the oak-wood at the back of it, from which it took its name, looked so extremely well just now. No, there must be some different arrangement; could not they drive up the valley as far as Oakenshaw? It would make no difference to the horses, and then return to Mr. Derwent's to tea; and as to the view from his window it would be sufficiently light for them to see that, because the opposite opening in the hills left him the advantage of so much longer twilight than most other places in the valley."

Mr. Derwent was more than satisfied, for he would thus be able to keep the party much longer with him. Honour and her mother were charmed with the prospect of so unexpected a pleasure. Honour played and sang, and Mr. Derwent accompanied her on his flute, on which he performed extremely well. The music was fine and well selected, but it had no connection whatever with the deceased Mrs. Elworthy.

Mrs. Mildmay devoted herself to Mrs. Dutton, who felt much fatigued and in want of rest. It seemed very long to her till nine o'clock, and spite of all the cushions which were piled around her, and the easy footstool which supported her feet, she found the sofa very uncomfortable, and she said she should go to bed as soon as she reached her brother's.

She had cause for anxiety, if her fears were just. It appeared to her as if scales had just then fallen from her eyes, and that she now saw, as plainly as day-light, that Honour Mildmay, with her school-teaching, and her simplicity, and her singing, was a most dangerous rival; that perhaps she had already laid a deep scheme to entrap the wealthy possessor of Wast-Wayland, and that perhaps he, with his enthusiasm about schools, and his poetical notions about female refinement, might be simple enough to be caught. She felt sick with apprehension and anger. She kept her eye fixed upon them, behind the hand-screen which she held between her eyes and the candle to protect them, as she said, from the light; she tried to discover if any secret intelligence passed between them, either of look or tone, but she saw none.

The full moon shone in at the little window, and Mr. Derwent, willing to please, played on his flute in the garden under the birch-tree; the window was opened, and they leaned out to listen to it. Something was said of walking in the garden by moonlight—it was Mr. Elworthy who proposed it—but Mrs. Dutton strenuously objected; "the autumnal dew," she said, was dangerous, and she would not allow Honour, who was not strong, to run any risks." The window, therefore, was closed, and Mr. Derwent, who found no pleasure in playing without an audience, soon came in; and as the conversation after this happened to turn upon the autumn of the poets, Mr. Elworthy asked Honour to read certain passages from Thompson's "Autumn," which he indicated, and then listened, with his hand shading his face, so that his countenance was concealed from Mrs. Dutton's scrutiny; not so Mr. Derwent, who listened with all the rapt devotion of a lover.—As far as he was concerned, Mrs. Dutton was satisfied; every unmistakable sign of love, on the knowledge of which she prided herself, was there; his feelings were as easy to read as an open book; her brother's were less intelligible. The carriage came before the reading was terminated, and Mr. Elworthy interrupted Honour in the middle of a paragraph; he evidently did not care much about her reading, at least so Mrs. Dutton thought, and from this small circumstance she derived great consolation

Beautiful as the preceding day had been, and brilliant and calm as the moonlight evening, yet the weather suddenly changed in the night, and the next morning was wet and cheerless. Again Mrs. Dutton had satisfaction; for if weather like this continued, even for a short time, there would be an end of Mr. Elworthy taking the party to Ellerdale, and showing Honour the picturesque situation of Oakenshaw.

A week of terrible weather succeeded; the autumn had been so singularly fine and dry that every one prognosticated a continuance of wet and storm, of which there seemed every appearance. Seven or eight days entirely destroyed every trace of that Turner-like beauty of which Mrs. Mildmay had spoken. No one apparently felt the disappointment so much as Honour and Mr. Derwent although from very different causes.

Mrs. Dutton was very anxious and uneasy; she never lost the unpleasant consciousness of Honour Mildmay's dangerous proximity to Mr. Elworthy, yet to that gentleman she now never mentioned her name. Day after day of wet weather went on, and Mrs. Dutton, who kept a strict watch on all her brother-in-law's movements, had the satisfaction of knowing that he had not once been down to the cottage. How gladly would she have believed that she had alarmed herself by a phantom! Never, at any time, had she so studiously endeavored to make herself agreeable to him as now, and he seemed to second every effort of her good-will. She sat with him in the library, where a good fire burned daily, at her netting, for she was netting a set of curtains for Ellinor, and he read to her. Nothing could be more cheerful, more self-possessed and heart-whole, than he appeared, and Mrs. Dutton, who prided herself on her skill in love-affairs, said to herself, twenty times in the day, that her anxiety had conjured up a causeless terror; nevertheless, she was determined not to leave the Dale until she had seen matters brought to a favorable issue between Honour Mildmay and Mr. Derwent. If she could only once get this dangerous young woman safely out of the way, she resolved, immediately after Ellinor's marriage, to remove into Waylanddale, even if she had to live in Dale-town, that she might be on the spot, and superintend the management of the school herself, and have the nominating of the new teacher.

CHAPTER IX.

During the continuance of the bad weather, the Cartwrights' party, together with the Miss Duttons, returned from Paris, and unwilling as Mrs. Dutton was to leave Wast-Wayland in the present unsatisfactory state of affairs she found that her presence at home was desirable, and began to prepare for her departure.

One day, therefore, when the rain had somewhat subsided, she drove down to the cottage, to bid Honour and her mother good-by. She looked in at the school, but her interest in Bible questions, and wholesome punishment, had greatly abated by this time ; and after a few commonplace remarks to Honour, who promised to join her as soon as school was over, she hastened to the cottage to Mrs. Mildmay. That good lady, who had not seen her since their pleasant drive into Ellerdale, received her with the utmost kindness. Mrs. Dutton, at her request, took off her cloak, and drawing her chair toward the fire, sat down, with all the cordial familiarity of a true old friend. As she had an important point to carry, there was no longer either hauteur or condescension in her manners : she was perfectly charming. Mrs. Mildmay compared her, in her own mind, with "dear Mrs. Woodley," who had been so kind a neighbor to them at North-bridge.

Mrs. Dutton inquired after Mr. Derwent, for of course they had seen him, spite of the bad weather. Yes, he had been there twice, if not thrice, Mrs. Mildmay said : he was a very good neighbor ; he was reading German with Honour, and that caused him often to come, for Honour having been in Germany two years, had a much more living knowledge of the language than he, and she was, of course, glad to aid him in any way, for he was an excellent young man.

Mrs. Dutton then spoke of his attachment to Honour, of which, she said, both herself and her brother were aware. Mrs. Mildmay replied, that as Mrs. Dutton had mentioned it, she would confess that this had been a cause of great anxiety to herself and her daughter. They both feared that Mr. Derwent had such views, but his manners were so guarded and so respectful, that it was hardly right for them to speak of it; she said that Honour was very conscientious on such subjects; she had not the vanity or the ambition of some girls, who like to make every man a lover; and as to Mr. Derwent, Honour hoped he understood, though not a word had been said on the subject, that she wished him to entertain for her no warmer feeling than that of friendship.

Mrs. Dutton was amazed, she felt vexed, but she concealed the feeling. Was it possible, she said, that Honour did not respond to Mr. Derwent's affection? To her it had appeared as plain as daylight, that they understood each other perfectly; every body must have thought so; she did not doubt but that Mr. Elworthy believed it, and was quite pleased that it should be so. Did not Mrs. Mildmay remember how anxious he was to include Mr. Derwent as one of the party to Ellerdale, and had even made a point of their going back to tea at his cottage? To be sure he did! and he and she had had conversation on the subject; he was quite delighted with the idea, and thought that Miss Mildmay would make an excellent clergyman's wife.

"She would unquestionably make a good wife for a clergyman or any other man whom she might marry," replied Mrs. Mildmay; "but she would never marry unless her affections entirely responded to his. She has very high and pure views with regard to matrimony, as every young woman ought to have, and besides, she does not wish to marry at present."

"You must allow me," said Mrs. Dutton, with warmth, and yet with a new hope in her heart, "to speak freely to you—to use a friend's privilege, although I am not an old one. Permit me then to ask, are Miss Mildmay's affections pre-engaged? because, you know, that quite alters the case; and so handsome and accomplished a young lady must have had many suitors."

"Her affections are not pre-engaged," replied Mrs. Mildmay, with perfect candor "both hand and heart are free."

"Then do you really mean to say, my dear lady," said Mrs. Dutton, "that your daughter would be so regardless of her own interests as to refuse Mr. Derwent if he proposed to her? Are you aware that he is not only a very excellent young man, but of good family, and with good expectations? Surely you do not mean what you say? I have great interest in Miss Mildmay; I sincerely wish her well. She is quite too good for this situation, which is not a position for a gentlewoman; and nothing would gratify me more than to know that she was likely to become the wife of so worthy and respectable a young man as Mr. Derwent. I am sure these are my brother's sentiments also."

"I mean what I say," replied Mrs. Mildmay; "Honour and I have weighed this subject deeply. If she could have loved Mr. Derwent, I should have been well pleased, for I believe he deserves all you have said in his praise. Both my daughter and myself think highly of him, and we have seen a good deal of him since we came here."

"I should have thought," said Mrs. Dutton quickly, "that Miss Mildmay was extremely well-disposed toward him. I consider myself a pretty good judge on these matters, for I have four daughters of my own, and love-affairs and marrying have kept me employed for the last several years, and I never saw any young lady appear better pleased with a gentleman's attentions than, it appeared to me, Miss Mildmay was with those of Mr. Derwent. You may depend upon it he is not disposed to despair," said she, smiling; "I know I should not, if I were in his place. Why, she was delighted with the thoughts of the little excursion, and the drinking tea at his cottage! Of course she was; and she'll come around in time. Oh, yes! that I know is the way with some young ladies: they take a deal of wooing. But here she comes: she shall answer for herself."

And with great gayety and kindness of manner Mrs. Dutton began to rally Honour about the prudery which her mother had avowed on her part; declaring that nothing would persuade her that she could be foolish enough to reject so agreeable and excellent a young man as Mr. Derwent, and one who had, at the same time, such good expectations. No, indeed, she would not believe it; and laughing, she declared that she would not leave the cottage until she had disposed her favorably toward her young clerical friend.

Honour laughed at first, and then grew serious. She reiterated all that her mother had said, dwelling very strongly on the fact that Mr. Derwent must himself have long felt that he had not any warmer response to expect from her feelings than friendship. Had it not been so, she said, he would long since have declared himself; on the contrary, not a word, amounting to a declaration of love, had been spoken, and yet their intimacy remained, and would remain, she trusted; she hoped that they would continue to be friends for years. There were, she said, many points, both as regarded character and intellectual pursuits, in which they could be useful to each other; he was as much aware of this as she was, and it was evident that he considered this merely friendly intercourse to be worth making a sacrifice for on his part; he had already made it, she believed, and could now regard her with equanimity merely as a friend or sister. Those were the terms on which they now were—terms which were in every way conducive to their mutual happiness.

Mrs. Dutton laughed. She said that she was satisfied, for that all would come right in time. Friendship between men and women always ripened into something much warmer; but of course it was an excellent basis to found love upon. Oh yes! mutual esteem, mutual confidence, mutual love—that was the way the passion grew!

"I understand it perfectly," she said; "my second daughter, Emma, talked of friendship for Mr. Cartwright: she would not hear of love at first; I was quite satisfied with it and so was he; and in twelve months she was his wife. Yes, my dear young lady, I know perfectly well how it will be, and I promise you, that after my youngest daughter is married, next spring, I will come here to your wedding, and my unmarried daughter, Natalie, shall be your bridemaid.

It was no use disputing the matter with Mrs. Dutton. Honour saw that; she therefore merely smiled, shook her head, and said that the day when she should marry Mr. Derwent was much further off than next spring.

It was now getting dusk, Mrs. Dutton therefore put on her cloak, bade her dear friends an affectionate good-by, and drove away very much dissatisfied in her own mind.

The road which led to the cottage joined the high road from Ellerdale at a few hundred yards distance, and at this very point who should be met but Mr. Derwent, with a quantity of books under his arm, evidently on his way to the cottage. Mrs. Dutton at sight of him, ordered the carriage to stop, and most kindly invited him to take a seat by her. She was about to leave the country, she said, and should be glad thus to bid him good-by. Perhaps, indeed, he would go on with her to Wast Hall, and spend the evening with herself and her brother. Mr. Derwent declined the latter invitation, but cheerfully took the seat by her side, saying he would drive on with her a mile or two, as the walk was nothing to him.

"I am glad to have met with you," said Mrs. Dutton; "I am just come from the Mildmays, and have something particular to say to you."

Mr. Derwent, who was a very sensitive and modest young man, colored to the eyes, but as it was dusk, Mrs. Dutton did not see it, and went on in a tone which was meant to be jocular. "Perhaps you do not know, my dear sir, that I am a very knowing person with regard to affairs of the heart, and that I can tell at a glance who and who have likings for each other?"

Poor Mr. Derwent felt breathless, and was at a loss for an answer, but none was needed, and Mrs. Dutton continued, "Now, I tell you candidly, that you have very good friends at the cottage, whither you were bound when I met you, and where you will go when you part from me. Ah, you lovers! you are more easy to see through than you think. But, to be serious, they are excellent women, real gentlewomen, and Miss Mildmay is not only good-looking but very accomplished. Where in the world do they come from?"

"From a little town called Northbridge, in Kent," replied Mr. Derwent—"they were in very good circumstances until lately, when they lost their property by a great commercial bankruptcy."

"Northbridge, in Kent!" repeated Mrs. Dutton, recollecting instantly that this was the native town of Frederick Horrocks, and that from him she could learn all particulars regarding them. "Indeed! Northbridge!—I know a gentleman from that place. Yes, they are excellent women; I like them much! And what I wanted to say to you, my dear Mr. Derwent," said she, speaking very kindly, "has, of course, reference to them, or rather to Miss Mildmay. It is rather a delicate subject, but you must not feel it as an impertinence on my part; you must receive what I am about to say as a proof of the friendly interest I take in you, and which my brother takes also, I am sure."

He took her hand for a moment, and expressed his grateful sense of the kindness of both.

"I am going to speak quite candidly to you," said she, "as I would speak to a son of my own, Of course, then, I am aware of your attachment to Miss Mildmay."

He said hurriedly that he believed it to have been a secret within his own breast.

"Oh! you can't deceive a person as well-read in these matters as I am," said Mrs. Dutton, again smiling; "I saw it immediately, almost the first time I saw you in her company, and I mentioned it to my brother. He was quite pleased with it, I assure you; he is a man of but few words, but he said he knew no one who would make a better clergyman's wife than she."

"Did he indeed?" said Mr. Derwent quickly; "I am glad to hear that. Do you know, my dear madam, I have had a suspicion that he liked her himself; she is so beautiful, so pure, so noble. She is so deserving to be the wife even of Mr. Elworthy! You indeed relieve me."

"Good heavens!" exclaimed Mrs. Dutton, feeling as if a knife had been thrust into her heart, "what could put such an idea into your head? My brother marry!—not even an angel from heaven! He will never marry; he will carry his love to his first wife inviolate with him to the grave! I am amazed at the idea,! No, *he* will never marry; never, never!"

"So I have heard some people say," returned Mr. Derwent; "others think he may; but of course you know best."

"Of course I do!" said she; "I know perfectly well that he will never marry again. I know how all his affairs are settled, how his will stands. Besides, poor man, he has that dreadful heart-complaint which may carry him off any day; he lives as in the hourly presence of death. But, of course, these things are not to be talked of. Only let me dispossess your mind of any such notion: and I hope to heaven that Miss Mildmay has no such absurd, such wicked ideas, in her head!"

"Miss Mildmay!" repeated he, "God forbid that I should say any thing of the kind! But knowing her excellence as I do, her nobility of character, her many and rare accomplishments, to say nothing of her beauty, it was but natural that I might fear the influence of all these on a person like Mr. Elworthy, who, in so many points, bears so strong a resemblance to her—more especially as I had not the happiness to believe that she was likely to respond to my affections."

"Nonsense!" said Mrs. Dutton, feeling exceedingly angry and alarmed; "for heaven's sake do not talk such nonsense! Miss Mildmay is very handsome and very clever, no doubt, but she is not going to be Mrs. Elworthy; and as to her not responding to your affections, pray, my dear sir, have you ever given her an opportunity of so doing? You must not think my interference impertinent, but I have been having some talk with both mother and daughter about it. I know exactly how the affair stands."

Mr. Derwent, in the secret of his own heart, and according to his reading of Honour's character, thought it *was* impertinent, but he did not say so; and Mrs. Dutton, assuming again a jocular manner, said; "I have been speaking a good word for you, as the country people say, for I thought you were too modest, or rather, perhaps, to humble, to speak for yourself, and I can tell you that you have no reason to despair."

"This is a serious affair with me," said Mr. Derwent; "I almost wish that nothing had been done in it by a third party, but, nevertheless, your intentions were kind; the ice is now broken; it must now be decided whether I am to be loved as I desire, or not! To me it is a very serious thing; it may altogether unsettle my peace of mind—that peace of mind which it has cost me so much already: an explanation must now come. I have had reason to believe, although not a word has passed on the subject, that she could not entertain any tender sentiment toward me; painful as that idea was I have tried to reconcile myself to it. I believed I had succeeded, and our present *friendly* intercourse caused me great happiness. Now, if I am right, this must cease—"

"But if *I* am right!" interrupted Mrs. Dutton; "if merely for some reasons of her own—perhaps, because she wishes to do something really efficient in the school before she engages herself in any matrimonial way—she prefers that no declaration of love should be made at present, then, of course, all is right. I certainly have no business to say that she loves you with a passion equal to your own; women, you know, are diffident in expressing their feelings, and Miss Mildmay, as I interpret her character, is a very cautious person; but you may take my word for it, that if you only act wisely you have no need to despair. I do not think there needs any formal declaration of love. You understand one another; and I tell you candidly, that I shall think she uses you extremely ill if she does not marry you. I am very sure, from what she has said to me, that she has a very *warm* regard for you; she has confessed it to me. But she is cautious; perhaps, she wishes to study your character more fully; ladies, nowadays, are philosophical, you know; and allow me to say without flattery, that I think yours is a character which will bear study. At all events keep a good heart in the affair; remember, girls like a cheerful lover, and don't you let any body come between you and her—remember that! And if I don't find you two comfortably jogging on toward matrimony before this time next year, when I shall again be at the Hall, then I'm no conjurer. But here we are at the Hall; you must come in with me; you must ask my brother how he is!"

Mr. Derwent excused himself; he could not go in, he could not see Mr. Elworthy that night; he thanked Mrs. Dutton for the warm interest she had taken in his affairs, and receiving from her, as a parting injunction, that he was to be careful and not ruin all by a hurried declaration of love, but to keep a good heart and look on Honour Mildmay as his future bride, he wished her good-by and a happy arrival at home, and walked quickly amid the gathering gloom of evening down the valley.

He had much to think of. His feelings were composed as of light and darkness which would not mingle. If Mrs. Dutton had just grounds for what she said, then Honour, his pure, noble, single-minded Honour, was less single-minded than he had imagined her, and there was a degree of duplicity even in that stern womanliness by which, without words, she made it understood that love was interdicted between them, and which, though it was as a death-sentence to him, had excited his deepest respect and admiration. Yet still, was it for him to quarrel with his happiness on any terms—was it not felicity enough that she loved him, that she would permit his addresses at some future time, if he only proved himself worthy? Yes, indeed, that was a joy beyond words, beyond belief; *but was it so?* His own inner sense of truth told him no—it was not so! A dreadful crisis in his life was at hand; a meddler had come in between his own soul and its yet only now dawning peace, and unspeakable sorrow and disappointment seemed to lie before him. He could not, in his then state of mind, call at the cottage; therefore, in mist and rain, and facing a cold autumnal wind, he passed the turn of the road where the tempter had met him, crossed the Lower-Fells, and sadly wearied and dispirited by uncertainty and disquietude of mind, reached his home late at night.

In the mean time Mrs. Dutton had work to do at Wast Hall. She found her brother busied with his lawyer about the purchase of the little estate of Oakenshaw in Ellerdale. As soon as the lawyer was gone, he laughed, and said that he had made up his mind to be the possessor of Oakenshaw, although Miss Mildmay had not seen it. He spoke in an unusually cheerful tone, and as he stood with the map of the estate in his hand, the full blaze of a large fire and a bright lamp upon him, he looked singularly handsome. Mrs. Dutton was struck by it. Was this the man that was likely to die so soon—that was never to marry again? Why, if such a man had presented himself as a suitor to one of her own young daughters, would not she have regarded herself as the most fortunate of mothers? She would; and she knew it. A most painful apprehension that there might be truth in Mr. Derwent's words, that Mr. Elworthy loved, and might even marry Honour Mildmay, made her feel absolutely sick and faint.

"Bless me," she said, "what has Miss Mildmay to do with

your purchasing, or not purchasing Oakenshaw! And by-the-by," said she, drawing her chair to the fire. "I have a little news to tell you about this young lady." Mr. Elworthy leaned his elbow on the chimney-piece, and with the map of Oakenshaw still in his hand, immediately gave his attention.

"I told you, some time ago," said she, "that I was sure Mr. Derwent was in love with Miss Mildmay. I have just had a long talk with her and her mother about it. I hope she is not playing with that young man's affections, for he is desperately in love with her, and she knows it, too, for she confessed as much, and said how much she liked his society, and that he spends three or four evenings a week with them. She is teaching him German now, or something of that kind; and evidently is giving him great encouragement; which is certainly very wrong if she does not mean to marry him."

"If she gives him this encouragement," remarked Mr. Elworthy, "what leads you to suppose that she does not intend to marry him?"

"Oh! she *does* intend, there is no doubt of that! Only, this I tell you in confidence—she confessed to me that she did not wish him to make the declaration at present. She is a very cautious young lady, take my word for it; and this confession of hers has sunk her very much in my esteem—for I was inclined to think very highly of her. Pray, my dear sir, who recommended these ladies to you, and how *did* you meet with them?"

"They are friends of a friend of mine in whom I repose great confidence," replied Mr. Elworthy. "And you think that Miss Mildmay is attached to Mr. Derwent, that she returns his affection, and will marry him?" asked he, evidently interested in the subject.

"I have not the slightest doubt of it!" returned Mrs. Dutton, "and if you remember, I mentioned it to you some time ago. I could see that she liked him the first time I was in their company; but she is very cautious; my idea is, that perhaps she thinks you might object to it, as interfering with her duties in the school; but this is mere surmise—as it is, she is playing with his affections and so I have as good as told her. However, there is no doubt how it will end, and I have promised to come to her wedding, whenever it may take place, for he is an excellent young man and has good expectations, and she is a very attractive young woman, with good sterling qualities, and, as you said, well calculated for a clergyman's wife."

"Upon my word, I had no idea that I had said so!" returned Mr. Elworthy; "but one thing, my dear lady, let me remark. Some little time ago, you mentioned that Mr. Derwent was in love with Miss Mildmay, and that you could see instantly by her manner, when in company with him, that she returned his affection. I admire the penetration of you ladies, and therefore, my curiosity being excited, I paid more than usual attention to Miss Mildmay's manners the other evening when we were all together at the cottage."

"I am glad you've mentioned that," said Mrs. Dutton, interrupting him—"so did I. Did you not see her joy in the prospect of his being of the party to Ellerdale, and drinking tea at his cottage? Any body with half an eye could see that she loves him, and she means to marry him. I tell you, she has herself, this very evening, confessed as much to me. Of course she means to marry him, unless she can catch some richer husband—" Mrs. Dutton had gone further in this last remark than she intended, and instantly recollecting herself, she continued, "I fancied, when first I came, that she had rather a liking for young Broadbent, the Quaker; he is a very handsome young man, and he evidently was smitten with her."

Mr. Elworthy burst into a loud fit of laughter, which disconcerted Mrs. Dutton.

"What is there so absurd in the idea? Young Broadbent, though he is a miller, and a Quaker, is rich, and she, though she may have had a gentlewoman's bringing up, is but a poor schoolmistress. She would do very well if she married young Broadbent, let me tell you!"

"Mr. Broadbent would not thank you for choosing a wife for him," said Mr. Elworthy; "for, poor fellow, he is over head and ears in love with that pretty Agnes Fothergill. He is ready to drown himself in his step-father's mill-dam for her sake; for his step-father and his mother, and his brother, who is a preacher among the Quakers, I am told, won't hear of it. Has not Mrs. Hawes communicated to you some intelligence of this unhappy love-passage, which bids fair to have a tragical ending, if the young people don't get married in defiance of every one? But I refer you to Mrs. Hawes for all information regarding young Broadbent. You may rely upon it, if you saw him at the cottage it was on business of no more importance than is contained in a meal-sack."

"As to that, it's of no consequence," said Mrs. Dutton, really vexed; "but as regards Mr. Derwent, I am confident that I am right. I have had, as I have told you, a long conversation this very afternoon with both her and her mother about it; and after what I heard from Miss Mildmay's own mouth, I thought there could be no harm in letting poor Mr. Derwent know that there was no reason for him to despair, however much she might enjoy tantalizing him. I have no notion of girls behaving in that way; there is a geat want of delicacy and self-respect in it, to say nothing of the cruelty of such conduct! We don't know, my dear sir, what this girl really may be; she may be a heartless flirt. Her former life may have been of the same character; and my dear brother, let me say one thing to you before I leave: you have taken these two ladies into your very family, as it were, yet you know nothing of them—nothing at all."

"I beg your pardon," interrupted Mr. Elworthy; "they were not so wholly unknown to me in character as you imagine."

Mrs. Dutton shook her head. "Very excellent ladies they may be," said she; "I was disposed to think most favorably of them myself. I am sure I have behaved to them as if they had been my own equals, every way. I thought most highly of them, but my faith is a little shaken, I assure you. I think, that under a show of more than usual womanly delicacy, and refinement, and nobility, that Miss Mildmay is a heartless coquette. I think that she is behaving infamously toward Mr. Derwent; at least, after what she has confessed to me, if she does not at once honestly accept him, even if the thing is kept quietly among themselves, she is greatly to blame. I understand these affairs perfectly, and I can see plainly what game she has been playing. Mr. Derwent was kept dangling just to be taken up or flung aside, as might suit her after-views, if she could catch a better lover; then, of course, he went overboard; if not, she had him safe. I know no conduct in a young woman more selfish, more heartless, than this; and I never would allow any of my girls to play thus with young men's feelings."

Mrs. Dutton had, she found, a very attentive listener in her brother. He had thrown the map of Oakenshaw on the table, and now stood, as before, leaning his brow on his hand, and his eye attentively fixed upon her. She continued:

"You see now her whole plan. She has, she told me, most studiously prevented him from making any direct declaration of love; for, had it been otherwise, it would have come to a decisive yes or no, at once, and he must have been taken or rejected; as it is, they read German together, sing together; he is there three or four evenings a week, loving her, adoring her, her most devoted servant; while she herself is as free as air, and if a richer man came to-morrow, she could, and *would*, throw him off from her with as much indifference as an old glove! The proverb, my dear sir, says that a feather will show us which way the winds blows; but when one sees the tempest driving a noble ship upon the rocks, one must be a fool, indeed, not to see the consequences, and worse than a fool, a thousand times not to warn it of its danger, and save it if we can!"

Mr. Elworthy understood her to mean that he was the noble vessel driving toward destruction, and hers was the friendly voice that warned him of his danger. He did not thank her; he stood like the man at the helm, who, having forgotten himself amid Elysian dreams, on a smooth sea, finds himself all at once in the midst of breakers. The voice that now warns him, seems like an omen of evil, and he wishes ten times rather that he had gone down in the midst of his delusion. He stood, still leaning his brow on his hand, but his eyes were no longer fixed on her face. She continued:

"Yes, my faith is a good deal shaken in these ladies. However, I shall make further inquiries. I happen to know a gentleman from Northbridge, where they lived; I can learn all about them from him, and I will report faithfully of what I hear. But after all," added she, speaking much more cheerfully. "I have perhaps said more than there was any occasion for. I have given her good advice, such advice as I would have given my own daughters, and my conversation with Mr. Derwent will not be without its effect, I believe. I shall have to come next year to the wedding, as I have told her, and you, my dear sir, will have to look out for a new mistress for your school, unless you will intrust it all to Natalia and me, which, when Ellinor is married, I would not object to. But we can talk of that another time, there's no hurry about it."

"No hurry at all!" repeated Mr. Elworthy, and rolling up the map, and gathering together his various papers, he left the room, and Mrs. Dutton did not see him again that night.

Mrs. Hawes always attended Mrs. Dutton to her chamber, and though, in a general way, that lady was not remarkable for her affability to domestics, least of all to Mrs. Hawes, who was by no means a favorite with her, she seemed disposed for a little chat tonight, which was the last night of her present stay at Wast-Hall.

"I have been telling Mr. Elworthy," said she, "that I shall be coming here next summer for a wedding. I shall be coming to see your young curate, Mr. Derwent, married to Miss Mildmay. I've long suspected something in that quarter. I think them admirably qualified for each other."

"He's a farrantly young man," said Mrs. Hawes, "and a rare preacher. But wae's to me! if Miss Mildmay leaves these parts; for I reckon, if he marries her, it will not be afore he gets a living of's own. But what will th' master do, and all th' poor children if she goes clean away?"

"Th' master?" repeated Mrs. Dutton, "why should Mr. Elworthy object to her going?—there are plenty of schoolmistresses to be had!"

"There's only one Miss Mildmay!" returned Mrs. Hawes. "Ask any body, Christie o' Lily-garth, th' folks at Birks-mill—though they and Christie have fallen out so of late, all about young Broadbent and Agnes, Christie's daughter; yet there'd be only one mind between 'em about Miss Mildmay. Ask the poor folks in th' Dale and in Dale-town, and hear what they'll say. If folks might have their way, they'd rather than any thing else that the master would marry her himself."

Mrs. Dutton felt again sick with apprehension and anger. It is not too much to say that she would have been glad to see Honour Mildmay dead at her feet. "That is going rather too far, Mrs. Hawes," she said, "my brother has not lived single all these years, and with a most affecting constancy, remained faithful to the memory of his adored wife, the sister of my late husband, to marry a schoolmistress! There are fitnesses in things, my good Mrs. Hawes; and, as I have just told you, she will have a much more suitable partner than Mr. Elworthy in your excellent young curate. I am astonished at your thinking of her marrying your master!"

"There's more than me who have thought of it," replied Mrs. Hawes, pertinaciously. "I know not what th' master's intentions may be; I only know 'at he's a very handsome man, young-looking for his years, for all he's had so much trouble; with a good heart and a liberal hand, and a fine house; and, please God, many a long year before him yet; and why folk should not think of his marrying again I know not! But ma'ppen, he doesn't think of it himself; and that's another thing; and if Miss Mildmay likes our curate, it's not for me to say nay; she marries to please herself, not me; and Mr. Derwent is as farrantly a man as any in these parts, and a rare preacher; and now I think of it, he's taken desperately to th' Temperance society and th' Lending Library of late; I reckon it's all along of Miss Mildmay!"

Nothing could well be more unsatisfactory than this conversation with Mrs. Hawes. Poor Mrs. Dutton scarcely slept a wink all night. She left Wast-Hall by eight the next morning; nor did the handsome present of money, more liberal even than common, which Mr. Elworthy put into her hand at parting, tend at all to decrease the anxiety and anguish of heart which she carried with her out of Wast-Wayland.

CHAPTER X.

It was soon whispered about in Wayland-dale and Dale-town, that Mr. Derwent and Miss Mildmay were going to be married. Mrs. Hawes took the liberty of speaking to her master about it the first opportunity. She inquired, when she carried in the letter-bag to his breakfast table, a few days afterward, if he had heard the news.

"News! no, what news?" asked he.

"Oh, the news about Mr. Derwent and Miss Mildmay, that they are going to be married." Mrs. Dutton had told her; and it was to be next spring, she supposed.

Yes, Mr. Elworthy said, coldly; he had heard the same thing. Mrs. Dutton mentioned it to him, and then he held out his hand for the letter-bag, which Mrs. Hawes had retained as a plea for staying in the room.

He took the bag from her, and yet she lingered, wanting to say more, but hardly knowing how.

He took out his letters, and looking at her, said inquiringly, "Well, Mrs. Hawes?"

She felt a little disconcerted, but she said, "as I told Mrs. Dutton, says I, he's a farrantly young man and a rare preacher, and they tell me he comes of a good family, and has an uncle, a Prebend of Durham, who will do something handsome for him."

"Mr. Derwent you mean," said Mr. Elworthy, breaking the seal of a letter, which he proceeded to read.

Mrs. Hawes brushed a few crumbs from the breakfast cloth with her hand, and then walked away quite annoyed. "He does not care any thing about it," said she to herself. "I fancied he had a liking for her but I reckon it were only my own conceit."

To compensate herself for her disappointment at home she made an errand that day to Lily-garth about some butter and eggs, and had a long comfortable gossip about it with Mrs. Fothergill. From Mrs. Fothergill it spread in twenty ways; it reached Tod's-gill in an amazingly short time. And Dannel, as he sat in his father's old chair on the hearth, "supping his porridge," said, "folks had talked of the squire marrying her himself, for at one time he seemed desperately taken with her; and, for his part, he should have had no objections, for he did not see what he was to get by either Richard Elworthy or the Duttons having the Wast-Wayland property."

Before long the little girls in the school knew of it, and wished that Mr. Derwent would come to ask them Bible questions, as he so often did, that they might see how they behaved to one another: but he did not come, and they could not imagine why.

The news also traveled over the Lower Fells into Ellerdale, and reached Mr. Langshaw in his study and Mrs. Langshaw in her bed, and they both thought it was an excellent thing. When the rector, therefore, next saw his curate, which, however, did not happen to be for some little time, he congratulated him on his prospects. He did not know any where, he said, a lady so admirably qualified, not only for a clergyman's wife, but to make a man happy, and he considered him a fortunate fellow.

There was something in Mr. Derwent's manner of replying to these congratulations which Mr. Langshaw could not understand; he told his wife so, adding that Derwent looked ill and any thing but happy. Perhaps, after all he had not been accepted: in that case he was very sorry for him.

Of course the news reached Birks-mill, and was discussed in the drab-curtained sitting-room by Caleb and Elizabeth Fothergill, both highly approving of it. Young Broadbent, who sat by and said nothing, thought how hard it was that the true-love course of others should run smoothly while his own was so vexed and crossed. Why were not he and Agnes Fothergill as fitting a match as the curate and the young schoolmistress? He began to rebel against Quakerism, and to determine that he would do as Agnes's father had done—marry "out of the society," and that in defiance of his mother and his step-father, and of his uncle, the preacher, or "ministering friend," as they called him, though he did expect money from him. He would go and talk to Mr. Derwent, the happy lover, about it; and as soon as he was of age, and got his own twelve hundred pounds into his hands, if he could bring his pretty Agnes into the mind, they would be married, and set off to America, where they could buy plenty of land, and live happily, as William Penn had done, and Morris Birkbeck, and many another Quaker!

Thus the subject was pretty generally discussed and apparently pretty generally approved of, before the rumor reached the ears of the parties themselves. It was now some time since Mr. Derwent had been at the cottage. At first his absence was a relief; for after the conversation with Mrs. Dutton, a painful consciousness was left in the mind of Honour, which made the idea of seeing him unpleasant; but when day after day, and even two weeks passed, and he had been neither at the cottage nor yet at the school, and when the effect of Mrs. Dutton's remarks had a little worn off, surprise and anxiety filled her heart. What could it mean? Had Mrs. Dutton really been talking with him on this foolish subject, and had she misrepresented things? or what could she have said? Was he offended or piqued—or what was it? Ill he was not, for they had heard of his visiting a sick family in Dale-town, yet he had not been near them, nor had Mr. Elworthy. It was very strange and very painful, because the interference of Mrs. Dutton left room for such unpleasant surmise.

At length Mr. Walker, of the boys' school, called. He offered his congratulations on Honour's approaching marriage with Mr. Derwent; "two or three people," he said, "had mentioned it to him, and he had mentioned it to Mr. Elworthy, who had been that day at the school, and he also knew of it. Had not they seen Mr. Elworthy that day! It was the first time he had been down for a long while, and of course he expected that he would call at the cottage."

"No; Mr. Elworthy had not been with them," said Mrs. Mildmay. "But, indeed, there was no truth in the report; and, in proof of that, Mr. Derwent himself had not been at the cottage for near a fortnight."

Mr. Walker looked as if he hardly could credit this, and spoke very highly of the young curate.

Honour was greatly annoyed and perplexed. But Mr. Derwent's case was more painful and perplexing than hers. After carefully reviewing the whole of his intercourse with her, and every word and look of hers was daguerreotyped into his very soul, his reason refused to believe that he had any ground for a lover's hope. On the other hand, Mrs. Dutton, whom he was so willing to believe, assured him to the contrary, and that, too, on assertions from Honour's own lips. Could he, a lover, then refuse to hope? But even here was a something which presented a painful conviction, and which no effort of his could overcome. If it were possible that Honour had made such an avowal to Mrs. Dutton, he had, in a great measure mistaken her character; there was a something in Mrs. Dutton's representation of the case, however flattering it might be to his vanity, which wounded his nice sense of delicacy—of that very delicacy and sincerity of character, which had appeared to him as one of Honour's most inimitable charms. And what was the line of conduct which was so emphatically laid down for him? He was to regard Honour Mildmay as his bride; to be careful that no one came between himself and her, yet to withhold for the present any declaration of love! Was this, indeed, the course prescribed by Honour for him? It might be flattering to him as a lover, but he felt at the same time as if the pure gold were stripped from his idol.

For two weeks he neither went to the cottage nor yet to the school. He preached in his turn at Dale-town church, and saw Honour, pale and pure in appearance as an angel, in her pew, with her little Sunday scholars around her; his heart seemed to die within him at the sight, and, for a few moments, utterance seemed impossible. Some of his congregation remarked his manner, and many of them thought that he looked ill; they could not conceive why he should look so, and he and Miss Mildmay engaged to each other! Mr. Elworthy, too, was at church, but his pew was aristocratically curtained, and he could sit, if he chose, quite out of every body's view; so he did at this time. It was a cold, wet Sunday; there were no greetings in the church-yard; Honour went out with her scholars; her mother, who was an invalid in winter, and especially so now, for she had been used to a warmer climate, and a warmer house, was not at Church, and Honour had no opportunity of speaking to either of the gentlemen. She felt really dispirited and overcome by anxiety as she mentioned these little circumstances to her mother, adding that she feared greatly something was on Mr. Derwent's mind—if he were not ill; and as to Mr. Elworthy, she really could not understand him.

"I wish Mr. Derwent would come!" said Honour to herself the next evening; "but," added she, recollecting what a dreary evening it was, and listening to the wind as it howled round the cottage, "what a terrible walk he would have over those desolate wild Fells!"

Her mother, who continued very unwell, went to bed as soon as tea was over, and Honour sat down to read "As you Like It," a favorite play of hers, for she would not trust herself to her own thoughts over her needle-work. A book, and that book Shakspeare, was a better companion than herself at that time. Scarcely, however, had she got through the first act, when a well-known step on the gravel outside, and a knock at the door, interrupted her. Mr. Derwent was there.

Painful and difficult as this interview might prove, she was unfeignedly glad to see him. She said so with a voice and manner, at once cordial, simple and sincere. She was the same Honour Mildmay as ever. He felt this. Her true, cordial womanliness restored all the glory and fascination to his idol; she was pure gold again; and it was but a false counterfeit that Mrs. Dutton had held before his eyes. This was the genuine Honour Mildmay whom he loved so devotedly—yet whom he as truly felt could not, and did not love him other than as a friend! An anguish as of death came over his soul; he had never loved her so tenderly, so passionately, as now. He was silent; he could not have spoken for the world. She saw it all; and bold though the step might seem, she determined to introduce the subject which was so near to the thoughts of both, yet one on which they felt so differently

"We have not met for a long time," said she, with a deep blush; "something painful, I am sure, has kept you away. It has, perhaps, been difficult for you to meet me; it would have been so to me but that I have been very anxious. But it is right that we meet, that we look this phantom, which a third person has raised, steadfastly in the face: it is but a phantom, and it has been raised by unholy means."

He made no reply, but gazed at her with an expression of unspeakable love and anxiety. "I stand on no idle points of delicacy, Mr. Derwent," continued she, again blushing, and with a slight hesitation of manner; "it is much better not, though some people might blame me, but *you* will not, for it is of vital importance to us both—to you even more than to me—I would spare you pain or sorrow: God knows I would!"

He still made no reply, but, taking her hand, grasped it between both his with almost convulsive force.

"I thought that we fully and clearly understood one another," she said; "I hoped—I believed that you knew how much I esteemed you, although a warmer sentiment was impossible."

"I understand all this," said he. "We have been very happy together. I regarded your friendship as the blessing of my life; it has been beneficial to me in a hundred ways. I expected nothing more, till Mrs. Dutton assured me that I had more to expect!"

"God in Heaven!" exclaimed Honour, carried beyond her usual equanimity of manner, "what mischief can not such busy meddlers do!"

"But," pleaded he, "can not, may not, good spring out of evil? A meddler has come between us—has torn the vail from our two hearts and laid them bare before each other; is there then no hope for mine? I ask it not now—at some future time—when you will, only do not deprive me of hope! Lay down any conditions you please—require from me any amount of devotion, of preparation—lay any penance on me, only leave me hope!"

"Oh, why is this trial needlessly laid on us!" sighed Honour.

"I am by no means without friends or without prospects in the world," said he; "say only that I may hope, and no man on God's earth will prove himself more worthy than I will. You know me, Honour—you know something of me at least; our views, our tastes, our desires in life are similar. If love, if devotion, if the truest esteem can make a wife happy, it shall make you so. Speak, Honour; tell me that I may hope; and, if it be in seven years' time, I will be patient, and will only endeavor to be more worthy of you!" Again he seized her hand, and held it as though life and death were in the grasp.

She had to bear a great trial—to remain true to herself by inflicting mortal anguish on a noble human soul. She did not withdraw her hand, and during a few moments, her own soul passed in severe scrutiny before itself. A deep momentous truth was impressed upon her which she dared not gainsay, and then she spoke with downcast eyes and in a low voice, in which, however, were tones of more than usual tenderness and sympathy, every one of which vibrated upon the hearer's soul. "Since the strange conversation," said she, "that Mrs. Dutton had with me, and which she has most singularly perverted—but more especially during you absence from us, which I believe had its origin in the same cause—I have subjected my heart to a deep and close scrutiny. I have even pleaded for you with myself; I have set before me all your many good and noble qualities—your virtues, your amiability—our accordant tastes, and our usefulness to each other. I have tried to think of you as a lover—as a husband—but my heart would not respond. God alone knows why the heart is so steadfast and wayward in such things; but it is the true dial finger, and we must trust it. It will not obey reason merely, but an internal sense within itself which is stronger than reason. There must be a responding in the inner life of the heart—which is God's voice within us as regards our affections, before we have any right to pledge ourselves to another. Had the true response come, I could not have disobeyed it; as it is not there, I dare not act without it; to me it would be a sin, a lie before God. Dear friend, I have even prayed that this voice might respond, but my heart has been silent as a tomb!"

"God's will be done!" said the curate, dropping the hand which he had held so tenderly. He sat down with his head resting on his hand, and his eyes fixed on the ground. At length he rose; he looked deathly pale; the struggle with himself had been very painful.

"Mrs. Dutton has done us a great unkindness—me, at least," said he, in a voice which, though it was calm, sounded strangely hollow. "It has been like calling back the soul to undergo a second time the pangs of death, which it had already borne. My life is of little value to me now; and yet, how beautiful it has been!"

Again he convulsively grasped her hand, and then, without another word went out. It was a dark, wild midnight, not a star in the sky; and the wind, and rain, and darkness, seemed like types of his own state of mind. There are times when the outward and inward are strangely illustrative and symbolical.

Honour, who saw him go forth into the night with his burden of sorrow, returned greatly agitated and depressed to the parlor fire side. There is no moment when the sympathetic heart of woman is so moved to pity and kindness towards a man whom she believes to be worthy and noble, as when she has inflicted the deepest wound on his self-love by rejecting his affections. Thus Honour felt. "Would that I could have given him my whole heart," thought she to herself, "but it was impossible! Strange is the mystery of this human heart! I have gone down into the depths of my own, and sought for love—for that love which at one time I gave to another, and which was flung back to me—but it was not there for *him*. I have inflicted on him—on my friend—on him whom I loved as a brother, a deep wound for which I can give no consolation! Wonderful mystery is this human heart of ours! Among the old ruins of a buried love, I could not find what I sought, and even prayed for, but, Heaven have mercy upon me!" exclaimed she, in the inmost recesses of her soul; "I have found, where there was no love for *him* who gave so much, love for another, who can give me nothing—who regards me with indifference, perhaps aversion! There is great truth, indeed, in the doctrine of compensation; for even here I see it—feel it! If I have caused deep anguish to a noble human soul, there is deeper anguish in store for me! The law of compensation is in force. Father in heaven, have mercy on me, and guide and sustain my weak and wayward heart, which, with all its mysterious springs of affection is in thy hand!"

She uttered a sigh, almost a groan, and leaning her forehead on her hand, bowed it to the table and wept bitterly.

It was past midnight, and her mother, alarmed by her long absence, rang to inquire the cause, and the little maid who was asleep by the kitchen fire, rushed into the parlor only half awake, thinking that something dreadful had happened. Honour said not a word to her mother that night of her visitor; she went to bed, but could not sleep. The wind howled down the chimney like a wailing spirit; the rain streamed down the window panes like torrents of human tears. Every thing seemed sad and depressing, yet the next morning Honour sat in the little school-room, mild as a good angel, among her little scholars, who wondered how it was that she looked so sad and thoughtful through the whole day.

CHAPTER XI.

When Mrs. Dutton arrived at home she found her daughters still at Fircoates, whither they had gone with Mrs. Cartwright on their return from Paris. She immediately, therefore, dispatched a note to Frederick Horrocks, begging him to give her half an hour of his company that evening. She was glad to have him quite alone on many accounts.

As soon as the mutual greetings were over she introduced the subject nearest to her thoughts. "I want you to tell me," said she, "if you know any thing of a young lady named Mildmay, who lived at Northbridge; Honour Mildmay is her name?"

This unexpected question was a great shock to him. He believed that it was asked with some fearful reference to himself. He did not answer it immediately, for he was thinking how best to evade it.

"Perhaps you do not remember her; perhaps you did not know her?" said Mrs. Dutton, who thus interpreted his silence; her mother is a widow; they lost a good deal of property some time ago, I believe."

"Yes, certainly," said Horrocks, considerably assured by her manner, which implied no suspicion; "I do remember: a widow lady and her daughter; but what of them?"

"I wish to know all you can tell me about them. I have a curiosity on the subject, and a reason for asking," said she.

Again he was tortured by apprehension. "I—I can tell you very little—next to nothing," said he.

"Tell me that little then," replied she quickly; "and you can write to your sister, can not you, and learn every particular from her? My idea is that she is an artful, scheming girl, always on the look-out to catch some man of fortune. I have heard a good deal of them while I have been in the north," said she, deeming it wise to disguise the truth, in some measure, and to speak rather of having heard of than having seen this young lady. She therefore merely said, that she had her reasons for believing that Miss Mildmay was a flirt who cared not how many lovers she could catch, meaning only to reward the richest with her hand.

"You will oblige me, therefore, greatly, dear Frederick," said she, "by obtaining for me some positive information regarding them: both mother and daughter, I mean. I wish to commit no one, but it will be a satisfaction to me to know whether certain suspicions of mine are correct or not. Or, shall I write to your sister?" said she, seeing still a hesitation in his manner; "I am sure she will do any thing to oblige me, and there must be plenty of people at Northbridge who know them well."

Frederick Horrocks hoped that his fears regarding himself were groundless, nevertheless he replied; "May I ask for what purpose these inquiries are made? It would seem strange to my sister, or to any one, to make them without a definite object."

Mrs. Dutton was now somewhat perplexed on her side, she would not, for the world, have created any doubts which might go forth to the world regarding the fidelity of Mr. Elworthy toward her own family, yet she was determined to leave no stone unturned which could furnish her with an argument against Honour Mildmay and her mother, therefore she replied, with a smile—"It concerns *me*, my dear Frederick, will that suffice you? You lawyers are so cautious! I will pledge you my word that you shall get into no trouble about it."

"Formerly," replied he, "my family used to know these Mildmays well, but I have been at Northbridge so little for these many years that I can hardly speak of them. They were very respectable people. The father was a good-natured, easy sort of man, who, at his death, left his property in the hands of a commercial firm in which he had been concerned; it failed, and the property was all lost. The mother and daughter have left Northbridge now some time. I know nothing of them now, nor does my family."

"What character did they bear?" again inquired Mrs. Dutton; "it was of their character I inquired, not their circumstances."

"I really can not say," replied he impatiently.

"Then I must write to your sister," persisted Mrs. Dutton, "or to somebody else. Let me see; there's your sister's god-mother, Mrs. Woodley; that's her name, as I remember."

"I don't think Charlotte can tell you any thing," returned Frederick Horrocks, "my family dropped their acquaintance long ago."

"Dropped their acquaintance!" exclaimed Mrs. Dutton, catching at the phrase eagerly. "Come, come; it's no use your being so very circumspect and particular; people don't drop their acquaintances without good reason. I shall really begin to suspect something! Tell me now candidly, Frederick, was not Miss Mildmay an artful, designing young woman, forever on the look-out to catch a rich husband?"

Horrocks thought he now understood the whole purport of this questioning. He believed that Mr. Elworthy had heard something unpleasant regarding his behavior to Honour Mildmay, and perhaps threatened to withdraw his consent; and now, therefore, this good Mrs. Dutton, his kind mother-in-law wished to clear him with her relative. This view of the case entirely explained her determination, her reserve, and her eagerness to throw blame of this kind upon Honour. His course was now clear.

"It is no use, my dear madam," said he, "skirmishing any longer with you on such a subject; you have the best of the argument, because you are so singularly near the truth. It is a painful thing, nevertheless, to bring a charge of any kind against a young lady; but your suspicions, or information, or whatever it may be, is very near the mark. She was, as you say, a flirt, and one of the most dangerous kind, because she had, apparently, so much modesty and single-mindedness, and was remarkably accomplished. She laid desperate siege to a member of our own family—connection, I should say—names need not be mentioned; but there was a great deal of unpleasantness on both sides. Of course, some of her friends blamed the gentleman, but it was entirely *her* doing; he had no idea of marrying her, and was obliged to draw off. After this, my family had no further intercourse with her or her mother. It was a very painful thing; involvements of this kind ought never to occur; but it was entirely *her* doing. I don't believe that the gentleman ever thought of marriage. But now, my dear madam," said he, earnestly, and with a certain anxiety of manner which was wholly misunderstood by Mrs. Dutton, "you must be aware that it would be the most painful thing in the world for my name, or the name of any of my family, to be brought up in this affair. I rely on your honor, and I am sure that I am safe in your hands. The affair I speak of is long past; such things ought not to be revived; the least said of them the better. Besides, the Mildmays have been unfortunate since then; but, I assure you, nevertheless, that what I have told you is perfectly true."

Mrs. Dutton was satisfied; she treated her son-in-law elect with the utmost kindness; she pressed him to stay supper, which he did, and she had the pleasure of telling him of the charming visit she had paid to her excellent relative, who had been kinder and more agreeable than she had ever before known him. She repeated many assurances which he had given her of the warm interest he felt in herself and her daughters, and finally showed Horrocks the substantial proofs of his good-will, in sundry bank-bills which he had given her at parting, principally to be devoted to wedding purchases for Ellinor.

"It is twice the sum he gave either to Caroline or Emma, but I told you that Ellinor was his favorite," said she, exultingly, "and I have promised that she and you shall pay him a visit this summer."

Mrs. Dutton had now, in the information which she had derived from Frederick Horrocks, a substantial foundation on which to erect a serious accusation; an accusation of the very kind most calculated to produce an effect on the mind of her brother-in-law, with all his "romantic and chivalrous notions about women," as she said.

She therefore wrote to him, without much loss of time, as follows:

"WOODBURY, Nov. 15.

"MY DEAR SIR—You would receive my letter, informing you of my safe arrival at home. I have now once more my girls about me, and we are settled down to our quiet but cheerful winter life, Woodbury being very gay just at this time. The girls are looking extremely well after their continental trip; they have greatly improved their French, and have a vast passion for German just now. Ellinor sends her love, and thanks you for your liberal gift. We are already beginning to make preparations for the wedding.

"But I must not gossip too long on these domestic matters, as I feel compelled to address you on a painful subject: but there are, you know, my dear sir, painful duties which admit of no choice, and this is of that class.

"I was, during the greater part of my delightful visit to you, most agreeably impressed, as you are aware, in favor of the young lady whom you have placed at the head of your school. I thought her, spite of the fine education she appears to have enjoyed, and the refinement of her manners, admirably calculated for the fulfillment of her duties. As you know, I devoted a good deal of my time to the school, and I hope with some good effect; and thus I had an opportunity of studying her character pretty fully. So agreeably, indeed, was I impressed by her, that I spent a good deal of time both with her mother and herself, and in this way it was that I came, by degrees, to see in her traits of character which at first surprised me, and then woke my unfeigned disgust.

"I mentioned to you the conversation I had had with her regarding poor Mr. Derwent; for, my dear sir, I am not often mistaken in character, and I soon saw that she was playing with this gentleman's affections, having no strong regard for him, although her manners were such as to lead him to believe the very reverse. I did not leave Wayland-dale without speaking very freely to her on the subject, telling her that unless she intended to marry him, her conduct was very blameworthy; she avowed to me her great liking for his society; her entire unwillingness to give it up; yet, at the same time, her determination to prevent him from declaring himself definitely; because that, you know, must end the thing at once one way or another. I also spoke to Mr. Derwent on the subject, as I felt myself in duty bound. Nor did I, as you may remember, omit to mention it to you—for it was but right that you should know how dangerous and blameworthy a person you had placed in so responsible a situation.

"I mentioned to you at the same time, as you will doubtless remember, that I happened to be acquainted with a gentleman from Northbridge, who would be able to give me information regarding the former character of this young lady. The information he gives me, I am sorry to say, so entirely coincides with my own suspicions, and so forcibly strengthens my apprehensions, that I should consider myself culpable by remaining silent.

"To come at once to the point, then: my informant, who is a gentleman of undoubted veracity, assures me, that the conduct of this young lady when at Northbridge, was precisely of the same character. She was a most notorious flirt, and drew at least one young man into a matrimonial engagement with her quite unconsciously to himself, which occasioned a great scandal in the place, and in fact obliged them to leave, for naturally enough, several families of high standing, dropped their acquaintance, and she and her mother were justly regarded as very dangerous people.

"I can not, my dear sir, in the short compass of a letter, communicate all the painful but well-authenticated details of which I have become possessed. But this I can do—I can hold up the glass of truth to your eyes, and show you how poor Mr. Derwent is likely to be treated, if she does not take warning by what I have already told her, and put you also on your guard, and beseech of you to be careful as to the influence which it may be the object of this artful young woman, to exercise over a mind as generous, as unsuspicious, and as frank as your own.

"And now, in conclusion, let me assure you, that after Ellinor's marriage, which will, as I said, take place in the spring—the young people talk of the 3d of May, which is her birth-day—would that we might hope for your company on the occasion! Nothing, I say, when this bustle is over, will give me greater pleasure than to spend some time with you again in your beautiful valley. I do not, my dear sir, stand on any ceremony with you, for I know that I am always welcome, and I flatter myself that, if you find it necessary to remove this young lady from the school, or if she removes herself, by becoming Mrs. Derwent, be assured that you can not confer a greater mark of regard than by placing it under the management of

"My dear brother, yours,

"Faithfully and affectionately,

"MARTHA DUTTON.

"To William Elworthy, Esq."

This letter, as was intended, produced a great effect on the mind of him to whom it was addressed. His first feeling was displeasure against the writer and suspicion of her motives. His second was anxiety and unhappiness, as regarded his new friends themselves. "How and with whom," questioned he, "had these injurious accusations, on which Mrs. Dutton now founded her charges, arisen? Was there ground for them? or were they the foul and false aspersions of envy and malice?"

He immediately wrote to his friend, Mr. Wilbraham, to inquire regarding these past events at Northbridge. But before the letter was finished he destroyed it, for he felt it as an offense against virtue and womanly purity even to seem to credit such a report. "If she is pure and noble," said he, "as I believe her to be, I will not injure her by appearing to think otherwise; if not, let my own judgment, at least, have some conviction before I take so decided a step against her."

Both Mrs. Dutton's words as well as her letter had warned him of Honour's designs against himself; this led him to take a scrutinizing review of her whole behavior. From being at first reserved and almost shy in her intercourse with him, she had become cordial and frank, as one who had no fear and no guile; as one who acted alone from the sincere impulses of an upright soul. As to Mr. Derwent, whatever might be the nature of the intimacy between them, nothing had been suspected in the slightest degree derogatory to Honour until Mrs. Dutton herself had suggested it. It had seemed to Mr. Elworthy that she behaved to Mr. Derwent as a sister might to a brother; they had community of tastes and pursuits; their objects in life were the same; their daily duties brought them frequently together. Possible it was, and very probable too, Mr. Elworthy's own feelings soon convinced him, that Mr. Derwent might take a deeper interest in Honour and her occupations than the mere duties of a minister in the little school where she taught would warrant; and this idea once in his mind, he looked on with a much keener scrutiny—with an interest which had a painful intensity in it, as if his soul's peace depended upon the issue. He had long known that there were singular points of sympathy between himself and her, the influence of which was felt rather than expressed; their views of life were accordant; and her active and efficient co-operation in his schemes for the moral advancement of his poor dale's-people, had already produced so large an amount of good as to insure his lasting gratitude. He had looked at her, when she was least aware of it, from his great curtained pew in the church, as she sat with her mother, among the little children whom she was training up as lambs for Christ's fold; and his pure and noble heart had blessed her, and associated her in a sentiment of heart-reverence, as the dale's-people did with his long-since dead wife.

Such, indeed, was the nature of his feelings toward Honour at the time when Mrs. Dutton first mentioned to him the curate's attachment to her. A very little observation convinced him that she was right, and it thus became necessary to him, as we have said to ascertain what were her sentiments toward Mr. Derwent. He watched her, therefore, narrowly on that memorable evening when they were all together at the cottage. He and Honour, it is true, had been together alone before the party returned from Ellerdale. Their conversation, though on indifferent subjects had been of the most agreeable character. Honour appeared that afternoon to be singularly happy; a serene but heartfelt joy beamed in her countenance and permeated her whole being. She was filled with an unspeakable joy to be thus in friendly intercourse with one, who, though he knew it not, possessed an absolute power over her; who stirred the inner depths of her soul, and called forth its best and purest treasures. He felt the fascination that his own influence called forth, but to him it seemed that the magic power resided in her, and that he alone was its slave. He asked her to sing, to sing the songs that he loved best—the songs that his soul held sacred; and while she was yet singing, the party returned from Ellerdale, and with them, as we know, the man whom he considered to be his rival.

Profoundly impressed with the sincerest and noblest sentiment of love, as his heart was at that moment, he determined to remain there through the evening, in company with them both, that he might, if possible, discover of a certainty what were her real feelings toward Mr. Derwent. Not a look nor a word escaped him; and to him it appeared plain as daylight, that no electric touch vibrated in Honour's soul to word or look; she was calm and unimpassioned before him, and never had the young curate been more agreeable, or produced to greater advantage the wealth of a naturally rich and highly cultivated mind. Honour, though amiable and attractive still, was no longer the love-inspired woman whose every movement, and look, and tone, seemed only the outward response of an inward harmony.

"If there is truth in looks that express the soul, she loves me better than she loves him!" mused he, with an inward joy that no words could have given utterance to, as he sat silent, and apparently indifferent to all that went forward, and while Mrs. Dutton, from behind her hand-screen, was scrutinizing both him and Honour, with the most excited alarm, though the conclusion she finally drew, tended in some measure to abate her anxiety.

To ascertain still more clearly Honour's feelings with regard to Mr. Derwent it was, that Mr. Elworthy proposed and arranged the party to Ellerdale, of which the curate was to make one. This day, said he to himself, shall be decisive one way or another. That excursion did not take place, and Mrs. Dutton, as we know, left behind her a poisoned arrow, which was intended to be mortal, as far as regarded every sentiment of love in the heart of her relative.

"Mr. Derwent," said she, "is the *pis-aller*. If she can not catch a richer lover she will take him. I have from her own lips, the most unequivocal avowal of her regard for him; he is under the power of her fascination, so much so, indeed, that he dare not avow his love until she permits it, and she will only permit it if no better lover is to be had. Beware of the siren—of the fair, fascinating woman, who under the simple guise of a schoolmistress, is laying skillful traps to catch you—you, the honest, the true, the unsuspecting!"

Such was the spirit of her final warning. His natural caution was called forth; he remembered the plausible cunning and smooth guile of Richard Elworthy; he remembered that the most dangerous sin bears the nearest resemblance to virtue; he said, "If there is double-dealing in Honour Mildmay, who shall distinguish between truth and cunning? Nevertheless I will pause; if she has willingly drawn Mr. Derwent within the magic sphere of her fascinations, I withdraw from it; thank God! I have yet the power of free-will. If however," mused he, in another mood "she is true, and pure as I believed her, and this is but another phase of Mrs. Dutton's falsehood and selfishness, of which I have already had so many proofs, there needs but a little time to make it all right."

Then came Mrs. Dutton's letter. In a little while its unpleasant effect also became somewhat deadened, and he merely replied to her, that with regard to the charges against Miss Mildmay, he should in all probability, be able himself to test their truth or falsehood; for the present, therefore, he could say no more, than to warn her against propagating accusations, so injurious to the character of a young lady as these were. The letter was a vexation unspeakable, but Mrs. Dutton said not a word of it to any one. Not an individual of her family knew that there was any cause for anxiety or apprehension regarding Mr. Elworthy; they took such little interest in the young schoolmistress, of whom their mother casually spoke, that not one of them cared to remember the name. What need, indeed, was there that they should?

As regarded Honour, herself, after the terrible evening when she and Mr. Derwent came to a definite understanding, a cloud seemed altogether to fall over her life and prospects. Tidings soon reached her that Mr. Derwent was ill; that he was going immediately to leave, and that Mr. Langshaw was looking out for a new curate. The weather was intolerably bad; it was that broken, dreary winter weather, in which there is no stability; no continuance of frost to make the air fresh and invigorating; no pure cheerful snow; nothing but a damp, cold atmosphere, the dirty, forlorn earth, and the leaden, dreary sky; it was weather as depressing to the mind as to the body. The short light of the winter day, was entirely occupied by the duties of the school, which, though still conscientiously performed, seemed to Honour to have lost all their interest, all their productiveness of good.

Honour's heart smote her, as if she had, someway or other, been guilty of a crime, when in the now total absence of the young minister, she took up the book he had been accustomed to use, and went through the Saturday's routine of Bible questions. Tears fell on the page, and her heart seemed as heavy as lead; there seemed no longer any vitality in her instruction.

"There is no use teaching the children in this way!" said she to herself; "I must rouse myself, and put aside all these miserable thoughts. God knows that I have done what was right; but my duties must not be neglected. Better, by far, give up the school at once, than stand among the children self-absorbed as I do!"

A few moments sufficed for these thoughts; she closed the book and dismissed the class, which she was incapable of attending to.

"Miss Mildmay doesn't do the Bible questions well!" said the little girls, one to another. "Is it because Mr. Derwent is going? I wonder whether he will come to the school again before he leaves. I wish he would, it was so nice when he came!"

It was whispered here and there in the Dale, first as a great secret, and then it was openly talked of, that Miss Mildmay would not have Mr. Derwent, and therefore he was going. "Why would she not have him?" people asked. "Oh, what a pity it was!" said one. "What a shame!" said another. They wondered what Mr. Elworthy would say, for he liked him so much, and they were so friendly, how sorry he would be to part with him!

Other people said, there was something queer about it, for that poor Miss Mildmay looked quite ill, and somebody had seen her crying behind her prayer-book at church. It was certainly very incomprehensible, for every body had thought that they were just made for each other.

Young Broadbent, who, however, had not mustered courage to go and speak of his troubled love-affairs with Mr. Derwent, whom as the supposed fortunate lover, he had so greatly envied, now felt the deepest sympathy with him in his unknown trouble; nevertheless, it afforded him a little consolation to discover that there were other men crossed in love besides himself, and certainly even more seriously crossed; for his Agnes loved him, although their friends were for the present adverse, and though even Christie o'-Lily-garth had now taken it into his head that the lovers must wait two or three years before he would consent, which was quite a new trouble, for Christie hitherto had been as accordant as possible. Yes, even spite of all this, his case was certainly better than the poor curate's, whatever the real truth might be.

In the midst of this unhappy and agitated time, the indisposition of Mrs. Mildmay, though it did not amount to illness, still continued. She was wholly confined to the house, and principally to her bedroom, which could be made much warmer than the parlor, so that unless Honour sat wholly when at home in her mother's chamber, which that good lady would not permit on account of her being confined through the day in the close school-room, her evenings were spent alone in the little parlor, either in reading to herself, in silent needlework, or in music, to which she had no listener.

One Sunday, it was about a month after Mrs. Dutton's departure, Mrs. Mildmay was somewhat better; the weather had changed, and though there was the commencement of settled frost, the air was more refreshing even to a house-bound invalid. She said, therefore, that she would come down stairs and spend the evening in the little parlor. It seemed to Honour like an omen of better times; she closed every crevice about the window with folded paper; she let down the white muslin curtains to keep out the draughts in a slight degree; made up a good fire, swept the hearth, drew the sofa near to it, and soon saw her mother wrapped in a large shawl, reclining upon it.

Honour sat down also near her, and felt that deep joy which assured affection gives to every loving human heart. "Well, at least," thought she to herself, "there is one love which can never disappoint me; never cause me any pain or sorrow, and that is my mother's! Thank God, that she is spared to me! for without her, how desolate would my life become!"

"We must get Mr. Elworthy," said Mrs. Mildmay, speaking quite cheerfully, and interrupting her daughter's thoughts, "to let us have new fastenings to the windows, if we stay here another winter—they are so bad that they don't hold the casements tight; they are very bad in my bedroom, and if he would inclose the outer door with a little porch, which we could make very pretty in summer with creepers, it would be a vast improvement, and make the house much warmer, and it would not be very expensive either. I have been thinking over all these things as I lay in bed up-stairs. I fancy this must have been a common laborer's cottage at one time, it is so slightly built, although it looks so pretty in summer. But if we stay here another winter, we certainly must have it done, even if we do it at our own expense. But now play me something, will you, my darling," said she, after Honour had acquiesced in the proposed improvements. "Play me that beautiful part of the Messiah, and sing the words, 'Comfort ye, comfort ye, my people.' "

Honour sat down to the piano, and played the piece which her mother had asked for. She sang for some time, then suddenly ceasing, put her hands before her face and wept.

"My child! my Honour! my darling! what is amiss?" exclaimed Mrs. Mildmay, starting from the sofa. Honour rose, wiped her eyes, re-seated with gentle violence her mother, wrapped her again in the shawl, and then drawing a low seat, sate down by her side and took her hand tenderly.

"Do tell me, my Honour, what is amiss with you?" said poor Mrs. Mildmay, really distressed.

"Oh, I don't know; it is very foolish!" said Honour, "but I can not help it!" and dropping her head to the sofa where her mother lay, again she wept passionately.

Presently, however, she commanded her feelings, and said, "there is something in that beautiful piece of music which is very affecting to me. I played it so many times to Mr. Elworthy; and someway, dearest mother, every thing seems so changed here now. You are ill, and then there is all this unhappiness about poor Mr. Derwent, and all the trouble and misery which I have caused him; and I can not help thinking, but that that meddling Mrs. Dutton has said something to prejudice Mr. Elworthy against us. I feel sure of it! he never comes to the school now. The whole place, every thing, seems so changed now," said she with a deep sigh, "I even feel changed myself; my feelings about the school are changed; and it is such a miserable thing to lose confidence in ourselves! I used to think that I could do so much good by means of the school. I loved every little child in it, and I felt such great interest in many of the parents, even some of the very poorest and most neglected. But someway, as I said, every thing seems to have been delusion; as if I had been only deceiving myself with the idea of doing great things; and God, perhaps, to punish me, or to set me right, shows me that I can not; that indeed I have done mischief rather than good! Oh, these thoughts make me very unhappy, and I do not know even whether we ought to stay here; but then where are we to go? I pray earnestly that God will guide us right! and I am sure," continued she, "as I sat in church this morning—it was poor Mr. Derwent's turn to preach, and some stranger officiated for the time—and I felt that it was I who had driven him away from a wide field of such great usefulness, and where every body loved him, I felt humbled and ashamed;

but when I saw Mr. Elworthy so cold and stern, walk past me and the children, as though he too was angry, as most likely he is, into his pew, it quite went to my heart, and I thought that certainly I could not stay here, that I ought not to stay here!"

She paused; an expression of the deepest trouble was on her countenance, and in her large and now tearless eyes. Her mother pressed the hand which she still held with the tenderest affection; she looked down, as it were, into the very depths of her daughter's soul, and read there the secret which she had half suspected; there was the deepest, the most affectionate sympathy in her voice as she now spoke, but she spoke cheerfully.

"My darling," she said, "this is all a very natural reaction of feeling. You are over-fatigued, both mind and body; you have had a great trial to bear; you have suffered almost as much perhaps as Mr. Derwent, though in a different way; but that will pass over, and on his part, he is too conscientious, he knows his duty too well to himself and others, to sacrifice every thing to an unrequited attachment; he will rise from his depression perhaps a better man, and certainly with as many elements of happiness and usefulness within himself as ever; and as for you—thank heaven! that you have the Christmas-holidays just at hand; the relaxation and repose that they will afford you will restore all your interest in the school. As to Mr. Elworthy, whatever Mrs. Dutton may have done or said to prejudice him against us, I have too much faith in the uprightness and justice of his character to believe that any prejudice can ultimately influence him. Mrs. Dutton is a mischievous, match-making woman, and whatever she has said and done has, we know, had reference to Mr. Derwent, whom, as you remember, she was determined that you should marry. Her interference terminated the whole affair, that is all. Neither Mr. Elworthy, nor any one else, would blame you for refusing a man whom you could not love; the case is simply that."

The calm way in which her mother looked at these things reassured Honour greatly.

"Poor fellow!" she said, speaking of Mr. Derwent, "he left Wayland-dale yesterday—the children told me so. The last two days he spent at the Hall. Mr. Elworthy sent the carriage for him on Thursday. I am glad he was at the Hall, he liked Mr. Elworthy so much, they were such good friends, and he would be much more comfortable there than at his own cottage. Mrs. Hawes would take such great care of him, I am sure," said she, smiling; "and I dare say he and Mr. Elworthy would have beautiful conversations together! Oh! it seems so strange to me," continued Honour, again speaking in a voice of the deepest feeling, "to think of all the pain and trouble I have occasioned to that good young man, and every thing has come about so quickly, and has produced such a change in every body—every body but that good Christie o' Lily-garth. I saw him to-day as I came from church, and stopped to speak to him. It did me good to hear his strong, cordial voice, speaking a kind and respectful greeting out of that brave, stout heart of his. If ever I were in trouble and wanted aid or counsel from any one, I would ask it from Christie, rather than from any one else in the Dale, and I am sure he would give sound counsel and good aid, too."

Thus the mother and daughter sat and talked; they talked long of the past, and of the present, and of what the future might have in store for them, and through all was mingled a trust in God and a cheerful hope even in life, spite of the many sorrows and the many trials which it presented.

"But now we will have a little consolation from the great consoler himself," said Mrs. Mildmay, after that long conversation which had seemed to cement their hearts still closer to each other. "Read the Sermon on the Mount, as it is given in St. Matthew, and the two following chapters, for in them are wonderful things —the divinest wisdom and the profoundest philosophy."

Honour read, then closed the book and they sat for a while in deep silence, the blessed influence of those holy words having descended into their hearts.

The following day Mr. Elworthy called at the school. He rode down, and his groom held his horse while he staid. There was a degree of constraint in the manners both of Honour and himself, and he was very grave, though kind. He remarked that she did not look well, and regretted to hear of the prolonged in disposition of Mrs. Mildmay. He said that he had heard from Christie o' Lily-garth that Honour was not well, and he feared that the confinement of the school was too much for her. He did not, however, tell her what Christie had added as a probable surmise; he said "he feared that she had something on her mind; ma'ppen she was troubled for poor Mr. Derwent's sake, or ma'ppen it was for somebody else—there was no saying; only this was sure, her looks were not so lightsome as they were when she first came into these parts." Of this Mr. Elworthy said nothing. Ostensibly he had come to the school merely in consequence of Christie's information regarding the state of her health, and he now strongly urged upon her to break up the school a week earlier than had been proposed for the Christmas holidays, that she might the sooner be able to recruit her strength.

A few days afterward, on the first half-holiday, in fact, he called at the cottage to inquire after Mrs. Mildmay. The clear frosty weather continued, and Mrs. Mildmay was better; the cold, slant rays of the December sun were shining into the little parlor as he entered; Honour was at her needlework, and her mother was reading aloud. He had not been in the house since that eventful evening when the party had returned from Ellerdale. Again there was an evident constraint, and he addressed himself alone to Mrs. Mildmay, glancing, from time to time, at Honour grave looks of keen scrutiny, as he had done on the first evening of their meeting in the porch at Lily-garth.

Mrs. Mildmay was perfectly at her ease; she inquired after Mrs. Dutton, andr eceived satisfactory intelligence of her arrival at home and present health; she was very deep, he said, in marriage-preparations, which was an occupation greatly to her taste. There was nothing either bitter or angry in his manner of speaking of her, but the grave, searching expression of his eye as he turned it upon Honour, when he said these words, made her instantly cast down hers. Good Mrs. Mildmay, who saw nothing of this, ventured now to ask after Mr. Derwent, and Honour listened with breathless anxiety, without daring to look toward him, as he replied that Mr. Derwent was better; that he had himself taken him a couple of stages on his journey; that he had heard from him since his arrival at Durham, where he was staying with his uncle, and where he would probably remain till the spring, when he talked of making a tour into the North of Europe. "I have advised him to do so," said Mr. Elworthy, as though he were speaking of a stranger, for his wish was to convey pleasant intelligence to Honour, and to set her mind at ease, which was best done in this way: "the journey is one which he will greatly enjoy," said he; "and his present Scandinavian studies, to which he will devote himself with double energy this winter, will enable him to turn it to still greater advantage. On his return, it is probable that the living which his uncle has in store for him may be vacant; all, therefore, promises extremely well for him." Mr. Elworthy then said, that he was intrusted with messages of unfeigned respect from him to his friends at the cottage.

A deep silence ensued; and Honour, whose feelings were deeply excited, left the room. When she returned he was gone.

Although the December sun had set, and the chill dusk of evening began to gloom the earth, and even to penetrate into the little parlor, Honour felt unusually cheerful. A load was taken off her heart as regarded Mr. Derwent. She sang to her mother in the evening like a warbling bird.

"I have not heard you sing so well for these many months," said her mother, and then sank into a long train of thought, which at that time, she did not communicate to her daughter.

Honour played and sang, as though she would never weary; as though she would thus give utterance to an inexpressible joy in her own soul, and her mother mused still on many things with a growing hope and unqualified satisfaction.

The conversations which Mr. Elworthy had with Mr. Derwent during the two days that he spent in his company, had not only rendered Mrs. Dutton's assertions nugatory with respect to Honour, but had also substantially shaken his faith in his sister-in-law's truth and honor. Little, indeed had she calculated the effect either of the letter or of her interference. Her interference had hastened the catastrophe which she would have wished in every way to prevent, and the effect of her letter was more injurious to herself than to any one else. Nay, indeed, as far as Honour and her mother were concerned, it created a reaction in their favor, and Mr. Elworthy, who was as just as he was generous and warm-hearted, independently of his own private feelings, became impatient to retrieve the wrong which he had done to these excellent women, even by a momentary thought. But the principal agent in it all was Mr. Derwent himself.

"Elworthy," said he, on the morning of their separation, and while they were together in the carriage, "I can not part with you without congratulating you on your good fortune. Miss Mildmay loves you; I have thought so long—*feared* it, I might more justly say. She is the very wife for you. God has sent her here for that purpose; and pardon me, my friend, if I seem to have been a spy upon your secret feelings; but if I am not greatly mistaken, you also love her—have loved her long. I saw it directly—lovers' eyes are very keen and jealous, and many a time has this conviction made my heart die within me, for I knew which of us must be preferred. I believe I mentioned my suspicions of your preference for her to Mrs. Dutton, when she wished to persuade me that I was more fortunate than I believed myself to be. God knows how precious is Miss Mildmay's happiness to my soul, although mine is shipwrecked, and therefore, I will not part from you until

I have urged upon you to unite your fate to that of this noble, this inestimable girl. Your property must not descend unworthily—as it will, unless you marry. There is not one of your good dales-people—there is no one who knows you, far or near, who is not selfishly interested in your remaining unmarried, who would not rejoice that you should marry. People may talk of money; but what do you want with money?—you have more than enough; you want the noble wife to use it with you, to aid and carry out your good and beautiful plans for the aid and well-being of the people around you; you want a pure-minded, enlightened, and affectionate mother for the children who shall come after you. All this is very important to you; and she is the woman who would be all this, who would nobly grace you house and your name.

"Can I, my dear sir," continued he, speaking with a degree of enthusiasm which had sustained him through this parting trial, "can I give you a higher proof of my esteem and admiration for yourself, than by counseling you thus, or can I give a higher proof of my regard for her than by the same thing?—I can not! Some time or other, you can tell her of these, my farewell words to you, my earnest advice—but you need no advising; your own heart is your truest counselor, and it has advised the same—long before I spoke."

He was silent.

Mr. Elworthy pressed his hand. "God bless you, my dear fellow!" said he, "let no one say that the race of martyrs is at an end. This is true heroism. I know none greater. She shall know it, and we will both of us love you and bless you."

CHAPTER XII.

The children had holiday. It was now near Christmas, at which time the Dale would be full of festivity. As if in accordance with the spirit of the season the earth and the sky were bright and pure ; snow covered the Dale and the brown Fells ; the sun shone brilliantly by day, and a young moon, with all her myriad stars, by night, as if on purpose to light the social dalespeople from house to house, as they would progress in their great merry-making parties through the twelve nights of Christmas. For some time past, Honour and her mother had been invited to one of these old-fashioned social gatherings at Lily-garth, on the Saturday after Christmas-day, which fell this year on a Thursday, Mrs. Mildmay was to go there during the day, if she were well enough ; and warm rooms, and large fires, and a hearty welcome, insured her every comfort when she was once there, more especially as she was to remain all night. This invitation was of long standing, and Mr. Derwent himself had been included in it ; but things were strangely altered since then ; nevertheless Christie would not hear of the party being given up.

"We must show them as much kindness as we can ; we must try to make their lives pleasant among us," said he, "so I've a great mind to ask the squire to come too ; he likes a merry-making as well as any body, and as it's Saturday night, folks won't stay late. But I'm sorry for my poor lass, though, and young Broadbent, but I won't have him coming after her at present, as I've told him. They are both but young; in two or three years they'll know their own minds better !"

So the pretty Agnes, in the midst of the general joy, cried, because young Broadbent was not to be invited to Lily-garth ; and never did she feel so great an inclination as now to do as her lover prayed her—marry him as soon as he came of age, in spite of every body and set off with him and his twelve hundred pounds to America.

Two days before Christmas-day, Mrs. Hawes came down from the Hall in the covered market-cart, bringing with her a bountiful Christmas present of good cheer, which would supply the larder for many a day, and the cellar for twelve months at least. She also presented a note from Mr. Elworthy, containing an invitation for Honour and her mother to spend the twelve days of Christmas at the Hall; some other of his friends, both ladies and gentlemen, mostly from a distance, being also invited. They accepted this invitation with pleasure. It was a bright day in every sense, as bright and genial outwardly as a winter day could be; and Honour, now wholly released from her school duties, wrapped herself in furs and velvet, and went out for a walk.

She passed the church-yard and saw, as she had often before done, the white marble tomb of Mrs. Elworthy. She walked slowly as she read the inscription, though this was not the first time. She read :—" Sacred to the memory of Ellinor, the beloved wife of William Elworthy, of Wast-Hall, in this parish, who died 17th of September, 18—, aged 28 years; and also of William, the infant son of the above, who died 26th April, 18—, aged seven months."

The remainder of the tablet was uninscribed. It would only be filled up when the husband and father slept with his beloved ones.

While she thus lingered for a moment, she was joined by Mr. Elworthy himself. He made no remark as to what she had been looking at, but simply said, that if she were intending to walk, he should like to be her companion.

They left the church-yard, and crossing the bridge, took the road which led them over the Lower Fells toward Ellerdale, where as yet Honour had never been. As they were, however, now on foot, they could not do more than gain a distant view into this fine valley from the high and open ridge of the Lower Fells.

There was something, either in the pure bright winter air, or in Honour's own feelings, which gave an unusual elasticity to her steps, and wonderful brightness to her eyes, as she thus walked by the side of Mr. Elworthy. Both were silent, but to her the silence was agreeable. A deep peace, as regarded the past, had settled down upon her soul; she could now bear to think and even to speak of Mr. Derwent; she remembered him only as the friend who had suffered manfully for her; as one who had bravely combated through one of the great conflicts of life, and had gained the hardest victory—the victory over himself. Such conquerors win the true palms of life. Honour knew this, and she rejoiced for him, though she had suffered with him.

Thus she thought of him as she walked by Elworthy's side, and something akin to that old happy feeling filled her soul, which had caused her to rejoice when they first drove into the Dale, amid the sounds and scents of the summer-night, with the woodlarks singing round them, and the village chimes uttering a holy, melodious welcome.

"Yonder, where those oak-woods stretch darkly to the right, is Oakenshaw," said Mr. Elworthy, as they stood on the hill-top together, looking far beyond into Ellerdale, which now lay brilliantly white in the sun-lighted snow. "You can not see the house, but it is a small, dark-red brick house, built in very good style, with a great number of picturesque windows, which catch the sunset in a most extraordinary manner. I have bought Oakenshaw, and there is none of my property that pleases me so well as this purchase. I was fond of the place as a boy; an old, very distant relative, lived there at that time, and I spent many happy months of my boyhood there. My father expected the property would have been left to him, but it was left to his brother, who soon ran through it. It passed into various hands since then, and has had no regular occupant of late, so that it has fallen into neglect. But nothing could injure the beauty of its situation, and its own intrinsic and peculiar character as a house. When spring comes, we must go over to see it!" All this he said in the most natural manner as if he already associated Honour with him as co-proprietor of Oakenshaw.

They turned their faces homeward. Mr. Elworthy said something about the bright expression of Honour's countenance that morning, and the freedom of her step.

"There is a delicious influence," replied she, blushing still more deeply, "in a day like this; and besides the free, solitary spirit that seems to belong to these hill-tops, always does me good. I think the air here is very pure and invigorating, more so than in the south. I shall never forget," continued she, with animation, "the first evening when we drove into the Dale. All seemed so calm and delicious, so filled with a pure and happy life: it was the strangest effect; and I, who was not wholly well at that time, felt it deeply. Someway, it seemed as if we had left all our old sorrows and anxieties behind us in the busy world; as if in approaching this region we had passed by that cross which Christian found on his journey, and that in our case, as in his, the burden had dropped off at its foot. And then the next morning, when, because I could not sleep, I rose early, almost as early as the lark, and saw a silvery vail of mist lifted up from the valley, which lay before me so beautiful, so calm, and fresh! how happy I felt, and with so strange a happiness, I could not help praising God for it, and praying that he would make my life useful amid such heavenly scenes! But," continued Honour, "something must be deducted from this, perhaps, for the enthusiasm which mere novelty creates. Feelings of so exalted a character, are not the best for us. God sends the storm and cloud as well as the sunshine; how else could we enjoy the sunshine as we ought? And there is a grand, an immortal influence for good," continued she, after a pause, "even in battling with the storm. The oak-tree has strength for a thousand tempests, and the human soul is brought nearer to the godlike the severer the conflict through which it passes."

Honour was silent. She had spoken aloud some of her most inner thoughts; she had spoken as of old, in the old, cordial, confiding voice, every tone of which vibrated to Elworthy's heart; but since the times of that former familiar intercourse, though so few words and of such meagre intelligence had been exchanged between them, events had occurred which had drawn them closer than ever to each other. Her words had reference to this, and so he understood them.

He looked at her as she walked thoughtfully by his side, filled with youthful grace and strength—strength of mind as well as body—and he recalled the words she had just spoken. "I prayed God that he would make my life useful amid such heavenly scenes!" He recalled, also, the parting words of poor Derwent, not one of which was without its effect. Then a strange sort of waking dream passed over his soul, like a mysterious intelligence. It seemed to him as though he had known and loved Honour for years—as though the time had never been when he had not known and loved her—as though she were, in some incomprehensible manner, his dead wife restored to him. It was but for a moment, and then he seemed to wake from it into a still clearer knowledge of his own heart. He knew it well; he loved Honour with a deep, unutterable affection, even as he had loved his former wife; and a sincere joy filled his whole being, and that deep peace, which always accompanies the acknowledgement of truth, sunk down upon his soul.

Honour and her mother passed the Christmas week at the Hall, with a number of other guests. It was a formal rather than a familiar visit; Mrs. Mildmay still continued an invalid, and this circumstance, together with the number of visitors who were at the Hall, disappointed Christie and Nelly Fothergill of their company at the less ambitious Saturday-evening party at Lily-garth.

There was a deal of cheerful, seasonable occupation for the visitors at Wast-Hall—for the gentlemen, skating on Wast-water, shooting on the hills, or riding and driving for all, into some of the beautiful, though now wintry scenes of the neighborhood. Mr. Elworthy was the best of hosts; the ladies were delighted with him, and yet wondered why none of the Duttons were of the party. They had not been invited. Honour took a high place among the guests; for though but the poor schoolmistress of the Dale, her beauty, her great natural talents, as well as her many accomplishments, made her necessary for the general entertainment, while the tone of high breeding about her, and the unpretending simplicity of her manners, caused no one to be offended by her admission into their society.

Mr. Elworthy secretly prided himself upon her presence among them. He rejoiced to see her, humble school-mistress though she was, in universal request; and he delighted to hear her praise spoken by all. Yet no one of the guests suspected his love for her. There was, in fact, a constant succession of guests going and coming; few, if any, remaining there through the whole week, so that none had very much time to become censorious critics. Every one left speaking in her praise; one or two gentlemen were suspected of having lost their hearts, and not a few of the ladies said, that if Mr. Elworthy were at all likely to marry again, this Miss Mildmay was just the right person for him; but, of course he never would! they were quite sure of that! but if he did, what *would* the Duttons say!

The Christmas gayeties and the Christmas holidays were over, and Honour and her mother returned to the cottage. The day before the school recommenced, Honour went to Lily-garth to inquire after poor Nelly Fothergill, who, having fallen down on the ice in the back-yard, on the very Saturday evening, as she was fetching a bowl of cream out of the dairy, for the use of her guests, had been laid up, poor woman, ever since. On Honour's return she was overtaken by Mr. Elworthy, who joined her. It was a dull afternoon; the frost was going, and a leaden cloud hung over the Dale, resting, as it were, on the Fell-head, on either side, and threatening to fall later in the day in heavy snow.

"This is a very different day," said Mr. Elworthy, addressing her in a low, earnest voice, "to the one when we stood together on the Lower Fell, looking toward Ellerdale. I know that you admit the wonderful similarity that there often is between the outward and the inward. My life, then, for many years resembled this valley, beneath the leaden sky, which seems to shut it in between barren, bleak fells; but the sun as you know, will dispel these clouds from the valley, and clothe the fells with verdure. There is, also, a sunny influence, a spirit, like the spirit of spring itself, which can produce a similar change in me, which has already even done so in part."

He gazed into her face, into her clear, truthful eyes, and continued:

"Comparatively speaking, I am old; I am considered so by some, I believe; it is true that my youth, and the spirit of my youth has long been past. I have had sorrows more than you know of, and these blighted my youth. But, of course, you never knew me then; never knew me other than I am. You have seen me under the gray, leaden cloud; grave, earnest, and perhaps severe. But I have flattered myself that the sun may yet dissipate the gray cloud, and that I may yet be happy—happy as I have ever coveted to be, in the power of making others happy. Will the sun wholly dissipate the cloud; tell me, Honour?" said he, addressing her thus familiarly, for the first time, and yet with a voice low and solemn. "Tell me, Honour—for you are the sun that can alone brighten the path of my declining life? Honour," continued he, as if he loved to repeat the name; "you know something of me; you know, at all events, what my views are, my wishes, and the purposes of my life. Will you aid them effectually—more than you otherwise can do? Will you become my wife? Will you permit God thus to accomplish your prayer, by spending your life, as my wife, among my poor dales-people?"

The crimson glow which had suffused the countenance of Honour at the commencement of this address was now gone, and the marble paleness of intense feeling had taken its place. She stopped; they stood face to face, and his fine deeply-marked countenance was pale and earnest as her own.

"I will!" said she, with perfect simplicity and truth, giving her hand at the same time, while tears filled her eyes, and again a crimson blush overspread her face.

"May God Almighty bless you!" said he, with more passion than was common to him, "and enable me to make you as happy as you deserve!"

He would have sealed this prayer with a kiss, but at that moment a female form appeared in sight. She was walking rapidly, wrapped in a large plaid shawl, and her old black silk gown, now very shabby, was draggled in the mire of the road. She started at the sight of Mr. Elworthy, for she knew him, and would have turned back, but that she was perceived. Agitated as she was by meeting Mr. Elworthy at that moment face to face, she stood and gazed at him from head to foot, and then at Honour, with such a peculiar expression as riveted at once the attention of Mr. Elworthy. It was Isabel Garr, sent hither out of Swale-dale, as we shall afterward relate, to ascertain for Richard Elworthy whether it was really true, as he had heard, that his relative was about to be married.

Mr. Elworthy knew that it was Isabel; but he was then too happy for the unexpected sight of her to cause him any disturbance.

It was not generally known in Wayland-dale for three months, that Mr. Elworthy was to marry Honour Mildmay. Christie o' Lily-garth was the first that knew of it, and it afforded him and his family the greatest satisfaction. Christie had said, times without end, to his wife, that if the squire married again it would be to Miss Mildmay.

The first thing that gave the dales-people an idea of some change being at hand, was that Mrs. Hawes told somebody that the Hall would be finished this summer. Some people thought that Mrs. Dutton was coming down to live there; some said that it was Squire Cartwright and his lady; but these surmises pleased nobody.

At length the truth came out. The squire was going to be married to Honour Mildmay, and they were to be married on May-day!

Mr. Elworthy was impatient for the marriage to take place. He said, and justly, that they knew each other well, although they had been strangers to each other till within twelve months. But his life was wearing on, he said, and he had no time to lose, therefore he would not have their union deferred.

Honour knew that this unlooked-for marriage would be displeasing to Mrs. Dutton and her family. She would not therefore be satisfied until she obtained a promise from Mr. Elworthy, that her introduction into the family should not utterly destroy every hope of advantage from the Wayland-dale property which the Duttons had so long cherished and confidently built upon. Mrs. Dutton's annuity, she insisted, should be still continued, and the daughters well remembered in his will.

The promise was made to her. A handsome settlement was fixed upon herself, and Mr. Wilbraham, who paid a visit at this time to both parties, being again on the northern circuit, was consulted by Mr. Elworthy on these matters, and ultimately made one of Honour's trustees under the new will.

It was in consequence of these monetary arrangements that Honour learned, for the first time, the name of Ellinor Dutton's intended husband. The discovery was one of painful astonishment, and the true history of her former engagement to Mr. Horrocks was now made known to Mr. Elworthy. In Horrocks, Mr. Elworthy recognized the authority for Mrs. Dutton's malicious accusations against Honour; "She will be nobly avenged!" said he, "for fortune, if no higher power, has made her the unconscious agent in defeating his selfish ambition!"

It was a curious question now, whether Mrs. Dutton knew of her intended son-in-law's former engagement to Honour: and it was decided as the wisest and best, to act as if no such knowledge existed. Mr. Elworthy had a secret pleasure in the singular position of all parties.

When all these business arrangements preparatory to the marriage were made, Mr. Elworthy resolved to write to Mrs. Dutton, announcing to her, as a matter of form, his intended marriage with Miss Mildmay.

Every thing, in the mean time, had gone on remarkably smoothly at Woodbury. Frederick Horrocks had taken a house and furnished it handsomely; his mother-in-law elect having nearly as much voice in the selection of furniture and other things as the young bride herself. His sister had come from Northbridge to direct the new arrangements, and was to remain over the marriage, and she having been duly instructed by her brother, confirmed all that Mrs. Dutton had already heard from him relative to Honour Mildmay.

Mrs. Dutton wrote a second letter to Mr. Elworthy on the strength of this new ally; but, to her surprise, received no answer. She persuaded herself that as he was the very worst of correspondents, there was no cause of alarm. She had, besides great confidence in her powers of diplomacy, and she doubted not, but that by keeping his suspicions alive, all would be safe, until after her daughter's marriage, when she would at once, without waiting for invitation, go to Wayland-dale,and there make herself not only so agreeable, but so useful, that she should be sure of a welcome for an indefinite term; and then she determined that it should go hard with her, if Honour Mildmay was not dismissed on one plea or another.

In the midst of these schemes and plans, when nothing was talked of or thought of in her family, but the approaching nuptials, the terrible letter from Mr. Elworthy arrived. Mrs. Dutton was sitting in her dressing-room, before a table covered with ribbon and lace, with her milliner, the most gossiping woman in Woodbury, who was preparing a wedding-cap for her, when the servant entered with this letter.

"From my brother-in-law—Elworthy," observed she, taking it, and slowly breaking it open, while she said, "I told you Miss Wadhams, I think, of Mr. Elworthy's handsome present to Ellinor; he is the most generous creature in the world. I hope this letter is to say, he is coming to the wedding, as we wish him to do, for he was always extremely fond of Ellinor."

She said no more, for her eye had already caught a few terrible words. She read it through without fainting, without hysterics—without evincing any outward sign of the pang of rage, and of the consternation which it occasioned. She read it a second time, not because she had failed in understanding it the first, but because she could not help it. She was fascinated by it, as the bird is said to be fascinated by the snake; and as the bird falls dead into the serpent's jaws without any outward sign of injury, so seemed it now. Without any outward sign of the terrible death within, Mrs. Dutton sat and talked to the milliner about ribbons and lace; and then, rising calmly, went to her own chamber when, bolting the door, she sat down and gave way to the astonishment—to the indignation—to the agony—to the anguish, like death, which this letter had communicated.

There was then an end of all her hopes—of all her daughters' prospects! At first she thought of keeping no terms, but of shouting forth, as it were, the injury which she and her children were about to sustain, through an interloping woman, whose character she believed she had the power of ruining forever. This was her first impulse; her second was to conceal the tidings from every living soul, at least until after Ellinor's marriage, which otherwise it might fatally interfere with. And, besides, a faint hope whispered to her that perhaps, after all, he might not marry. Marriages, which appeared settled, often did not take place. The old bitter hatred arose tenfold in her heart toward Honour, and she again determined to prevent the marriage, if possible, at any cost.

Accordingly while keeping this terrible secret within her own breast, and acting the hypocrite to all the world; talking almost more than ever of her dear, kind brother Elworthy, and his great affection for her daughters, she wrote to him such a letter as her excited and really wounded heart dictated.

She upbraided him with the desertion of those who had been as children to his former wife, and who had looked up to him as to a father. She upbraided him with being false to the memory of his former wife; with having deceived herself and her children. She made a formal claim of heirship on their behalf, as if in virtue of some old promise. She drew a touching picture of the effect which his estrangement, through this marriage, would produce upon them all; and then she told how she had hoped to have become useful to him and his good dales-people; she said how much she loved them, and how she intended to have devoted the remainder of her life—as she always understood he had wished—to himself and his works of goodness! She said that she had been willing to make any sacrifice for him, but that he had cruelly deceived her.

Then she altered her tone. She reminded him of what the world would say. That he was no longer young; that there was always a degree of absurdity in an elderly man marrying—but now to marry an adventuress—a person little better than a servant; and one whose character was not faultless, as those who knew her best could testify—would make him ridiculous in the eyes of the world! It was the act, she said, of a man in his dotage!

This was, Mrs. Dutton thought, an irresistible letter. It would shame him, if it did no more; and she wept tears of passion over it.

It was a very busy house, that of Mrs. Dutton. There was such a going and coming in it; there was so much to occupy every body just then, that there was not much time to notice each other's looks. Still one said to another: "How ill and out of spirits mamma seems! Is she ill? Is she cross? Has any body vexed her? Sometimes she was seen weeping, and then the cause was demanded, but she replied petulantly, that she was not well, and that she should be glad when all this bustle was over!

Mr. Elworthy, though Mrs. Dutton called him a bad correspondent, replied instantly to this letter. He entered, however, into no other subject than as regarded Honour's character.

It was, he said, the second time that she had thrown out these insinuations. He would not suffer Miss Mildmay's name to be attacked. What did she mean by calling her an adventuress? by saying that they who knew her best did not esteem her? He demanded an explicit reply.

The letter was one which admitted of no trifling; and Mrs. Dutton, therefore, without taking counsel of any one, not even of her intended son-in-law—wrote to Mrs. Woodley as she had thought of doing before, for, independently of her being the very kind and liberal godmother of Miss Charlotte Horrocks, she had a slight acquaintance with her, having two summers before met her at Cheltenham.

She wrote, requesting immediate information regarding one Miss Mildmay, who, with her mother, had formerly resided at Northbridge, whose character she had understood was not wholly without blame, as related to some gentleman there.

Mrs. Woodley, full of astonishment, showed the letter to Mrs. Walpole, and they called into counsel both Mr. and Mrs. Bellairs. They were all indignant at the contents, but they fancied it could easily be explained. They explained it thus. Mrs. Dutton had heard of the shameful behavior of Frederick Horrocks, her intended son-in-law, to Honour Mildmay, and had charged him with it, and to clear himself he had been base enough to throw blame upon Honour. It was like him, they said, for he was cowardly and false; they had never liked him, and they had always said he was not worthy of Honour, but then it was such a long engagement, having been begun when they were mere children! They said that all the Horrocks were so set up with the prospect of Frederick marrying a great heiress that there was no bearing with them; that, however, might have been excused, but nobody could excuse his throwing blame upon one so pure and good as Honour Mildmay!

Mrs. Woodley wrote back immediately. It was a very civil letter that she wrote; but it said plainly that Honour Mildmay was almost an angel; that there was nobody in Northbridge that was more respected than both she and her mother. That Frederick Horrocks had been engaged to her for many years, ever since she was quite a girl, but that when their misfortunes came he deserted her; and that he would not have dared to have done so if she had had either a father or a brother. Mrs. Woodley then apologized for having spoken thus of a gentleman who was about to be so nearly allied to Mrs. Dutton; but, as Miss Mildmay's character was in question, of course, there could be no standing on ceremony, and the writer was reluctantly compelled to speak these unpleasant truths.

Here was a dreadful blow for poor Mrs. Dutton! Again she was silent. But this time she could not keep up. She confessed that she was ill, and she was confined to her bed for many days.

She made no reply to Mr. Elworthy. She gave up the struggle now as hopeless, and she almost wished she were dead, so terrible seemed the discoveries which were about to be made.

Mr. Beauchamp could not understand the poor lady's malady. He said that it was in the nerves, and that she must have something on her mind. She said that she was much overdone; that she wanted rest, and that then she should soon be better.

How she wished now that Frederick Horrocks had never come to Woodbury; that he had married Honour Mildmay, as he ought to have done, and then she would never have interfered between them and their prospects! The thought of it almost drove her mad.

CHAPTER XIII.

It was very pleasant now up in Wayland-dale. It was the mildest and the most lovely of spring weather. Perhaps east winds had blown and late frosts had nipped some blossom, but our friends noticed it not. The birds sang, as it seemed to them, sweeter and more wildly than ever. The strongly-marked branches of the larger trees were garlanded with tender green; brown catkins swung on the tender twigs of the birch, and the homestead-orchards were white with the snowy blossoms of the pear and the cherry. It was very lovely.

And not only nature, but man seemed full of rejoicing and hope. A happy anticipation filled the hearts of the dales-people, of all such, at least, as wished well to William Elworthy; and very few indeed were there who did not, for he was to be married on May-day, in the old church at Dale-town, to one who was worthy of him—to one whom they all loved, and who loved them—to Honour Mildmay.

This approaching marriage, which would, as we know, cause such consternation to every member of the Dutton family, was, strange to say, without any concert between the parties, fixed to take place only two days before that of Ellinor Dutton, who was to be married on her birth-day, the third of May.

Honour's wedding-day came. It was like the May-day of the poets. The birds sang like mad; thrush against thrush, sky-lark against sky-lark. They seemed to partake of the general joy. The little lambs bounded on the fell; the little river sang of love and happiness as it leaped over the mossy stones that lay in its course, and like the good dales-people, now dressed in holiday attire, it was hastening onward toward the little church, where the happy wedding was to take place.

"May God bless him! May God bless him, and send him a long and happy life with his lady!" were the words that passed many an honest dales-man's lips that morning, as he spoke of the honored bridegroom.

And I wish you could have seen the children—the little lads

and lasses of the Dale, how they came trooping up, all in their best, with baskets on their arms, filled with flowers, which they had been early abroad to gather. It was a pleasant sight to see them with their rosy, happy faces, standing in two lines from the church-door to the church-yard gate, waiting for the bride to come forth. And then when she came, in her simple white dress, with her sweet, modest face, looking so happy, and yet so pale—leaning on him who was now her husband, and her dear old mother and Mr. Wilbraham, and many another friend of the bride and bridegroom beside, and Christie and Nelly o' Lily-garth, and other good dales-people coming after; the little, joyful children threw handfulls of flowers before them, that thus they might walk upon flowers. With that, the bells of the little church burst forth into such a peal of joyful harmony, that the sunny air quivered with it, and it seemed as if there were voices somewhere between heaven and earth, shouting forth an acclamation.

"And what a handsome gentleman th' squire is, after all," said many a dales-woman that day; "I never knowed 'at he were so handsome; he looks quite young, and as likely for life, as e'er a man in th' dale."

"Long life and much happiness to them!" and "may heaven bless th' squire and his lady!" resounded through the valley. The very birds seemed to sing it; the very river to murmur it.

Honour had, as we know, once before driven along the Dale, and been very happy; and now once more, crowned by a surpassing happiness, she drove along—no longer poor and dependent, but the beloved wife of the man to whom the greater part of this lovely valley belonged, and better still, who was the friend and the benefactor of all.

We must now look after another wedding. It was Saturday morning, the third of May, and all the town of Woodbury was astir: for Mr. Horrocks was to be married that day to the pretty Ellinor Dutton.

The Beauchamps were up early, and now the Cartwrights' handsome carriage was at their door. The Cartwrights were already at the Duttons', and had sent their carriage, as had been arranged, to bring the Beauchamps to the house of rejoicing.

"Happy the bride that the sun shines on," said many a gossip; and the sun shone as brilliantly as it had done two mornings before on the wedding in Wayland-dale. The street before Mrs. Dutton's house had been swept and watered, and now three handsome carriages stood at the door to take the bride's party to church, where Horrocks and his friends would meet them in equal style.

Poor Mrs. Dutton! spite of her wedding attire, she looked ill. Every body said so. No one could conjecture what was amiss with her. It was remarked that she had not been cordial for some time toward Frederick Horrocks, and they wondered whether she were dissatisfied with the match, or what *could* be the cause.

Ellinor was splendidly dressed. She had her wedding clothes from London, and her vail, a real Chantilly, was the gift of her sister, Mrs. Cartwright. Mr. Cartwright was to give her away at the altar; for he and Horrocks were at that time great friends.

But now the wedding ceremony is over; the church bells are ringing merrily; the clergyman breakfasts with the bridal party at Mrs. Dutton's so does old Cheatham, and many another friend of the family.

"How ill poor Mrs. Dutton looks!" people could not help saying to each other.

Mr. Venables, one of the friends of the family, was a great politician; his copy of the "Times" was sent down to Mrs. Dutton's for him, for he could not eat even a wedding breakfast without his paper. He glanced at it, his eye was arrested, and then touching Mr. Cheatham on the shoulder, he said, "Cheatham, a word with you."

The two rose and went into another room. Nobody thought it strange at the moment, but Mrs. Dutton, who was alive to every thing, turned pale, felt almost dizzy with apprehension.

Another person was called out, and then Mr. Cartwright; Frederick Horrocks followed, and all the wedding guests were now in excitement.

"For heaven's sake! what is amiss with Mrs. Dutton? she has fainted!" said somebody.

Cartwright came storming in with the "Times" in his hand, and marched up to the fainting lady. "By Jove! we are to have weddings enough," said he. "Here's Mr. Elworthy's marriage in the 'Times!'"

"Not my uncle Elworthy's!" exclaimed the nieces in one breath.

Cartwright read, in a tone of extreme bitterness, "Yesterday, May 1st, at Dale-town, Westmoreland, William Elworthy, Esq., of Wast-Hall, in the same county, to Honour Mildmay, daughter of the late Mark Mildmay, Esq., of Northbridge, Kent."

Frederick Horrocks had seen it already. He said not a word; he stood there as pale as death, and seemed to support himself against the grand wedding breakfast-table. Mrs. Dutton was gone to her own room: there was an end of gayety for the time.

And yet what had happened? A worthy gentleman, to whose property they had only an ideal claim, had married; he had done what Frederick Horrocks had himself done this morning. But he had taken from them neither love, nor life, nor friendship, nor intellect, nor the means of insuring peace of mind—why then did they act as though he had blighted their existence? To see and hear them, you would have thought that he had deprived them of all that made life desirable.

The plan of the wedding trip was now changed, in so far, at least, as concerned their taking Wayland-dale on their return from Scotland. Ellinor was angry and mortified at the strange, down-cast, disordered look of her bridegroom. She wept bitter tears. Mrs. Cartwright came in from her mother's dressing-room, where she had been made the confidante of all that poor lady's long anxieties. She rushed into the room where the young couple sat, he sincerely doing his best to console his bride.

"It is all owing to you, Mr. Horrocks," she said; "and we have nobody but you to thank for it. *You* were engaged to this Miss Mildmay, we now find, and they say that you behaved shamefully to her! She has married Mr. Elworthy on purpose to spite you, and I should be glad of it, were it not that poor Ellinor and all of us must be the sufferers! It is a poor compliment on your wedding morning," said she, in rage which she could not control, "but the worst I wish is that we never had known you. What will Mr. Cartwright say? what will Mr. Cheatham say? what will every body say?" and Mrs. Cartwright cried for vexation.

Frederick Horrocks never forgave this outbreak.

We will pass over what all the worthies of Woodbury said, and the nervous fever of poor Mrs. Dutton, and the terrible discovery that the Cartwrights were in difficulty; that they must retrench or go abroad, "or do something:" and the coldness that ensued between Mr. Cartwright and the Horrocks, and all the domestic unhappiness of poor Mrs. Cartwright, who talked of leaving her husband and insisting on a separate maintenance; only he was so stingy as regarded her that he would not allow enough for her and her children to live upon. The Beauchamps were the only branch of the family that kept up at all. He, however, was gifted with excellent animal spirits, and now professed never to have had much faith in "old Elworthy." His wife, however, still deplored and resented, but only, as she said, on account of her large family—she was one of those good women whose olive branches increase every year—and for the sake of poor Natalie, who had now no chance of getting married, and had such a dismal prospect before her, with poor mamma and her bad spirits. But they had been shamefully used, there was no doubt of that; and she was inclined to be of Mrs. Cartwright's opinion, that they had nobody to thank but Frederick Horrocks and so she should have told him plainly but for poor Ellinor's sake, for he had a bad temper, and it would not do to say too much to him. So, like her husband, she thought that it was wisest to make the best of a bad bargain, and not to give the wretched people of Woodbury more occasion to talk than they had already.

Mrs. Beauchamp in so doing, showed her good sense, certainly.

CHAPTER XIV.

One day, nearly twelve months after these terrible convulsions in the Dutton family, and when the nine days' wonder in Woodbury had become rather stale, a shabby-looking man in rusty black with a seal-ring on the little finger of a thin white hand, with thin black hair, black whiskers, sallow complexion, sunken eyes, and very white teeth—having altogether the look of a needy gentleman, who had been long put to his shifts, presented himself at the office of Cheatham and Horrocks, solicitors in Woodbury, requesting to see Mr. Horrocks on very important business, and giving at the same time a card on which was neatly engraved the name of Mr. Richard Elworthy Elworthy.

After waiting some time, he was admitted into the private room of Mr. Horrocks. That gentleman received him very coldly, rising as he entered, and planting himself with his back to the fire, and taking at the same time a coat-lap under each arm; with a short, "Sir, I'll thank you for your business, as my time is short," waited for his communication.

An hour afterward, the two were still together. Mr. Horrocks being then seated as well as his visitor, and both leaning toward each other, each with an arm on the table that stood between them. They were evidently engaged on interesting business.

"It is of small consequence to you, or to any of the other branches of the late Mr. Dutton's family," said Richard, "how the will came into my hands. It was, as I have told you, by a mere accident—one of those lucky chances that do occur sometimes. It is enough for you to know, that the will is safe, safe in my hands, and he believes it to be in his own keeping. He will not live long; that heart-complaint will carry him off one of these days; and then the property will fall into my hands; excepting such small portion as the law awards to the widow, I am the direct heir-at-law."

"But there may be children," said Horrocks, "I have heard that there is such a prospect."

"Nothing of the kind!" returned Richard, "I assure you that

you are totally misinformed. I have my friends in the Dale, and the whole events of the family are known to me, and on my honor, I assure you, that there is no danger of this kind. The property is very great; he has lately bought land in Ellerdale, besides the Oakenshaw estate; and all this, together with the Wast-Wayland property, will drop into my hands—every pennyworth of it! nothing can prevent it! Now I have made you an unexampled offer; I have dealt candidly with you, because I consider you to be a man of honor, and have concealed nothing from you. If you will advance to me the trifling sum of money which I have named, I will then enter into such a bond as will secure to you one half of this immense property, which will, I again repeat it, be mine. What do you say now? It is such an offer, let me tell you, as you will never have again."

Horrocks thought so too; nevertheless he replied, "you are, sir, in my power. What prevents me from informing Mr. Elworthy of this, your proposal; from warning him of the loss of the will, and putting him doubly on his guard? I may thus, in the fairest way, find my own advantage."

"You have no witnesses," said Richard, coolly. "I have never committed myself on paper. Besides, what can you gain by advising the preparation of a new will? You sacrifice your only advantage which I offer you, for I know," said he, in a sarcastic tone, "in what estimation Mr. Horrocks is held, both by Mr. and Mrs. Elworthy. There were some old affairs at Northbridge, if I mistake not, which may be remembered no way to your advantage; you'll pardon my freedom," seeing an angry cloud gathering on Horrocks's brow, "but there need be no ceremony between us, and it is as well for you to understand every side of the question. You have therefore, I tell you plainly, no chance with the Wast-Wayland Elworthys, take what step you may. The simple question therefore is, will you, or will you not, accept the offer I make you. It is an offer which does not come to one man in a million. Look at it fairly. If you accept it, you have one half of this fine landed property—property sufficient to maintain a title. If you will not accept it, there are others that will. I have nothing to do but to make the same proposal to Cartwright. *He* will see no obstacles in the way. Nevertheless, I candidly tell you, I prefer dealing with you to Cartwright. You are the surer man of the two, besides which, you have cash, and he has none, and cash I must have. Now, in fine, will you or will you not? I will give you till to-morrow to decide—longer than that I can not wait. And by-the-by, perhaps in the mean time, you can accommodate me with a couple of sovereigns. I am hard up for ready money just now, and for the sake of your wife's family, I wish to get creditably out of Woodbury. I can drop a hint to Mr. George, of the King's Head, where I am staying, that, after all, a good share of the Wast-Wayland property may come to your wife. Mrs. Dutton always gave it out that she was the old gentleman's favorite."

"Not a word of the sort," said Horrocks sternly, for he wished in no case, more especially if he entered into this scheme, that the subject of this property should be again revived in his wife's family. "Not a syllable; call yourself any name but Elworthy; and never dare to breathe a whisper of this subject to living soul, or—by heaven! you shall find yourself in a worse position than you think of."

He gave him a couple of sovereigns, and bade him return at the same hour on the following day.

It is now necessary, that some explanation be given of this strange affair, and to make it altogether intelligible, we must go back somewhat in our story, to the time, in fact, when it was supposed that Richard was gone off with the embezzled property to America, and William Elworthy was, in consequence, summoned to London, as the responsible person.

Although nothing was easier than to prove the unprincipled and utterly-abandoned character of the man into whose hands the unlucky patentee, and his cousin, the baker in Bishopsgate-street, had fallen, and though the forgery upon William Elworthy was clearly substantiated, yet, to prevent the disgrace which must attach to the family name, if the injured parties prosecuted, as they seemed disposed to do, and in the belief that his unworthy relative had left the country, and probably might never return, William Elworthy refunded the money of which they had been robbed, and was laughed at by the lawyers on both sides as a good-natured dupe.

But Richard Elworthy was not gone out of the British dominions. After undergoing various personal alterations, he hastened, as the Whitehaven trader had said, to the Isle of Man, where he already had some acquaintance, and became a frequenter of a well-known gambling-house at Douglas. Richard, who had left London in considerable alarm for his personal safety, intended altogether, to abandon Isabel Garr, fearing also that he must now forever resign any hope of advantage from the Wast-Wayland property. But his cousin's lenity, of which he was speedily informed by associates with whom he was still connected in London, somewhat modified his views; he laughed at his cousin as a dupe, looked on the whole affair as a capital joke, and seemed to see the opening into a new Eldorado.

While poor Isabel Garr was trying to persuade the people of Tod's-gill and Swale-dale that he was a great man, holding a government appointment abroad, his ill-gotten money was spent, and in consequence of debts which he had contracted, as well as foul play at the gambling-table, he was thrown into prison at Douglas. The horrors of this Isle of Man jail had at this time no parallel in England. This was the most rigorous punishment which Richard had ever undergone, and in the midst of it he remembered the poor, faithful, deserted Isabel Garr. To her he wrote, therefore, a letter of penitence, confessing where he was, telling her of his sufferings, and begging a small sum of money, by which to mitigate the severity of his imprisonment.

It was enough for Isabel to know that he was suffering and in want; she sold her fine clothes, therefore, and sent him all the money she could raise, leaving herself almost pennyless. In process of time he was liberated from his miserable imprisonment, but his name was so much damaged, even among his late associates in the island that it was impossible for him to remain there. The walls of Douglas had been placarded, before his imprisonment was generally known, by large bills, offering twenty pounds to any person who, then or thereafter, would enable a certain well-known Colonel Trent to meet Richard Elworthy Elworthy, so that he might administer to him the chastisement of the horsewhip. Such had been the words of the placard, and though many months were now passed, Richard Elworthy, on his liberation, soon found that his stay in the island was neither agreeable nor safe. Accordingly, he left it; and one dreary, January day, foot-sore, emaciated by his long confinement and subsequent want, almost in rags, and yet with his seal-ring on his finger, he made his appearance at Cousin Thomas's door, where he knew that Isabel Garr was to be found.

Isabel was by this time quite established with Cousin Thomas, who, spite of his miserliness, had a real liking for her. She had managed to give a more cheery aspect to the whole place, and even to call forth occasional sparks of humanity from the heart of the hard old man.

On the day when Richard Elworthy made his unexpected appearance, Cousin Thomas was from home: he had set off early in the morning to a considerable distance, to the house of a relative lately deceased, from whose heir he was that day to receive about a hundred and fifty pounds, the amount of a mortgage now paid off, and would return before dusk with the money.

Poor Isabel, who was thus alone, received her prodigal in the spirit of the forgiving father in the gospel. Regardless of what the miser might have said, had he been there, she set before him all that the house contained; she washed his feet on her knees, while he ate and drank; she wept and bemoaned over him. Nothing but affection was in her heart; she uttered not a hard nor a reproachful word; and when he urged her immediately to set off on foot to Dale-town, to ascertain whether it was true, as he had heard, that William Elworthy was about to be married, she did not hesitate further than as regarded his own comfort. But no time was to be lost, she must go and be back before Cousin Thomas's return; therefore, urging Richard to lie down and sleep on the old man's bed in the parlor, she set off, though not before she had given him every farthing of money which she herself possessed.

She had mentioned to him the errand on which the old man was then from home, and the money he would bring back with him, and as Richard lay on the bed in the parlor, wearied but not sleeping, the idea of this hundred and fifty pounds, which, as Isabel had said, would remain but that one night in the house, so great was Cousin Thomas's fear of being robbed, seemed to haunt him; and strange tempting thoughts crowded about his mind like evil demons. He rose; looked at the old oaken desk, now locked, which stood in the chamber; noticed the fastenings of the casement, and thought to himself how easily any one might enter the room from without through the window, more especially if divers little preparations were made beforehand by a person from within. Cousin Thomas's house was the most solitary in Swale-dale; there was not another house within a quarter of a mile; it lay in a hollow, too, and was almost buried by old plum and pear trees. Richard had been struck with this circumstance as he this morning approached it; nor was there a dog about the place. Richard's brain seemed teeming with these ideas and suggestions: he sat down again in the kitchen, on the wooden settle by the good fire that Isabel had made for his comfort, and soon in the warmth and gloom of the confined hearth, dozed heavily. He roused himself, and to him it seemed as if he had been asleep through a long night. He looked at the clock, it was only two; Isabel had hardly been gone a couple of hours.

The old thoughts were again in his brain: he rose up, feeling bodily very stiff and weary, and with a dogged, yet strange agitation of feeling—

"Misers," said he to himself, "hide their money in queer places: in the clock-case perhaps—or in an old tea-pot, or even in their Bibles," and as he thus cogitated, his eye glanced round the room, as if in search of the objects he named. He looked into the clock-case, into various old tea-pots, mugs and jugs, under the cushion on the settle, and on the old man's chair, and finally into the Bible, which lay in its old green baize cover, on a shelf over the door. Leaf after leaf, he turned, not failing to be struck by the circumstance, that it was now years since he had looked into a Bible before. "What are the first words I shall see?" thought he to himself; "it is thus that people sometimes seek for guidance!"

He read, "Lead us not into temptation, but deliver us from evil!" He closed the book, and sat down again on the settle. "It is no use!" said he to himself, after a while, and rose to restore the Bible to its place. "He may have hidden a ten-pound note between the green baize cover and the binding," was suggested to his mind as he lifted the book to replace it. Instead of doing so, he held the two covers of the Bible back, that he might slip one of them out from the baize; there was nothing. Most singularly, however, out from the thus opened leaves, fell a folded paper; he lifted it from the floor. It was a five-pound bill! A thrill of exultation passed through him: the next moment he saw that it was a local note of old date, and of a bank in the north, which he remembered had stopped payment some years before. With a feeling of disappointment that amounted to anger, he put the worthless note again between the pages of the Bible, threw it upon the shelf, and sat down overcome by the Evil One.

It was four o'clock, and getting dusk. He no longer wished to see Isabel; therefore, locking the door and putting the key under the big stone, where he knew she would find it, disappeared from the place.

Isabel returned from Dale-town with the tidings that she had herself seen William Elworthy and the lady he was going to marry, walking and talking together, as lovers only walk and talk, but to her surprise the door was locked and Richard gone. It was all right, however, she thought, for she had no good news for him; and as it was now dusk, Cousin Thomas's return might be looked for every moment; besides, she had given him sufficient money to keep him from absolute want for a little time at least; and she would prepare the old man for his return before he next made his appearance. Not altogether dissatisfied, therefore, and glad to remember that he had eaten and drunk and rested, she made Cousin Thomas's bed, and set every thing in order. She put the pot on the fire, and placed the little round table on the hearth, with the meal tub and porringers ready, that the old man might have his supper as soon as he returned.

It was eight o'clock when he came back, and had been now more than three hours dark; Isabel had become extremely anxious, and had looked out the way he would come, many a time. At length he came; he was quite elated and talkative, for he had been regaled with plenty of good cheer and strong ale, and these unusual potations had called forth, even in him, a great hilarity. As he sat in the blaze of his own fire, his hard old countenance beaming with something like geniality, he laughed and talked as Isabel had never heard him before; and drawing forth his canvas bag of money, told her exultingly that it contained a hundred and fifty-seven pounds; fifty seven sovereigns, five ten pound bills, and ten fives. He wanted to count them out to her, but she would not let him; and as he presently afterward became drowsy, she persuaded him to take his money, lock it up in his desk, and go to bed.

"Ay, wench! ay wench! I will, I will!" said he "and to-morrow I'll tae it to th' bank."

He locked the parlor door upon himself, and Isabel heard his keys jingling as he opened his desk to put away the money. She then heard him get into bed, and knew that he had put out his candle, because the chink under the door became suddenly dark. At a little after nine, she herself went to bed in the chamber over the kitchen where she slept. She could not sleep for two or three hours so much was she still excited by Richard's return; at length she dropped into an uneasy slumber, from which she was suddenly awoke by sounds which at first seemed to her to be a part of a dream. A moment, however, sufficed to convince her that they were not imaginary; they were strange, terrible sounds from below stairs, from the parlor where the old man slept, and at once she concluded that, in his tipsy foolishness, he had probably boasted of the money he was bringing home, and now robbers, perhaps murderers, were in the house.

Hastily, therefore, throwing something on, and with a light, which she had the precaution to put into a lantern, she stole softly down stairs, with all the courage of a true dales-woman, taking the kitchen poker in her hand, and stealing across the kitchen to the parlor, burst open the door, which had been locked over night, and by the light of her own lantern, saw, as she expected, the old man thrown backward on his bed, murdered, as she at that moment believed, and a man rifling the contents of the open desk. The sudden sound of the door bursting open, the dim light, and the figure that rushed in resolutely with the upraised poker in its hand, seemed for a moment to fill the burglar with sudden terror. Grasping the bag containing the money in his hand, he was about to make his escape by the window through which he had entered, when Isabel seized him. She was a powerful woman, naturally, and at this moment seemed filled with super-human strength. She wielded the poker with intent to strike him down, but at that moment his countenance came within the light, and the blow she had intended fell harmless.

"Oh, my God!" groaned she, still keeping hold of him with a grasp like that of an iron vice. He spoke not a word, but ground his teeth.

"Have you killed him?" groaned she out fiercely. "Oh, if he is not dead, leave him his money!" and seizing on the bag struggled violently for it.

The old man, who was not dead, though he had been so sorely mishandled by the thief as to be rendered, for the time, insensible, now somewhat recovering himself, and recognizing Isabel's voice, raised himself slowly from the bed, and, though it was utterly useless, began to scream for help, as though the house had been full of inmates, and neighbors were close at hand.

Isabel's strength was prodigious; the bag was in her hand, when at once a violent blow from the ruffian felled her backward, and he made off with his booty.

She lay bleeding and insensible for some time: when she recovered consciousness, the old man, now partly dressed, ghastly pale, and with patches of blood about his person, was leaning over her with the candle which he had taken from the lantern in his hand. He was crying like a child. She raised herself with a confused remembrance of something dreadful having happened, and feeling very faint and sick.

"T'ou art alive, art ta?" said the old man; "well, thank God! I thought t'ou wert dead; but they've ta'en my money, they've ta'en my money!" and again he cried like a child.

The next morning the news of the robbery spread far and wide, and people came hurrying to learn the particulars and to render what help they could. Intelligence was sent to the district police, and officers came to receive the deposition of the two inmates, both of whom having seen one of the burglars at least, could give important evidence.

Cousin Thomas confessed that he had come home rather merry with liquor, which he was not in the habit of drinking, but he positively denied having spoken to any person on the road respecting the money that he had with him. He had gone to bed early first putting his bag of money into the desk in his bedroom ; he might have left his keys in the lock, but he could not say ; he slept soundly as he always did, but was nevertheless awoke suddenly by somebody entering his room by the window ; there was an iron stanchion in the casement, but by some means this had been loosened. He sprung up and made for the chimney-corner, where he always kept a gun loaded, but in his confusion he could not find it ; he screamed for help, but the thief knocked him down and threatened to murder him if he made any noise ; he was quiet for a minute or two, but when he saw him at the desk he could not keep his peace, and made at him. The thief had no pistols, but he had the iron stanchion out of the window, and with this he knocked him down and beat him on the head ; his face was blackened, he was not sure whether he should know him again, for though he had a light of some sort, he managed to keep himself in the dark ; one thing, however, he could swear to, he was a tall man, and had very black hair. He, the deponent, lay insensible for some time, and when he came to himself, his relation, Mrs. Elworthy, or Isabel Garr, as some people called her, who had broken in the door and came to his aid, was struggling with the thief to save the money, but he knocked her down and then made off. He believed for some time that Isabel was dead ; she looked so, and bled very much from the back of her head. He was greatly distressed, and not knowing what to do, shouted for help through the open window ; but there was no use shouting, for the house lay off the road and had no neighbors ; he took water and sprinkled it on Isabel's face, and at length she came to herself.

Such was the old man's report. Isabel, who appeared to be suffering very much, though the doctor said the hurts she had received were not dangerous, had very little to add to the above ; but in one important particular she differed materially ; she said that the hair of the burglar was of a reddish brown, that he stooped in his shoulders, and had a cast in one eye. She persisted in this;

and as the old man was equally strenuous in his assertion, it was supposed by many that there must have been two persons concerned in the robbery.

All was done by the authorities that was possible in the case; the newspapers reported it far and near; it was the one absorbing subject of conversation in every house in all the surrounding dales. A reward was offered for the apprehension of the burglars, as they were now generally considered, but no positive information was gained; the burglar or burglars were never apprehended.

Never at any time had Cousin Thomas's house been so much visited as now; every body came to see the place and to hear over again the account from the old man's mouth. Isabel was very reserved on the subject; she said that her nerves had received such a shock as she should never get over; and truly it appeared like it, for she was altogether an altered woman.

As Isabel expected, in her own secret heart, she saw no more of Richard Elworthy for the present, and as none of the many people, whom curiosity brought to the place, spoke of having seen him, she was convinced, and in some measure satisfied, that he was gone entirely out of that part of the country.

She became now, according to her best endeavors, a woman of a religious life; she was extremely self-absorbed; worked like a slave for the old man, dug the garden, and even cut peats on the Fell; and this, in fact, became almost necessary; for after the first excitement of his loss was over, it was evident how deep a hold it had taken upon him by his failing health and faculties.

Without any apparent illness, his strength left him, and paralysis commenced, which gradually impaired his mind. He often cried like a child for the loss of his money, and distressed himself by the dread of dying in poverty. As autumn and the lengthened evenings came on, the fearful recollection of the past terrors took strong hold of him. One day he called Isabel, as he was sitting in the sunshine outside the door.

"Isabel," said he, "what is Richard Elworthy doing, that he doesn't come to take care of us? Let him come, wench, let him come! He is thy husband, isn't he—why doesn't he come? He can take care of things, and I've left all to him and thee—I have lass!—all the little that's left I've left to him and thee!"

Isabel was in a great strait. She said at first that she did not know where he was. She thought that the old man, who now maundered over many things, and forgot them again, would forget this—but he did not. "Let Richard Elworthy come and take care of us," he said. "He is thy husband, isn't he? Let him come, for I've left all to him and to thee!"

Isabel went down on her knees before the old man, and confessed what she had hitherto denied, that she was not married to Richard Elworthy. She told him many a sad story of ill usage and desertion; she cried and said that she had no friend but God and him, and that rather than live with Richard Elworthy, she would throw herself into one of the black pools in the beck.

The old man fell into a great rage; he called her many evil names, then cried and said that he should be murdered that winter, having no one to take care of him. Isabel's faithful kindness to him was beyond words, and in proportion as his feebleness increased the hardness of his nature abated, and he acknowledged as an humble child, how greatly he was indebted to her. But with these newly-awakened and better feelings, a new trouble possessed him, which for some time did not become fully intelligible. His mind was often so clouded, that he could not command his ideas; he would sit for hours in a sort of waking stupor; his eyes open and gazing fixedly, but without intelligence, and his large bony hands laid upon his knees rigid and paralyzed. He could not bear Isabel out of his sight, and his feeble cry was now ever about his will. "The will's wrong!" he said, in his hard, unmodulated voice; "I tell thee, it's wrong! It's all thine, wench! —all. But it's wrong!"

Many times in the day were these words repeated, whenever, indeed, the mind had power to raise itself from the lethargy of the body they fell from the sluggish tongue. At length Isabel sent for the lawyer whom she knew he had employed, and the old man, after gazing at him stupidly for a few moments, seemed to make a violent effort to bring together the fragments of his mind. He repeated vehemently that the will was wrong, and that all was to be left to Isabel.

He was right: the will had been made in favor of Richard Elworthy and Isabel his wife, and some little portion had also been left to Dannel o' Tod's-gill; now all was unreservedly bequeathed to Isabel Garr. The old man was wonderfully collected through the whole making of this new will; his paralysis seemed gone for the time; he could lift his hand and command his thoughts. The lawyer could not believe that he was as infirm as Isabel had stated. But the effort was too much for him. That same night he had a second paralytic stroke, which wholly deprived him of speech, and laid him on the bed which he never left until when, more than a year afterward, he was carried to his grave.

After this second paralytic stroke, which occurred in the early spring, Isabel took a relation and his wife to live in the house with her. She had already virtually come into the possession of the old man's property, which was more considerable than was expected. She bought a couple of cows, had a horse and cart of her own, and there was an air of life, and even prosperity, about the place such as it had not known for years. But in herself she was stern and grave, and remarkably taciturn. She rarely entered voluntarily into conversation, gave her orders in a few stern words, and devoted herself with child-like duty to the poor helpless creature who was now dependent upon her for every thing, and to whom she owed so much. Every way Isabel was changed; not a trace of the old London life remained about her. She dressed as a middle-aged dales-woman of the yeoman class, wore a plain cap, a blue linen apron, and a stuff gown. No one could have recognized her as the wild Isabel Garr o' Tod's-gill, and still less as the so-called Mrs. Richard Elworthy of London.

William Elworthy, of Wast Hall, had now been married about twelve months. Isabel had not interested herself in this marriage, nor did she now seek to know any news regarding any of the Wayland-dale people.

One day, during the spring, when she came out of the parlor where she had been attending the old man, she was startled by the sight of Richard Elworthy, with his usual genteel mendicant-air standing in the kitchen. He asked her for money, in a bland, gentlemanly voice, as he would have asked it from a stranger. She closed the door, and then standing sternly before him, she replied, that for one moment only she would speak to him and no more; and then, recalling to his mind the awful time when she had last seen him under that roof, she took down the Bible from the shelf above the door, that Bible which he so well remembered, and solemnly swore upon it, that if he remained longer in the house, or returned to it again, she would give him into the hands of justice. "I saved you," said she, sternly, "alone by a lie! Had you taken the old man's life, I would have appeared against you; as it was, you took his money and I helped you to escape! I owe you nothing more, Richard Elworthy, and I thank God now," said she, with fierce exultation, "that you never married me! Villain that you were to me—cowardly villain, I have you now in my power, and I will rid myself of you—or crush you!"

Having delivered herself of these words, spoken in a low but determined voice, she opened the door wide, and let in a gush of sunshine.

"There are people about the place who shall hear what more is to be said between us!" she exclaimed. "It is not now unprotected as it was; I have a fierce dog in the yard, a man-servant in the house at night, and a brace of pistols loaded, which I can use!"

Richard Elworthy stood pale before her; he had retreated a few steps—he then paused; spoke in a low and humble voice of his poverty, and said that he had not broken his fast that day—would she not give him a morsel of bread?

She was hard as iron. No! she said, she would neither give him to eat nor to drink. She had fed him, and warmed him, and washed his feet, and given to him her last penny once before under that roof, and gone out to do his bidding, and what had been her reward? No, no, she repeated, she owed him nothing now; her heart had grown hard since then, and it should remain so; and that if he lay dying at her feet, at that moment, and a drop of water from her hand would save him, she would not give it!

She went out into the yard, called the man from the cow-house, and Richard, not knowing what her intention might be, walked leisurely away.

She watched him as he went slowly up the Fell, where there was no regular path, and not a spark of pity or shadow of tenderness remained in her soul toward him, "I am one of the old Garrs," said she to herself, with hard resolution, "who never forgive!"

He sat down on the Fell-head within sight of the house, as if in very bravado, and there he remained for the greater part of the day. The Fell was solitary; not a soul might pass that way for days; and there he sat, distinctly visible from the kitchen windows, from the very door by which she had expelled him. At noon he was there; all through the afternoon; at sunset he was there. Isabel was haunted by the consciousness of his near presence; not a single half hour passed but she looked out to see if he still remained; she felt the dogged malice that was in his soul, and she hated him fiercely. At length he was gone; which way she knew not, for she had not seen him depart, and that was a source of dissatisfaction to her.

The following day brings us to that strange event, which enabled the penniless mendicant, Richard Elworthy, to stand as the tempter of the junior partner in the respectable firm of Cheatham and Horrocks, solicitors, Woodbury. As he sat on the Fell-head in the sunshine, all that summer's day, a nuisance and a torment, as he knew he should be to Isabel, he took counsel with himself what was best for him to do in the present difficult state of his affairs. It was true, as he had told Isabel, that he was penniless, that he had eaten nothing that day and had no prospect but to die by the road-side.

He turned over twenty schemes; he was a man of wonderful resources, and was wont to boast that when once at the bottom of Fortune's wheel, she always lifted him up again. In the present emergency, therefore, he determined to apply to his relative, William Elworthy, whose kindness and forbearance had so often been proved.

Two roads lead from Swale-dale into Wayland-dale. The shorter, which, in fact, is only a foot-road, leads over the Fells, and falls into the high road of the valley somewhat below Lily-garth, so that a person coming in this direction to Wast-Hall would be, for some time, within sight of the house and grounds before he reached it. The other, which is the high-road, makes a circuit through the wild district at the back of Hibblethwaite, and then joins that very road by which Mrs. and Miss Mildmay first entered the valley. Considerable sycamore plantations, through which the road runs, shroud the lower base of Hibblethwaite; and here the traveler passes the court-yard of the Hall, by the gates of which he may arrive at the house quite unnoticed; or, going onward about fifty yards, he may enter by a small gate, which leads likewise to the back, or rather side, of the house, through thick shrubbery.

Wast-Hall and its approaches were as familiar to Richard Elworthy as to the proprietor himself: therefore, on the day succeeding the one on which he had his interview with Isabel Garr, we must see him under a July sun, and at about four o'clock in the afternoon, advancing toward Wayland-dale by the high road, and then, having walked under the cool shade of the sycamores for some little time, entering the premises of the Hall itself; not by the court-yard, where he expected to encounter grooms and other men-servants, but by the more retired shrubbery-walk, which would enable him, as he well knew, to reach a side-door which opened into a lobby leading to the very centre of the house. He chose this entrance because he knew that he could, when this door was once opened to him, make his way directly to the library, where he doubted not but he should find his cousin, and thus, forcing his way to his presence, should, without any parley, secure at least an interview with him.

It happened to be the time of hay-harvest, and the hay was at that very time being made in the great meadow, which adjoining the grounds of the Hall, lay on two sides of Wast-water. Singularly enough, many of the household were out at work, and Mr. and Mrs. Elworthy themselves, and dear old Mrs. Mildmay, attracted out also by the beauty of the weather, and the pleasantness of the scene, were seated under a group of sycamores amid the fragrant hay near the water, enjoying every thing around them to the full. Mrs. Mildmay was busied with some light female work. Honour was reading aloud Waverley, which was a favorite book of her husband's, while he, reclining on hay, and with his head on her lap, lay with his eyes closed, the very personification of that calm, human enjoyment, which, while it lays up no repentance for itself, has no fear from others.

The place seemed deserted as Richard Elworthy approached it; he heard the bees humming in the sunny air, and the poultry in the distant poultry-yard, but not a human sound. Mrs. Hawes, who unfortunately happened this very day to be busy over her preserves in the kitchen, which lay in a distant part of the house, had left her own house-keeping parlor, which otherwise lay very near this entrance, unoccupied. All was quiet as a house of the dead, or as one of those fairy palaces where every body lay in enchanted sleep. Little did good Mrs. Hawes know, little did any other domestic, male or female, know, that while they were thus occupied this still, slumberous afternoon, Richard Elworthy, after having knocked once at this side door without receiving a reply, had quietly opened it, and advanced softly up the matted lobby, first to Mrs. Hawes's parlor, where he expected to find her, and then to the library, where, after pausing a moment, knocking softly, but receiving no answer, he walked in.

The library was empty. Richard looked on all sides; he was amazingly cool and self-possessed. He walked to the window and saw the people at work in the meadow below, and the unconscious group under the sycamores. He now breathed rapidly; here was an unlooked-for opportunity which offered instant temptation. He softly closed the door by which he had entered, and turned the key to prevent interruption if it came. There stood the escrutoire in which of old he knew that money and papers of value were kept. Could he but find the key! The operations of his mind were like lightning, and his action equally prompt. Formerly the key of this large escrutoire was kept in a secret drawer of the desk which stood open on the writing-table. He looked: it was there!

No one heard him. No one interrupted him. The escrutoire lay open before him; money he did not find; but by a strange fatality he found, among other papers, the large, properly inscribed, and attested will of William Elworthy, of Wast Hall, bearing date a month or so before his marriage. At once he saw the advantage which the possession of this valuable document might give him. Money if he had now found, he would not have taken, penniless though he was, so unwilling would he have been to have excited the slightest suspicion of any minor theft which might have prematurely led to the discovery of this greater one.

All was done with breathless rapidity; he put the will within his waistcoat, which he buttoned to his chin, locked the escrutoire, replaced the key, and then softly left the room still unseen. He stole down the matted lobby to the side door, which, admitting the broad summer sunshine, stood open as he had left it. He placed his hand on the lock-handle, as though just entering in case of surprise; and now, for the first time feeling agitated, he waited, he knew not how long, it might be for a few seconds only, or it might be much longer, for he felt like one who has been saved from drowning, or in some other terrible situation, and can not measure time.

Any body but Richard Elworthy, after the Evil One had given him this unlooked-for advantage, would certainly have escaped, but his cool audacity was unparalleled. He was still penniless, and he knew not whom to ask for money but his relative; he must therefore yet see him.

He knocked loudly at the open door, and this time heard Mrs. Hawes shout from a distance, "Martin, go to the garden-door; there's somebody there!"

Martin, a young lad of about fourteen, in the dress of a page, made his appearance, and never having seen Richard Elworthy before, did not, of course, recognize him. He inquired for the master, and was told what he already knew, that he was in the hay-field; perhaps he would walk down to him, as it was not far, and he, Martin, would show him the way.

Richard Elworthy bade him run on, and he would follow. He did so, keeping, however, considerably behind him. Midway in the meadow, he stopped near some other trees; watched the boy go to the group under the sycamores, and presently saw his cousin rise and come slowly toward him. He remained himself partially unseen, watching all that took place, and made his observations on William Elworthy as he approached. He was a handsome, vigorous man, and to all appearance likely to live for many years. Richard could not help remarking, that he looked not only well, but happy—as happy as he had done during the short period of his former marriage.

A sudden cloud of surprise and displeasure settled on William Elworthy's brow when he saw who the stranger was, and with a voice of stern severity, he demanded what his business was, and how he had dared to show himself in his presence.

Richard assumed the manner suited to his outward circumstances; he made no attempt to extenuate the past, and told of poverty, suffering, and long sickness; to all of which the pallor of his countenance, and the squalor of his dress, bore testimony. He said that he was just come from Swale-dale, where he had to ask a morsel of bread from that she-devil Isabel Garr, who had now got all the old man's money into her hands, and she would not give it him. He said he had not slept in a bed for many nights, and that a morsel of bread had not crossed his lips for two days. He said that now he was sincerely humbled and penitent; that all he wanted was money to buy him present food, and to convey him back to London, where he had friends; that he would from this time forth apply himself industriously to his profession. He made eloquent promises of amendment; made eloquent appeals to his cousin's mercy, and declared that sorrow and sickness had made an altered man of him. He even wept, and then told such a history of woe and suffering as was enough to wring any heart. But William Elworthy though the good and merciful man, which his relative declared him to be, was not duped by all this. He had been too often deceived before; he put no faith, therefore, in any protestation of contrition and amendment, but the poverty and need were evident enough. These he consented to relieve, though he denied any claims which the other had to seek relief from him; and even sternly assured him that he should take measures to prevent his thus thrusting himself in future into his presence.

A couple of sovereigns were all that Richard Elworthy could obtain from his cousin, and with these he departed.

It was some time before William Elworthy returned to the two beloved women under the sycamore trees. He felt as if he had been suddenly forced into the presence of evil, and he stood looking after Richard, as he walked up the meadow, as he would have looked after a venomous snake, and then, slowly following in the same direction, did not lose sight of him until he saw him upon the high road on his way out of the Dale.

Within a few days after this time, as we have seen, Richard Elworthy stood in the private room of Frederick Horrocks; and the day following, Mr. Horrocks entered into an agreement, whereby a certain sum of money should be paid, according to after arrangements, by the said Frederick Horrocks to Richard Elworthy Elworthy, in consideration of one half of the Wast-Wayland and Ellerdale property, now belonging to William Elworthy, becoming the sole property of the said Frederick Horrocks, in case this said property of Wast-Wayland and Ellerdale descended to the said Richard Elworthy Elworthy, as heir-at-law, or by any other means. Both parties solemnly covenanting not to make known to any other parties this transaction between them.

Frederick Horrocks introduced into this agreement the words, "heir-at-law or by any other means whatever," because Richard Elworthy had said, in reply to the suggestion of Horrocks, that there might be a subsequent will made; that nothing would be easier than to prepare a deed of gift in that case, for that he could at any time produce a signature so like his cousin's, which was a very peculiar one, that it should never be known from the true. This was merely said to prove that he had many resources, but after this Horrocks regarded him as a very dangerous man, over whom the strictest guard must be kept.

CHAPTER XV.

Things went on smoothly at Wast-Hall, nor was the important theft which had been committed there, discovered. Hay-harvest was finished, so was the corn, and now the winter was at hand, the second winter of the happy married life of the much honored master and mistress.

How happy they were it is impossible for us to say. But now it was early spring, gusty, vigorous March, and the dales-people talked with joy of the crowning event of the late spring—the birth of a child at the Hall—the child of their beloved Honour, the heir of the beloved "master;" and again, as two-and-twenty years before, every one who loved these excellent people, felt as if a personal joy were before them.

The news reached Richard Elworthy in London, where he was again living in chambers, well dressed, and supplied with money; studying antiquities in the library of the British Museum, boasting of his many aristocratical friends, and wearing once more his large seal-ring upon a white and well-kept hand.

The news reached Woodbury—there is no knowing how such tidings spread—that there would soon be an heir to the great Wast-Wayland property. "Well," said the Beauchamps, the Cartwrights, and the remaining Duttons, "let it be so! It matters very little to us, whether an heir is born sooner or later."

But Frederick Horrocks's feelings were quite different. It was from him that Richard Elworthy first received the news, and of so momentous a nature did he consider the circumstance, that he hastened to London, and had an interview with him on the subject. He was extremely incensed; said that he had been deceived, vowed to stop all further payment, and to destroy the agreement between them. Richard was, in his turn, no little chagrined. Things at this moment seemed about to take a position beyond his hand; still he said, "faint heart never won fair lady;" that the child was not yet born, that it might die; that Elworthy himself might die; that it was too early, in short, to despair yet. Nevertheless, both he and Horrocks were very near despair, as far as any advantage to be derived by them from the Wast-Wayland property went; while Horrocks looked upon the money which he had already advanced to his partner in guilt, as so much money thrown away.

The birth of the child was expected in May, and now, at the commencement of April, Mr. Wilbraham came again to Wast-Hall, on a visit to his friends. He had been with them three days, during which Mr. Elworthy had frequently spoken to him of the future; for the birth of the child seemed to make it very bright to him. On this third evening they sat together late into the night, talking of many things, which were at that time deeply interesting and important to Mr. Elworthy. He told his friend that he should revise his will, and make still more liberal provision for his wife; that he intended his favorite Oakenshaw, and the other Ellerdale property, to be her jointure in case of his death. This, he said, should be done on the following day, when he solicited the best advice and assistance of his friend, which was cheerfully promised. His mind, that night, seemed unusually active; he was full of magnificent schemes of good on all hands, and he spoke of his wife with unbounded affection, and repeated many times that his life had been unspeakably happy with her.

It was about one o'clock in the morning, when Wilbraham left him.

It had been Mr. Elworthy's practice, for many years, to read daily a portion of one of the Gospels, which were his favorite study in the Scriptures. There was no parade in his devotions: they were an act between God and his own soul.

Wilbraham had letters that night, to write. He was one of those who work in the night, often till morning, and had left his friend for this purpose. At about three o'clock, being in want of certain papers, which he believed himself to have laid down in the library, he proceeded thither in search of them. What was his surprise to find the lamp still burning, and his friend, sitting in his chair, as if asleep, with the open Bible before him. He thought that he must have been overtaken by sleep; he spoke to him therefore, but received no answer. He looked closely at him, and the most dreadful apprehension seized him. Could it be death? Yes, yes, it was that sudden death which had been so long anticipated!

He had died in the midst of his simple devotions, and the last words which human ear had heard him utter, were blessings on his wife.

A dreadful task devolved on Wilbraham. He was sufficient of a surgeon to know that there are means to be made use of in a case like this. He loosened the neck-kerchief therefore, and tearing up the coat sleeve, seized a pen-knife, and endeavored to open a vein, but without success. He must have been dead some time, and his death had been like an infant's sleep, for not a muscle of his countenance was distorted; love and devotion seemed to have stamped upon it an expression which was almost angelic.

Wilbraham was a strong-nerved, hard-headed lawyer, not used to emotions of any kind, but he now wept. He had known Elworthy for years, and was greatly attached to him. But it was not his own loss that most affected him. His heart was wrung for Honour, for the beloved, adoring wife, and she so soon to become a mother.

But he did not give way to his feelings, however intense. He summoned his own servant, a steady and experienced man; and a messenger was immediately dispatched for the family physician. The chamber occupied by Mrs. Elworthy, was fortunately in a distant part of the house, and these alarming movements were not at first heard by her. Mrs. Hawes was called up also, and Mrs. Mildmay. What dreadful tidings for them all!

The whole household knew that the master was dead before the tidings were communicated to the wife. Her mother was now in her room, commissioned to communicate the dreadful intelligence, and all were alarmed for its effects upon her.

They told Honour, that her husband was ill; that the physician was sent for, which was true.

She started up from her bed, pale as death, and throwing round her a wrapper, was hastening out, when her mother held her back.

"What would you do, Honour?" said she; he is very ill; you can not see him—at least not now. Remember your yet unborn child—his child. You must be calm; oh Honour, my beloved one, you must be patient, but indeed you can not see him now!"

"Then he is dead!" said the wife, with a sense of sudden misery that seemed enough to break her heart.

Her mother hesitated to reply.

"Tell me at once," said Honour, speaking in a voice that seemed hollow; "do not deceive me. The dreadful truth must come out at last. If you tell me that he lives I shall hope. I shall believe you, for you never deceived me. I will go to him, and let it cost what it may, I will be with him; no one can wait upon him as I can; but, if he is dead—the shock can not be greater than it has been already, and, with the help of God, I will try to bear it, for his sake, and for the sake of his blessed child.

And now, my mother, speak!" said she, laying her hand on her mother's arm, and looking into her face with pale expectation, "Speak!—but tell me the truth!"

"God help you, my beloved child!" said the mother, in a broken voice.

Honour understood all. She spoke not a single word, but fell back upon her bed.

She did not speak again for hours, and the physician, who had left the dead body of her husband, sat by her side. She had not yet shed a tear. Her mother seated herself by her bed, and told her all that she had just heard from Mr. Wilbraham regarding their last conversation. His expressions of love and gratitude to her seemed to unseal the stony anguish of her heart, and she wept. Those assurances of his love and his last wishes, which were to provide still more for her happiness, were like drops of balm to her wounded heart.

When she was told of the delight and hope with which he spoke so lately of the child, and of the joy it afforded him to think of its inheriting that noble property which involved the happiness of so many honest and worthy people, and when she remembered that all this now devolved upon her, as well as the well-being of that child, the sole representative of her now deceased husband, a superhuman strength seemed given to her—the strength of love and duty; and with a bleeding heart she prayed that God would give her strength to bear this great trial, and to control her natural grief for the sake of the child which had been his latest thought, and on the life of which so much depended.

The joy which the marriage of William Elworthy had occasioned in the Dale has already been described. But no words can tell the consternation of sorrow which seemed now to still every pulse and silence every voice when the strange tidings went abroad that William Elworthy was dead. There were more tears shed that day, tears of genuine sorrow, than had ever been shed before on any one occasion. The dismal sound of the death-bell, as it tolled through that long day, seemed to ring a knell into every heart.

There had been a very general sorrow, two-and-twenty years before, when the first Mrs. Elworthy had died, but it was nothing to that which was felt on the present occasion. It revived all the old sad memory of the past, and people grew almost superstitious, for it seemed as if the coming of an heir was the precursor of death in Wast-Wayland.

The news of William Elworthy's sudden death soon reached Woodbury. All the Dutton family were in the greatest excitement; he had died, as they always expected, from that terrible heart-complaint; and now, would his death bring them any advantage? They hoped it would; for Mrs. Dutton's annuity had been continued, and he had assured her that, in this respect, his marriage would make no difference. Mrs. Dutton had cheered up under this, and once more figured among the Woodbury people, as a lady of respectable income and first-rate connections, although little was now said of future expectations, and therefore poor Natalie, as Mrs. Beauchamp had foretold, seemed to have small chance of a husband. Of course all the Duttons went into mourning—and these mourning preparations revived the old regrets. How different would it have been had he still remained unmarried, and what a heart-felt satisfaction there would then have been under their bombazine and crape!—a fat sorrow is so different to a lean one!—and nobody would have conducted herself more admirably as a mourner than Mrs. Dutton, if she could but have mourned as the mother of four co-heiresses. As it was, it must be excused her that the tears she shed were those of bitterness, and that her aversion to her son-in-law, Horrocks, was very great.

A coldness had grown up between him and his wife's family from the day of his marriage. They could not tolerate him because he had not married Honour Mildmay. People are very moral on occasions of self-interest. Again, there had been hard money-dealings between Mr. Cartwright and his lawyers, and that gentleman seemed to have now less power on his own property than Cheatham and Horrocks. It was for the benefit of his family that it was so, they said; but it had occasioned a great quarrel, which had settled down into a formal coolness. The beautiful unity of the Dutton family was thus from various causes, broken up. Mrs. Dutton still suffered from her nerves, and Natalie had a dull life of it, as Mrs. Beauchamp had foretold.

To Mrs. Frederick Horrocks one thing appeared very astonishing—namely, the remarkable good temper of her husband at this time. He could not have been more cheerful, she thought, if the Elworthy property had now been theirs. Well, men were unaccountable creatures! she thought.

Of course he did not tell her what particular reasons he had at this time for satisfaction. Women had nothing to do with professional secrets, he said, and this was of that kind; it remained in his own breast, therefore, and it sufficed to her to wonder at the unusual sunshine that seemed to irradiate from him. He left home for London two days after the news, as he was summoned there, he said, by important business. It was for a conference with Richard Elworthy that he went.

Richard was now a member of the Reform Club, and there they met.

"My calculations have been right," said Richard, triumphantly, "he has died of this heart-complaint! I have received intelligence from friends I have in the Dale, that Mrs. Elworthy is dreadfully ill; the first intelligence was that she also was dead; but that the child should live is impossible!" And Richard Elworthy swore by the Divine Presence, that he had never expected it to turn out so well!

"No will can be found!" continued he, exultingly; "rumors of that, I hear, are already abroad. This will be a great blow to Mrs. Elworthy. What can they do without a will? The property is as good as mine already! I congratulate you, my dear Horrocks, on your luck in sailing in the same boat with me. And I'll tell you what," said he, in the imprudent assumption of his success, "I should not mind marrying your wife's sister—she's not as pretty as your wife—but in this way we should be a snug family party. What do you say to it?"

Horrocks had a thorough hatred of Richard Elworthy, and he would have expressed it, if he had dared; as it was, he laughed, and said that it *would* be a snug family party with a vengeance!

Richard continued: "I shall go up myself to the funeral, nobody can prevent that; I shall demand to hear the will; and when no will is forthcoming, I shall make my claim as heir-at-law. If the child is not still-born, by that time we shall not have much to fear. I shall soon take possession as heir-at-law. What do you say to going down with me, Horrocks? It would be a merry jest, and as pretty a piece of malice on your part as any one could wish for. It would excite and agitate her to see you. What do you say, now? Will you go with me? or we can wait till after the funeral if you prefer it; we can afford to wait, when we know where the will is, and they do not; or, go when you will, I know the house perfectly; I'll take you in by a side-door, and lead you at once to the room where she sits. Our sudden appearance there—I as heir-at-law, and you as my solicitor—would make a pretty little surprise. What do you say?"

Horrocks said, no; he would not be a party to violence, and he warned his associate to be careful what he did.

"As you will, as you will!" said Richard; "but I'll bet you any money, that in one month from this time, I am the Elworthy of Wast-Wayland!"

Even before the funeral—before Mr. Wilbraham had conveyed the alarming intelligence to Mrs. Mildmay and to Mr. Elworthy's lawyers, that there appeared to be no will, nor any testamentary document whatever among that gentleman's papers at Wast-Hall: and while neither the lawyers nor any of the other anxious friends of the deceased, had whispered the fear of so unforeseen a misfortune, it became rumored in the Dale, from mysterious sources which could not be traced up, that this was the case, and that the property would unquestionably pass into the hands of the heir-at-law, Richard Elworthy Elworthy. Such being, as was believed, a possible chance, a gloom and despondency, greater even than was occasioned by the death itself, prevailed every where.

Among the tenants whom this change of proprietorship would most seriously affect, was Dannel o' Tod's-gill, whose long lease depended on three lives, the last of which, the late William Elworthy's, had expired with his death. The time which Isabel Garr had foretold, hardly three years before, when in her indignant and wounded affection, she strove to uphold the greatness of Richard Elworthy, seemed now come, and Dannel and his family were, to use her very words, ready to kiss the hem of his garments. Dannel who, as he said, "was no great hand at writing," "now put pen to paper," to offer his services in any way to aid the probable new heir. If money was wanting, he offered him "a matter of a hundred pounds or two," invited him to take up his quarters at his house, if it suited his convenience to come to Wast-Wayland before he got possession of the Hall. In fact, Dannel gave him to understand, as plain as words could speak, that he and his were ready to do his bidding, and that, no doubt, when they came to the bit of a settling, that he reckoned there must be about the new lease, there should be no words between them.

Of course, Dannel meant that he was to have his advantage when the new time of bargaining came, and Richard was no niggard of fair promises. Nothing could have pleased him better, indeed, than such an auxiliary at such a time. He came down to Sedburgh that he might be near at hand to watch all that went forward; took up his quarters at the inn there, and though

Horrocks had already given him a further advance of money, accepted the proffered loan from Dannel of two hundred pounds, and began to feel how true it is that the rising sun never lacks worshipers. Henceforth Dannel was established as his agent and spy at Wast-Wayland.

The funeral took place; it was attended by a long train of carriages from far and near; for all respected William Elworthy, and the peculiar circumstances of his death created a more than ordinary interest for his widow. A small number of his more immediate friends assembled at the Hall after the funeral, and to them Mr. Wilbraham, in presence of Mr. Entwistle, the late Mr. Elworthy's solicitor, announced the sad intelligence, that as yet no will had been found. Mr. Entwistle, who had drawn up the will, previous to Mr. Elworthy's marriage, proved that such a document had at one time existed, and Mr. Wilbraham, who was one of the trustees under that will, stated that, only a few hours before his death, Mr. Elworthy had spoken of his will as in existence at that time, and had mentioned to him sundry alterations which he contemplated making with a view of providing still more liberally for his wife, and also to give her an increased power under it. It was feared, perhaps, that he himself might have that night destroyed it, in the fatal intention of substituting a second; or if not destroyed, it might have been, in consequence of the confusion attending his death, mislaid among other papers. It was determined, therefore, to institute the most rigid search, and in the mean time, to keep this untoward circumstance from the knowledge of the widow.

Mr. Wilbraham, spite of the professional demands on his time, remained yet a few days after the funeral, determined, if possible, to discover among the papers of the deceased the missing document; but in vain. His presence, however, was valuable in another way. It was well known at Wast-Hall, that Richard Elworthy was in the neighborhood, ready on the first occasion to assert his hostile claims, and his presence was even expected at the funeral, but he had the good sense to absent himself. On the following day, however, he drove up to the principal entrance in a post-chaise, requesting to see Mr. Wilbraham, as the confidential friend of the deceased, and the adviser of his widow. He was dressed in a suit of deep and handsome mourning, and conducted himself in the most gentlemanly manner. The mildness of his demeanor, and, legally speaking, the reasonableness of his demands, quite disarmed Mr. Wilbraham, who met him with a mind full of the most decided prejudice. Richard Elworthy said that, of course, it was well known to Mr. Wilbraham, that himself and his late cousin had not been for some years on amicable terms, which was now greatly to be regretted, and for this reason, and also owing to the peculiar relationship into which the death of the deceased, under existing circumstances, had thrown him with regard to the widow and her unborn child —he had, from motives of delicacy, absented himself from the funeral. Nevertheless, considering in what position he stood with regard to the property, in case no will was found, and no living child was born, it was but right that he should have every opportunity given him of making such inquiries as he might consider necessary, and he was sure that Mr. Wilbraham himself, to whose high legal standing and character he took the liberty of bearing his testimony, would afford him every opportunity of doing so satisfactorily.

Mr. Wilbraham bowed, and assured him that that would be the case.

Richard then said, that of course Mr. Wilbraham would understand the observation he was about to make as mere matter of business, and as bearing no indirect implication whatever. He said he had no doubt but that the conduct of the opposite party would be of the most upright and honorable character; nevertheless, many rumors were abroad, and, of course, on an occasion of this kind there was no means of preventing rumors being circulated; he felt therefore justified in stating them to Mr. Wilbraham, and in demanding to know if there were any foundations for them. He heard, he said, from those who appeared to be unquestionable authority, that Mrs. Elworthy had been extremely ill, and subsequently had given birth to a still-born child. There was nothing, he said, incredible in the circumstance; in fact, from what he had heard of the shock she sustained in consequence of the sudden death of her husband, it appeared highly probable to him. "Was this, or was it not the case?" he inquired.

Nothing of the kind had taken place, Mr. Wilbraham most cheerfully assured him, nor was likely to take place, he hoped. Mrs. Elworthy was in excellent health, and had been able to preserve her mind wonderfully calm under the late painful circumstances.

Richard Elworthy expressed a wish to see her, were it only at a distance.

To this Mr. Wilbraham made a decided objection.

Richard bowed. "Pardon me, sir," he said, "but the precaution is not altogether unnatural in my case; there are people who apprehend—but let me remark, sir, that this is no suggestion of mine; it has come quite from another quarter—there are parties, I say, who have hinted that even if Mrs. Elworthy were delivered of a still-born child, a living one would be substituted in its place, and produced as the legitimate heir."

"Absurd!" said Mr. Wilbraham, looking angry.

"The assertion is not mine, my dear sir, I beg to repeat," said Richard; "I simply mention to you what appears to be an opinion abroad. The property is of no trifling importance, and unfortunately Mrs. Elworthy's mind is, I am sorry to believe, greatly prejudiced against me. Such things have been done, as the substitution of a living for a dead child to secure a valuable inheritance, as your own legal knowledge must tell you. My situation is a very delicate and peculiar one: I have my own interests to secure, and without reference to one person or another, I have a right to make sure of fair play."

"By all means," said Mr. Wilbraham, speaking very calmly; "but as regards the present state of affairs here, I can assure you that Mrs. Elworthy is in perfect health, and please God, will in due time become the mother of a living child. This affair, Mr. Richard Elworthy, is not taking place in a corner, nor are Mrs. Elworthy and her yet unborn child of so little consequence as to have no friends who will stand by her and see right done; besides, sir, we have not yet given up the hope of finding the will; once find that, and the whole thing is beyond your power or mine; in the mean time, we can not permit Mrs. Elworthy to be harassed or annoyed or agitated in any way, and perhaps the best thing will be for me to refer you to Mr. Bethune of Sedburgh, her medical attendant, who sees her every day, and who will report to you, as I have done, regarding her health. And further, considering the peculiarly painful circumstances of the case, I would suggest to you whether, as a matter of common humanity, to say nothing of feelings of delicacy, it might not be better for you to withdraw from the neighborhood, or at all events, to refrain from making your appearance at Wast-Wayland for the present; and I must hold you responsible, as a gentleman, that no measures shall be taken by yourself, or by any of your friends, which may create in any way disturbance or lead to violence."

"Certainly not!" said Richard, "certainly not!" and then thanking Mr. Wilbraham in his most affable manner, he took his leave.

Even Mr. Wilbraham was for the time deceived; there was apparently so much more reasonableness in the disposition, and so much more suavity in the style and demeanor of this formidable opponent than he was prepared for; but no report, favorable or unfavorable, was allowed to reach Mrs. Elworthy. It was beautiful, and at the same time very affecting, to see the calm submission and self-possession which she enforced upon herself in the great strength of love and faithful duty. He who was more to her than all the world beside, though dead, seemed still to be near her, strengthening her to bear with fortitude, for his beloved sake, all this great sorrow, so that his child might live to be worthy of him. Thus she sat in the silence of that large, solitary house, which it was expected would have been filled with rejoicing, but over which so dark a sorrow and such an uncertain fate had now fallen, in a sort of charmed circle of profoundest quiet, while around her was gathering a terrible storm, of which not even the mutterings for some time reached her.

Richard Elworthy withdrew again to Sedburgh. And so much more agreeable than he expected had been the impression made by his visit on the mind of Mr. Wilbraham, that that gentleman left Wast-Wayland in very good heart. Mr. Bethune prognosticated most favorably of his patient, and for the moment all appeared calm and full of assured hope.

But Richard Elworthy's mind was teeming with sinister designs, and as regarded the widow nothing was further from his wishes than that she should remain in a state of calm assurance. His money flew in all directions; and it was really amazing and sorrowful to see, spite of the general love and reverence felt for William Elworthy and his wife, how great a number of people were ready to swell the tide of Richard's fortune when it appeared likely to turn in his favor. Even in Wayland-dale there were many found who were willing to eat and drink at his cost, and to bluster with big words about his rights. But the head of his party was Dannel o' Tod's-gill and his eldest son, now about twenty—young Dannel as he was called—a wild young chap and a convicted poacher, ready for any mischief; who, with about a dozen others like himself, loved nothing better than a spree of any kind, and who now found it extremely amusing to lounge about the door of the Bull's Head, in Dale-town, where Richard very soon took up his quarters, and where he permitted a free tap and bread and cheese to all his partisans. From the conclave at the Bull's Head, therefore, proceeded all kinds of rumors, both as regarded the present state of Mrs. Elworthy, and the ultimate success of her opponent.

It was a singular circumstance that now, in this strife for the Wast-Wayland property, Isabel Garr set herself in determined opposition to Richard Elworthy and her brother Dannel. Dannel was offended at being wholly cut off from any participation in the property which Cousin Thomas had left, and which, turning out so much more than was expected, at once placed Isabel in circumstances better than his own; and Isabel, who transacted her own business at fairs and markets, like many another stout dales-woman, always carried it with a high hand against her brother whenever an opportunity occurred. Now, therefore, when Dannel was the sworn partisan of Richard Elworthy, Isabel, from a double motive, as violently espoused the other side. The whole district, indeed, was divided into two factions; all who loved license rather than order, all who found their pleasure in idleness and drunkenness, rushed in to reap the harvest of the heir-at-law's present popularity. From Tod's-gill and from the Bull's Head, therefore, circulated the most astonishing rumors, all of which it was intended should reach the ears and harass the mind of the widow herself, and probably produce their realization. Sometimes it was asserted that there was no prospect at all of an heir; again, that the child was still-born, and that, in either case, Mr. Bethune was bribed to produce a spurious heir. It was asserted that Richard Elworthy would dispute the possession to the last farthing; that the first lawyers in the land gave it already in his favor: and in three days from the present time, armed with the authority of law, he would take forcible possession; and if there was to be an heir, like the bishops and the great lords of the land, when an heir to the crown was born, he would himself be cognizant of the birth.

What a scene of disorganization and riot was this formerly peaceful and orderly Dale! The off-scourings of the country thronged to it, and there was such drinking and rollicking, and such floating rumors pregnant with mischief abroad, as roused the old sober inhabitants to a pitch of indignant resistance. At this sorrowful and alarming crisis, Isabel Garr made her appearance in Wayland-dale, determined to raise such an active spirit of opposition as should, at least, if it would not substantiate the right, annoy and inconvenience the wrong. She went to the blacksmith's shop, to the baker's, to the barber's, to every spot where people congregated, and declaring that she herself would give twenty pounds to the poor of Dale-town parish, and ten shillings to the bell-ringers, out of her own pocket, if a child was born to inherit the Wayland-dale property. This created quite a reaction, and even the crowd at the Bull's Head gave three cheers for Isabel Garr and the lady of Wast-Hall.

Before Isabel Garr, however, had made her appearance on the scene, a stronger alliance had taken place on behalf of Mrs. Elworthy and the true heir. Nothing has been said for some time of the untoward love affair of the pretty Agnes of Lily-garth and the young Quaker miller. They were not yet married; and so far from that, indeed, that though the young people remained as much attached to each other as ever, the two families had not spoken for a year and a half, much less shaken hands. Thomas Broadbent was gone from the Dale, and Agnes had displeased her father by refusing to marry another lover, in whose case there was as much money, without any sectarian prejudices. Thus it unfortunately happened that, at this very time, when the respectable inhabitants of the Dale should have all banded together, hand and heart, on behalf of the right, that the two best men in it stood aloof from each other, while they would separately have upheld it to the last gasp with the true Quaker steadfastness. But the case grew desperate, and even these two, so long dissevered by unbrotherly ill-will, met and shook hands, and laid their heads together to consider what it was in their power to do in the present emergency.

Nelly o' Lily-garth, who had none of the old Quaker inflexibility in her, cried for joy when she saw her good brother in-law, Caleb Fothergill, once more in her house.

"Ay, what a good sight this is for sure!" said she. "Sit thee down, Caleb, sit thee down; thou'rt as welcome as flowers i' May! Ay, to be sure! we must mae up all our quarrels and stand by th' mistress."

Christie brought word that there was a strong rumor of Richard Elworthy taking possession of Wast-Hall by force, that he might know with his own eyes that he had fair play, and that there was no deception. Somebody down at Dale-town had heard Richard Elworthy say so himself. If that was the case, Mrs. Elworthy ought to be removed, Christie argued, and putting on his better coat to do honor to the purpose of his visit, as well as to the new reconciliation, he set off to Birks-mill to consult his brother.

There was truth in the rumor; inasmuch as Richard Elworthy, who was now attended by a lawyer from London, had sent to the

Hall a written notice that, in three days from the date thereof, if a properly attested will were not found, he should demand admittance into the house as presumptive heir-at-law. These tidings soon spread beyond the Dale, and Mr. Entwistle, and other of Mrs. Elworthy's friends, began to be seriously apprehensive lest he should proceed to violence, which, in Mrs. Elworthy's state, might prove fatal to her or the child, or even to both. Pressing invitations were not wanting from persons of high standing in the neighborhood that she would remove to their houses, where she would be cordially welcome, as well as in perfect security. But she shrunk from removing herself; in fact, she did not know by how much danger she was threatened.

Nobody knew exactly what was to be done, for the most contradictory rumors were afloat. This, however, was soon very certain, that any violence or outrage on the part of Richard would be as violently resisted and opposed by a very formidable party that was now organized in the Dale, with Christie o' Lily-garth and his brother of Birks-mill at its head. These two, and half-a-dozen other Wayland-dale and Ellerdale farmers constituted themselves into a little guard of honor to defend their beloved lady and her yet unborn child.

There was a wonderful excitement in every body's mind, yet outwardly things were still. Mr. Entwistle had been at Wast-Hall, where he had a long conference, the purport of which had not transpired, further than that it was his wish that Mrs. Elworthy should be quietly removed. Richard Elworthy also was away from Dale-town; the morrow was the day on which his violent entrance at Wast-Hall was expected. It was said that a detachment of police were coming down to be stationed at the Hall, others said soldiers; however that might be, a number of young dales-men, among whom were Christie o' Lily-garth's son, a handsome youth of eighteen, and a young fellow named Michael Satterthwaite, who lived at the mill with his uncle, vowed that Richard never should set foot within the Hall—that they would resist his entrance to the utmost. These young men really enjoyed the excitement, and frightened Mrs. Hawes and the maid-servants by a show of fire-arms and much talk of the terrible deeds they were ready to do. Isabel Garr was again seen in the dale, going from point to point, promising every where money, and plenty of good beer for the men, and tea-drinking for the women, if an heir were born to the lady of Wast-Wayland. It was reported that Isabel Garr would spend a hundred pounds if things only went as they ought to do; and it really was wonderful what enthusiasm she every where excited.

On this important day, Christie o' Lily-garth presented himself before Mrs. Mildmay.

"I am not come," said he, "only on my own head and for my own sake, but we've all talked it over among ourselves, and as we hear that the mistress will not leave the Dale—and yet she should leave the Hall before to-morrow, when there's no knowing what yon villain may do—we all want to get her nicely away to Lily-garth to-night, and nobody know any thing of it. There's only about half-a-dozen of us as knows of it. I've wrote to Mr. Wilbraham about it, and to Mr. Entwistle, and I've got his answer, and he approves of it altogether and so, no doubt, will Mr. Wilbraham, when his letter comes, only there's no time to be lost."

"It is an excellent idea, my good friend," said Mrs. Mildmay.

"And," continued Christie, "Nelly has got th' rooms ready for her—capital rooms they are!—they've been airing ever since yesterday. There's th' best bedroom for her, with th' old family-bed in it, as wer' never taken away, and ma'ppen she'd like to know sometime that th' master himself wer' born in it. However, that's not much to do with it, only she would be safe there. Nobody dare come there without my leave, for I've a lease of th' place, and it's all still and quiet, and Nelly and Agnes will tae great care of her, and she can have as many of her friends with her as she likes; we can make up four beds, and five at a pinch."

Christie looked very grave and anxious. "Now, you'll persuade her," continued he, "for if any thing happened here, either to her or to th' child, I think I should never get over it."

Mrs. Mildmay was affected by his zeal; she gave him her hand, thanked him, and said that she was sure her daughter would see the desirableness of this proposal.

"Mr. Entwistle thinks," said Christie, "that all had better be done on the sly, as it were; we'll get her away in the dusk—and that reminds me of what I had clean forgotton. I went over to Sedbur' last night, and saw Mr. Bethune, and he approves of it too, and he'll come to-night if it is agreeable to all, in his carriage, about dusk-hour, and so go with her to Lily-garth himself, and see her all safe. There's nothing, you know ma'am, uncommon in th' doctor coming, he does that every day; and he'll drive off again, and nobody be th' wiser; so then Richard Elworthy and all his villainous set, they'll think that th' mistress is still here, and if they make any disturbance, let them—we can laugh when we've got her all safe at Lily-garth."

Honour, to whom as much of Richard Elworthy's threats, as was thought proper, were communicated, made no opposition to the removal of herself to Lily-garth; indeed, independently of a letter which was received that day from Mr. Entwistle, by Mrs. Mildmay, urging upon her to accept this proposal of Christie's, there was nothing in it at all unpleasant or undesirable in any way. It was but selecting for the place of the child's birth, the old family home, where his father, and his ancestors before him, had been born for many generations.

Mr. Bethune's carriage drove up to the Hall toward dusk, and Christie and his few stout-hearted coadjutors, who were alone deemed worthy to know the secret, stood at a respectful distance, unseen by her, with their hats off, and saw Honour enter the carriage in her deep, deep mourning, and in that condition of near maternity which so readily excites the sympathy of every good-hearted married man; and there was not one of them but who felt his heart touched, and the tears spring to his eyes.

"Now drive carefully, drive as if for your life," said Christie to the coachman, rushing forward the moment he saw the door closed on Honour, her mother and Mr. Bethune; "drive carefully, my good man, pray do!"

CHAPTER XVI.

It was not known to Richard Elworthy and his partisans that Mrs. Elworthy had left the Hall. No sooner, however, was she safely off, than the doors and the windows were carefully secured, and Mrs. Hawes was ready to put herself at the head of the men-servants, who alone formed no inconsiderable defense.

News was brought about noon the following day, that Richard Elworthy, and a whole army of men, were on their way to the Hall to take possession. The greatest excitement prevailed both within and without; the young men posted themselves in the court-yard to wait the event, being now strengthened by a couple of the police, who had been sent by Mr. Entwistle, to see that the peace was kept. The great gate-way, which formed the principal entrance, and the gate leading to the shrubbery, were secured against intrusion, so that there was no access to the house, but by the court-yard. There was something exciting in all this, and it is questionable whether these young men did not long to come to close quarters with the detested heir-at-law and his allies.

But neither the heir-at-law nor any of his allies were seen, and toward evening, it was found that he had not even been at Daletown, nor any where in the Dale that day. People knew not what to think.

The following day they were again expected ; and again the court-yard at the Hall was filled with the same eager little group, who now were growing very restless for want of something to do.

About ten o'clock, a chaise drove rapidly up ; it contained only Mr. Entwistle and his principal clerk. He was received by our young Dale friends with enthusiasm, and from them he learned the existing state of affairs. He made very little remark on all he heard, and seemed to take every thing so coolly, and so much as a matter of course, that the young men, who wanted nothing more than action, were a little disconcerted. They entered the house, and were soon seated at an abundant breakfast supplied to them in the library, by Mrs. Hawes. From her they learned that Mrs. Elworthy had been gone two days, and that her removal to Lily-garth was as yet unknown to any but the household, and the parties immediately concerned in it. Mr. Entwistle appeared much satisfied.

Mrs. Hawes, like the good men in the court-yard, was dissatisfied with the cool and undemonstrative lawyer. She wanted him to assure her that all was safe for Mrs. Elworthy, but he did not do so, and therefore she was compelled to speak.

"Pray ye, sir, do ye think 'at this Richard will get the property, and the mistress be turned out?"

"If we are fortunate enough to have a living child—no certainly!" was his reply.

That was all the answer he gave, and poor Mrs. Hawes knew as much as that before. He went on with his breakfast, and the discomforted housekeeper, who felt as if her appetite were quite gone, wondered how he could swallow such mouthfuls of hot buttered rolls and tongue. She felt as if the news were come that the child was dead, and that the now disinherited widow must be despoiled of all.

"What's th' use of lawyers," said she, indignantly, "if they can not make just and common-sense laws? I wish they were all of them in the Red Sea, and 'at I had the settling of this business. I'd soon make short work of it, that I would."

Another chaise was now seen driving up. If it contained Richard Elworthy, he was come in a much more sober state than was expected. It drew up at the court-yard, after having pulled up a moment at the great gates, where the chain and padlock sufficiently intimated that there was no entrance. A gentleman, whom nobody knew, alighted; Richard Elworthy was with him, but kept his seat, after the two had exchanged a few inaudible words with each other.

The strange gentleman looked very brisk and cheerful, and seemed quite ready to return any salutation of the young dalesmen, who now, with the stout old butler at their side, stood ready to oppose his entrance, or at all events to hold a parley, He asked in a civil, but rather peremptory voice, to see Mrs. Mildmay.

"You can not see her, sir," returned the butler, shortly, "but Mr. Entwistle of Kendal is here."

"Good!" said the other, not appearing in the least surprised, and giving his card, desired that it might be presented to that gentleman.

The card of Mr. Steele, solicitor, Lancaster, was handed in.

"Ah, well!" said Mr. Entwistle, handing over the card to his clerk. "I am glad that we have to deal with a respectable man. Tell Mr. Steele that I shall be happy to see him."

The lawyers had a long conference, a small part of which reached the ears of Mrs. Hawes, as she sat in her parlor, with the door open, that she might watch all that went forward.

"You are mistaken, my dear sir," said Mr. Steele, who now interposed between Mr. Entwistle and the door, which that gentleman opened, as if about to leave the room, having just said, "then there is an end of the conference between us, and I wish you a good morning; only remember that any entrance here on the part of your client will be dealt with as a breach of the peace."

How these words delighted Mrs. Hawes! But Mr. Steele replied, "My dear sir, you are mistaken. Pardon me, my dear sir, but you are too hasty! You take an incorrect view of the grounds upon which my client acts." The head clerk here spoke. He, too, seemed to be mollifying Mr. Entwistle, and Mr. Steele proceeded:

"My client," said he, "demands nothing unreasonable, nothing more than I think you would feel yourself justified in demanding for a client of your own under similar circumstances. If this child lives—if it can be proved that a living child is born, he retires from the contest; the child becomes a ward of chancery, and the thing is removed from our hands. But until then, he stands as heir-at-law, and is justified by the law in protecting his property from spoliation or fraud. I claim for him, then, as heir-at-law, and you can not, my dear sir, nullify his claim. The case may be hard, as you say, but we make not the hardship, we merely assert our legal rights. I demand for him the power of wardship of his property until his claim is nullified by the appearance of a direct heir. But we must have the birth of this heir properly attested."

"Of course, of course," said Mr. Entwistle. "The Lord Chancellor has had the case laid before him, and takes great interest in it; it will be well looked after. But it is our present imperative duty to protect the unfortunate lady in question from any aggression, or from any mode of annoyance and disturbance. We must have fair play, Mr. Steele, we must have fair play!"

Mr. Steele acquiesced. Again the library door was shut, and the lawyers again sat down to their conference, of which, as Mrs. Hawes could hear nothing, nothing transpired.

It was not long, however, before Mr. Entwistle's clerk went out, and to the surprise of every body, returned with Richard Elworthy himself. Richard had occupied himself with reading the "Times" newspaper, after his agent had left him, while young Fothergill and his friends stood outside the gate talking about him, and saying many bitter, and as they thought, witty things, which were intended to wound and mortify him. Like Mrs. Hawes, they were infinitely dissatisfied, but they were much more than dissatisfied when Mr. Entwistle's agent stepped to the chaise door, and opening it, said in a civil voice, "I'll trouble you, sir!" at the same time, letting down the steps, and intimating to him to alight.

They all thought that there must be treachery within doors. Both Fothergill and Satterthwaite started forward to oppose Richard's entrance, but the clerk, who was a positive man, put them aside, saying, "By your leave, gentlemen!" and thus the two entered.

"What does it mean?" asked Satterthwaite from Mrs. Hawes, into whose parlor he now walked. The butler was there also, and three or four other domestics, all asking the same question.

"Goodness only knows!" said poor Mrs. Hawes, ready to cry.

A loud ringing of the library bell startled them. Mrs. Hawes answered it. She found the gentlemen all standing, and all talking together, so that for some time they did not notice her; but she gleaned up, that Richard was really to be permitted to remain there. The discussion now was, how far he should be limited in action. He demanded for his own use this room in which they were standing, namely, the library; but that was resolutely opposed by Mr. Entwistle. The head clerk was at this time engaged in placing seals upon all the locks in the room, and this Mrs. Hawes understood was to be done throughout the house.

Mr. Entwistle at length called Mrs. Hawes aside, and told her that Mr. Richard Elworthy would remain there for the present. She was about to interrupt—to beg an explanation—to remonstrate—but he silenced her, saying that they knew what they were about.

"It is a good thing, then," said she, "for it's more than I do."

"That is possible," said he, good-humoredly; "but in the present state of affairs, we can not have every thing our own way. You must provide a private room and necessaries for Mr. Richard Elworthy."

"I hope he has brought his own cook with him," interrupted she, "for there is nobody here 'at will do it, that I can tell you! I, for my part, should think it sin and treason, Mr. Entwistle."

Mr. Entwistle must have had great power of persuasion, for

presently Mrs. Hawes listened quietly. "We are doing all for the best," said he, in conclusion; "we are keeping things quiet. Please God we get a *living* child, all then is settled! There is no saying what violence might have been committed if we had not yielded a little. You have done right in removing Mrs. Elworthy; she must be kept apart from every disturbing and annoying cause."

Mrs. Hawes said something about the triumph that Richard had gained; that all he wanted was to get his nose in, and now they never would get him out again.

Mr. Entwistle laughed; he said that she would soon see that Richard had no great triumph—that he was bound now to keep the peace—and any breach of it, which was what they had principally to fear, because of its effect on Mrs. Elworthy, would subject him to punishment. He had thus become interested in the maintenance of peace and order, and thus he was made to aid them in the most effectual manner.

Thus it was concluded. Richard was to have the drawing-room and a chamber; Mr. Entwistle's head clerk was also to remain as a representative of the other party. Seals were fixed upon every lock; the rooms were locked, and the keys placed in the hands of Mrs. Hawes, who received orders not to leave the place.

Mr. Entwistle and Mr. Steele took luncheon together, after which they drove off in their respective vehicles.

The news that Richard Elworthy had got possession of Wast-Hall spread through the Dale, and caused the utmost consternation and dismay. It was feared at first that, some way or other, the law had given it to him, and so great was the popular indignation, that, had it been so, there is no doubt but that they would have been ready to pull it down over his head.

On the other hand, the wild rabble who had attached themselves to Richard, and who were regarded by him merely as the coarsest tools wherewith to rough-hew, as it were, his work, and then to be cast aside, now finding no demand for their rude energies, contrary to their expectations, sat drinking at the Bull's Head until they were all a-fire for action, and for any mischief which might come into their heads.

One of these fellows proposed, therefore, as a capital joke, that they should go and make a bonfire at the Hall in honor of the new squire. It was thought to be a very bright idea, and young Dannel Garr, and three or four other foolish, half-drunken fellows, set out toward evening to accomplish it. Young Garr, who knew the ground well, led them to an old oak copse adjoining Hibblethwaite Force, in which brushwood had been cut this spring, and now lay tied up in fagots. Of these fagots they collected a sufficient number to form an immense bonfire, and conveyed them by dusk-hour to a little dingle, forming the extremest corner of the Tod's-gill land, and only at a short distance from the Hall itself, to the front of which they intended to remove them as soon as the darkness would render it safe to do so.

Under the strict surveillance of the police in-doors, as well as of the most stringent orders from Mr. Entwistle's head clerk, the household at the Hall went early to bed, and the insurgents outside might have carried their plan into execution without interruption, had not the dogs kept up such a tremendous barking the moment they approached the house with their bundles of fagots, as obliged them to desist from this part of their scheme. But they were not disposed to give it up altogether ; accordingly clambering over a wooden fence into the stack-yard, they found a stack of fagots ready to their hands, and piling up of these an immense heap, loosely put together, so as to make a monstrous bonfire, they soon had it all a-blaze.

It was long past midnight, and pitch dark, there being no moon, when a fierce light flashed through every chink of the closed shutters of the back windows of the Hall, and awoke such of the startled sleepers as lay on that side of the house, with the idea of lightning. But the light continuing, a more terrible idea instantly suggested itself, and one nearer the truth, that the Hall was on fire.

"It is that villain's doing ! He thinks the mistress is here !" exclaimed Mrs. Hawes and the butler, and all the other servants in a breath.

They rushed to the chamber which Richard Elworthy occupied, and met him at the door, apparently as much alarmed as themselves.

"Where is the fire ?" he demanded.

They charged him with it, and hurled out volleys of hatred and indignation against him, every one seeming glad to have an opportunity of speaking his mind.

He took no notice of them or their opprobrium, and even ordered the police to be immediately summoned, and to them he gave the strictest orders to search out and seize any one who might appear to be the originator of the mischief, although in his own mind, he suspected them to be his own friends. The setting fire to the Hall.

had once before been proposed as a means of alarming the poor lady, and Richard Elworthy, had, at that time, laughed at it as a capital joke. He feared now that some of his friends were acting on this suggestion, in the idea of doing him good service.

The windings of the dale prevented the Hall from being seen at any great distance, and this, together with the early hours kept by the dales-people themselves, caused the alarm of fire not to be spread immediately from one end of the valley to the other; neither did the light from the burning, nor indeed any knowledge of it, reach Lily-garth until all danger was over,

Richard Elworthy, who, above every thing, wished to avoid any breach of the peace, was unspeakably annoyed at this occurrence; and disregarding the torrents of abuse by which he was assailed by the congregated household, rushed down stairs, and issued peremptory orders to have the fire-buckets taken down, and the fire-engine brought out. But this was already done; there was neither man nor woman about the place who was not prompt for action, and whose activity and energy was not roused still more by the determination not to receive orders from Richard Elworthy.

It was soon ascertained that there was no danger to the Hall; but the fire having been made too near the stack from which the fagots were taken, it also caught fire and soon became one mass of flame most terrific to witness. A new cause of apprehension then arose from a hay-rick which stood near, and which adjoined the stables, from which the horses were immediately removed.

Richard Elworthy, as we have said, was most assiduous on this occasion; rushing from point to point, and giving orders as though he were the master of the place.

His zeal, however, defeated its own object; the people who resented his interference even though his directions were the wisest that could be given, exerted themselves with redoubled voluntary energy and forethought, that they might render his commands unnecessary by forestalling them. It afforded a great deal of amusement, even amidst the first terror, when one of the maid-servants, a stout dale-lass, who, when directing the leathern pipe of the engine, was peremptorily ordered by Richard Elworthy to make some alterations in her movements, at once cut short the speaker's words, by turning, as if accidentally, the stream of water upon himself, and drenching him from head to foot. It was done as if in the twinkling of an eye, and the next moment the water was deluging the hay-rick. There was a loud roar of laughter which the incensed heir-at-law thought it best not to notice, and as it was soon after ascertained that there was no longer any danger of the fire spreading, he quietly retired from the scene, while several of the ring-leaders in the mischief, among the rest young Dannel Garr, were already in the hands of the police.

Is was during this night that Richard Elworthy learned that the widow was no longer at the Hall. This was a piece of intelligence that startled him. Where, then, was she, asked he, and how long had she been gone? Nobody would give him a satisfactory answer, and he was filled with many suspicions and apprehensions, which led, within the next several days, to active correspondence among the lawyers.

The news of an incendiary attempt upon Wast-Hall spread far and wide, and did more to damage Richard Elworthy's cause than any thing else. It was universally attributed to his agency; it was said that supposing the widow to be in the house, he had caused this diabolical outrage to be committed, in the hopes of its producing the most disastrous effects upon her. He was really guiltless of the affair, but he bore the blame. It was in vain, as far as popular opinion went, that he was extremely indignant; that he disclaimed all knowledge of the attempt, and even, to prove his innocence, did his utmost to bring the true offenders to justice. Young Dannel Garr and several others were taken up on the charge, and for the present committed to prison.

But Richard Elworthy gained nothing by all this. He was indeed in a most difficult position, between two very formidable horns of a dilemma. He must either prove himself guiltless of this outrage, and thereby incense his own party by convicting them, or he must allow himself to be considered guilty of this breach of the peace, and become, therefore, in his own person, amenable to the law. He infinitely preferred the former, and now the reaction began. And while he cursed the lawless people who, when left to themselves, had committed a fatal outrage, which had essentially damaged him in the eyes of all, they, in their turn, cursed him as a sneaking Judas, who would betray his own friends when they were doing their best to serve him.

CHAPTER XVII.

WHILE the violent passions of the Tod's-gill Garrs and others, were raging almost to madness, and while all the Dale and the country round was ringing with the strange news of this incendiary outrage, Mrs. Elworthy was calmly passing the early weeks of May in the seclusion of that shady old house, where all was as still as in a castle of enchantment. She asked not for tidings of what occurred without, well knowing that she had wise and warm friends to protect her interests, and that her present duty was to wait and be still. She walked daily in the quiet garden at Lily-garth, but knew not, that at such times, a faithful sentinel, Christie or some one else, kept watch near. Christie said, from her first coming to his house, "she shall never know, poor thing, how we never have her out of our sight, lest, ma'ppen, she might not feel so free and easy."

The only thing they told her, was that Lord Lonsdale and many other influential people had written, immediately on the news of the fire, most kind letters. They read her only such parts as did not refer to the outrage, and she made no inquiries regarding the rest, for she knew that a time would come when nothing would be withheld from her. Lord Lonsdale, as well as the others, expressed the warmest interest in her behalf, and offered aid and countenance if any emergency occurred in which they could be available to her. This was very cheering and consolatory. Mr. Wilbraham had also written to assure them of what Mr. Entwistle had told Richard Elworthy, that the Lord Chancellor took deep interest in the case, and that the child and its mother would find the most favorable, and the most kind wardship, under this Head of the Law.

"And pray ye how's th' mistress? And have ye heard ought fra' Lily-garth?" asked the dales-people of each other many times in the course of each day.

Christie came home one evening in high delight, for he had met Matthey o' Brockside, who was just come out of Rosendale, where lived the famous dumb wife that every body consulted about their dreams. Matthey's sister, Ally, who lived in Rosendale likewise, had dreamed a wonderful dream. She dreamed that she saw a beautiful white dove, sitting on a rock amid raging waters; people in boats were trying to get at her to save her, but they could not, and then, all at once, there rose up from beside her a young eagle, and took her on its outspread wings, and lifted her from the rock, and soared with her far into the blue sky, away and away through golden sunshine, and all the people in the boats, and crowds that were looking on, set up a great shout of joy, with which Ally awoke.

Ally was so astonished by the dream that she went at once to the dumb wife to get it interpreted, and she, without a word about Mrs. Elworthy, showed them as plain as if it was in a glass, a lady lying in a bed with a "lad-bairn" in her arms. Ally, therefore, knew in a minute that it had reference to Mrs. Elworthy. It was a dream of good omen, as the dumb wife had given her to understand.

Ally went from house to house in Rosendale, and her brother Matthey o' Brockside did the same in Wayland-dale, telling every where the wonderful dream and the interpretation which was given of it by the dumb wife—she who never spoke, yet knew so much, and whose interpretations of dreams were acknowledged true both far and wide.

It was now somewhat past the middle of May.

One morning, Christie o' Lily-garth called up his son before day-break, and told him to ride with all speed to Sedburgh, and bid Mr. Bethune hasten there without delay.

"Thou mae tae my mare," said Christie, calling again to his son from his chamber door; "she'll go better than th' black filly."

This permission showed to all who knew Christie, how much his heart was in the errand. This mare was his pride and his glory, and his son would not have dared to ask the loan of her, but now she was volunteered for this hasty ride.

Such of the dales-people as saw young Fothergill o' Lily-garth riding at this early hour at full speed, understood the errand, and it soon spread from house to house, that the doctor was sent for to Lily-garth, and before night they should have great news one way or another.

Young Fothergill returned for a late breakfast, according to dale hours, and Mr. Bethune arrived in his carriage almost as soon.

Christie said that he would rub down the mare himself, for that he did not feel in spirits to go far from home that morning. And yet when hour after hour passed, and he saw nothing but the anxious faces of the women in his house, it was more than he could bear. He now said he would go up the Fell and look after some black Scotch cattle which he had grazing there. He did so, and hoped that, as he had been away now for some hours, there would be glad tidings for him on his return.

Nor was he the only one so waiting; a crowd of people was literally before the house, keeping at a respectful distance; some sitting, others walking about, and others going and coming. There never had been such an excitement and anxiety before. Christie inquired for his wife, and found her in the back-kitchen scouring a cheese-pan.

"Wae's to me!" said Nelly, rather snappishly, in reply to her husband's inquiries, "she's very badly!—to my thinking, *very* badly!" Nelly rubbed at the brass pan more energetically than ever, and continued: "I wonder 'at women are fools enough to marry! Th' finest man 'at ever was, isn't worth what it costs a woman! I wish, for my part, that I do! 'at having bairns was turn and turn about, as would be more fair like, and then th' man, when he'd had his turn, would know how to set store by's wife!"

Nelly's intense sympathy made her very cross.

Christie did not reply, but walked back to the stable where his favorite mare stood, and leaning against the stable door-post, thought over past times. He recalled that dreadful day, now so long gone by, when the first Mrs. Elworthy died, and his Nelly, then his blooming young wife, suddenly took to her bed, and the terrible agonies of child-birth succeeded. He remembered his feelings at that time as livingly as if it was now; when the intensity of his sympathy made him suffer with her, and it was a bitter grief to him that he could not bear all for her. His heart at this moment was very heavy; a foreboding of evil oppressed him, and he felt almost as weak as a woman. He thought of the dumb wife, and how she had interpreted Ally o' Rosendale's dream; but it could not sustain his hopes now—it even seemed like a tempting of Providence.

Tears coursed down his sunburnt cheeks. "What an old fool I am!" thought he to himself, but he could not shake off the depression.

He was one of those simple, earnest souls, who believe that no prayer can be efficient unless presented kneeling. It seemed disrespectful to the Almighty, according to his feeling, to present a petition otherwise than in this humble position. He now needed the consolation of earnest prayer ; therefore, mounting to the hay-loft, he knelt down among the hay, and prayed fervently for the woman who was then in her hour of need, and for the child about to be born, and on whose life the well-being and happiness of so many depended.

His prayer was ended, and he came down; but just as he reached the outer door of the stable he heard the voice of his daughter, shouting, "Father! father! there's a lad bairn! a bonny lad bairn!"

The joyful news flew among the people outside; there was a buzz, a murmur, almost a shout of joy.

Christie said nothing, but again mounting the hay-loft, dropped once more upon his knees, and poured forth his genuine overflowing soul in thanksgiving; and when he came down again, he was as mad as the rest.

Nelly was in the parlor, setting out the tea-things, with cold meat various sorts of pies, and the great stand of spirits, the three bottles of which had been filled that morning for the occasion. Every body must now eat and drink, and the doctor was coming down for that purpose.

Nelly was crying for joy as Christie came in.

"Thou must nae think ill o' me for what I said just now, Christie," said she; "if th' woman has a' th' pains to bear, so has she maist joy over her bairn. Oh! there is no joy like that of a mother over her new-born bairn; and I never thought, when it wer' all over, 'at I had borne too much either for thy sake or th' bairn's; so thou must think nought of what I said."

Christie gave his wife a hearty kiss. He could just then have kissed all the world. He declared he was so pleased that he could forgive Richard Elworthy, and even the very devil himself, all the mischief that he had tried to do.

Christie said he could not stop to eat any thing, for that he must go and tell the good news. "But, pray ye, Nelly woman," said he, speaking mysteriously and in a whisper, "is th' bairn all right and sound?"

"For sure it is," replied Nelly, looking as bright as her words were satisfactory; "as sound and perfect a bairn as ever wer' born; a big thumping chap 'at knows how to cry, I promise thee!'

"And there's no fear 'at it may die then?" said Christie, now venturing to speak in his natural voice.

The doctor at this moment came in, looking very cheerful.

"Well, Mr. Fothergill," said he, offering his hand to Christie, "we've managed our affairs very satisfactorily up-stairs. Mrs. Elworthy is famously, and we have a beautiful little boy."

Christie shook the doctor's hand so vigorously that the gripe was felt long afterward. He then went to an old-fashioned desk, the key of which hung to his watch chain, and taking out thence a little roll of something in white writing-paper, opened it, and laid ten golden sovereigns and a half before the doctor.

"There, doctor," said he, "those are yours; we've had them laid by in readiness these many weeks. There's my brother at Birks-mill, and Mr. Walker o' th' school, and Matthey o' Brock-side, and one or two of th' folks in Ellerdale—but you'll find all th' names written upo' th' paper—we said 'at we'd mae you this little compliment among us if there wer' a likely bairn—we mattered not much whether it were lad or lass; so you can put it in your pocket, doctor, and you'll be none the worse of it, I reckon. But I'll go now and carry th' news to th' Hall," said he, impatient to be off.

"Willie's gone there," said Nelly; "he set off as soon as th' bairn wer' born."

"Then I'll go to Dale-town," said Christie.

"All Dale-town knows it by this time," said Nelly; "besides, Michael Satterthwaite's there long afore this; he set off when Willie did. Thou art getting an old man, Christie," said his wife, laughing; "th' young fellows all get th' start of thee!" and then springing up from her chair, she set the parlor-door wide open, saying, "Hark ye, Christie, my man, there's th' bairn a-screeching! There's no mistake in that!"

The doctor, who was well pleased with the unexpected fee, which he had placed in his pocket, began, in high good-humor to explain that crying in a new-born child was a sure sign of health, and was necessary to expand the lungs, &c., &c.; during which long speech, for the doctor made it both long and learned, poor Christie, who could listen to nothing but the child, felt himself quite unmanned. The voice of this new existence, so welcome and so precious to him, seemed to stir the very depths of sentiment and affection within him. He thought again to himself, "what an old fool I am, for sure!" and then, who should walk in but Mrs. Mildmay herself, looking very happy and yet very pale.

She had received every body's congratulations but Christie's. He, poor man, however, seemed in no condition to offer them, for the very sight of her at that moment brought such a choking sensation into his throat that he could not speak a word. Fortunately Mrs. Mildmay bore him company; they shook hands without saying a word, but their looks and their very silence were intelligible to each other.

The grand meal, whatever it might be called, was now ready, and the doctor was eating away with an amazing appetite from various of the many good things with which "the big table," as it was called, and which was only used on great occasions—weddings and such like, was now so abundantly furnished.

"Sit thee down and tae a mouthful," said Nelly to her husband, "for thou'st not eaten any thing to speak of to-day."

"And you must drink to the health of the lady up-stairs, and our young heir," said the happy, and proud doctor.

Christie filled a bumper, and drank a happy recovery and long life to Mrs. Elworthy; then filled again, and drank long life and prosperity to the young heir of Wast-Wayland.

He ate something standing, for he said he must be off. He must go down to Dale-town and set the bells a-ringing; for though they might hear them up to the Hall, yet they would not disturb the mistress at Lily-garth, for Bow-fell kept off the sound of the bells, as he had often noticed.

Christie was in such an excitement of joy, that he was ready to ring the bells himself.

When he reached the church-yard gate, however, the bells began to ring as of themselves; somebody had been before him, that was evident. Besides Michael Satterthwaite, there were plenty of others to set them on; even Isabel Garr, who by some unaccountable means, was on the spot to hear the first tidings, had been there, and left ten shillings for the ringers, as she promised, vowing more vehemently than ever, that there should be such tea-drinkings, and such merry-makings, as had never been known before, even if it took fifty pounds out of her own pocket.

The bells were ringing, as though they would shake the old church tower down, and all Dale-town was a-stir as well as the valley itself, from one end to the other, when a chaise was seen driving rapidly through it, on its way out of the valley. It contained Richard Elworthy. Where he was going nobody knew; but hardly was he through the street and out of sight, when the landlord of the Bull's Head rushed to his door-steps to look after him, exclaiming loud enough for every body to hear, "The villain! and he has left his bill unpaid."

Christie was a great and happy man. Every body thronged about him for days, and would shake hands with him, not only because they loved and honored him, for his own sake, but because he had always been the friend of the mistress, and because it was under his roof that the young heir of Wast-Wayland was born, when he and his mother were almost outcasts from their own.

The general joy and satisfaction was so great, that there was a daily throng at Lily-garth, to inquire after the young child and his mother, to make little offerings to both, and, if possible, to get a sight of him. A few favored mortals had seen him before he was many days old, and these became oracles on this popular topic. The most wonderful reports of the surpassing beauty and intelligence of this child, were in circulation; no nurse nor mother in the Dale had ever seen any thing equal to him.

His birth, of course, was in the newspapers, and many copies of such papers are carefully preserved, by such of the dales-people as have a turn for the chronicling of events, to this day.

The spirit of this general rejoicing, which had in it the spirit of conciliation, produced a remarkable effect at Birks-mill. The good Quakers, Caleb and Elizabeth Fothergill, were, in some mysterious manner, brought to consent to the marriage of Thomas Broadbent and the pretty Agnes o' Lily-garth. They said that they would no longer oppose his marrying out, of the Society, seeing that Agnes and he were so much attached to each other; or perhaps, suggested the good step-father, Agnes might come into the society before they were married. He thought "'Friends' would not object to receiving her, seeing that her father had been a 'Friend' himself."

The news of this concession on the part of his family, soon reached Thomas Broadbent, and he hurried into Wayland-dale, with a heart so full of joy, that no other besides Agnes's could equal it. It was delightful coming home—after the miserable leaving it that there had been. The step-father broached the idea of Agnes becoming a "Friend," for this was a sort of middle course for the good Quaker to take. Thomas and Agnes took this matter into consideration. They said that this would take a deal of time; it would have to go from one monthly meeting to another; for "Friends" were always so slow about such things; and, perhaps, after all, they would not receive her, because she was not "a convinced Friend," but only applied for membership because she wanted to marry a "Friend."

They determined, therefore, as the shortest and safest way, to go to church, as Agnes's father had done before them, and get married at once. They did so.

Caleb and Elizabeth Fothergill looked very grave when they heard what the rash young people had done. They said, "'Friends' would be very angry about it; perhaps would 'even deal with *them*' for having sanctioned it; but as it was done, it could not be undone; there was no crying for shed milk." So they kissed and shook hands with the young couple, and in the bottom of their hearts felt very well satisfied.

The young heir of Wast-Wayland was baptized William, after his father. The dales-people said among themselves that, of course, his christening would be very grand, and that no doubt Lord Lonsdale, or the Lord Chancellor, or perhaps both, would be his godfathers. They said that he and his mother should be taken back to the Hall with a grand procession of all the neighboring gentry in carriages and on horseback; and that all the tenants should follow with music and banners; they said that the bells of Dale-town should ring for a week, and that there should be a general holiday, with bonfires and fire-works; that an ox should be roasted whole for the men, with plenty of good ale, and that the women should have tea in the meadow by Wast-water; and that there never should be so much honor done to a young heir and his mother as should be done on this occasion to Mrs. Elworthy and her infant son.

So talked they in their enthusiasm; but they forgot that the young mother was a widow, and that she could only return to her child's home to feel in its desolate solitude that the child's father would never enter it more.

Honour wept over her child, her beautiful first-born. Now, for the first time, she might give way to her grief, so many, many things pressed the sense of her bereavement upon her. A strange, deep agony stamped it upon her soul, when forgetting for a moment the death of her husband in the ecstatic joy of her child's birth, she thought instinctively, as it were, how great would be his joy also, and then sank down, remembering as if with the fiery wing of lightning, that he would never, never behold it in this world—never could fold it in his arms—never encircle it with his love—that it was fatherless—that she was a widow!

No one at present could speak of hers as joyful feelings. She had yet to be allowed the indulgence of grief before her time of joy arrived. There was again, however, healing for her in her maternal duty. Again she must curb her sorrow for the sake of her child. Oh! the wisdom and the sustaining power of duty! She was calm and still, and at times her pale and sorrowful countenance was brightened by a smile of maternal love, only too often dimmed by tears.

Christie, who was desperately bent upon her triumphal return to the Hall, could not be convinced of its utter impracticability, not to say impropriety, until he had seen Honour herself; then he said no more.

She returned quietly, very quietly, one evening about the middle of June, and the few friends she loved best, they who had stood by her in former trials, were there to receive her, and to remove, if possible, some sadness from her desolation. After this, all the families of distinction and influence in the neighborhood vied who should show her most kindness and most attention.

But if she could not rejoice with a full-hearted joy, that was no reason why there should be no rejoicing at all. Christie o' Lilygarth, his brother, Caleb Fothergill, his happy son-in-law, Thomas Broadbent, the good Mr. Walker, and even Isabel Garr, took care that there should. The bells of Dale-town now rang because the young heir had taken possession of his father's house; the children, both boys and girls, had holiday, and tea and plum-cake under the sycamores in front of Mr. Walker's school; an ox was roasted and distributed one day, with plenty of good beer, to all the poor people for miles round, who would fetch it, Christie officiating as seneschal on the occasion. The following day, that there might not be a surfeit of good things, a grand tea-drinking was held in a beautiful meadow below Birks-mill, after which, in the evening, every body hastened to a field near the town, where an exhibitor of fire-works, who had been sent for from Lancaster, had set up his great machinery, and where, as soon as it was dark, every body, old and young, gentle and simple, from far and near, were transported by the wondrous beauty of Catherine-wheels, Roman candles, blue fire, rockets, stars, and every possible fiery device which the mechanist could imagine, and, to end all, there was a dance in the open air for the young people—Christie, and two or three others of the more respectable dales-men, being, of course, masters of the ceremony.

All this was any thing but amusing to the people of Tod's-gill. Young Dannel was in jail, betrayed there, as they said, by Richard

Elworthy; and more than this, Dannel himself had lost that two hundred pounds which he, miserable man that he was! had volunteered as a loan to the now penniless and absconded heir-at-law.

The lease of Tod's-gill was not, of course, renewed to Dannel Garr. He and his family set off, as soon as young Dannel's trial was over, with what money they could raise, to America, whither young Dannel was to follow them as soon as the twelve months, the term of imprisonment to which he was sentenced, was expired. The old dismal house at Tod's-gill was pulled down, a substantial one built in its stead, and here Thomas and Agnes Broadbent settled down, instead of going to America, as they had talked of, and thus a new and most respectable name was added to the tenantry of the young heir.

The Duttons, of course, were anxious lookers-on, not knowing how deeply interested and implicated Mr. Frederick Horrocks was in the disgraceful part of the affair. To them it was rather satisfactory than otherwise, that a true heir was born; for seeing that all possible advantage to them was lost, they had a pleasure in knowing that Richard Elworthy was defeated. Little did they think that advantage to any of their own family could have accrued by the success of that unprincipled adventurer.

Horrocks was enraged beyond measure; and but for his share in the business, he would have betrayed the base thief whose accomplice he had allowed himself to become; as it was, he knew that he was in this man's power, and it was only by the sacrifice of another considerable sum of money that he sent him out of the country, and bound him to remain there.

The Lord Chancellor was an able and indulgent guardian, both of the widow and her child. Mr. Wilbraham was his intimate friend, and every suggestion from this excellent man had its full weight. As far as possible, the wishes and views of the late Mr. Elworthy, when they were known, were carried out. Mrs. Elworthy's income was on the most liberal scale, and this enabled her to do an act of generous kindness, mere justice, she called it. She continued to pay Mrs. Dutton's annuity out of her own income; but that lady, not wishing to consider herself in any way indebted to Honour Mildmay, accepted it as an allowance made to her by the Lord Chancellor, in consequence of her claims on the Wast-Wayland property; and, though she knew to the contrary, she always spoke of it as such. Honour never objected to this piece of self-deception; it was enough for her that this unhappy lady could be benefited in any way.

At the present moment what is the state of affairs at Wast-Hall? Mrs. Elworthy in the tenth year of her widowhood, seems the impersonation of all that is lovely and graceful in woman. Her hair, though she is still young, is gray; her calm and thoughtful countenance is remarkable for its expression of heart-felt goodness, and that joy which springs from the peace within. It is the countenance of one who, having passed through a severe conflict, has come out, though wounded, yet victorious.

She is devoted to the well-being of her beloved dales-people and her young son. Many have been the splendid alliances which have been offered her; but she has remained steadfast to her widowhood, and to the fulfillment of present duties in which her whole soul is engaged.

Of the child, I know not how to speak, lest I should seem to be as extravagant as Christie o' Lily-garth, who firmly believes that human perfection exists in him. It is enough to say that this young William Elworthy is not only gifted with extraordinary personal beauty, but with rare natural endowments both of the heart and the head. Mrs. Mildmay still lives, hale and active, the happiest of mothers, the proudest and fondest of grand-mothers.

Scarcely any person of consequence in our story has died within these ten years. Caleb and Elizabeth Fothergill still live at Birks-mill. And even though Thomas Broadbent did marry out of the society, "Friends," dealt gently with his mother for the offense; so gently, indeed, that when five or six years were passed, and she occasionally dropped a few good words in meeting, there was so much unity felt therewith that she was advanced up into the gallery, and thus took her place among the established preachers, or "ministering Friends," as they are called.

Thomas and Agnes Broadbent flourish immensely at Tods-gill. There are now many little rosy-cheeked children running about, and Agnes, though she obliged Thomas to take her to church to to be married, now always goes to meeting with him, and has even put on the neat little Quaker cap, which amazingly becomes her. Her father is delighted with her in this costume, for she brings back, with her bright blooming face, the remembrance of the whole class of young "Quaker lasses" who, when he was a young man, had great fascination for him, though he married, after all, "out of the Society." He has occasionally taken to going to "Friends'" meetings himself, but he says he shall never go back again into the old fold, because they are sadly too quiet for him, spite of his old liking for them. Christie is as full of energy and activity as ever, and he hopes that he and every body else who loved " the master," may live to see the day when the young heir shall be one-and-twenty, and then, he declares, there shall be such a jubilee held as will put every other out of remembrance.

THE END.

LIGHT READING FOR TRAVELERS,

PUBLISHED BY

HARPER & BROTHERS, 82 CLIFF STREET, N.Y.

Harper's Library of Select Novels.

No.

1. PELHAM. By Bulwer. 25 cents.
2. THE DISOWNED. By Bulwer. 25 cents.
3. DEVEREUX. By Bulwer. 25 cents.
4. PAUL CLIFFORD. By Bulwer. 25 cents.
5. EUGENE ARAM. By Bulwer. 25 cents.
6. THE LAST DAYS OF POMPEII. By Bulwer. 25 cents.
7. THE CZARINA. By Mrs. Hofland. 25 cents.
8. RIENZI. By Bulwer. 25 cents.
9. SELF-DEVOTION. By Miss Campbell. 25 cents.
10. THE NABOB AT HOME. 25 cents.
11. ERNEST MALTRAVERS. By Sir E. Bulwer Lytton. 25 cents.
12. ALICE, OR THE MYSTERIES. By Sir E. Bulwer Lytton. 25 cents.
13. THE LAST OF THE BARONS. By Sir E. Bulwer Lytton. 25 cents.
14. FOREST DAYS. By James. 12½ cents.
15. ADAM BROWN, the Merchant. By Horace Smith. 12½ cents.
16. THE PILGRIMS OF THE RHINE. By Sir E. Bulwer Lytton 12½ cents.
17. THE HOME. By Miss Bremer. 12½ cents.
18. THE LOST SHIP. By Capt. Neale. 25 cts.
19. THE FALSE HEIR. By James. 12½ cts.
20. THE NEIGHBORS. By Miss Fredrika Bremer. 12½ cents.
21. NINA. By Miss Bremer. 12½ cents.
22. THE PRESIDENT'S DAUGHTERS. By Miss Fredrika Bremer. 12½ cents.
23. THE BANKER'S WIFE. By Mrs. Gore. 12½ cents.
24. THE BIRTHRIGHT. By Mrs. Gore. 12½ cents.
25. NEW SKETCHES OF EVERY-DAY LIFE. By Miss Bremer. 12½ cents.
26. ARABELLA STUART. By G. P. R. James, Esq. 12½ cents.
27. THE GRUMBLER. By Miss Ellen Pickering. 12½ cents.
28. THE UNLOVED ONE. By Mrs. Hofland. 12½ cents.
29. JACK OF THE MILL. By William Howitt. 12½ cents.
30. THE HERETIC. By Lajetchnikoff. 12½ cents.
31. THE JEW. By Spindler. 12½ cents.
32. ARTHUR. 25 cents.
33. CHATSWORTH. By Ward. 12½ cents.
34. THE PRAIRIE BIRD. By Charles A. Murray, Esq. 25 cents.
35. AMY HERBERT. By Miss Sewell. 12½ cents.
36. ROSE D'ALBRET. By James. 12½ cents.
37. TRIUMPHS OF TIME. By Mrs. Marsh. 25 cents.
38. THE H—— FAMILY. By Miss Fredrika Bremer. 12½ cents.
39. THE GRANDFATHER. By Miss Ellen Pickering. 12½ cents.
40. ARRAH NEIL. By James. 12½ cents.
41. THE JILT. 12½ cents.
42. TALES FROM THE GERMAN. 12½ cents.
43. ARTHUR ARUNDEL. By Horace Smith. 25 cents.
44. AGINCOURT. By James. 25 cents.
45. THE REGENT'S DAUGHTER. 25 cents.
46. THE MAID OF HONOR. 25 cents.
47. SAFIA. By De Beauvoir. 12½ cents.
48. LOOK TO THE END. By Mrs. Ellis. 12½ cents.
49. THE IMPROVISATORE. By H. C. Andersen. 12½ cents.
50. THE GAMBLER'S WIFE. By Mrs. Grey. 25 cents.
51. VERONICA. By Zchokke. 25 cents.
52. ZOE. By Miss Jewsbury. 25 cents.
53. WYOMING. 25 cents.
54. DE ROHAN. 25 cents.
55. SELF. By the Author of "Cecil." 25 cents.
56. THE SMUGGLER. By James. 25 cents.
57. THE BREACH OF PROMISE. By the Author of "The Jilt." 25 cents.
58. THE PARSONAGE OF MORA. By Miss Fredrika Bremer. 12½ cents.
59. A CHANCE MEDLEY OF LIGHT MATTER. By T. C. Grattan. 25 cents.
60. THE WHITE SLAVE. 25 cents.
61. THE BOSOM FRIEND. By Mrs. Gray 25 cents.
62. AMAURY. 25 cents.
63. THE AUTHOR'S DAUGHTER. By Mary Howitt. 12½ cents.
64. ONLY A FIDDLER! AND O. T. By H. C. Andersen. 25 cents.
65. THE WHITEBOY. By Mrs. Hall. 25 cts.
66. THE FOSTER BROTHER. Edited by Leigh Hunt. 25 cents.
67. LOVE AND MESMERISM. By Horace Smith. 25 cents.
68. ASCANIO. 25 cents.
69. THE LADY OF MILAN. Edited by Mrs. Thomson. 25 cents.
70. THE CITIZEN OF PRAGUE. Translated by Mary Howitt. 25 cents.
71. THE ROYAL FAVORITE. By Mrs. Gore. 25 cents.
72. THE QUEEN OF DENMARK. By Mrs Gore. 25 cents.

Harper's Library of Select Novels, *continued.*

No.
73. THE ELVES, ETC. By Carlyle. 25 cts.
74, 75. THE STEP-MOTHER. By G. P. R. James, Esq. 50 cents.
76. JESSIE'S FLIRTATIONS. 25 cents.
77. CHEVALIER D'HARMENTAL; or, Love and Conspiracy. By Sue. 25 cents.
78. PEERS AND PARVENUS. By Mrs. Gore. 25 cents.
79. THE COMMANDER OF MALTA. By Sue. 25 cents.
80. THE FEMALE MINISTER. 12½ cents.
81. EMILIA WYNDHAM. By Mrs. Marsh. 25 cents.
82. THE BUSH RANGER. By Charles Rowcroft, Esq. 25 cents.
83. THE CHRONICLES OF CLOVERNOOK. By Douglas Jerrold. 12½ cents.
84. THE CONFESSIONS OF A PRETTY WOMAN. By Miss Pardoe. 25 cents.
85. LIVONIAN TALES. 12½ cents.
86. CAPTAIN O'SULLIVAN. By William H. Maxwell. 25 cents.
87. FATHER DARCY. By Mrs. Marsh. 25 cents.
88. LEONTINE. By Mrs. Maberly. 25 cents.
89. HEIDELBERG. By James. 25 cents.
90. LUCRETIA. By Bulwer. 25 cents.
91. BEAUCHAMP. By James. 25 cents.
92, 94. FORTESCUE. By Knowles. 50 cents.
93. DANIEL DENNISON, &c. By Mrs. Hofland. 25 cents.
95. CINQ-MARS. By De Vigny 25 cents.
96. WOMAN'S TRIALS. By Mrs. S. C. Hall. 25 cents.
97. THE CASTLE OF EHRENSTEIN. By G. P. R. James, Esq. 25 cents.
98. MARRIAGE. By Miss S. Ferrier. 25 cents.
99, 100. THE INHERITANCE. By Miss S. Ferrier. 50 cents.
101. RUSSELL. By G. P. R. James. 25 cents.
102. A SIMPLE STORY. By Mrs. Inchbald. 25 cents.
103. NORMAN'S BRIDGE. By Mrs. Marsh. 25 cents.
104. ALAMANCE. 25 cents.
105. MARGARET GRAHAM. By G. P. R. James, Esq. 6¼ cents.
106. THE WAYSIDE CROSS. By E. H. Milman. 12½ cents.
107. THE CONVICT. By James. 25 cents.
108. MIDSUMMER EVE By Mrs. S. C. Hall. 25 cents.
109. JANE EYRE. By Currer Bell. 25 cents.
110. THE LAST OF THE FAIRIES. By G. P. R. James, Esq. 12½ cents.
111. SIR THEODORE BROUGHTON. By G. P. R. James, Esq. 25 cents.
112. SELF-CONTROL. By Mary Brunton. 25 cents.
113, 114. HAROLD. By Bulwer. 50 cents.
115. BROTHERS AND SISTERS. By Miss Fredrika Bremer. 25 cents.
116. GOWRIE. By G. P. R. James. 25 cents.
117. A WHIM AND ITS CONSEQUENCES. By G. P. R. James, Esq. 25 cents.

No.
118. THREE SISTERS AND THREE FORTUNES. By G. H. Lewes, Esq. 25 cents.
119. THE DISCIPLINE OF LIFE. 25 cents.
120. THIRTY YEARS SINCE. By G. P. R. James, Esq. 25 cents.
121. MARY BARTON. By Mrs. Gaskell. 25 cts.
122. THE GREAT HOGGARTY DIAMOND By W. M. Thackeray, Esq. 25 cents.
123. THE FORGERY. By James. 25 cents.
124. THE MIDNIGHT SUN. By Miss Fredrika Bremer. 12½ cents.
125, 126. THE CAXTONS. By Sir Edward Bulwer Lytton. 37½ cents.
127. MORDAUNT HALL. By Mrs. Marsh. 25 cents.
128. MY UNCLE THE CURATE. 25 cents.
129. THE WOODMAN. By James. 25 cents
130. RETRIBUTION. By Mrs. Emma D. E. Nevitt Southworth. 25 cents.
131. SIDONIA THE SORCERESS. By William Meinhold. 50 cents.
132. SHIRLEY. By Currer Bell. 37½ cents.
133. THE OGILVIES. 25 cents.
134. CONSTANCE LYNDSAY; or, the Progress of Error. By C. G. H. 25 cents.
135. SIR EDWARD GRAHAM; or, Railway Speculators. By Miss C. Sinclair. 37½ cents.
136. HANDS NOT HEARTS. By Miss Janet W. Wilkinson. 25 cents.
137. THE WILMINGTONS. By Mrs. Marsh. 25 cents.
138. NED ALLEN. By D. Hannay. 25 cents.
139. NIGHT AND MORNING. By Sir Edward Bulwer Lytton. 25 cents.
140. THE MAID OF ORLEANS. By the Author of "Whitefriars." 37½ cents.
141. ANTONINA; or, the Fall of Rome. By W. Wilkie Collins, Esq. 37½ cents.
142. ZANONI. By Bulwer. 25 cents.
143. REGINALD HASTINGS. By Eliot Warburton, Esq. 25 cents.
144. PRIDE AND IRRESOLUTION: a new Series of the Discipline of Life. 25 cents.
145. THE OLD OAK CHEST. By G. P. R. James, Esq. 37½ cents.
146. JULIA HOWARD. By Mrs. Bell Martin. 25 cents.
147. ADELAIDE LINDSAY. Edited by Mrs. Marsh. 25 cents.
148. PETTICOAT GOVERNMENT. By Mrs. Trollope. 25 cents.
149. THE LUTTRELLS. By F. Williams, Esq. 25 cents.
150. SINGLETON FONTENOY, R.N. By James Hannay. 25 cents.
151. OLIVE. By the Author of "The Ogilvies." 25 cents.
152. HENRY SMEATON. By G. P. R. James Esq. 50 cents.
153. TIME, THE AVENGER. By Mrs. Marsh. 25 cents.
154. THE COMMISSIONER. By G. P. R James, Esq. 50 cents.
155. THE WIFE'S SISTER. By Mrs. Hubback. 25 cents.
156. THE GOLD-WORSHIPERS; or, The Days we Live in. 25 cents.

Mount Hope;
Or, Philip, King of the Wampanoags. An Historical Romance. By G. H. HOLLISTER. 12mo, Paper, 62½ cents; Muslin, 75 cents.

The Heir of Wast-Wayland.
A Tale. By MARY HOWITT. 12mo, Muslin.

The Moorland Cottage.
By the Author of "Mary Barton." 12mo, Paper, 25 cents; Muslin, 37½ cents.

Yeast:
A Problem. By the Author of "Alton Locke." 12mo, Muslin.

Alton Locke,
Tailor and Poet. An Autobiography. 12mo, Muslin, 75 cents.

Jane Bouverie;
Or, Prosperity and Adversity. By CATHERINE SINCLAIR. 12mo, Paper, 50 cents; Muslin, 62½ cents.

Eastbury.
A Tale. By ANNA HARRIET DRURY. 12mo, Muslin.

Maurice Tiernay,
The Soldier of Fortune. By CHARLES LEVER. 8vo, Paper.

Roland Cashel.
By CHARLES LEVER. With Illustrations by Phiz. 8vo, Paper 75 cents; Muslin, $1 00.

Standish the Puritan;
A Tale of the American Revolution. By ELDRED GRAYSON, Esq. 12mo, Paper, 75 cents; Muslin, $1 00.

The Shoulder-Knot:
Or, Sketches of the Three-fold Life of Man. A Story of the 17th Century. By Rev. B. F. TEFFT. 12mo, Paper, 60 cents; Muslin, 75 cents.

Lavengro:
The Gipsy—the Scholar—the Priest. By GEORGE BORROW. 8vo, Paper, 25 cents.

Home Influence.
A Tale for Mothers and Daughters. By GRACE AGUILAR. A revised Edition, with a Memoir of the Author. 12mo, Paper, 75 cents; Muslin, $1 00.

The Mother's Recompense.
A Sequel to "Home Influence." By GRACE AGUILAR. 8vo, Paper, 25 cents.

Godfrey Malvern;
Or, the Life of an Author. By THOMAS MILLER. With numerous Illustrations. 8vo, Paper.

Vanity Fair.

A Novel without a Hero. By W. M. THACKERAY. 8vo, Paper, $1 00; Muslin, $1 25.

The History of Pendennis:

His Fortunes and Misfortunes, his Friends and his greatest Enemy. By W. M. THACKERAY. With numerous Illustrations. 2 vols. 8vo, Muslin, $2 00

Raphael;

Or, Pages from the Book of Life at Twentv. By ALPHONSE DE LAMARTINE. 12mo, Paper, 25 cents.

Memoirs of my Youth.

By ALPHONSE DE LAMARTINE. 8vo, Paper, 25 cents.

Additional Memoirs of my Youth.

By ALPHONSE DE LAMARTINE. 8vo, Paper, 12½ cents.

Genevieve;

Or, the History of a Servant Girl. Translated from the French of A. DE LAMARTINE, by A. R. SCOBLE. 8vo, Paper, 12½ cents.

Jane Eyre:

An Autobiography. Edited by CURRER BELL. Library Edition, 12mo, Muslin, 90 cents

Shirley.

A Tale. By the Author of "Jane Eyre." Library Edition, 12mo, Muslin, 90 cents.

The Children of the New Forest.

A Novel. By Captain MARRYATT, R.N. 12mo, Paper, 37½ cents; Muslin, 45 cents.

The Bachelor of the Albany.

A Novel. By the Author of the "Falcon Family." 12mo, Paper, 37½ cents; Muslin, 45 cents.

Now and Then.

A Tale. By Dr. WARREN. 12mo, Paper, 50 cents; Muslin, 60 cents.

Mary Grover;

Or, the Trusting Wife. A Domestic Temperance Tale. By CHARLES BURDETT. 12mo, Paper, 30 cents; Muslin, 40 cents.

Wuthering Heights.

A Novel. 12mo, Paper, 50 cents; Muslin, 75 cents.

The Tenant of Wildfell Hall.

A Novel. 12mo, Paper, 50 cents; Muslin, 75 cents.

The Peasant and his Landlord.

A Novel. By the Baroness KNORRING. Translated by MARY HOWITT. 12mo, Paper, 50 cents; Muslin, 75 cents.

Agnes Morris;

Or, the Heroine of Domestic Life. 12mo, Paper, 25 cents.

Angela.

By Mrs. Marsh. 12mo, Paper, 75 cents; Muslin, 90 cents.

Lettice Arnold.

By Mrs. Marsh. 8vo, Paper, 10 cents.

Edward Vernon:

My Cousin's Story. By Edmund Childe. 12mo, Paper, 50 cents; Muslin, 75 cents.

The Image of his Father.

A Tale of a Young Monkey. By Henry Mayhew. With Illustrations. 12mo, Paper, 50 cents; Muslin, 75 cents.

Model Men, Women, and Children.

By the Brothers Mayhew. With Illustrations. 18mo, Paper, 50 cents; Muslin, 62½ cents.

The Fear of the World;

Or, Living for Appearances. By the Brothers Mayhew. With Illustrations. 8vo, Paper, 25 cents.

The Green Hand.

A "Short" Yarn. 8vo, Paper, 25 cents.

The Professor's Lady.

Translated from the German of Berthold Auerbach, by Mary Howitt. With numerous Engravings. 8vo, Paper, 18¾ cents.

Adelaide Lindsay.

A Novel. Edited by Mrs. Marsh. 8vo, Paper, 25 cents.

An Easter Offering.

By Fredrika Bremer. Translated from the Unpublished Swedish Manuscript, by Mary Howitt. Contents: The Light House, Life in the North. 8vo, Paper, 6¼ cents.

Miss Fredrika Bremer's Novels.

Comprising The Neighbors; The Home; The President's Daughters; Nina; New Sketches of Every-day Life; The H— Family; The Parsonage of Mora. One Vol., 8vo, Muslin, $1 50.

Life and Adventures of Martin Chuzzlewit.

By Charles Dickens. With numerous Illustrations. 8vo, Paper, 50 cents; Muslin, 75 cents.

Dickens's Christmas Tales:

Comprising The Haunted Man; The Cricket on the Hearth; A Christmas Carol in Prose; The Chimes; The Battle of Life. 8vo, Muslin, 50 cents.

W. G. Simms's Works:

Comprising Guy Rivers; Martin Faber; Mellichampe; The Partisan; The Yemassee; Pelayo.

Fielding's Works

The History of Amelia, with Illustrations by Cruikshank; The History of Tom Jones, with a Memoir of the Author, by THOMAS ROSCOE, illustrated by Cruikshank.

Smollett's Works:

Roderic Random, with Illustrations by Cruikshank; Humphrey Clinker, with a Memoir of the Author by THOMAS ROSCOE, with Illustrations by Cruikshank; Adventures of Gil Blas, translated from the French of LE SAGE, with a Memoir of the Author, by T. ROSCOE, with Illustrations by Cruikshank.

Georgia Scenes.

With Original Illustrations. 12mo, Muslin, 90 cents.

Scenes at Washington.

A Story of the Last Generation. By a Citizen of Maryland. 12mo, Paper, 37½ cents; Muslin, 50 cents.

The Diary of a Physician.

By Dr. WARREN. 3 vols. 18mo, Muslin, $1 35.

The Vicar of Wakefield.

By OLIVER GOLDSMITH. 18mo, Muslin, 37½ cents.

Recollections of a Housekeeper.

By Mrs. C. GILMAN. 18mo, Muslin, 45 cents.

Recollections of a Southern Matron.

By Mrs. C. GILMAN. 12mo, Muslin, 90 cents.

Love's Progress.

By Mrs. C. GILMAN. 12mo, Muslin, 65 cents.

Miss Edgeworth's Tales and Novels.

With Engravings. 10 vols. 12mo, Muslin, 75 cents per Volume. The Volumes sold separately or in Sets.

VOL. I. Castle Rackrent; Essay on Irish Bulls; Essay on Self-Justification; The Prussian Vase; The Good Aunt.

VOL. II. Angelina; The Good French Governess; Mademoiselle Panache; The Knapsack; Lame Jervas; The Will; Out of Debt, out of Danger; The Limerick Gloves; The Lottery; Rosanna.

VOL. III. Murad the Unlucky; The Manufacturers; Ennui; The Contrast; The Grateful Negro; To-morrow; The Dun.

VOL. IV. Maneuvering; Almeria; Vivian.

VOL. V. The Absentee; Madame de Fleury; Emily de Coulanges; The Modern Griselda.

VOL. VI. Belinda.

VOL. VII. Leonora; Letters on Female Education; Patronage.

VOL. VIII. Patronage; Comic Dramas.

VOL. IX. Harrington; Thoughts on Bores; Ormond.

VOL. X. Helen.

Miscellaneous List of Novels and Romances.

ADVENTURES OF A YOUNGER SON: by Trelawney. 85 cents.

ALLEN PRESCOTT: by Mrs. Sedgwick. $1 25.

ANASTASIUS: by T. Hope. 50 cents.

THE ATLANTIC CLUB-BOOK: by Paulding and others. 50 cents.

BERNARDO DEL CARPIO: by Montgomery. 50 cents.

BLACKBEARD: a Page from the Colonial History of Philadelphia. $1 25.

BURTON: by Ingraham. 75 cents.

THE BOOK OF ST. NICHOLAS: by Paulding. 62½ cents.

THE BUDGET OF THE BUBBLE FAMILY: by Lady Bulwer. 90 cents.

THE CABINET MINISTER: by Mrs. Gore. 85 cents.

CALEB WILLIAMS: by Godwin. 85 cents.

CAPTAIN KYD: by Ingraham. 75 cents.

THE CAVALIERS OF VIRGINIA: by Caruthers. $1 25.

CHEVELEY: by Lady Bulwer. 90 cents.

Miscellaneous List of Novels, *continued.*

CHARLES VINCENT: by Willis. $1 25.

CHRONICLES OF THE CANONGATE: by Sir W. Scott. 70 cents.

THE CLUB-BOOK: by James. 45 cents.

CONTI THE DISCARDED: by Chorley. 90 cents.

THE COUNTESS IDA: by Fay. $1 50.

COUNT ROBERT OF PARIS: by Sir W Scott. 90 cents.

THE COURTIER of the Reign of Charles II.: by Mrs. Gore. 50 cents.

CYRIL THORNTON: by Hamilton. 87½ cts.

DARNLEY: by James. 85 cents.

DEERBROOK: by Miss Martineau. 90 cents.

DE L'ORME: by James. 70 cents.

THE DESULTORY MAN: by James. 90 cts.

DE VERE: by Ward. 90 cents.

DIARY OF A DESENNUYEE. 45 cents.

DREAMS AND REVERIES OF A QUIET MAN: by Fay. $1 12½.

ELKSWATAWA, the Prophet of the West: by French. $1 25.

FALKNER: by Mrs. Shelley. 62½ cents.

FRANK ORBY. 80 cents.

THE FROLICS OF PUCK. 90 cents.

GENTLEMAN OF THE OLD SCHOOL: by James. 90 cents.

GEORGE BALCOMBE: by Tucker. $1 25.

THE GIPSY: by James. 45 cents.

GODOLPHIN: by Bulwer. 90 cents.

HENRI QUATRE: by Mancur. 50 cents.

HENRY OF GUISE: by James. 90 cents.

HENRY MASTERTON: by James. 87½ cts.

HERBERT WENDALL: a Tale of the Revolution. $1 25.

HOBOKEN: a Romance of New York: by Fay. 45 cents.

HOME; or, the Iron Rule: by Mrs. Ellis. 25 cents.

HOPE LESLIE: by Miss Sedgwick. $1 25.

THE HOUR AND THE MAN: by Miss Martineau. 50 cents.

THE JACQUERIE: by James. 90 cents.

JAPHET IN SEARCH OF A FATHER: by Marryat. 45 cents.

JOHN MARSTON HALL: by James. 85 cts.

KONINGSMARKE: by Paulding $1 25.

LAFITTE; the Pirate of the Gulf: by Ingraham. 75 cents.

THE LINWOODS: by Miss Sedgwick. $1 50.

LORD ROLDAN: by Cunningham. 45 cents.

LOUISA MILDMAY. 10 cents.

MAHMOUD. 90 cents.

MARIAN: by Mrs. S. C. Hall. 50 cents.

MARY OF BURGUNDY: by James. 85 cents.

THE MAYOR OF WINDGAP: by Banim. 42½ cents.

MELMOTH THE WANDERER: by Maturin. 90 cents.

MEPHISTOPHILES IN ENGLAND. 50 cts.

MERCHANT'S CLERK: by Warren. 45 cts.

MICHAEL ARMSTRONG: by Mrs. Trollope. 90 cents.

MIRIAM COFFIN: by Hart. $1 25.

MORLEY ERNSTEIN: by James. 45 cents.

MORTON'S HOPE: by an American. $1 40.

MOUNT SOREL; or, the Heiress of the De Veres: by Mrs. Marsh. 12½ cents.

MY LIFE: by Maxwell. 85 cents.

MYSTERIES OF PARIS: by Sue. 56¼ cents

THE NEVILLES OF GARRETSTOWN: by Dr. Lever. 12½ cents.

NORMAN LESLIE: by Fay. $1 25.

NOVELLETTES OF A TRAVELER: by Nott. $1 25.

ONE IN A THOUSAND: by James. 45 cents.

THE OUTLAW: by Mrs. Hall. 90 cents.

THE PARTISAN: by Simms. $1 25

PAUL ULRIC: by Mattson. $1 25.

PELAYO: by Simms. $1 25.

PHILIP AUGUSTUS: by James. 85 cents.

PREFERMENT: by Mrs. Gore. 90 cents.

THE QUADROON: by Ingraham. 75 cents.

THE REFUGEE IN AMERICA: by Mrs. Trollope. 85 cents.

ROMANCE OF HISTORY—FRANCE: by Ritchie. 70 cents.

ROMANCE OF HISTORY—ITALY: by Macfarlane. 70 cents.

ROSE OF PERSIA: by Spring. 50 cents.

SALMAGUNDI: by Paulding and Irving. $2 50

THE SCHOOL OF FASHION. 85 cents.

THE SELF-CONDEMNED. 45 cents.

SHEPPARD LEE: by Himself. $1 50.

THE SKETCH-BOOK OF FASHION: by Mrs. Gore. 50 cents.

THE SMUGGLER: by Banim. 85 cents.

SOUTHENNAN: by Galt. 70 cents.

SPECULATION: by Miss Pardoe. 50 cents.

STORIES OF THE SEA: by Marryat. 37½ cents.

ST. PATRICK'S EVE: by Lever. 6¼ cents.

THE STUDENT: by Bulwer. 80 cents.

SYDNEY CLIFTON: by Strong. $1 25.

TALES AND SKETCHES: by Stone. 70 cts.

TALES OF THE EARLY AGES: by Smith. 70 cents.

TALES OF THE GOOD WOMAN: by Paulding. $1 25

TALES OF THE PEERAGE AND PEASANTRY: by Lady Dacre. 50 cents.

TALES OF THE WOODS AND FIELDS: by Mrs. Marsh. 45 cents.

THREE ERAS OF WOMAN'S LIFE: by Mrs. Smith. 45 cents.

THE THREE WISE MEN OF GOTHAM: by Paulding. 62½ cents.

TWO OLD MEN'S TALES. 80 cents.

THE UNFORTUNATE MAN: by Chamier. 80 cents.

VALERIUS: by Lockhart. 85 cents.

VILLAGE BELLES. 80 cents.

THE WANDERING JEW: by Sue. 50 cents. New Edition, with over 500 Illustrations. $5 00.

WAVERLEY: by Scott. 70 cents.

WILD SPORTS OF THE WEST: by Maxwell. 50 cents.

YOUNG MUSCOVITE: by Chamier. 90 cents

www.ingramcontent.com/pod-product-compliance
Lightning Source LLC
LaVergne TN
LVHW050514100826
845148LV00002B/336

9781425521707